# THE JANE AUSTEN DATING AGENCY

## FIONA WOODIFIELD

Print ISBN 978-1-913419-31-8

*To my family with love*
*and to all those out there dreaming of romance...*

# CHAPTER 1

Oh God, it's him. I jump nervously as my phone zings into life, buzzing and trilling around the desk like a half-crazed beetle. I grab it, trying to stop its erratic movement, as people around me look up outraged at the interruption. I hurriedly press the reject button, staring dumbly at the screen, wishing for the thousandth time I'd never given him my number.

The phone bings, proudly announcing to the world that he's left a voicemail. The third today and it's only 9am. That's not including five texts and the bouquet of flowers drooping sadly at my desk. I try to rustle through my papers in a businesslike manner, picking out the next sales leads, attempting to distract my anxious mind. Perhaps if I hide the phone away in the bottom of my bag, somehow he will have gone. I scrabble about in its cavernous depths, trying to avoid the wrapper containing a half-eaten SlimFast bar from the day before. It's melted, oozy little bits of molten chocolate smeared over my notebook. Great, that's my favourite one – I scrub at it ineffectually, trying to remove everything carefully without getting chocolate on my new suit.

My phone sings out again, causing me to drop it back into the bag like a hot potato, then frantically rummage around to check the caller ID on the screen. It's a love-hate relationship, a bizarre fascination – I have to know if it's him... It isn't.

'Hello?' I whisper, removing myself and my bag from the desk and hurrying out into the hallway, attempting to look inconspicuous.

'Sophie, are you okay?' It's my flatmate, Mel. 'You sound a little breathless.'

'Hardly surprising. I'm stuck between the window and a very large pot plant.' I wriggle about a bit to find a more comfortable position. 'If Amanda discovers I'm on a personal call at this time in the morning, I'll be out of the running to win free tickets to the Yves St Laurent Spring Show.'

'You shouldn't go in any case; I think they use real animal fur. It's disgusting. Anyway, Dean's phoned the flat again. You're going to have to change our number. I'm sick of hearing his creepy little voice several times a day.'

'It's going to take more than that; he keeps trying my mobile.'

'Buy another one.'

'But he knows where we live and we'll never afford anywhere else in Islington.'

'For God's sake, why do you always attract complete weirdos?' Mel snorts. 'Mike was bad enough but honestly, Dean's raised the bar to a whole new level.'

'How was I to know he's a stalker with a history of attachment issues? I can't help it if I attract these people.'

'You're too nice. Like you never tell them to get lost.'

'I do try, I just don't like to hurt their feelings.'

'And they can tell. You might as well have "puts up with total losers" written on your T-shirt. It's not like it's only one or two; you attract them in droves. Thank God you got yourself locked out of Tinder. Otherwise the issue could have gone global.' Mel laughs in spite of her grumpy mood.

'I'm not that bad, Darren was quite nice.'

'Yes, he was lovely but gay.'

'Nothing wrong with that, as you know.'

'No, but as a boyfriend it's a bit of a fundamental issue. And he stole all your clothes. He was a complete kleptomaniac.'

'I loved that Monsoon top, it was really special – we bought it that day at Camden Market,' I lament.

'Don't remind me, that horrible old bag was trying to sell hundreds of caged birds.'

'I admit it was upsetting, but I wish you hadn't gone and picked a fight with someone that scary. I've never run so fast in my life.'

'I had no choice; it was disgusting the conditions she was keeping them in. How would you like to be locked in a tiny cage, like a prisoner, and barely–'

'Mel, I've got to go,' I interrupt – there's no stopping her once she's started one of her rants. 'Amanda's just walked into the office, I'll speak later, bye...'

'Don't forget to deal with Dean!' Mel repeats desperately as I click off the phone, shove it in my bag and scramble from my cramped hiding place, brushing stray pot plant leaves from my skirt, and saunter casually back into the office, hoping no-one will notice anything is amiss.

I think Mel is overreacting a bit about Dean. I mean, I know I haven't had the best history of dating in the world but they aren't all weirdos. Some have been sort of okay. Though to be perfectly honest, none have been great really. I just don't seem to have much luck with guys at all, like ever.

Why can't it all be a little more simple? I just need someone single, tall, dark and handsome who will well and truly sweep me off my feet. Charming, gentlemanly like Mr Darcy, although he was a bit moody. I always had a sneaking suspicion that he was pretty grumpy a lot of the time, and used to having his own way. Hot though. Or Mr Knightley was pretty nice and I always had a sneaking liking for Mr Tilney. Mel would give me a lecture on feminism if she heard this wish list of idealised masculinity. I can hear her now, saying, 'You sound like one of those women who can only define themselves by being with a man.'

Of course I'm not like that at all. I am a proud feminist, a totally modern woman – I believe in equality and all that stuff. Yet there is a sneaky little part of me, which I keep very well hidden of course, that desperately wants a man to show some good old-fashioned chivalry, to look after me a little, even if I can really look after myself. Is that so wrong even in the twenty-first century? Maybe this type of guy no longer exists; except captured for eternity in the novels of Jane Austen.

My phone bings again. It's a text from Mel.

*This is so you* – attached to the message is an e-card saying... *Jane Austen – giving women unrealistic expectations since 1811.* (Oh ha ha, maybe I don't keep my dreams that well hidden after all.) *And make sure you deal with Dean xxx*

My brother, Ben, always says I have such unrealistic expecta-tions of men due to an alarming overconsumption of romantic novels as a teenager. Maybe he's right, I know I love to escape into a book – I should probably at least try to live in the real world. But right now it feels pretty inadequate.

As I walk back into the office, the sales team is hard at work, barely flicking me a glance from under their perfectly sculpted eyebrows. The room has a productive buzz about it, making me feel more than usual like a fish out of water.

Amanda's already writing the sales targets on the board, adding and removing brightly coloured ticks, and crossing through percentages – the only visible evidence of our never-ending stream of phone calls. It's as though she is playing a glori-fied form of noughts and crosses all by herself.

I slide quickly behind my desk, gathering work around me like a protective wall to look as though I was here slaving away for hours. A couple of calls later and it feels as though I have been.

It had sounded so glamorous when I spotted the ad in the

*Graduate Review.* They were looking for dynamic graduates to source and pitch advertising in the classified sales department of the iconic *Modiste Magazine.* I applied, thinking the interview would be good experience, though the trip to London frightened me. Coming from Bampton, a sleepy seaside town, it was all so noisy yet captivating and I was fascinated by the buzz, the air of excitement.

Two interviews later, shortlisted from over four hundred applicants, and to my amazement, I reached the final listing. The only problem is, I think I was so caught up in trying to win the position, I'm not really sure I wanted it when it was offered.

My mum isn't impressed either. She thinks I'm wasting my time in sales (probably true), as I should really like to work in Editorial. But those jobs hardly ever come up. Anyway, you would think I work in B&Q (not that there is anything wrong with that but you couldn't exactly call it glamorous) for the amount of respect my mum gives to the fact I work for Modiste.

'It doesn't matter how you dress it up, love, you're essentially a cold-caller. Whether it's a glamorous glossy magazine or a double glazing company you work for, you basically phone people who are innocently minding their own business, trying to sell stuff to them they don't want and aren't interested in.'

The whole experience was so incredibly exciting though, being whisked off to Harvey Nicks with Amanda Beale, Head of Classified Advertising, to sip from tall elegant flutes of champagne at 11am. It was all so glamorous and sparklingly captivating, I was entranced right from the start.

'Sophie,' Amanda had said, 'I'm pleased to say you have the position, absolutely super interview. Simply thrilled to have you. Welcome to Modiste, darling.'

I was amazed and sort of in shock. Of course I accepted the position, there was no question. You don't turn down a job somewhere like Modiste. Naturally I had to go out and spend a fortune on an entire new wardrobe, as you can't wear any old suit to the offices of Modiste each day. What's a student loan for anyway? The problem is, my salary doesn't reflect the glamour of the job. Actually, I could have earned loads more as an administrator in my hometown and that wouldn't involve the exorbitant costs of living in London.

My rent on the flat is pretty high but I like living in Islington and it's not that far to the Modiste office in Hanover Square, once I got over my fear of the daily tube journey that is. When I first started I was so scared I took a taxi to work each morning but rather unsurprisingly, I couldn't afford to keep this up. In fact, now I've got used to it, the tube is okay; it's just all the people and I've got this thing that the train might start going before I get in the door so I end up hustling inside it really quickly.

But this is Modiste and I'm in, which is pretty amazing. Of course it means I get in quite late in the evening, something like eight, after a long day, which doesn't leave much time for socialising. But I'm sure there will be loads of opportunities to go to really glamorous premieres and other amazing events. Not that there has been yet, but I've only been there a couple of weeks. There's bound to be, because this is Modiste after all.

I hate to admit it but my mum does sort of have a point re. the cold-calling. The position is selling advertising space in the back of Carter Whitrow publications. It isn't really cold-calling though; it involves phoning specialist shops and offering them the amazing opportunity to advertise in some incredibly popular publications.

The only thing is, they don't always really want to advertise, or they are already advertising somewhere else cheaper or they just don't want to be bothered by us, like at all, ever. So, calling them up and pestering them gets them annoyed and they start telling you to go away, not very politely either. I was told to 'f' off three times in one week, and not all by the same person. So you can see, it isn't quite as glamorous as I thought.

The training when I first started was intensive; we spent an entire week writing and practising sales scripts. There were six of us trainees, all pretending to phone and persuade each other to buy extremely expensive advertising space. I didn't really enjoy it, acting can be fun but sales role-play is pretty boring and was bordering on the patronising. But it was okay because I had a plan. I was going to just be my normal polite and friendly self and as soon as I heard or could sense someone was not interested, I would apologise for bothering them and ring off to phone another poor victim, I mean 'lucky prospective customer'.

There was just one terrible flaw in my plan. I didn't realise this until the Monday of the week after training had finished. We were shown the slightly daunting sales room, with its open-plan desks and row after row of phones and headsets.

'Right,' Amanda had trilled. 'You're now the best-trained sales team Carter Whitrow has ever known. Remember you work for Modiste, one of the most prestigious magazines in the world. You are offering these people the most amazing opportunity of a lifetime. I want to hear the pride in your voices as you sell the UK's most glamorous and exclusive advertising space. Remember the script and keep to it. The script is your law, your creed. Always, always stick to the script, we don't want any mavericks in here.'

She paced up and down the room restlessly on long spidery legs, feet clad in what I have recently discovered to be Manolo Blahniks, slapping her hand with the all-important scripts. 'I, meanwhile, will be nearby at all times, popping in on the other line to listen to your conversation and add any suggestions in your left ear with my handy little headphones here.' She waved a cream pair of headphones ominously at us.

My heart had started to beat rather fast all by itself. I'd never ever thought that someone could be listening to my sales conversation and then telling me what to say in my other ear. But there was nothing I could do but rather fakely mutter 'great' and go and sit down at my desk looking suitably enthusiastic.

'Now, Sheena, Gina and Kelli – you are working on Modiste. Here are your copies of the classified ads, pricing lists and terms and conditions. Caitlin and Sophie, you are on *Modiste Brides*. Marie, you can start with *Modiste Traveller*.' Amanda flicked copies of the relevant magazines and price lists towards us. 'And before I forget, the first person to sell an advertising space, wins...' And she paused dramatically while I thought, *yes! It's going to be something designer and cool from Modiste...* until Amanda finished with, 'A bottle of bubbly.'

Oh, a bit of a let-down but it was quite a nice prize, I supposed, and it wasn't going to be me in any case. I tried my first couple of calls on the Bridal Directory as quickly as I could to get a bit of practice in before Amanda got to me. I was ducking down behind the screen, hoping not to catch her eye; it reminded me of being back in maths class at school. Hah, that's a shame, the first couple of people weren't answering; this list wasn't going to take long. But the third lady did.

'Surrey Brides,' she answered in a happy and helpful tone. 'How may I help you?'

'Oh, good afternoon, this is Sophie calling from *Modiste Brides* magazine. How are you today?' I recited in my best Queen's English.

'I'm fine, thank you.' The lady didn't sound quite as cheerful now – I could hear a hint of reserve creep in. I knew how she felt, I hate people trying to sell me things.

'That's wonderful,' I gushed nervously. 'I am phoning today to ask if you would like to take up a fantastic opportunity to advertise your fabulous shop in the UK's biggest and most glamorous bridal magazine, *Modiste Brides*, thus reaching a huge audience, thus achieving greater footfall in your shop, thus maximising your profits?'

I became a little discombobulated during this last spiel as Amanda, beaming widely, had plonked down in the chair next to me and plugged in to my call.

'Not really.' The voice became uncompromising. I flapped at my sheets, realising that I shouldn't have asked the question in that way as it allowed a 'yes-no answer'.

'Ask why not,' hissed Amanda in a loud stage whisper that made me wonder if she had swallowed a voice projector. Oh no, I really didn't want to do this, now was the time to say, 'Oh okay, thank you very much for your time, have a good day, goodbye.'

But Amanda was in my other ear, listening to every word. So I said rather falteringly, 'Erm, why not?'

'Because I don't have the budget for it,' came the terse reply.

At that point, I wanted to apologise for disturbing her, finish the call and move on. But Amanda was whispering in my ear again, 'Ask her how much she has in her budget.'

This was going to blow it. 'Sorry to ask, but how much do you have in your budget?' I asked, cringing inwardly.

'I'm not going to discuss that sort of question with you!' the woman snapped. 'Bloody cheek ringing me up and asking me how much money I have!' And she slammed down the phone.

'She was in a hurry!' Amanda tinkled. 'Never mind, next number, back to selling. And in future...' She stuck her immaculate blonde head close to my face to emphasise her point, 'remember, stick to the script, darling.'


I'M KIND OF GETTING USED to it now, although the lady on that call was one of the politer responses. As I said, I'd really like to move to Editorial and hope this might happen if I work hard. Writing is much more my thing and I have so many important issues I would like to address like 'Should women over forty wear short skirts?' To be on the Modiste editorial team would be amazing. I see them waft into the entrance lobby at Modiste House looking stunningly untouchable, off to premieres and exclusives with incredible people. They are like higher beings to us mere mortals down in Classified Sales. Actually though, I'm beginning to notice they're all someone who knows someone important. Aaahhhggghhh, perhaps I'm going to be stuck in Classified Sales my whole life because I don't know anyone important at all.

My phone buzzes again, thankfully I'd remembered to put it on silent. *Sophie, I'm begging you, please stop ignoring me… I need to talk to you, Dean xxxxx*

I look about surreptitiously as, ironically, Amanda is pretty strict on the no-phone rule in the office and I have enough problems right now. I quickly tap in a reply: *You need to move on, Dean. This isn't going to work, we're different people…* I think for a moment then harden myself to add – *If you don't stop contacting me, I'll have to involve the police.*

Hopefully that would get rid of him. It made me feel bad as he wasn't horrible really, just very weird. His taxidermy collection. I shivered remembering it. I think that had been the moment I realised he needed to go. I guess Mel has a point, I do seem to attract total weirdos. The one before Dean was so much fun but when he started to wear my clothes and make-up, I knew we had a problem. The guy before that, Mike, turned out to be married and an alcoholic. In short, my life so far is a catalogue of dating disasters. My solution: every night I retire to bed to read a nice happy romance – generally Jane Austen, and lose myself in the world of Elizabeth and Darcy while consuming a worrying amount of chocolate.

'Sophie!' My reverie is broken by Mark who works in Account Management and is a complete sweetie. He is quite simply a rose in a bed of thorns. 'Some leads for you, darling.'

'Thanks,' I say rather absently. 'I could do with those.'

'What's up? Prêt a Porter have a flash sale and you missed it?'

'No.' I smile in spite of myself. Mark always makes me laugh –

he's the only one who is half normal in the office. 'Just ex-boyfriend trouble.'

'Marvellous, this calls for an early lunch break.' He sweeps my chair from underneath me, grabs my stuff and propels me towards the door. 'You know how good I am at solving your problems.'

'What about Amanda?' I ask half-heartedly.

'Stuff Amanda!'

We leave the office, giggling like a couple of naughty children. A few of the sales team seem to have already gone for lunch so I don't feel too guilty. We walk companionably downstairs into the lobby.

'Oh, I've left my phone! I'll catch you up.' I run back up the sweeping staircase and across the landing into the sales room. It seems to be momentarily deserted; I've never seen it like this. I cross the floor quickly to grab my mobile and get out again before anyone returns, when I'm halted by one of the desk phones. It's tempting to leave – it won't be for me anyway – but something stops me. I have to answer it.

'Good afternoon, Carter Whitrow Publications, how may I help you?' I actually manage to make it sound quite natural for once.

'Oh, hello, good afternoon. I wonder if you can, I'm looking to place an advert in *Modiste Brides* magazine,' says a well-spoken lady in a pleasant tone.

'Yes, of course, you would like to book a slot in the magazine?' I repeat her words like a loon, unable to believe my ears.

'Yes, this is the right number, isn't it?' The poor lady sounds confused.

'Definitely,' I reply, pulling myself together. 'A 5x3 ad in the back of *Modiste Brides* is £350 for one insert, then £200 for the next couple of months as we are offering a promotion at the moment.'

'That's fine, what would I need to do next?'

'If you'd like to send the details through to Modiste, my e-mail is sophie.johnson@modiste-magazine.com and I'll get you booked in for a three-month slot. Please could you give me your payment details.'

The lady has all the info ready and rings off, seemingly happy with her transaction. I put the phone down and do a two-minute victory lap of the office, my arms high in the air, whooping until I'm suddenly stopped by the sight of Amanda walking past the door, followed closely by my fellow recruits.

'You okay, Sophie?' Amanda asks, peering round the opening. 'Is there a mosquito or something?' The immaculate girls either side of her smirk knowingly at each other.

'Erm, no, sorry I erm...' I stutter like an idiot. 'Oh, I er... I've made a sale.'

'Oh my gosh, Sophie! Everyone,' Amanda claps her hands together, 'gather round, we have our first sale. Sophie Johnson here has sold the first advertising slot in *Modiste Brides*. Well done.'

She stalks rapidly to her desk... 'And here is your very-much-deserved bottle of Moët. Enjoy, darling!'

I sheepishly walk to the front of the room to claim my prize, wishing the ground would swallow me up, trying to ignore the fake congratulatory smiles of the rest of the sales team. God, I feel a fraud.

Having managed to fight off the not-very-sincere well dones/barely concealed scowls from the rest of the team, I escape gratefully to join Mark down in the foyer.

'Where have you been? I thought you must have fallen asleep at the desk or something.'

'No,' I reply innocently. 'You're only talking to the highest achieving sales recruit of the century!'

Mark laughs when I tell him what happened, but in spite of my amusement, I feel a total fake as I know it was nothing more than luck. It's lifted my mood for a while though and we sit and enjoy our favourite lunch at Yo Sushi on the corner.

I tell Mark about Dean and even manage to laugh off his weird behaviour – he hasn't phoned again so perhaps the message has finally got through.

'You just don't have high enough standards, darling,' Mark states categorically, chomping his way through his fourth yasai roll. I don't know how he always manages to eat so neatly. I've already dropped soy sauce down my shirt.

'I do,' I protest, trying without much success to remove the stain. 'I order Prince Charming but instead I keep finding trolls.'

'Then you're not looking in the right places.'

As usual, he's flicking through a magazine he's found on the table, expertly critiquing the designers, the photography and the style. Mind you, Mark has excellent taste and always looks immaculate, I think he has his suits handmade at Lock and Co.

I peer over his shoulder, checking out the latest fashions. 'You really ought to be a designer,' I say. 'You're wasted in Account Management.'

'Maybe one day.' Mark smiles. 'At the moment, this job pays the bills and Tim's enough of a diva for both of us!' Tim is Mark's long-standing, long-suffering partner who works at a top London fashion house.

Mark turns to the classified ads at the back.

'I don't want to look at those,' I protest. 'I've been trying mostly unsuccessfully to sell them all morning.'

'You should be studying other magazines. Check out the competition.'

'Oh my God!' I grab frantically at the mag as Mark continues, mechanically turning the pages. 'Stop, stop. Go back!'

'What? Why? You made me jump.'

I take the magazine and finally manage to find the ad that had attracted my attention.

'Look at this.' I point triumphantly at the page.

*Exclusive dating agency for ladies to meet real gentlemen in beautiful settings – only the truly romantic may apply! Dine like Elizabeth and Darcy at Chatsworth aka Pemberley, picnic like Emma and Mr Knightley on juicy strawberries and sparkling champagne on Box Hill. The possibilities are endless... Fed up with looking for Mr Right? Bored with dating complete blockheads whose idea of romance is asking what you are cooking them for dinner? Then look no further than The Jane Austen Dating Agency... Call 0207 946 0801 for more info or check out our website on janeaustendatingagency.com*

'The Jane Austen Dating Agency,' I repeat slowly. 'It's like a dream come true.' And it is... I can't believe it. Just imagine, Regency Balls, champagne picnics, men in tight breeches and maybe even a Colin Firth wet shirt... OMG, book me in now.'

'Sounds utterly fabulous. I'd join if I were single.' Mark is the best friend ever. Even though I've only known him a short while, he's totally supportive. He also loves Austen – in fact, he always says *Pride and Prejudice* is one of the best heterosexual love stories he's ever read, which is quite a compliment I think.

'So, what you gonna do?' he asks, winking at me dramatically. 'I should phone now quickly before there is a crowd of desperate damsels queuing down the street, beating the door down for Mr Darcy.' Mark grabs my phone and starts dialling the number.

'No, give it back.' I laugh, snatching it from him. 'I need to think about it first. After all, I'm not sure about a dating agency. I'm not that desperate yet.'

'Believe me, girl, you are! And anyway, this is something special; it's The Jane Austen Dating Agency.'

I smile enigmatically, trying to conceal my excitement, while inside my mind is going crazy with fantasies of arriving at the ball at Pemberley in Regency dress.

You know, I think The Jane Austen Dating Agency is exactly what I need in my life.

# CHAPTER 2

'Miss Johnson?' A stylish and expensively dressed young woman, probably in her late twenties, appears from nowhere and wafts elegantly across the room wearing this season's pale lilac Jimmy Choos. Looking at her, I begin to wonder if I should have worn something a little more designer, and I squirm uncomfortably in my seat.

'Yes?' I leap to my feet, trying ineffectually not to appear like an overexcited puppy. *Keep it cool, Sophie, slow it down.*

The woman gingerly takes the tips of my offered hand and shakes it limply, releasing it far too quickly for politeness.

There's an awkward silence as she scrutinises me from head-to-toe, her eyes narrowed, making me feel completely out of place. I brush my top randomly, pretending to remove a stray hair which doesn't really exist. This woman is the limit; I hate it when people deliberately look you up and down – don't they realise they're doing it or are they just plain rude?

'I am Miss Palmer-Wright, Head of Membership at The Jane Austen Dating Agency. My colleague, Miss Emma Woodtree, who processed your online application, is currently off-site shooting locations for our annual ball.'

'Oh, how exciting!' I gush. I always gush when I am ill at ease. 'That must be so romantic!'

'Yes, the ball at Pemberley is a splendid occasion,' Miss Palmer-Wright gives me another glance, 'but it is only available to our Gold members.' She eyes my outfit from the high street with undisguised distaste. 'I shall continue to explain our terms and conditions in my office. Follow me please.'

I wonder if this woman is for real. Her tone has made it quite clear it's highly unlikely I'll qualify to be included in any invitation to the ball. I'm feeling worryingly like Cinderella dealing with her wicked stepmother. I'm not sure what I'd expected, Regency dress perhaps, but I'd incorrectly assumed that anyone who loves Jane Austen would be nice, not a prize bitch.

'You will need to complete some more forms so we can assess your suitability for the agency,' Miss Palmer-Wright states decisively, striding out along the corridor.

I find myself trotting at her heels, stammering, 'Yes please, thank you very much,' as gratefully as though she is offering me a thousand-pound Prada suit for nothing. I hate that about myself, I'm just so Miranda Hart. I don't look like her, but the whole thanking someone even when they are being rude thing. Even if someone told me to get lost, I would probably thank them very much a la Mrs Bennet in *Pride and Prejudice*, 'Thank the gentleman, Jane.'

In fact, I blame my mother, for my ridiculous politeness in the face of blatant bitching is all her fault. Manners were a huge part of my childhood, and as for older people, they were always right, the same for doctors, teachers and policemen. I think it's a generation thing; her mum, my gran, was always the same. So Victorian. Then my mother spends her whole life saying, 'You need to learn to stand up for yourself. Don't let people push you around,' while she tells me what to do and pushes me around.

Miss Bitch-Face, no I must remember not to call her that, not at all Jane Austen, strides out in front of me as though her stilt-like heels are ballet pumps, while I totter after her. Her crisp little suit, Louis Vuitton of course, spring collection, sits beautifully on her perfectly gym-toned silhouette. There's not an ounce of fat anywhere; this woman has probably never eaten a croissant in her life.

I'm beginning to wonder if this whole thing is a good idea. As soon as I got home from work the other day I'd checked out the website. Partly because Mark keeps nagging me to see if I had done it but mainly because I was hooked on the idea. The site is simple with beautiful images taken from various film versions of Austen: Emma Thompson, Matthew Macfadyen and of course good old Colin Firth, all interspersed with quotes from Austen's novels.

There are also gorgeous photos of people dancing in a vast ballroom, in Regency dress and most remarkably good looking I noted. Either way it had inspired me to fill in the application form, although I must admit I saved it a few times as I was still a bit nervous about the whole joining an agency thing. The people on the website didn't look like weirdos, however, but with my track record, you never know. Either way, I was amazed to hear back so soon and before I'd known what was happening, here I am at this extremely daunting interview with Miss Palmer-Wright.

I follow her into an office which is as pristine and immaculate as she is, and nearly as intimidating. 'Take a seat,' she coos, though it's an order not an invitation. I sit, ever obedient, in the vintage wooden chair.

'This is so beautifully decorated,' I enthuse, looking round the room at the pale blue walls. 'Are those real first editions of Austen's novels?' I point at the impressively antique-looking collection of Austen's works carefully and strategically arranged on the window ledge.

'Oh no.' She laughs, a horrible fake and tinkly sound which immediately sets my teeth on edge. 'Those are just for show, sweetie. It doesn't need to be the real thing, their job is to create the ambience our clientele would expect.'

I wonder idly if she has even read any of the books and can't resist asking. 'Which was your favourite novel?'

'Oh, I haven't read them.' In fact, I can tell Miss Palmer-Wright is incredulous at my absurdity in asking such a thing. 'I don't have time to read novels. Of course, if I had tried I could have been a very successful scholar but when one has so many better things to do, there isn't any necessity to read books.' She leans forward in her chair. 'Just think, darling, this is the age of technology – we have Kindles and Google, no-one reads fusty old books anymore.'

This idea floors me and I sit momentarily silenced. I can't be bothered to explain to this woman my absolute love of books; they are my friends, my refuge. To try to describe the excitement of buying a brand new edition, smelling the leaves of the pages; books are so incredibly tactile. I guess a Kindle is more useful on a plane. One of my friends used to complain I used up my entire luggage allowance on books, but I can't be without them.

'I love books,' is all I can state lamely, sounding pathetic even to my own ears.

'If you lived in the busy social whirl I am accustomed to, you simply wouldn't have the time, darling,' replied Miss Palmer-Wright disparagingly, and I notice her write in an elegant flowing hand – *loves books* with a big exclamation mark next to it on the form sitting in front of her on the desk. I don't get the impression it's meant as a compliment.

There's no way on earth I want to spend any more time with Miss Palmer-Wright. Restlessly, I look about the room, wondering if I can think of an excuse to get out of there and brush it all off as a mistake. What's the point of someone working in a Jane Austen dating agency if they haven't even read her books? Surely they should be a fan of her work. Before I'm able to ask, Miss Palmer-Wright fires questions at me.

'Just short answers to these please; I am aware you have filled in the online application form but these are designed to assess your personality.' She peers at me, her expression intimating that she is already fully aware of my character and it is totally inadequate.

I give myself a little mental shake. *Come on, Sophie, don't let this woman get to you.*

'So, what are your favourite hobbies, other than reading?' she asks in a bored tone.

'Erm, I think I filled all this in online?' I say tentatively.

'No, I don't think you have.' Miss Palmer-Wright leafs through the papers on her desk, glances momentarily at the computer screen, and shakes her head. 'No, I can't see it here.'

'Oh, okay. I enjoy dancing, though I don't have much opportunity to go at the moment. I used to do contemporary dance.'

'I don't think we can put things down you used to do. What do you do now in your spare time, or do you read and do nothing else at all?'

'Work takes up most of my life currently, I've just started a new position at Modiste.'

'Yes, I saw that on your form.' Miss Palmer-Wright's tone is dismissive, disbelieving almost.

'I also enjoy socialising with friends, going for a run...' She doesn't need to know I only run if I'm late for the tube – it's still running. 'I also enjoy singing.'

'Professionally?' suggests Miss Palmer-Wright, brightening a little.

'Erm, no. Just for fun.' I mean what does she expect? Adele?

'Any charity work, marathons, gap years?' She reels the list off dismissively as though she already knows the answer.

'No.'

'Never mind, we can't all be debutantes in *Country Life* magazine, can we?' She smirks, that insincere self-satisfied smile which makes me want to slap her. 'What made you want to join The Jane Austen Dating Agency?' she asks.

'I obviously love Jane Austen and...' I hesitate, not wanting to share my disastrous history of dating with this judgemental piece of work.

'And...?' she asks, her eyes suddenly focused, glitteringly intent like a snake.

'I haven't had the best experience with men,' I reply in a rush. Oh no, why did I say that? It's as though she's given me a truth serum or something.

'What a shame.' Miss Palmer-Wright's smile and tone are both insincere, patronising even. 'Why do you think that is?'

I don't really want to get into a psychotherapy session right now, especially not with Miss Palmer-Wright. 'I don't know,' I reply casually. 'I guess I just haven't met the right person yet.' Thank God she moves on quickly.

'And what are the most important things you look for in a man?'

'Kind, sympathetic, reliable...' *Preferably single, not a liar, not into weird dressing up, not as a woman anyway...* I add silently.

'What about rich?' she asks deliberately, flashing that fake smile again.

'It would be nice, but it isn't that important to me.'

'That's a bit of luck then,' she mutters, typing something on her keyboard.

'Pardon?' I ask, wondering if I've heard her correctly.

She ignores me and continues with the questions. 'And if you could choose the ideal man, who would it be? Doesn't have to be a character from Jane Austen,' she adds as an afterthought.

'I guess it would be Mr Darcy. No, actually I always liked Henry Tilney – he had a great sense of humour.'

'So, your ideal man only exists in books written two hundred years ago. We may just about have found why there might be a problem with your previous relationships.' Miss Palmer-Wright smiles delightedly with herself and gives that irritating tinkly little laugh of hers.

'No, I like lots of other real men.'

'Like...'

'Like Colin Firth, Matthew Macfadyen, Aiden Turner...' I share my list of favourite actors.

'Basically any guy in breeches then, who's acted in a period drama.'

*That just about covers it, I think. God, am I really that shallow?*

'This might prove a little tricky as I believe most of those are pretty busy right now.'

I glance at her uncertainly; this is no time for her to develop a sense of humour.

'No, I mean that would be my ideal, I know they're not available. I just don't really know that many men,' I mumble, trying to hold on to any shred of dignity.

'Of course not,' she snaps, glaring. 'My little joke. Anyway...' She sweeps round in her chair and presents me with a large glossy brochure. On the front is a picture of the BBC 1995 production's Jennifer Ehle gazing up at Colin Firth with the caption... *You must allow me to tell you how ardently I admire and love you...*

'Inside you will find details of how to join the agency, how to download the app on your mobile, our fees, and the Bronze, Silver and Gold Membership schemes,' recites Miss Palmer-Wright. 'If you sign up for the Bronze Membership in the next week, I am able to offer you ten per cent off your first date which is usually one of the following: a tour and stroll in the park at Luckington Court aka The Bennets' House, afternoon tea with the Collinses if you prefer something a little less full-on, or a Regency dancing lesson at Chawton Village Hall.'

Miss Palmer-Wright finishes reciting the list, which she has obviously learnt by heart, and looks at me awaiting my response. I hesitate, this was not really what I'd been expecting from The Jane Austen Dating Agency – it wasn't what I thought it would be like. Of course I have constantly daydreamed about being transported into all the film versions of Austen's novels but I guess that isn't reality. I don't know what I had thought but this just isn't it. It all feels so weird, kind of fake, like playing at being in Austen, a bit like going to a French group but with English people who are all speaking in French so it doesn't really work. And I mean, realistically, what kind of guys are going to want to have a date involving a cup of tea? This is not exactly *Love Island*, or *Dinner Date* for that matter.

Miss Palmer-Wright leans forward in her chair. 'We are extremely popular, you know. This is why there is an incredibly comprehensive questionnaire. We, as an agency, are renowned for connecting the right sort of people, creating lasting and successful relationships which are for those in the same, shall I say, income bracket as each of our clients. Of course we wouldn't want a lawyer from Goldman Sachs matched with a cleaner from Bristol now, would we?' She tinkles again.

I recognise this sort of sales script – it sounds all too familiar. I also feel it's time for me to make my excuses and leave, but while she was talking I have been flicking nervously through the brochure. It looks good actually, the ball is at the beautiful Chatsworth House, strawberry champagne picnics sound amazing and the people aren't bad looking. Some of them are quite fit; they don't appear to be total weirdos, although of course they could be actors.

My phone suddenly rings loudly. Darn, I thought I'd put it on silent.

'Sorry.' I apologise to Miss Palmer-Wright who glares impatiently at me as I quickly check the screen. Yep, it's Dean again. For goodness sake, this guy just doesn't give up. Then I have a sudden thought – perhaps I'll give him the number for the agency. He might find himself someone else, and if not, Miss Palmer-Wright would certainly know how to deal with him! I shove my phone back in my bag, having firmly turned it off.

'How do you find people their perfect date?' I ask, suddenly having images of computer matching and random blind dates.

'We pride ourselves on our personalised matchmaking service. Emma and I, as the agency chaperones, personally review each candidate's resumé and work out their perfect match. It is a rather old-fashioned approach but we like to be traditional here at The Jane Austen Dating Agency.'

*Apart from when it comes to reading*, I think.

'It is only possible to go out with someone if introduced by the chaperones. That way there is no room for unsuitable matches and you are more likely to have things in common. We do have an app as we like to keep up to date, but it is really a log of dates you have been on and forthcoming events.' Miss Palmer-Wright has it all mapped out.

It kind of makes sense, yet I'm not convinced I want her matching me with anyone. Still, it might be worth having a look at the brochure when I get home and perhaps her colleague Emma might be nicer. She simply couldn't be much worse.

I get up from my chair in what I hope is a businesslike manner. 'Thank you for your help. I shall read the brochure, fill in the form, and return it to the agency.'

'Please allow plenty of time for us to assess your application,' says Miss Palmer-Wright. 'I don't like to point out the obvious but I do like to try to avoid any confusion. We do not necessarily accept all our applicants as we are an extremely exclusive agency.'

I trot out of the door behind her, trying not to feel like a naughty schoolgirl.

As we return to the front desk, I notice a huge wall-mounted advertising screen with images of glamorous and good-looking couples in Regency dress. They look deliriously happy, posing in front of dreamily romantic backdrops of ruined abbeys and wild moorland.

'This is impressive.' I point at the screen.

'Yes, just a few of our incredible success stories. Penelope Smith-Klein's wedding to Andrew Huntingdon was in last month's edition of *Tatler*, absolutely stunning occasion.' Miss Palmer-Wright looks as pleased with herself as though she has achieved all this single-handedly.

As I stop to admire the images, an impossibly good-looking guy comes up on the screen. He's dark and handsome, slightly swarthy and, oh yes, brooding with a hint of dark stubble smudge on his finely chiselled cheekbones. He isn't dressed in Regency costume but an extremely expensive-looking dark blue tailored suit, moulded tightly to his obviously fit body. In fact, this guy is so fit, I have a job not to stand there and gawp.

'Is this one of your clients?' I ask hopefully, thinking if he's on my list, book me in now.

'Gosh no!' Miss Palmer-Wright retorts in utter disdain at my total ignorance. 'That is Darcy Drummond,' she pauses dramatically. 'He is CEO of the agency. But surely you have heard of Darcy Drummond – of Drummond Associates? I thought you said you work in London. Huge business, darling, mother is loaded; family friends of ours. It's not what you know but who you know in this world.'

'Oh,' I reply, making a concerted effort to drag my eyes away from Darcy Drummond's image. And he's called Darcy – it must be a sign! I've never heard of Darcy Drummond, but I would certainly like to get to know him a whole lot better. Although, I bet he is surrounded by eligible women, probably Jessica Palmer-Wright at the top of the list, trampling on the others in her lethal heels. Money always attracts money, as my dad often says. It's only in the novels of Jane Austen there is any variation on this theme.

But where better than The Jane Austen Dating Agency to find

both love and money at the same time? As Lizzie says to Jane in *P and P*, 'Take care to fall in love with a man of good fortune.'

I say goodbye to Miss Palmer-Wright with barely disguised relief and a renewed determination to check out the glossy brochure. Who knows, perhaps I might be going to Pemberley after all.

# CHAPTER 3

A couple of days later, I'm back at work and the world of Jane Austen is a million miles away. I've spent most of the morning making fruitless calls with a variety of responses from not answering or not interested, to the downright rude and aggressive. I also haven't even had a chance to check out the agency brochure properly. I tried last night with a glass of wine when the phone had rung and I'd left it, thinking it might be Dean and his repetitive messages, or my mum, which would definitely mean no evening left for anything. It turned out it was my mum, who continued to phone until finally our dodgy answer machine had kicked in.

'Sophie, are you there? I need to speak to you, it's very urgent,' she'd said, sounding so agitated, it had made me scramble to the phone, scattering the brochure and its contents onto the floor.

'Hi, Mum, sorry, I was just sorting out some stuff. Is everything okay?'

'Oh, thank goodness. I've been needing to catch you. Have you sent Great Aunt Flo a birthday card?'

Oh no. My heart sank. I'd completely forgotten Great Aunt

Flo's birthday and not for the first time. She's so sweet and about ninety. I can't have missed her birthday again.

'Oh, Sophie – you knew it was today, I reminded you on Friday. Didn't you send one?' My mum always treats me as though I'm about ten.

'It's okay, Mum.' I tried to adopt a bright and cheerful every-thing-is-under-control-here tone. 'I'll send it tomorrow. I'm sure she won't mind.'

'That's not the point. I'm always telling you how important it is that the card gets there on the day. It's not much to ask. I gave you a birthday book last year. Haven't you filled it in?'

'Erm, yes? I'm just not quite sure where it is. I expect I'll find it when I've finished unpacking.' I actually can't remember where it is and I don't think I ever got around to filling it in. I'm hope-less when it comes to birthdays and other communications. It's really embarrassing but I have drawers full of unsent thank you letters and birthday cards and even worse, a sympathy card, all of which I wrote or started writing and have never sent.

I'm not joking but people have literally died waiting for a thank you card from me. I have one which I wrote for my Uncle Jim, who is now sadly no longer with us (see what I mean), when I was about twelve, and I still feel a pang of guilt when I read it. As you can imagine, it was a very long time ago and I'm sure he would have loved to have known how pleased I was with his glove puppet, though I expect I said thank you when I next saw him.


No-one ever sends cards these days anyway – a text is so much quicker and easier. Although no good with Great Aunt Flo as she hasn't got a phone. Actually, maybe that gives me an idea – I wonder if she would like one, she could probably deal with Dean for me once and for all.

'Are you listening, Sophie?' Oh no, my mum had been continuing to chat and I hadn't heard a word she'd said.

'Of course,' I replied as convincingly as possible.

My mum carried on undeterred. 'Ben did his yesterday and Chloe said she sent hers last week.'

'I expect Ben only signed yours,' I said indignantly.

'Of course he did, and I said you could too if you had been here.' Mum always has an answer for everything. Quite honestly it never occurs to her that Ben could actually go and buy his own card. He's twenty-seven, after all.

'Okay, Mum. I'll deal with it tomorrow and send it out. It'll only be a couple of days late.'

I had felt a bit rubbish; my sister Chloe is ridiculously organised even if she is busy, which is always. She remembers every card and every birthday. She does her Christmas shopping all year round so when it comes to the actual season, it's done. She makes me feel totally inadequate.

'How's Ben?' I asked, trying desperately to change the subject.

'Okay, I suppose, though he isn't at all himself.' Mum sounded worried.

'No, I suppose he's not going to be for a while.' Ben's wife, Libby, had run off with another guy last year.

'I know, he's still heartbroken, poor lad. And to think we made Libby so welcome. She was always included as part of the family. I can't understand it. And now he brings home all these different girls, disappearing off to his room with them for hours. Most embarrassing. I never know whether to call him for dinner or just leave it in the oven for later. It's so awkward.'

'I s'pose it is a bit.'

'I've been asking your dad to have a word with him but you know what he's like. He says it's interfering. Leaves it all to me, as usual.'

I made soothing noises and, thank goodness, after some time and a significant amount of chat covering most topics, including the redevelopment of the local community centre, Mum had rung off. Then Mel had walked in, so I'd pushed the brochure under the sofa – I don't think she would understand the point of a Jane Austen dating agency. It wouldn't conform to her feminist ideals.

So, the long and short of it is, I'm still none the wiser about the whole thing.

AND IT'S NOW Monday morning again. I hate Mondays, the whole working week stretching ahead and the only thing on my desk is a pile of bridal shops to phone. Today I'm in no mood to be bothering any more people who don't want to advertise with us. In fact, the whole day had started badly before I'd even got to work; the tube was extra busy and I had to run the last bit of the journey, never a good beginning as I felt dishevelled and at a disadvantage from the outset.

To add to my rubbish mood, the immaculately groomed girls in the sales team are all discussing the wonderful things they did over the weekend. Like meeting up on Saturday night at Lush – the cool new restaurant in Knightsbridge. They didn't invite me officially, which I was kind of relieved about as I could never afford £80 a course. Kelli had mentioned it casually in passing but after muttering a lame excuse, which no-one had listened to, the subject had been dropped. It sounded fabulous, if utterly pretentious, but I did feel even more than usually left out. Mel and I have difficulty scraping together the rent and certainly don't have the money for this kind of venue. I find myself wondering for the millionth time how on earth they afford it on our salary.

I'm about to pick up the desk phone and ring yet another wedding shop when my sister's number bings up on my mobile. After a quick glance to check Amanda isn't around, I grab it.

'Sophie...' Chloe sings out cheerily. 'Are you at work?'

'Of course. Where do you expect me to be on a Monday morning?' I whisper. Chloe's completely ditzy but I love her to bits.

'Ooh I thought you might be in a glamorous spa somewhere lounging round, drinking cocktails as part of the fabulous London lifestyle.' She laughs.

'I wish! Look, I can't talk long, Chloe. I've a load of calls to make. Can I phone you back at lunch?'

'I just wanted to tell you my exciting news,' she says coyly.

'Oh okay, fire away.' I flick absentmindedly at the sales list.

'Kian's moving back in.' Chloe rushes the words out, probably trying to get it over with.

'Oh my God, he's what?' I blush as I realise I've shrieked and everyone in the office is staring.

'I know he's been a bit of a... you know, a...'

'A complete and utter bastard,' I chip in, and then realise everyone is peering at me again. Obviously my conversation is a lot more interesting than theirs. I really hate open-plan offices. How's anyone meant to have any kind of private chat?

'That's a bit harsh,' she says. 'At any rate, he says he's sorry, he's changed. It was because he felt pressured and he was so sweet. You should hear what he said.'

I'm thinking *please not* as I already feel quite sick, but let her finish anyway.

'He says he'll always love me and I have to give him another chance,' she continues pitifully. She's got that dreamy note back in her voice, the one she had when she first met Kian.

'Chloe, you really can't do this; you've got to have more self-respect. You can't take him back, not after how he's been, and what he did to you. He was hideous to all of us, Mum, Dad. Kian's a nasty bit of work.' I stop because I can hear muffled sobbing on the other end of the line.

'But the thing is... I still love him.' Chloe sniffs.

'Look, I understand, and you know I'm always here for you,

whatever you decide, okay? But I'd better finish my sales list – I'll phone you back at lunchtime.' I feel bad but Chloe seems okay, saying something about buying bits for dinner, and rings off.

I sit there staring blankly at my computer. I can't believe Chloe's going to take this guy back. He's her second husband and worse than her ex. He'd sounded a really bad idea right from the start – apparently his wife didn't understand him, he was nearly divorced/separated – whatever crap he told Chloe. Most people would have avoided him, but Chloe who is really kind-hearted and always rescuing someone, whether it's dogs, old ladies or husbands, fell for Kian hook, line and sinker. After a short while of marriage to Chloe, he started being out all hours. Worse still, he took all of Chloe's confidence away with his mood swings and neurotic behaviour.

It turned out he was having an affair with someone at work and Chloe became the wife who didn't understand him. She was devastated of course and threw him out, and has been trying to move on with her own life for the last few months. She's so strong, and I thought she was succeeding, but she can be pretty stubborn – there's nothing I can do but show her some support when she needs it.

I half-heartedly pick up the phone and call a couple of salons. Neither is interested in buying any advertising space even though I've finally managed to perfect my pitch to a fine art.

I look up and am pleased to spot Mark coming towards me. 'Morning – just came along to find out how you got on at the agency, darling?'

He says the word agency in a loud stage whisper, which makes me want to either giggle or squirm in my seat as subtlety is not exactly his speciality.

'It was all right.'

'Sounds great.' He smiles sarcastically. 'Come on, let's go get some blinis and you can fill me in on the goss.'

I jump up, glad to escape my desk. This is the most motivated

I've felt all morning. Modiste is simply too posh to have bacon butties or coffee mid-morning; smoked salmon blinis are brought in by courier from Harrods.

SITTING GOSSIPING TO MARK, munching a yummy mouthful of blini, the world suddenly looks a brighter place. I recount the details of my visit to The Jane Austen Dating Agency, my raucous impression of Miss Palmer-Wright causing him to go off into fits of laughter.

'I simply can't wait to meet her,' he hoots, wiping tears from his eyes. 'You have to get me in there somehow... and as for Darcy Drummond, he sounds delicious.'

'I don't know. I'm not sure if I'm going to join,' I reply pensively.

'Why on earth not? You can't let one bitchy cow put you off. You've been a crazy Jane Austen fan ever since I've known you, you can't miss out on this incredible opportunity. It's perfect for you.'

'You've only known me a few weeks,' I tease, 'but yes, I'm going to think about it. God, it's 11.30, we'd better get back to the office.'

We walk slowly towards the sales floor. Mark scrutinises me with his intense blue eyes, pulling his tousled blond hair back with his hand. He's making me nervous staring like that.

'You need an escape, a distraction, darling. You're young and single yet you have mal de vivre. Why aren't you out partying?' He shrugs comically. Everything Mark does is exaggerated, as though he's playing a part on the stage.

'Mal de vivre?'

'You're just too serious, like you're carrying the burden of the world on those shoulders. All work and no play can make life pretty damn boring.'

I smile sheepishly. 'Yeah, I know, but by the time I get home

I'm tired and you know, blah blah.' I try to defend myself, aware it sounds like empty excuses. Mark's a total party animal, always out at some premiere or other. I don't know how he does it. He's got to be ten years older than me but he seems to have boundless energy. He's the kind of guy who appears to know everyone in the room within about two minutes of being there, and is often in someone or other's photo looking tanned and fabulous. Mark's life seems so relaxed and above all, fun.

'As you aren't going to help yourself, it's a good job I have the cure for your ennui right here.' Mark waves a smart-looking envelope at me.

I open it and pull out a very elegant embossed card. It's an invitation for the GQ Grooming Awards at the Royal Opera House. There's an awards dinner, dress code formal of course.

'Sounds very nice,' I say noncommittally. 'Are you going then?'

'Yes of course, and you, darling, are coming with me.'

'Me?'

'Yes, you, Cinderella, are coming to the ball. Well, not a ball exactly but it'll be a pretty amazing night.'

'How come?'

'Yours truly has been given an extra ticket. Tim's busy that evening with Fashion Week stuff so who better to come with me than you?'

'Sounds fun,' I say carefully, trying not to sound too ungrateful or unenthusiastic.

'Fun... fun, darling?' Mark leaps about, gesticulating, causing those around us to stare and tut at the noise. 'It's *the* social event of the year! Half these snotty cows would do anything to get in. In any case, you'll so want to go when you know who's going to be there! Look at the invitation again.'

I peer at the card, unseeing until I suddenly spot, written in small print at the bottom, 'Sponsored by Drummond Associates'.

'Oh.' I blush. 'Do you think he'll be there?' I ask shyly, referring to Darcy Drummond of course.

'You bet he will, so no more playing hard to get,' Mark scoffs. 'Now, we just need to talk about what you're going to wear, darling.'

I guess it sounds a bit sad stalking a man I've only seen in a photo once, but I have been spending rather a lot of my waking and sleeping hours thinking about Darcy Drummond. I've googled him a couple of times too, perhaps more than a couple – in the name of research of course. And to go to an awards ceremony, dress up in something stylish and maybe appear on TV. It's a hard job but someone's got to do it.

Anyway, I hate to admit it, but I've often secretly thought Mrs Bennet was kind of right to send Jane to Netherfield on horseback so she had to stay overnight. Pushy yes, but it put Jane right under Bingley's nose and without her knowledge, it brought Lizzie even more to the attention of Mr Darcy. They had some pretty snappy and electrically charged exchanges during that stay.

More to the point, in spite of all the evidence to the contrary, I still hope that maybe one day, I – like Jane Austen's heroines – can create my own happy ever after.

# CHAPTER 4

It's really late by the time I stumble in from work, as right at the end of the day, Amanda found a load of sales leads that needed documenting and in my usual way, I didn't feel able to say no. You never know, it might help me get a good reference just in case I ever get noticed by someone in Editorial, although somehow I doubt it. And to top off my perfect day, the Victoria Line was disrupted again due to emergency works, so it's well past nine when I get in the door.

'Your mum phoned earlier,' Mel calls from the bathroom.

'Oh God, not again. What did she want this time? I haven't forgotten someone else's birthday, have I?' I shout back.

'No, it was something about a teaching course she's found near Oxford.' Mel comes out from the bathroom, her head in a towel.

'Not that flipping PGCE course again. Will she ever give up?' I ask, throwing myself down in a chair. As part of the better-job prospects thing, my mum has this idea I should be a primary school teacher, probably because she loves her job and also due to the long holidays. I do think that bit sounds good but I can't imagine teaching in a school every day. Anyway,

Mum works every hour there is. When she isn't at school, she's preparing lessons, marking, writing reports and there's no such thing as a tea break – too much time spent on first aid and paperwork.

'I can sort of see her point in some ways,' Mel says, vigorously drying her mop of curly hair with a towel. 'You're not exactly happy in this job at Modiste, are you? Sounds boring as hell.'

That's one of the things I love about Mel, she always says it how it is. She's also easy going, arty and doesn't give a stuff what other people think about her, to boot. She's studying at the Royal College of Art and is awesomely talented. Mel's one of those enviable people you could give a piece of scrunched up paper and a plastic bag and she'd create something amazing out of it. She's always fabricating incredible structures out of the most unlikely articles.

Lately she's been concentrating on texture so I keep finding bits of knitting, weaving and other scraps of fabric round the flat. That's the only thing; she is kind of messy but then I'm not the tidiest person in the world either. Every so often we get fed up with it and run round with bin bags, chucking stuff in and hiding it in the car or behind the sofa. (That's usually only when someone's coming round though.)

The other thing about Mel is, she's really modest about her work; it's as though she doesn't really know how good she is. I think it's because her siblings all went to Oxford or Cambridge, I can't remember which, but her parents give her a hard time about it. They seem to think she's the failure of the family, just because she isn't academic; people can be so weird sometimes. I don't understand why they aren't able to celebrate how talented she is. It's like Mel has to constantly try to prove herself to them and she's wasting her time because they're the ones with issues, not her.

'Oh, by the way,' Mel grabs a vibrant pink Post-it with a scribbled note on it, 'speaking of boring, some woman rang from The

Jane Austen Dating Agency. What the heck is that, for goodness sake?'

'Nothing really,' I say casually, 'just something I heard about in a magazine.'

'Her name was Emma Woodtree. She wanted to know if you've filled in the rest of the forms yet as she doesn't seem to have received them?' Mel laughs. 'Have you joined a historical dating agency? I know you're crazy about literature but this sounds bizarre. I can picture you dressed like ladies drinking tea and reading Austen!'

'Oh erm, yeah, I mean no.' I find myself blushing with embarrassment. Of course, I'd given the agency my new home number as well as my mobile, having finally changed both in an effort to stop Dean's stalking. Darn, now Mel will think I'm a totally sad case. I clear my throat and slope off into the kitchen to pour a glass of wine. 'Yes, I was thinking about joining, it sounded quite good actually.'

'This Emma person seemed nice, but what do you do for dates? Dress up in Regency costume and prance about pretending to be characters from Jane Austen's novels?' Mel's doubled up with laughter. 'You do realise all the guys will either be complete weirdos or gay?'

She's probably nearer the truth than she realises. 'I thought I might give it a go,' I say casually. 'In any case, I may not need a dating agency, something a tad more exciting might have come up.'

'Really?'

'Guess who's going to the GQ Best Groomed Men Awards? You never know who I might meet.'

'Oooh you go, girl! Come on spill, tell all. What are you wearing, who's going?' Mel jumps off the sofa in her excitement. 'I want to hear every detail.'

'There isn't much to tell yet, but I'll fill you in on the story so far over a takeout. I'll order the pizza, you grab some more wine.'

. . .

A COUPLE OF DAYS LATER, I'm getting a bit panicky about this whole awards evening. The reality is, no-one goes out in London without major getting ready first. I've learnt this the hard way as my usual routine is a bit slap dash, to put it mildly.

For the girls at Modiste, pampering and being well groomed is a serious and full-time occupation in itself. They all spend several hours preparing just to go out for a drink, their hair immaculate, make-up flawless and Prada bags at the ready.

'Do you know any good beauty salons?' I had asked Heidi one day at work. She can be slightly kinder than the others.

'Yes, Bliss is amazing – I go every week, just to keep on top of the tan and my eyelash extensions,' she had replied enthusiastically. 'You must go – they're so good in there. Make sure you tell them I sent you, then I'll get a reduction next time.'

'Isn't it really expensive?' I had asked nervously.

'Not really, and it's so important to keep yourself looking good, don't you think?'

It's all so simple for these girls as it never occurs to them that a world without regular facials might exist. My mum doesn't wear make-up. 'Soap and water' she always says is more than fine. I can hear her now, 'Your gran always swore by splashing her face with cold water, it closes the pores you know, and she always had beautiful skin.' As a matter of fact, my mum also has great skin for her age, so perhaps there is something in it after all.

There are times in life, however, when a girl really needs to impress and the GQ Awards is definitely this occasion, especially if the delectable Darcy Drummond is going to be there. He must be used to beautifully groomed and manicured women throwing themselves at him the whole time, so I need to look amazing.

I check out the website for Bliss which is in Oxford Street, but the prices are out of my reach. After much angst, I book myself into the quite well-reviewed Allure on Lower Richmond Road.

The prices, though high, are at least possible. The awards ceremony is this evening and I'm really nervous, but figure that all it takes to boost my confidence is a complete makeover. That's the idea anyway.

ALLURE TURNS out to be a little less exciting than the lounge back at our flat and the girl who does my nails is rather worryingly goth-like, dressed in dreary clothes with black fingernails and purple make-up.

A couple of hours later, however, I walk out with freshly waxed legs and a face full of make-up, which looks pretty good I think.

My hair has been professionally washed and styled on big curlers without mishap, and when revealed at the end, is majorly BIG hair. I kind of like it as it gives me a sort of pampered well-groomed look and I don't look anything like my usual self, which is definitely a good thing.

UPON ARRIVING BACK at the flat, Mel is impressed, 'Wow! Someone's swapped my roomie for a supermodel.'

'Shut up!' I return. I know she's exaggerating but inside I'm secretly quite flattered. I'm ready... move over, Lizzie... Darcy Drummond, here I come...

# CHAPTER 5

'Can I have your ticket please?' asks an intimidating burly security guy on the door of the Royal Opera House.

'Oh yes, of course.' I scrabble about in my tiny bag, scattering tissues, a concealer stick, and lippy around me while I desperately try to find the elusive card Mark had rather ill-advisedly given me for safekeeping.

'Here it is.' I pass the ticket to the doorman with relief. 'But my friend Mark's vanished.'

'He'll have to catch you up, won't he, or you'll have to meet him back here in a while. Look, will you move aside, lady, we've got the press team coming through any minute.'

I am unceremoniously squashed against the wall as half a coach load of motley television crew bundle past through the entrance doors. It always amazes me how much room television cameras take up, this is meant to be the digital age where everything seems to have got smaller and more compact. Phones, computers, everything that is except TV cameras, and as for those great big furry mikes, they're like something left over from the seventies.

A stunningly beautiful woman swathed in a simple sheath dress, which I know must have cost thousands in the way simplicity always does, sweeps in behind the crew. She is surrounded by make-up artists still dabbing at her already perfect, flawlessly made-up face.

'That's enough, Harper,' she snaps, swatting at her assistants as though they are a couple of irritating and particularly persistent flies.

'Christie?' calls a large thickset man with a beard who I figure might be the producer. 'Ready for intro, darling?'

'I suppose so.' Christie frowns. Or she would have frowned but her forehead appears suspiciously immobile. 'This is a pain in the arse. It says in my contract I was to have a day's prep and you've given me two bloody hours, Zach. I won't do it again, next time you can get Davina to present the awards.'

'It'll all be fine. You look incredible as always, darling, you know you do,' Zach placates expertly.

'Yoohoo, Christie!' someone calls from the doorway. It sounds familiar but I can't quite place the voice.

'Jessica, darling, how lovely to see you.' Christie is air kissed by a tall raven-haired, elegant in a skeletal way, woman dressed in a heavenly Louis Vuitton beaded dress.

I can't believe it, it's Jessica Palmer-Wright. I shrink back into the shadows, thinking please don't let her see me. Fortunately, Jessica is too busy hobnobbing with Christie, whoever she is.

'Darling,' she breathes, 'another divine little piece of couture you're wearing, you lucky thing.'

Christie visibly preens herself, attempting to return the compliment. 'Look at you. Louis Vuitton, I presume?'

'This old thing?' Jessica Palmer-Wright dismisses her frighteningly expensive dress with a nonchalant sweep of her arms.

I'm still hiding, half transfixed by their ridiculous charade and half terrified they will spy me standing alone in the shadow of the door frame. Thank goodness the two of them sweep off into the Opera House together and I finally spot Mark wandering about inside the foyer looking relaxed and on fleek as usual.

'Mark!' I shout across the doorway as he comes into view again the other side of a pillar. 'Thanks for waiting.'

'Sophie! Looking fabulous, darling. You scrub up well after all.' Mark saunters over and air kisses me four times on either side of my face in true Modiste fashion. I've never got used to this habit although it finally dawns on me that the reason for such a seemingly pointless practice is so make-up is left intact. I guess it's never occurred to me before as I don't normally wear it. 'Sorry, darling, amazing coincidence, I just bumped into Will, my old chum from the good old days of working at *Men's Fitness* magazine. And pretty fit he is too I can tell you, such a shame he's straight. Would have done for you though, darling, if you hadn't set your heart on Mr Darcy! Speaking of which, have you spotted him yet?'

'No.' I shush him, flushing bright red as we're surrounded by crowds of people thronging into the building. 'You're so embarrassing, Mark.'

'Why? Might as well let him know you like him from the start. No point faffing around.'

I begin to have second thoughts about this whole idea as Mark is about as subtle as a blow to the head with a sledgehammer. Not that I haven't been fantasising about how I will meet Darcy. First it might be a discreet glance across a crowded room. He would suddenly notice me and be irresistibly drawn to my side, making his way across the floor, a bit like Matthew Macfadyen with Keira Knightley in the 2005 *Pride and Prejudice*, except they were outside in a field and it was misty. I want him to gaze at me, although maybe not in a creepy stalker way, and not controlling either. Just romantic – you know what I mean.

'Miss Johnson,' he would say in a really deep sexy voice,

taking my hand in his and drawing it to his lips, 'would you do me the very great honour of dancing with me?'

'Sophie? Hello?' Oops, awkward, Mark is trying to attract my attention... 'Shall we go in or are you intending to hide in the doorway all evening?'

He takes my hand and we walk into the Opera House.


THERE ARE handsome men in black tie everywhere, beautiful women in long glittering dresses and flashing lights dazzling us as press photographers snap important people as they enter. We're efficiently ushered by elegantly attired waiters to the Paul Hamlyn Hall and once inside, I have to remind myself to remember to breathe.

The room is like a giant conservatory with large round tables swathed in elegant white cloths, the chairs covered also. The lighting is subtle and, I desperately hope, flattering. I'm still not really comfortable with wearing this much make-up. I'd like to stop and just drink it all in but am propelled instead towards a table as everyone is sitting themselves down. I find my name and go to take my seat before noticing with dismay that Mark's name is not next to mine.

'Are you sitting the other side of the table?' I ask hopefully, but he shakes his head.

'I did think I might be over with the guys from GQ,' he says, 'but you're a big girl now, Sophie, so I'm sure you'll be fine.' He leans in towards me and adds in a loud stage whisper, 'Make sure you network. That's what these things are all about. I've got you in here, don't waste the opportunity.'

I plonk myself down with a sinking heart, that horrible feeling washing over me, the one I used to get when I was the new girl at school in the canteen at lunchtime with nowhere to sit. I thought I'd forgotten what it felt like but the sense of abandonment flooded over me as though it were yesterday. If only I knew someone from somewhere, but glancing around there aren't any familiar friendly faces. Then I take a deep breath, tell myself firmly to get a grip, and hold my head up. I have a degree from Oxford, for goodness sake, I can handle one little awards dinner.

'Hello,' I squeak to the rather gruff-looking old man next to me. 'I'm Sophie, nice to meet you, er...?'

'Henry.'

Oh sigh of relief, it's worked, he's talking to me. 'Sir Henry Greaves, Corporate Banking. And you are?'

'Sophie, Sophie Johnson.'

'And what do you do, Sophie Johnston?'

'It's Johnson actually. Erm, I work for Modiste, it's a fashion magazine.'

'Yes, I know,' he returns abruptly. 'Haven't been living in a hole my entire life, y'know. What position do you hold there?'

I sweep away a childish desire to reply, 'None of your business,' but I don't. Instead, I force myself to smile pleasantly, 'I work in Classified Sales.'

'Oh,' he says with an air of finality and turns back to continue his discussion with the lady on his other side about shares and mergers. And that's it, the conversation is at an end.

And I'm not joking, that's the last time he talks to me all evening, which is kind of awkward as he's sitting on my right, leaving me with only the man on my left to talk to, if he's vaguely normal. I peek casually at him. He's younger and, oh hello, quite nice looking actually. And he smiles at me when I catch his eye.

'Hi,' he says. 'We'd better introduce ourselves if we are sitting together this evening. I'm Rupert.'

This is more like it. I relax a little. 'Hi, Rupert, I'm Sophie, pleased to meet you.'

'You too. These things can be a bit of a bore but the food's top notch and there's always plenty of Bolly.'

'That's something, I guess, and hopefully you don't need to ask me what I do.' I laugh. Oh dear, perhaps I've had rather too much wine already.

'Why would I do that? Though I guess it is something to start a conversation.'

'And end it.' I eyeball in a totally non-subtle manner towards the old chap the other side of me. 'I hate it when people make irrational judgements on what I do. What does he know anyway, the old duffer?'

'He's the MD of Zenton Banking in the City, and also my uncle actually.'

'Oh.'

And that's the end of that conversation. This just gets worse.

I DON'T KNOW how I get through dinner. It seems to go on forever as there are several courses and interminable choices to make, such as which cutlery to use next. My coping strategy is to try everything put in front of me and down each different drink offered, probably not a good idea as I have a habit of slurping wine more frequently when nervous, and the attentive waiter keeps topping it up so I've lost track of how much I've had.

Having blown all chances of reasonable conversation in my immediate vicinity, I smile at the elegant and stylish lady opposite, hoping to find an ally, but she's far too busy trying to impress Rupert, nephew of rich old duffer. I look across at Mark, trying to catch his eye, but he's having a whale of a time as usual, laughing and joking – the life and soul of the party.

While I am gazing wistfully, one of the paps come up and snap some pics of him and his smiling comrades. I make a mental note to look for these in the next edition of *Hello*. I have been craning my neck, in a subtle way of course, to try to spot Darcy

Drummond, but can't really see much except the people talking and laughing on the tables around me.

Just as I'm thinking I could maybe escape to the ladies at least for a respite from looking like Norma no mates, and also for something to do as I'm pretty bored, there's a chinking of a glass and the chatter dulls to a quiet murmur.

'Pray silence for your hostess, Christie Salvatore!'

The sickeningly beautiful Christie, whose arrival and diva tendencies I'm well acquainted with from earlier, sashays onto the platform, smiling dazzlingly at the room. She looks totally different from before as she's now on a charm offensive. Effortlessly taking the stage, she flirts, teases and woos her audience. I have to admire it in spite of my dislike for her. She's not only made presenting a fine craft, she's truly captivating, having just the right amount of intro to each product, building the suspense to the big reveal of each category winner who is rewarded with multiple air kisses.

I try to view the proceedings by edging slightly higher in my seat, ignoring the disapproving glares of Sir Henry Greaves on my right. There's a table near the front where a glamorous older woman catches my eye. She must be about sixty, with long diamond earrings and huge jewels sparkling on her fingers, enormous like knuckledusters. She's very attractive in a carefully made-up way, her hair is smartly coiffured and she looks rather like a 1940s film star with impossibly raven hair, impeccably defined brows, bright red lipstick and long black gloves.

I glance at the man sitting next to her, then start in my seat. It's Darcy Drummond and, oh my, he's absolutely gorgeous. Even better looking than his pics, if that's possible. He has dark, casually arranged, windswept hair and slight stubble. He's fit too, especially in black tie. As I gaze at him transfixed, I notice his lips are firmly closed together and he appears thoroughly bored by the proceedings, although I can understand that. He's fiddling with his napkin like a little kid.

The expensively dressed woman on his left touches his arm and tries to engage him in conversation. On closer inspection, I realise it's Jessica Palmer-Wright, the cow; she would be there right next to him. She always seems to be everywhere I don't want her to be. In fact, she always seems to be everywhere full stop. I gaze at her, trying not to notice the flirty long eyelashes, her hard, insincere smile, the tiny gap in her front teeth, the somehow intimate gestures as she pats Darcy's hand, laughing coquettishly at the tiniest thing he says. God, I've got to stop obsessing like this, he's not mine after all, he doesn't even know I exist.

Christie Salvatore's voice breaks through my distracted thoughts. 'And to present the award for best wet shave is our very own Darcy Drummond, CEO of our wonderful sponsors Drummond Associates.'

Darcy removes Miss Palmer-Wright's hand from his sleeve, folds his napkin neatly onto his side plate, and strides up to the podium to be embraced by the delectable Christie. He does look more cheerful all of a sudden, but I guess I don't blame him; she is captivating. He must have said something suave and amusing to her, as she laughs, showing all her pearly white teeth and he grins back, transforming his features from stern and remote to boyishly handsome. I would give anything for him to smile at me like that.

Darcy eventually returns to his seat, having presented the award to an ironically extremely beardy guy who's won the best wet shave award. I'm not quite sure how that works. From that point on, I drift off into a pleasant little daydream of my own involving Darcy in a pair of swimming trunks and a sun-kissed beach, while a whole host of famous award winners are presented, and finally it's time to leave our tables and mingle.

It only now dawns on me that there's a huge flaw in my plan to meet Darcy Drummond. Things haven't changed all that much in the two hundred years since Austen. At these evenings you don't present yourself to someone without being formally introduced, otherwise you end up in the embarrassingly awkward situation of Mr Collins. Just as money begets money, rich people meet other rich people, and I'm about to go home like a saddo on my own again. I don't belong here.

All through dinner, everyone on my table had been discussing business. The price of shares, profits, mergers, it was a foreign language to me and at least I can speak some of those. I am out of my depth, I've been bored to tears. I feel like chipping in with, 'Did anyone see *Victoria* last night?' but manage to stop myself.

I decide to escape to the ladies and then somehow slip off. I can always text Mark later to let him know I've gone home early, saying I had a headache or something.

I manage to stand up without stumbling or removing the tablecloth, which is always a bonus. I definitely feel a little wobbly, all those top-ups taking their toll. Thankfully the toilets aren't too far away and I take the opportunity to chill out a minute and peer in the mirror.

This proves to be a mistake as I find, as usual at this time in the evening, my lipstick is non-existent and my eye make-up is mostly below my eyes rather than on them. I reapply my lippy, half-heartedly scrape at my smudgy eyes with a tissue, and give it up as a bad job. In any case, I have my escape route planned: I'm going to leg it through the hall, round to the entrance, and make fast my exit.

THIS PLAN IS WORKING fine until I come face to face with, oh God, you've guessed it, Miss Palmer-Wright. And standing next to her is the utterly delicious Darcy Drummond. I give a vague smile in his general direction and concentrate on Miss Palmer-Wright to steady my nerves. I don't think she'd have recognised me but like a blundering idiot, I hail her in a bizarrely false hearty manner. 'Miss Palmer-Wright, jolly nice to see you!'

'Oh.' She recoils. It's almost comic, you can see she's trying to remember where she's met me before, checking her mental log of important people to see if I'm on it. Of course I'm not. 'Oh, Sophie, isn't it? You were applying to become a member of the dating agency. I didn't expect to see you here.'

*I bet you didn't*, I think, but instead bluster, 'No, I haven't been here before, jolly nice though.'

'And what a charming dress, but what's this?' She pulls at the designer gap in the waist of my Versace dress with a perfectly manicured hand. 'You seem to have lost half of it, darling!'

I excuse myself, seething inwardly. Trust her to be lurking by the door. And she didn't introduce me to Darcy, but then that doesn't surprise me.

Reaching the exit with relief, I rummage through my bag for my mobile so I can text Mark and let him know I'm leaving early. For goodness sake, I must have left it in the ladies while looking for my lipstick; I knew I should have tidied out my bag before I left home. For one wild moment I consider leaving without my phone. No, it contains my entire life. There's nothing for it but to sneak back to the loo, grab my phone, and get the heck out again.

I REACH the ladies room unscathed, I guess that isn't surprising as I've been pretty much ignored by everyone since I got here. I grab my mobile and am about to re-enter the hall when I hear the familiar dulcet tones of Miss Palmer-Wright. I reverse back behind the studded hall door before I can even think what I'm doing. I can't face meeting her again this evening.

'Of course, most of our clientele at the agency are far superior,' she is saying, 'been to Marlborough College, then gap year, you know the sort of thing. That's the calibre of client we are looking for. But then we do have to include some plebs, they usually join on the Bronze Scheme, keeps them happy and out of the way of our more salubrious guests. Show them a bit of

Regency dancing and where Jane Austen lived and they're perfectly satisfied.'

Her voice goes lower but I still manage to make her out. 'Sophie is one of those spinster types who lives in a book. I expect she models herself on Jane Austen. Sad really because she's not bad looking, I suppose, if you like that sort of thing. Could be quite pretty if she bothered with her appearance, although she'll put most clients off by twittering on about novels. Probably one of those dreadful feminists! Says she works for some fashion magazine but I should think she makes the tea.' She gives her hideously annoying tinkly little laugh.

I strain my ears to hear if Darcy says anything in reply. I don't catch the first bit but then, 'We'll talk about targets at next week's meeting.'

I like his voice, it's deep and sexy, purposeful.

'But for God's sake, we need some kind of marketing meeting asap. We don't want to attract any more crazy feminist Austen fans who wouldn't know reality if it jumped up and hit them in the face. It's bad for business, that's not the clientele we're looking for at all.'

I reel back in shock, unable to believe his words. What a complete and utter chauvinist pig. What does he mean by calling me a feminist just because I love Jane Austen? Although it was Miss Palmer-Wright who started it, he could have defended me, not that he knows me, but still. And as for living in the real world, of course I do, it's just I enjoy a bit of escapism sometimes. Okay, quite a lot of the time. What's wrong with that? Anyway, it's more fun than Darcy's sad boring world of old men, mergers and figures. In any case, why on earth is he running a Jane Austen Dating Agency if he doesn't even like what she represents? It makes me want to laugh out loud at the ridiculousness of it.

I'm so angry I'm determined not to stay hidden any longer. Why should I hide from such people? Flouncing out from behind the door, flicking my long skirt behind me, I glance at Darcy as I go past, shooting him a dazzling smile. It's hard not to laugh at his surprised face, demonstrating he's been in ignorance of my proximity. I keep on walking. Okay, so my heel wobbles and I nearly face-plant in the middle of the dance floor, but I hold my head high in spite of wanting to shrivel up inside, and leave the building.

# CHAPTER 6

The next morning, I wake up feeling worse for wear, gingerly opening one eye, then the other. My bleary gaze falls on the black Versace dress with the offensive designer gap in the waist, and my discarded sparkly shoes all lying in a depressing heap in the corner. I hate cheap shoes, I'm never wearing them again, they were excruciatingly uncomfortable. Perhaps I'll save up for some L.K. Bennett heels. I have had my eye on the beige court shoes Princess Kate wears so frequently. She always looks incredible, then again she'd still be stunning in an old pair of flip-flops.

Oh God, I hate the all-too-familiar sinking feeling I get after a rubbish night out. The anti-climax is so much more acute this time following the exhilaration of planning the outfit, getting ready, dreaming of being on TV, chatting suavely to celebrities and being a whirlwind social success. The reality had been brutal, with me spending half the evening feeling invisible and the rest of it wishing I were. I'm kind of used to being disappointed on the dating front but this social ineptitude is new.

I lie in bed, brooding over why the evening had been such a disaster. I mean, I hadn't even been able to carry out a normal conversation on my table. Usually I'm quite chatty and can talk to pretty much anyone. I was a member of the debating club and Social Secretary at St Elena's College for the whole of the second year, for goodness sake. Yet last night, I'd been unable to rub two words together without either saying the wrong thing or offending someone.

I guess I have to face it; I didn't fit in with this crowd full stop. I can't get rid of the nagging feeling that maybe my mum is right (she often is unfortunately), that the glamorous world of fashion and bling is just not me. Although last night was more like a board meeting, nothing to do with anything as frivolous or entertaining as fashion. What was it some famous person said about the loneliness of being alone in a crowd? Whoever it was, I know how they felt.

And as for Darcy Drummond, I feel my face flush with toe-curling shame at the remembrance of his words. I'm an embarrassment, not the sort of client they want at The Jane Austen Dating Agency. Anyway, there's nothing wrong with being a feminist, he should know most women are these days. Move into this century, Darcy. We have equal rights so you'd better get over it. And for his information, I do live in the real world, I have a job and pay rent, and only fantasise occasionally about being one of the heroines of Jane Austen's novels… Maybe sometimes… okay, quite a lot actually. But so what if I do, it makes me happy. Well, maybe not that happy but it's more interesting than sitting and talking about stocks and shares.

It's typical that bitchy Jessica Palmer-Wright reports back to Darcy, pouring poison into his ear. And she doesn't know anything about me or books or Jane Austen for that matter. How dare they run a Jane Austen dating agency when they have no respect for her or people who enjoy her writing or anything else. Then it dawns on me, of course, it's another money-making scheme, probably a tax scam of some kind or other. Talk about me living in a world of reality, The Jane Austen Dating Agency is no more than a sham. And Mr Drummond is an arrogant stuck-up male chauvinist pig.

'Anyone awake?' Mel knocks softly on my bedroom door. 'How did last night go? I meant to stay up to hear all the goss but fell asleep over my art project.'

'Come on in,' I manage, and Mel sits on the bed, looking sickeningly glowing and healthy after her usual early morning run by the river.

'Oh dear.' She smiles. 'Someone is a bit worse for wear. Want a cuppa?'

'Yes please.' I'm definitely in need of tea. I probably should have something healthy and detoxing but all I fancy is something strong and caffeinated.

Mel, bless her, goes off and soon returns with a wonderfully sweet cup of tea and small toasted soldiers smothered in Marmite.

'Come on then, what went wrong? It's no good you protesting it wasn't a crap night because we've lived together long enough now for me to know your woebegone, could things possibly get any worse, face.' Mel knows me all too well.

'I was a complete disaster,' I confess and give her a blow-by-blow account.

'It's not that bad,' says Mel in her usual cheerful way. 'You had to spend an evening with people you have nothing in common with and you weren't really interested in. So you didn't enjoy their company. D'uh, not surprising really considering your background. And Darcy is a bit of an arsey after all. He won't be the first or last loser you've liked the look of only to find out, what a shock, that he really is actually a total loser.'

'He hurt my feelings though. I could have forgiven him for being such an arrogant sod or laughed it off if he hadn't been so bloody personal,' I grumble.

'If he can't see how lovely you are, then more fool him. Shame though as he's disgustingly rich and I have a feeling marrying money is the only way you're going to fund all those expensive tastes you have.'

This makes us both laugh and I giggle away about Arsey Darcy so much that I nearly fall off the bed, which all means I begin to feel a bit more human again until my phone pings the arrival of my Facebook notifications full of images of Kian and Chloe, his weaselly face horribly smug. I log out as I feel really sick by now and relieve my feelings by singing 'I hate men' at top volume. Fortunately, Mel can't hear as she's plugged into her headphones, back at her art desk once more.

Bizarrely for me, I feel inspired to sort out my room. Maybe if I'm a bit more organised generally, perhaps the rest of my life might start miraculously working out. God, that's the sort of thing my mum would say. Anyway, I give it a go.

Keeping busy seems a good idea. I shove things out of my cupboard onto the bed. This is usually my idea of tidying up, then I get bored after an hour or so, wander off to do something else, then come back at bedtime, really tired, and end up shoving the stuff back in the cupboard, leaving a lethal trap for the next time I open the door.

While trying to find the bottom of my desk, I come across the brochure for The Jane Austen Dating Agency and go to throw it into the recycling bin. It hovers there in my hand a moment too long. I can't quite bring myself to let go of the glossy brochure, or my dreams for that matter. Idly I flick through the pages. I haven't actually read it properly, or studied the terms and conditions yet, I just sat daydreaming over the pics of Colin Firth as Mr Darcy.

Reading the small print, I become engrossed in spite of myself, studying the different levels of membership, the Bronze Scheme is the most basic: learn to dance in the style of Austen in Chawton Village Hall and afternoon tea at Hunsford Parsonage. Obviously for the die-hard Jane Austen fans. For the Silver Scheme there are strawberry champagne picnics in various locations and a trip to No. 1 Royal Crescent in Bath. Included in the Gold Scheme, which is the most elite membership I'm apparently not eligible for, is a personal guided tour of Chatsworth House and the potential to meet some of the actors from the 1995 production of *Pride and Prejudice* at a conference celebrating different editions and performances of the novel. All of this culminates in The Grand Ball at Pemberley.

I reread the blurb, explaining how it all works. Contrary to Miss PW's comments, the main difference between the schemes seems to be money. What a surprise. But peering at it again, ignoring my aching head, the sentence reads, 'Applicants are to understand that The Jane Austen Dating Agency holds the right to withdraw membership to any client, should their behaviour not meet with the rules of etiquette stated by the agency. It should also be understood that membership is by application only, at the discretion of Miss Palmer-Wright, Head of Membership, or Miss Emma Woodtree, Publicity Manager, and they both retain the right to refuse admission of membership at any time.'

My addled brain attempts to understand the jargon. Surely that means it isn't just up to Miss Bitch-Face or Arsey Darcey which membership scheme I'm able to join under.

I ponder this thought while struggling through the shower, half-heartedly checking out my previous week's non-existent sales figures for Modiste in readiness for work the next day, and while walking to the shop and back in the hope it might clear my aching head. The price difference between the bands is quite high and I must admit the Gold Membership is beyond my mediocre monthly salary, but I'm beginning to feel a growing and steely determination to prove those two miseries wrong. At a stretch, and going without that gym membership I've been half-heartedly toying with (I hate the gym), and forgoing the holiday I've been considering taking to Spain (also a sore subject as Mel is broke in the style of all struggling artists trying to scrape a living in London), I can just about get the funds together for the Silver

Membership, and why shouldn't I try for it? I am going to bloody well show those two that Sophie Johnson, up and coming Sales Executive at Modiste, can kick butt.

WHILE EATING yummy takeaway from the local Chinese with Mel that evening (will definitely need to go to the gym now), my phone announces the arrival of a new e-mail. 'Listen to this,' I chortle. 'You are cordially invited to a Regency Evening at The Jane Austen Dating Agency, ticket includes complimentary glass of bubbly, free entry for two friends and a taster lesson of Regency dancing.'

'Sounds like a riot,' Mel remarks drily. She's not exactly a literature fan and although a feminist, she's more the kind who chain themselves to the fence outside the Houses of Parliament to protest against animal cruelty rather than Austen addict. Incidentally she's also a veggie and makes all her own clothes out of environmentally friendly recycled fabric. I smile to myself, wondering what Arsey Darcy and Miss PW might make of her.

'It would be so amazing,' I exclaim, 'and I can use it to dip a toe in the water to see if I want to join the agency.'

'Great, good idea,' Mel mumbles, halfway through a mouthful of tofu and rice.

'But I don't want to go on my own... I can't face that evil duo again... that is, unless I have major backup...' I leave off wistfully, hoping Mel might fill the silence.

'Some friend you are,' she says. 'Give me one good reason why I should ever be seen dead at an Austen convention, sounds like a load of freaks to me.'

'Because you're my best friend ever...' I can see Mel isn't convinced. 'And I'll cook dinner for a week.' She's wavering. That would give her a lot more time to complete her latest creation.

'Two weeks,' she states firmly, 'and you owe me big time. And I'm not under any circumstances wearing Regency dress.'

'You're the best, Mel.' I envelop her in a bear hug.

I'm in the middle of the washing-up, somehow this seems to have been thrown in as part of the bargain as well, when the phone goes.

'Sophie, hellooo.' It's Chloe again, but she sounds glum in spite of her usual sing-song greeting.

'What's up?'

'Oh nothing,' she replies brightly, but I can tell something's wrong because I know Chloe too well.

'Kian okay?'

'Oh yes, he's fine. It's just he's really busy at the moment, lots on at work, and he's having to cover someone else's extra shifts so he's out most nights.' Chloe sounds pretty down.

'You can come over here any time, you know that,' I offer.

'I know. Are you okay, Soph? You don't sound quite your usual cheery self. And a bit croaky. You been out partying all night?'

I can never hide anything from Chloe for long. 'Yes, I'm fine, just had a rubbish night which I was hoping was going to be a social triumph but it turned into more like social disaster of the year.' I tell Chloe the whole sorry tale.

'Oh, poor you.' She giggles. 'You must admit it's quite funny though, you upsetting everyone on your table.' She's disgusted in true sisterly fashion, however, when it comes to hearing about Darcy. 'I should ignore him next time you see him, and refuse to join his stupid little agency even if he begs you to on his knees.'

'I think I can safely promise you never to accept any proposal of this Mr Darcy at any rate but I am thinking of going back into the lion's den. Hair of the dog and all that.'

'What do you mean? You do make me laugh.'

'Are you doing anything Saturday night?' I ask, having a sudden brainwave.

'I don't think so, in fact Kian's working the late shift so he's out.'

'Great, because I need you to come and help me deal with Arsey Darcy and Miss Palmer-Wright at a Regency soiree.'

'Oh, Soph,' Chloe protests, 'I don't think that's my thing at all. I don't know anything about Jane Austen except that I quite enjoyed *Pride and Prejudice* at school. And I'm not sure Kian will like me going out without him.'

*All the more reason to go*, I think, but leave it unsaid. There's no getting Chloe to see Kian's faults at the moment. So instead, I just add, 'You'll probably enjoy it when you get there and there's free bubbly.'

'As long as I don't have to wear Regency dress!' she says, and on that note of finality, Chloe rings off.

# CHAPTER 7

'Would madam like a glass of champagne?' A rather solemn butler with a face like a kipper appears soundlessly at my side, expertly balancing a silver tray of breathtakingly fine glasses in the palm of his hand.

'Oh, yes please,' I reply, attempting in vain for an air of nonchalance to convince him that I drink Moët & Chandon at every social occasion with my friends. The butler passes me a full glass but I can tell by his demeanour that he isn't fooled one bit.

It's just the same in Harrods. I love wandering round the store for a browse but the assistants know there's no chance of me affording any of the clothes I'm looking at. Apparently, while they are staring at you, they're mentally calculating the cost of your outfit. That's what Mel thinks anyway, and I'm sure she's right. In my case that's probably a maximum of one hundred pounds, which would possibly just about buy a cheap non-designer T-shirt in Harrods, or half a pound or so of steak from the food hall.

Once, I was touching a pair of Jimmy Choos in the shoe department because I wanted to discover what was so amazing about a five hundred pound pair of shoes, when a hard-faced shop assistant materialised from nowhere asking, 'Can I help you?' in a tone that implied she knew I couldn't afford the shoes and needed to put them down immediately. I ended up dropping the precious footwear, fumbling to put them back on the stand, stuttering over my apologies while getting out of the department as quickly as possible.

THE BUTLER MOVES on to Mel, who is doing a better job at keeping cool, carelessly sipping out of her glass in an unusually ladylike manner.

Chloe is already halfway through her glass. I feel kind of bad dragging them both out like this. It's so not their thing but I hope the champagne and entertainment value of people watching might make up a bit. We're rather awkwardly huddled at the edge of the beautifully decorated room in our own little group. The space is enchantingly atmospheric with romantic candles and there's a pleasant murmur of chatter.

I was worried before we came that we might be the only people there, but actually it's quite busy. There's a mix of ages and personalities, which surprises me as I had stupidly assumed it would all be young people. I notice Miss Palmer-Wright is in the corner, chatting mechanically to a group of rather superior-looking, but slightly older, clients. She's obviously on full charm offensive.

I glance idly across the room, then freeze at the sight of a horribly familiar, overly smart young man who is chatting rather awkwardly to an elegant lady with a chignon. It's none other than Dean.

'Mel,' I hiss, jogging her elbow, making her spill her champagne. 'Oh my God, look who it is.'

'What, who?' Mel was deep in the middle of a conversation with Chloe about her Twitter account and is obviously annoyed at my bizarre antics.

'Look over there,' I hiss again.

She follows my frantic gaze. 'Oh God no, not Dean. What's he doing here?' She glares at me. 'You didn't tell him you were coming?'

'Of course not, I'm not that stupid... though I might have given him the number for the agency,' I confess sheepishly.

'Why the hell would you do that?'

'Shhh,' Chloe says. People are staring. 'I don't think a Regency soiree is the place to start a scene.'

I ignore her. 'I may have sent him the number of the agency out of the kindness of my heart, in the hope he might find someone else to stalk,' I say casually. I glance across at Dean again. He doesn't seem to have noticed me yet, thank goodness.

'That's it, we'll have to leave before he sees us,' Mel states categorically.

'I'm not doing that after all this effort. He might not recognise me anyway.'

We're still whispering about the situation when an attractive young woman sweeps confidently into our midst.

'You must be Sophie Johnson and guests,' she says, smiling. 'I'm Emma Woodtree. I don't think we have had the pleasure of meeting but how do you do?'

Emma Woodtree is tall, blonde and willowy but not in the aggressive food-restraining gym-obsessed way of Miss Palmer-Wright. Emma looks naturally slim. She has a lovely rose complexion and the relaxed and confident air of one of those people who have always had money and never known the disappointment or constraints of not having enough. In spite of this, I really like her, she's warm and friendly and the complete opposite of Miss PW in manner. I smile and introduce Mel and Chloe.

'Have you had some canapés?' Emma asks, offering us a plate of yummy-looking delicacies, which are actually as delicious as they look. Before we have time to finish our mouthfuls, she grabs an amiable-looking man who is walking past. 'Nick, have you met these charming ladies – all ardent Austen fans?'

I spot Mel backing away as though to prove she is not into Austen at all, but Chloe appears as though she can overlook this minor detail for once.

'Come on, I must introduce you,' continues Emma. 'Sophie, Mel and Chloe, this is Nick Palmer-Wright.'

I start suddenly, managing to spill champagne all down my front. 'Allow me,' says Nick, chivalrously grabbing a napkin from a nearby table and passing it to me to dab my top.

'Oh thanks.' I can't believe it, I'm so clumsy. 'Thanks so much. Er, Nick, can I ask, are you related to Jessica Palmer-Wright?'

'Just a bit.' Nick grins. 'She's my sister, though we're not really that similar. She's a little more full-on than me.'

*You bet she is*, I think, but instead smile politely if somewhat enigmatically.

'So, are you involved in the agency?' Chloe asks.

'Gosh no. I'm here to support my sister, but Austen's not really my thing. In fact, I don't really read that much at all, although I'm not sure she does either. No, I have my own company left to me by my late father, and Jess persuaded me to get involved with the agency as an investment. Surprising really as she was never into literature...'

*Don't I know it*, I think, smiling to myself.

'But it seems to be a success, largely due to Jess's endless social contacts and Emma's hard work and attention to detail. Jess and Emma went to school together.'

'Are you a big Austen fan then?' I turn to Emma hopefully.

'Oh yes,' she enthuses. 'I love all her writing, I've read every book over and over, and watched the movie versions several times each.'

'Me too.' I laugh. 'And if I ever feel a bit fed up or ill, I curl up on the sofa and watch a DVD of *Pride and Prejudice* or *Sense and Sensibility* and it's better than any medicine.'

'I know. I was at boarding school and used to read the novels to take my mind off how homesick I was.'

'And now it's your job! Lucky you!'

'Well, yes.' Emma smiles. 'Though like all jobs it has its ups and downs.'

At that moment, Jessica Palmer-Wright's tinkly laugh filters across the room and for a second, Emma looks a little irritated before she recollects herself, adding hurriedly, 'But most of it is lovely. Anyway, enough about me. What do you do? Talking of lucky, I hear you work for the very glamorous Modiste Magazine?'

'It's not quite what you might imagine.' I launch into the rather ridiculous reality of my position at Modiste, causing Emma to go off into fits of laughter. She's so nice and we both seem to have the same sense of humour. It's strange how with some people you can feel as though you've known them forever, even if you've only just met, yet others you may have known for years but it's as though you hardly know them at all.

I'm in the middle of an interesting conversation with Emma about her favourite Austen novel when I become aware of someone's steady gaze burning into my back from across the room. I look round to see if I'm imagining things and catch Darcy staring at me. He looks away immediately and I continue to chat to Emma.

I still can't escape the feeling I'm being watched and look round again. I become aware of Darcy's disconcerting gaze once more. Has no-one told him it's rude to stare? The real Mr Darcy might have got away with lovelorn looks at Lizzie, but Darcy Drummond is obviously totally glaring. Probably because he can see a deluded Jane Austen fan on the loose and he's annoyed I'm here, especially as he's made it pretty clear I'm one of the agency's least desirable clientele.

Finally, Emma excuses herself to go and mingle with the other guests, leaving me with Mel. Chloe is still deep in conversation with Nick. I think they've found some mutual old school acquaintance and are getting on really well. He's just what Chloe needs to get her confidence back; she lives like a recluse under Kian's control. Glancing across the room again, Darcy's moved slightly to get a drink but I still think he's looking at me rather a lot. Perhaps I've become paranoid.

'I'm sure Darcy keeps staring at me,' I huff to Mel.

'Ooh, is that him?' she asks, trying to peer inconspicuously at Darcy from behind my shoulder. 'Hmmm, handsome *and* rich, straight in my basket. He doesn't look intimidating to me, maybe a bit awkward. Looking at his body language, I'm not quite sure this is his usual crowd.'

I laugh. 'You're a nightmare since reading *Body Talk, 50 Ways to Know What a Person is Thinking.* You analyse everyone.'

'You've got to admit I'm bloody good at it though,' Mel says defiantly. 'Darcy does look at you a lot, Soph.'

'I wish he hadn't come. He should have stayed at home as he doesn't like Jane Austen or her fans, and is totally weird and disagreeable.'

'Perhaps he feels a bit out of his depth here. Maybe he's studying you as an example of a rampant feminist Jane Austen fan. He's probably worried you're going to start quoting novels, or try to set up an illicit book club or something dodgy like that.'

We giggle like a couple of naughty schoolgirls until Emma returns once more and we wipe the smiles off our faces and try to look normal.

'I wanted to come and continue our chat,' Emma says. 'It's so rare for me to find someone to discuss things that I enjoy. I'd have loved to study literature at uni but my parents wouldn't let me. Thought finishing school would be better for a young lady, they don't really see the point of academic pursuits.'

'That's a shame,' I sympathise, unable to really believe that there are still parents with such Victorian views. 'I guess you sort of get some kind of second-hand involvement through running the agency?'

'Not that much actually, the majority of clients are city high-fliers, jumping on the mass marketing popularity of remakes of Austen's novels.'

'And films like *Emma*,' Mel says, clearly really pleased with herself for being able to add to the conversation.

Emma smiles. 'Yes. I haven't been to see it yet and I can't wait, especially as it's about my namesake. If anyone fancies a girly trip, let me know.'

'Ooh yes,' I enthuse. 'I'd love that. It's not really the sort of thing my colleagues at Modiste are into. I can't afford their nights out.'

'I have a friend who works on the editorial team at Modiste,' Emma says thoughtfully. 'Her name's Miffy Pemberton-Smythe.'

'Oh my gosh, that's amazing,' I gush, which I've managed to refrain from doing so far but this is majorly exciting. 'I've always wanted to work on the editorial team but we don't even go up to their floor, we're the plebs downstairs on the sales team.'

Emma laughs at my enthusiasm. 'Miffy's totally crazy and I don't know if I've ever read much of her work, but she's really nice. Went to school with her yonks ago, but I can give her a call, perhaps I could introduce you sometime?'

'That would be so cool, thanks very much.' I wonder if this could be my big break; finally I would know someone important and perhaps if she likes me, I might even get to escape the sales floor.

'Meanwhile, have you signed up to the agency yet?' Emma asks in a businesslike tone. 'A little bird told me you hadn't, so there's no time like the present. I know we'll have someone who will suit you perfectly. Now, which scheme are you thinking of? Personally for you, I would recommend the Gold Membership, which includes the Ball at Pemberley, it's the most amazing experience.'

'Oh, erm, I wasn't sure whether I'm supposed to apply for that scheme.' I glance round uncertainly in the general direction of Jessica Palmer-Wright and Darcy Drummond. Darcy's moved, however. What a relief. Hopefully he's gone home. Oh no, I've spoken too soon, I spot him. He's coming over. *Oh God, Sophie, try not to pass out.*

'Darcy,' Emma calls pleasantly, 'have you met Sophie Johnson? She's a huge fan of Jane Austen, you know, and works at the incredibly glamorous *Modiste Magazine.*'

'Good evening, Miss Johnson.'

I try in vain to stop my legs trembling at Darcy's deep voice and direct gaze. I'm startled by the intensity of his brown eyes, which contrast strangely with his finely chiselled face. He holds his hand out to me formally and I shake it in a bit of a daze. His skin is warm and firm but I try to push the thought of any kind of physical contact with him from my mind, it's far too distracting. 'I don't think we have met properly.'

'IIi,' I say rather awkwardly, my voice sounding unusually shrill to my ears. 'No, I don't think we have, if you know what I mean.' I stop abruptly, realising I'm sounding ridiculous.

'I was just suggesting to Sophie that she joins the Gold Scheme, Darcy, don't you agree?' Emma is oblivious to any atmosphere or thoughts to the contrary. She is used to getting her own way but in the pleasantest manner possible.

'Of course,' Darcy replies politely. 'I can thoroughly recommend the Gold Scheme, it offers some amazing social occasions.'

'Oh,' I say, my hackles up in spite of my awe at his proximity. 'So, you're happy for deluded feminists who don't live in the real world to join the Gold Scheme then? I must have misunderstood.'

Oops. I shouldn't really have said that but I don't have anything to lose, the guy doesn't like me anyway. To be fair to him, Darcy looks momentarily disconcerted but he manages to collect himself, murmuring politely, 'We would be most happy to have you in the Gold Scheme.'

Turning to Emma, I say wryly, 'Darcy is very polite, but it's not possible.'

Darcy smiles stiffly and excuses himself under the pretext of being waited for, striding away to chat with a group of smartly dressed suits at the other end of the room.

Emma's looking a bit puzzled at this exchange. I smile apologetically and say quietly, 'I'm afraid I'm unable to afford the Gold even if I were eligible to join. But perhaps the Silver would be nearly as good? And surely we are allowed to upgrade if we need to?'

'Yes of course, but you know you're welcome to join any scheme you like with us. I read and approved your application form, did Jessica not say?'

'Er, not exactly.'

Emma and I exchange glances and she nods understandingly. 'Yes well, Jessica does have an issue sometimes with clients living up to her, shall we say, rather exclusive standards? And I don't mean exclusive from a literary point of view, more a social one.'

I smile gratefully at Emma, she's so nice.

'We'll get that sorted out then,' she continues. 'Oh, it looks like your friend, Mel, has found someone to chat to. A new face by the look of it, just what we need.'

I look across to where Mel is standing near the appetisers. She's being talked at very enthusiastically by a short young man; he must be in his early twenties, with gel-covered dark spiky hair and pale skin. He has round thick-lensed glasses and generally looks kind of geeky but not in a good way. I approach rather hesitantly alongside Emma who's all smiles and welcome.

The man turns at our approach and thrusts his hand at her. 'Miss Woodtree, delighted to meet you, charmed. And who's this lovely lady?'

As he's looking expectantly at me, I shake his horribly limp hand – one of my pet hates. It's even more worryingly kind of damp too.

'Hi, I'm Sophie.' He's still staring at me as though he's expecting something else so I add, 'Sophie Johnson.'

'Hello, Miss Johnson.' He guffaws loudly. I've always wondered what a guffaw sounds like and this definitely is one; it's kind of like a cross between a laugh and a snort but very nasal. 'It's always a pleasure to meet beautiful ladies and you two little dazzlers are friends, aren't you?'

'Erm, yes,' I utter, trying not to catch Mel's eye as I'm sure I'm going to laugh. He's such an odd mix of arrogance and pretentious old-fashioned obsequiousness.

'And your lovely friend, Mandy isn't it, informs me you've a glamorous job working for Modiste. Are you a model then?' He leans in hopefully, peering at me in a totally obvious way, his horribly stale breath hitting me like a wall. I take a step back; I also hate people in my personal space – I have an invisible bubble round me that I need respected unless I really like the person. I glance at Mel whose red face makes it obvious that she's struggling to control herself. I send a silent message to her that I'm going to get my own back at some point, though I guess she has to have some fun, this was my idea after all.

'So, where do you work?' I ask politely, hoping this will distract the geeky guy. I couldn't have chosen a subject in which he excels more.

'I'm a technical programmer at Dafco Systems,' he says proudly. 'Name's Rob, Rob Bright. Bright by name and bright by nature.' He snorts at his pun, which is a bit of luck as no-one else finds it funny, especially not me as a little piece of his spit has landed on my cheek and I'm trying surreptitiously to remove it without seeming rude.

Rob continues, oblivious. 'Of course I'm blessed to have the MD, Richard Simms, as my advisor. You know, Richard Simms, Head of Dafco and heir to the Dafco fortune. He's my mentor and good enough to look out for me generally. I've been to his family estate no fewer than ten times for dinner and he always sends a car so I can have a drink.'

'Wow,' I respond, because there isn't a lot else to say. 'Does he live near here?'

'His estate is only three miles from my house in Marlow. Of course, he has several properties but that is his main residence. He's chess champion for Bromwich and we have some very exciting evenings, I can tell you, pitting our wits against each other.'

'Yes, I can imagine,' I murmur, desperately trying to avoid Mel's eye because I might burst out laughing.

'I used to go to chess club when I was at school,' Mel pipes up suddenly, rather surprisingly. It goes to show you never know about people really.

'Oh,' Rob says in a disinterested tone; he obviously likes to be top dog. 'Did you play for the county?'

'No not really, but I wasn't bad.' Mel winks at me.

*Welcome back to the Mel I know and love*, I think, smiling to myself. Only I could come to a Regency evening and meet the world's greatest chess-playing nerdy guy.

# CHAPTER 8

A violin strikes up the opening bars of a cheery melody played by a small group of musicians who have been inconspicuously setting up behind us. Emma claps her hands. 'Ladies and gentlemen, would you like to choose your partner and join us for a Regency dance lesson?' she announces.

'Not really,' Mel mutters, backing towards a nearby wall, presumably hoping to hide there unnoticed. To my amazement, Nick Palmer-Wright walks past with Chloe following, takes her hand and stands in the line of dancers already in the middle of the room.

Rob turns to Emma with an atrociously camp mock bow. 'May I have the honour of this dance, madam?'

'Oh no,' she says decisively. 'I'm afraid I don't have time to dance as I have things to attend to, but I'm sure Sophie or Mel might like to join in.'

'Of course,' Rob acquiesces, taking a step nearer me with an ingratiating smile, revealing a row of crooked slightly off-white teeth. Obviously dental hygiene isn't very high on his agenda. 'Would madam care to dance with me?'

'Erm, well…' Darn, I'm always rubbish at thinking up excuses on the spot, must make a mental note of reasons for not dancing for future occasions, write them in a notebook and memorise them. 'Oh yes, that would be lovely,' I reply. Oh God, now I'll have to dance with this creep. Why couldn't I think of an excuse?

Rob holds out his hand, which has slightly too long nails, and we walk to the dance floor.

A lady in Regency dress stands at the top of the room accompanied by a rather depressed-looking middle-aged bewhiskered gentleman in leggings and boots. 'Now John and I will lead the steps round the room, so keep your eyes on us. I will call out the next moves in a clear voice so you can follow.' I have no doubt of this; the woman is sturdily built with the kind of booming voice that could probably penetrate a soundproof room. 'I'm Jane and this is John.' For some reason this makes me unaccountably want to laugh.

The woman continues. 'We are going to do a Scotch Reel, a very popular dance step from Austen's time for all echelons of society. It is very simple, we need three or four people in a line, that's it, and if you follow me, ladies you begin the dance, put your right foot forward first.'

We're lined up, apparently in the style of most Regency dances with ladies on one side and men on the other. It feels all wrong in modern dress and I'm totally self-conscious. I used to do ballet but it was a long time ago and I haven't really danced properly since, apart from clubbing at uni. Then I was always the first on the dance floor and the last off when the night ended, not even needing a drink first. This, however, is a lot more formal and I've no idea what I'm doing.

I glance at Chloe down the line, but she's mouthing something at Nick opposite her, who's in fits of laughter at whatever she's just said. It's great to see her having such a good time – she hasn't looked so happy in ages. The music begins and Rob launches himself forward rocket style like a monkey with two left feet tied together.

'Remember, ladies first,' Jane booms. 'Now you men come to the middle, join hands with your partners and one two three four, and back two three four.'

We concentrate dutifully and don't do too badly, although I don't know how on earth the actors in Austen films manage to memorise dialogue, get the timing and intonation right, and achieve the correct dance steps. There's so much to remember.

Unfortunately Rob Bright is the most irritating and embarrassing dance partner in the world. He keeps trying to talk or catch the eye of the people around him because he has to be the centre of attention, which inevitably means he messes up the steps totally. He has a hot sweaty little paw too, which I have to grasp every so often as we meet in the middle of the dance, and I begin to long for the protection of long white Regency gloves. Perhaps that's why they wore them, in case of revolting partners with disgusting clammy hands, I think grumpily. I catch sight of Darcy watching from the corner of the room and I'm sure he has a slight smirk as he witnesses my discomfort with the worst partner in the room.

Thank goodness Rob's so unfit; he decides to sit out for the next dance and I'm delighted to be asked by Nick Palmer-Wright. Dancing with Nick is like riding a thoroughbred after having bumped around the field on a stubborn stocky old carthorse. Nick doesn't have a clue about the steps but at least he has some idea of rhythm and we laugh companionably at each other's stumbling attempts at these Regency moves.

I'm really enjoying myself and dance the next with a group of ladies all in a circle, which involves a lot of waltzing in and out under the raised arms of the others in the ring. I'm next to a lively young girl with a lovely complexion and long blonde hair. She seems really nice and bubbly and, tiring of the dance at the same time, we help ourselves to some of the refreshingly welcome glasses of fruit punch at a nearby table.

My new friend, having introduced herself as Izzy Fenchurch, is quite exuberantly chatty. 'Have you been with the agency long?'

'No, I've only just joined,' I reply, 'but judging by this evening, I think I'm going to enjoy myself.'

'Oh yes, it's really fun. I wouldn't have even thought of joining as it isn't my thing, but my stepmum paid my membership so I could meet an eligible man.' Izzy rolls her eyes dramatically. 'Of course, she's only trying to get me out of the house so she can have my dad to herself, but it's one of the better decisions she's ever made – most of her ideas are crap!'

'Have you met some nice guys then?' I ask naively. 'My friend, Mel, said that most men at a Jane Austen dating agency have got to be gay or totally weird.'

My companion bursts out laughing. 'That's so funny! Is your friend here tonight?'

'Er yes, she's the one propping up the wall over there, trying to escape the unwelcome attentions of the guy with the spiky hair.'

'Oh God, not Rob Bright! He's just like the most hideous geek. Don't get him on the subject of chess or which *Star Trek* movie was the best or you'll be bored to death. I met him earlier unfortunately.' Izzy pulls a face.

'Anyway, back to the subject of eligible men, are there any?' I ask hopefully.

'I've been on a few dates, most of them were quite fun but no spark, but there is this one guy, Josh, who I really like. We've gone out on a couple of dates and I feel like I've known him forever. He's most definitely not gay or weird, he's scrummy.'

'Is he here?' I ask, looking around the room.

'No, he's away at the moment, and I miss him terribly. He's so romantic. I've never met a man like him, they're normally just after one thing, but Josh is thoughtful, kind, organises picnics in the park and reads me Shakespeare's sonnets. I can talk to him about anything – he's amazing.'

'Wow, I'm impressed. I don't think I've ever met a romantic man before,' I say wistfully. 'I'll have to hope there's another one as nice as your Josh.'

Just at that moment, Dean walks past with a drink in his hand and I dash behind a nearby pillar.

'What are you doing?' Izzy laughs at my strange behaviour.

I pause for a moment before answering, making sure Dean really has gone. 'He's one of my ex-boyfriends.'

'Oh dear. Messy break-up?'

'No, he just won't break up. He's totally deluded, believing we're meant to be together forever.'

'God, what a nightmare, the stalker type.'

'Yep, that's about right. I don't seem to have much luck with guys.' I briefly recount my sad and short dating history.

Izzy is very sympathetic. 'You might meet someone nice here. We get some pretty hot guys at the big events, many come along looking for the bored rich women who join, wanting to fit in with the Regency revival going on right now. Regency dramas are pretty cool at the mo, so it's the thing to do, especially since Penelope Smith-Klein's marriage to Andrew Huntingdon. It was covered in *Tatler*, and *Hello* paid a cool half mill for the story. In fact, I think the clothes worn by the bridal party are currently on show at the V&A Museum.'

'Yes, I think Modiste covered that story. I remember seeing pictures of the hand-stitched Regency wedding gown.'

'I forgot to tell you about Regency Gaming Nights too,' continues Izzy. 'Josh is into those, although I do get a bit fed up trying to get him to leave the tables to come and dance.'

'Regency Gaming Nights?' I echo. 'Doesn't sound very romantic.'

'No, but they are a really good draw for guys who have loads of money to splash around. They're quite a racy crowd and some of the boys are pretty cute.'

'That's a redeeming feature, I suppose.' I smile but inwardly I feel that this profit-making scheme was bound to have been devised by Darcy. I change the subject. 'Do you know any of the girls here? I haven't met many yet.'

'I know a few who seem quite nice. Maria over there.' Izzy points at the elegant lady with the chignon who is sitting quietly talking to a lively young girl with carroty hair. 'She is lovely but quite shy. She's so nice when you get to know her though. I think she's in her thirties so she's older than the rest of us. They say she was jilted at the altar and has never got over it.'

'That's really sad. Hopefully she might meet someone nice here though. What about the young girl with her?'

'Louisa? She's quite nice too although a bit annoying sometimes, very immature I think, like she's got ADHD; always on the go and giggling about something but seems popular with the younger lads.' Izzy obviously believes in saying it how it is. 'The one you need to watch out for is Tamara, she's super rich, a bit of an Essex girl, and in your face but she's a real laugh... She's over there with the fit guy in the deep-blue suit.'

I follow her gaze towards a dark-haired girl with large doe eyes and a very short dress. She has her hands all over the man in the blue suit on the dance floor, her face pressed right up against him, even though the other dancers are further apart.

'She looks a bit of a character,' I venture.

'Yes... she's a flirt... but–' Izzy breaks off as we are interrupted by a fair-haired man who sweeps her a mock bow.

'Izzy, how are you?' he asks gallantly.

'Oh hi, Matthew. This is Sophie, a new arrival at the agency.' We shake hands and I note he has a nice open face, if a little stolid. He has to be at least thirty-five, but is quite fit for an older guy.

'Nice to meet you,' he says pleasantly. 'Have you been enjoying the dancing so far?'

'Yes, it's been lovely,' I reply enthusiastically, but before I can continue, I'm interrupted by a firm hand on my shoulder.

'Sophie?' For goodness sake, it's Dean. There's no escaping him now.

'Oh hi, Dean, fancy meeting you here!' I stutter.

'I took your advice,' he says excitedly. 'We can go on some trips together, just like before, won't that be amazing? Let's dance and we can chat.'

'No, I don't think I will, thanks, Dean. I've had enough dancing for one night, in fact I think it's time for us to go home.' I look desperately around the room for my backup team.

'Would you like to dance, Izzy?' Matthew asks gently.

'Oh, all right then, might as well,' she answers ungraciously and wanders off towards the dance floor with him, sneakily turning and grimacing at me as she goes. I guess Matthew's not her type, which is a shame as he's quite sweet, but maybe a bit mature for her.

'Alone at last,' Dean says, making me jump as he comes closer, well and truly crossing the line into my personal space.

'Not really,' I snap, stepping back. 'If you count the room full of people we're in. Dean, I'm not sure this is your kind of thing.'

'Nonsense, I'm enjoying it and I met a nice girl, Louisa over there, very friendly she is, not quite as lovely as you of course. Anyway, I need to talk to you, a very strange thing's been happening. I've been trying to phone your mobile and this old woman keeps answering.' Dean appears quite puzzled.

'Really? How odd,' I reply innocently.

'Yes. She was quite pleasant but seemed rather deaf. Do you know who she is?'

'Can't imagine,' I reply, trying not to laugh, and walk off under the excuse of needing to talk to Emma.

I sign up for the Silver Membership with the promise of strawberry champagne picnics and a trip to Bath. I also ask her surreptitiously if she can prevent Dean from joining the agency. She's a bit taken aback but when I explain the situation, she agrees to turn him down immediately. I feel kind of bad about it until she suggests a taxidermy group she knows, which her eccentric old uncle runs out in the country somewhere. Dean will be thrilled with that and hopefully it'll get rid of him once and for all. He certainly won't be able to get hold of me because he's on a hotline straight to Great Aunt Flo.

I'm quite pleased with my dancing, I've mastered some of the steps and figure that with practice, I might even cut a reasonably convincing impression on the dance floor if I do ever make it to a Regency Ball.


ALL IN ALL, the evening has been fun and we eventually leave. Mel's exhausted, Chloe flushed and radiant. I think she may have had a few glasses of champagne too many. But I'm happy, what with me finally ditching Dean and making some great new friends, it looks as though The Jane Austen Dating Agency might be a winner after all.

# CHAPTER 9

I sprint into the Modiste offices at a couple of minutes to nine the next morning. The tube had been late as usual so I'm compelled to run the last few metres in spite of my heels. Rushing through the huge entrance doors to the art deco building, I push past the elegant reception desk and leg it up the stairs.

Amanda has already started the usual Monday morning sales pep talk, which is supposed to motivate us to sell more advertising space. This always includes the carrot Amanda feels it's necessary to dangle in front of us to reward the person who sells the most advertising space that week. I really hate this system but I guess it's the way most sales people operate and that's why I don't really fit in.

I've always worked as hard as possible, whatever the position, because I like to do my best. Throughout my student days, I worked several jobs: serving in a café, cashiering in a bank (I loved counting out huge sums of money, pretending it was my own) and in an event company selling balloons and tacky room decorations, on the minimum wage of course. It didn't matter how much I was paid, I worked hard, so the idea of being bribed to sell is a bit like being a performing dog. I don't really like the competition and haven't been very good at winning much business since my initial flukey beginner's luck.

I hate being late. Amanda raises an eyebrow at me as I stutter my apologies and rush to my desk.

'I shall start again,' she announces, 'for the sake of those who are a little tardy.'

The rest of the sales team, who have probably been there since at least 8.30, all appear smug and self-righteous. I pretend to be very busy, starting my computer and making sure my stationery is all in place.

Amanda continues her motivational speech. 'This week we will be doubly hard working as it is the end of the financial year and I want our MD, the honourable Angelica Sassay, to be totally blown away. So I need you to sell, sell, sell. I want to feel those phone lines buzzing. Of course,' Amanda surveys us all as though she is about to do us a huge favour, 'as it is such an especially important week, the employee with the largest number of sales will win a very special prize indeed.' She pauses dramatically. 'They will win tickets to Victoria Beckham's Spring Summer Collection.'

There's an audible gasp amongst the team. We would all do pretty much anything to go to Victoria Beckham's show, her collections are incredible so this is a BIG deal. I sit up straight in my chair, as though this will somehow help me be more professional, and comb the leads I'd been given the week before.


By the end of the morning, after making endless phone calls and leaving messages for shop managers who I know will never phone me back – who I'll just have to re-phone and take any 'get lost's, polite or otherwise, on the chin – I feel less motivated.

It's nearly time for the obligatory smoked salmon blinis and I'm considering wandering off to grab a coffee to try to help me make more pointless phone calls when a tall sloaney-looking girl dressed in Burberry mooches up to my desk. I can immediately recognise she is a member of the editorial team, who I occasionally see with her own little 'it crowd' in the lobby.

'Are you Sophie Johnson?' she drawls in a frightfully well-spoken voice.

'Erm, yes?' I answer, sounding as though I even doubt my own identity. In fact, I'm worrying that somehow someone's discovered that I'm not very good at sales after all, and that sometimes I put the phone down before anyone picks up because I just can't face being told to 'f' off one more time that day.

'Oh jolly good!' she spouts, extending a bony hand. 'Miffy Pemberton-Smythe, Editorial. You know, we're the chaps who sit upstairs and write stuff.'

'Of course. I love your stuff. I mean I read every edition, great writing. I especially love the section on "Essential garments for every girl's walk-in wardrobe".'

'Oh, that piece,' Miffy smirks. 'Total trollop really, ran out of ideas that week, shoved a few bits together and Bob's your uncle. In fact, I think it was my PA who gave me the idea for the feature because she suggested I put my clothes in feng shui order.'

'Great,' I enthuse, 'such a fab idea.' I'm trying not to visualise my own wardrobe back in the flat where New Look stuff is shoved in with Primani and everything is so precarious that anyone opening the door risks serious personal injury. Not quite like Miffy's article, which I presume displays her own walk-in wardrobe back in her luxury mansion, with every designer item colour co-ordinated and placed in outfit order. Heaven!

'Right, yes, anyway, a very good friend of mine, Emma Woodtree, mentioned you work here and I couldn't believe it, any friend of Emma's, you know... Emma and I go way back, went to school together. Have you been here long, darling? Don't seem to have seen you round the place.'

'I started in February.'

'Oh well, you must have been hiding away down here in sales, darling. Fancy coming out for a snifter at lunchtime? The girls in Editorial are all going to Epicure for a working lunch.'

'Erm, I wasn't really going to take lunch today – huge pile of leads to get through and, you know,' I stutter lamely, trying not to look at the iconic image of Victoria Beckham's designer viewing, which I've pinned on my noticeboard in a sad attempt at self-motivation.

'God no!' exclaims Miffy. 'Can't work through lunch, sweetie. It's just not done. Don't be a spoilsport, come and meet the gang. Don't want to get stuck with this lot.' She lowers her voice and gestures towards the rest of the sales team, raising a perfectly groomed eyebrow. I smile to myself as the rest of the team are not exactly plebs, they're all genuine, bona fide owners of Louis Vuitton handbags and regular radiance facials, which is all more than I have.

'Fabulous, meet you in the foyer at 12.30.' Miffy takes advantage of my silence and totters off. 'Don't be late!' she calls, casually flicking her long fingers in a miniscule wave without bothering to look back.

The rest of the sales team, who have been ineffectually pretending they weren't listening, go back to work.

Amanda seems to appear from nowhere. 'I expect you might like to go to lunch a little earlier today, Sophie?' she asks, glancing at me speculatively.

'Oh, erm, yes that would be lovely, thank you, if it's not too much trouble,' I add hesitantly. 'I mean I don't have to if it is a problem.'

'Of course not, Sophie. Miffy has invited you, that means you must go and don't worry about being back on time.' Amanda tootles off to speak to someone else and I try to ignore the jealous and incredulous glares of the other girls, pretending to be busy checking out the next bridal salon on my list. But I simply can't concentrate; I'm too excited.

. . .

JUST BEFORE LUNCHTIME, I leg it into the toilet and try to tidy my look, but end up appearing exactly the same as I did when I went in, apart from refreshed lipstick. Oh well, it's as good as it's going to get.

I meander down the large sweeping staircase at the front of the office, trying to look casual, and spot Miffy with her usual squad of elegantly groomed women loitering in the doorway.

'Sophie, darling!' she bellows, and I smile and wave, rushing down the steps to join her to be dramatically air kissed four times on each side. I'm a bit taken aback as I only saw her about an hour ago, but I can go with this. It's my opportunity to blend with the big shots and I'm prepared to take this whole networking thing very seriously.

Miffy leads the way out of the gigantic gold revolving doors of Modiste, to where a huge black limo is waiting. To my amazement, the smartly uniformed driver, who has been patiently standing, opens the door and Miffy's brigade climbs in. 'Come on then, darling,' she calls to me. 'Haven't got all day, you know.'

I promptly close my mouth, which I think must have been hanging open like a goldfish, and clamber into the limo, struggling in my straight skirt as it doesn't allow my legs to move that far apart. I seem to remember hearing they give royalty, such as Princess Kate, guidance so they can learn how to climb in and out of cars elegantly, thus avoiding any disastrous flashes of knickers such as those demonstrated by Britney Spears many years ago. Perhaps I should try to get some lessons if this travelling in limos is going to become a habit.

I attempt to act nonchalant as I sit down in the huge car, but fail miserably as the seat is deeper than I expected and I end up sprawled inelegantly backwards with my feet in the air. Not very stylish but Miffy just laughs. 'Emma said you were hilarious,' Miffy snorts. 'Absolute classic.'

Miffy's friends don't look amused at all. There are only three of them in the end but I notice them exchanging bitchy smirks.

As the limo pulls away smoothly, it feels like being in an aeroplane and I have a job not to smile, it's all so surreal.

'This is Nina, Bunty and Natasha.' Miffy sweeps her hand in the direction of her three colleagues who smile in a fake flash of expensive dentistry. Actually, in comparison, Miffy is quite natural looking, a little horsey even with her long dark mane of hair, slightly aquiline nose and strong arched brows. She has money but shrugs it off with an easy natural country style in contrast to the others who look more Towie and fake than she does, in spite of their designer clothes. And Miffy is quite nice actually, as Emma had said. Although she's totally different from me, she's friendly at least.

Nina, who as it turns out is from Norway, is the daughter of an oil tycoon. She's wrapped expensively in layers of fur, real by the look of it. 'So, you work in Classifieds?' she asks in clipped accented tones.

'Yes,' I reply and that's the end of that conversation, but I'm getting used to these blunt disinterested responses so it doesn't matter quite so much and I'm actually more interested in thinking about where we'll be eating lunch.

Then a thought suddenly makes me go hot and cold; what if I can't afford the food? This group will hardly think twice about a hundred pounds per person for lunch and I've just spent more than half of my savings on the annual membership of the dating agency. I suppose I'll have to put it on my card but I hate spending money I don't have, it mounts up and needs paying just the same. It took over a year to pay off my initial student overdraft after leaving uni. That and the student loan is enough to depress anyone.

Miffy's phone suddenly rings out. 'Hello?' she answers, snapping open the Swarovski jewel-encrusted cover. 'Oh hi, Bree darling. Oh that's sooo annoying. I suppose it can't be helped. What did Michel say? Okay then, the truffles will simply have to be served at the end of dinner and we'll hope that Maria can source and deliver them before 8.30 this evening. Okay thanks, Bree, yes bye, darling... bye, bye.'

I look questioningly at Miffy, not wanting to pry.

'That was Bree, my PA,' Miffy explains. 'Absolute treasure but complete cock-up with the catering for this evening. Not her fault of course, it's my truffle supplier. Michel will be furious and I did want the truffles to be a centrepiece. These things happen I suppose but it's terribly frustrating all the same.'

'You're far too lenient with the staff,' drawls Natasha, who is Russian, judging by her accent. 'I would have her bags packed letting me down like that a few hours before dinner.'

'Yes, darling, that's why you have the highest staff turnover of anyone of my entire acquaintance,' Miffy remarks without turning a hair. I want to smile at her confident comeback but look out of the window instead as I can sense Natasha glaring in my general direction. 'I'm having a little soiree this evening with a few friends: Lady Victoria Hervey, Santa Montefiore and darling Jasper,' explains Miffy.

'Do you mean Santa Montefiore the novelist?' I gasp.

'Yes, as it happens, and a few others. Do you know them, sweetie?' she asks, to my bemusement.

'Erm, not exactly,' I stutter. I mean I read *Hello* magazine of course and check out all the celeb gossip but I absolutely love Santa Montefiore's books. Actually *The French Gardener* made me cry for ages but I wasn't going to divulge such embarrassing details in front of this group.

'She probably read about them in a magazine,' is Natasha's bitchy but accurate comment.

I smile enigmatically and continue watching the crowded lunchtime streets of Mayfair whizz past in a glorious technicolour blur. I love people watching and here is the most amazing place for it, everyone is so incredibly stylish.

. . .

WE DRAW up in front of the spectacular St George's Church and alight from our smart limo. I follow the girls across the road like a kid in the playground who's been asked to hang out with the cool group at lunchtime and ends up tagging along at the back because she isn't quite sure where to put herself. We enter a small but select restaurant with a beautifully chic cream interior. The girls arrange themselves at the stylish bar, long elegant legs draped over the chrome stools.

'Champagne cocktails,' Miffy commands a debonair young man with immaculate slicked-back hair and a pristine white apron, 'and we'll have the seat in the window.'

I'm in a quandary about whether I should explain that I don't drink at lunchtime, but decide it's going to look a bit sad and that if I have some mineral water as well, I might manage to get through the afternoon in the office without falling asleep.

The waiter returns with our drinks, which are absolutely yummy incidentally, and shows us to our table. The menu is a little daunting, to put it mildly, but the food on the plates of the other diners look delicious.

'Darlings, don't they do low carb?' Natasha snorts. 'You know I'm on a strict regime, Miffs. I have a photo shoot Monday and I still have three pounds to lose.'

'You're such a bloody nightmare to take anywhere to eat, Nat,' Bunty retorts. 'Why don't you go back to eating tissues or throwing up in the loo, for God's sakes, and give us all a break?'

'That's a bit harsh, Bunty,' says Miffy reprovingly after Natasha has flounced off to the ladies room to powder her nose. 'You know she has food issues and there's loads of pressure in her business.'

'We all know that, darling,' says Bunty crushingly, 'but it's not as though she has to do this job, is it? Her family's loaded, she isn't stupid, she knows the stakes. Why doesn't she just stick to Editorial and give up the whole clotheshorse thing? She's too old to carry on in that game much longer in any case.'

'Because she enjoys it and it's not really any of our business how she eats, sweetie, as long as she's happy, we just have to put up with her little scenes. To be fair, she always has one about something.' Miffy's obviously pretty immune to Natasha's drama queen behaviour.

AFTER A SHORT WHILE, Natasha returns to the table seemingly recomposed. 'While we're here I need to make some notes,' she remarks, whipping out a bright blue leather-bound notebook. 'At least it will be worth a couple of pounds of weight gain when I've unleashed my feature introducing this establishment to the monde. It will be the place to be and be seen when I have finished with it.'

I watch Natasha enviously. How amazing to have that influence over fads and fashions. It would be so cool.

'What genre of music has the smoked salmon been exposed to?' she asks the waiter in her thick accent when he returns to take our order. It makes me want to laugh and I wonder if she has been taking something during her trip to the ladies.

'Only the best, madam,' replies the waiter. 'All our smoked salmon has been serenaded at least once a day, mostly opera but also some classical music.'

Miffy glances at my bemused face. 'This restaurant only ever serves serenaded fish,' she explains. 'It's believed that it makes it taste nicer. Load of total bollocks, I think, but you must admit it is different, darling, and a huge USP. The elite will flock here in their droves so they can all boast to their friends that they've eaten it.'

I'm incredulous at this but also, in a bizarre way, desperate to try the amazing salmon to find out if it tastes different from your pre-packed supermarket stuff. I wonder what it's supposed to taste like. Does music have a flavour anyway?

We choose our food and sit sipping champagne cocktails and

I start to feel as though this is the life. My fish soup with aioli and croutes is delicious and melts in the mouth. The Cornish Cod with spiced aubergines, young spinach salad and quinoa with toasted seeds is spectacular. I can't say I notice anything musical about the taste of the fish, whatever it should have been like, but it's totally delicious.

I sit happily eating while the others discuss haute couture. Natasha, having picked at a salad with no dressing and a plain piece of smoked salmon, is still scribbling in her book. No wonder she's so thin and can fit in the designer labels. I'm not sure I can work in Editorial if it means eating so little.

Speaking of which, I can't resist dessert, and Miffy seems quite happy to join me, though the others sip daintily at herbal teas instead. I go for the warm chocolate mousse; it's against my principles not to have a chocolate dessert if there's one on offer, it would be plain rude.

I am about to check to see if I have chocolate smeared around my mouth or down my front, which is all too apt to happen to me as I am an extremely messy eater, when I feel a gentle tap on my shoulder. It makes me jump.

'Miss Johnson?' a man's voice asks, and I turn in my chair to come face to face with Nick Palmer-Wright.

'Oh hi, Nick,' I say, genuinely pleased to see him. 'What are you doing here?'

'Business lunch,' he says, and adds in a low voice, 'boring as hell but has to be done. Meeting with a couple of guys from the office. We come here quite often. They do the best steak and not too many people know about it yet. I tell you what, Darcy's with my party, you must come and say hello.'

'Oh gosh no, I mean... I would hate to push in,' I stammer, surreptitiously wiping my mouth with my napkin, still hoping desperately I'm not sporting a chocolate moustache.

'Nick, darling.' Miffy suddenly spots my companion and leaps up for the obligatory air kiss. 'You know the girls, don't you?'

Natasha, Bunty and Nina sit up in their seats, simpering and preening, rather like a group of performing seals when a tourist brings some fish scraps. Nick Palmer-Wright is obviously a piece of prime real estate.

'Do come and say hi to Darcy,' Nick persists, oblivious to their efforts. 'He was only talking about you the other day and will be sorry not to catch up.'

'I doubt it,' I mutter, feeling puzzled, but follow Nick to the back of the restaurant where Darcy is chatting to a group of smart-looking guys. It's so frustrating, I don't seem to be able to see him without my heart skipping a beat, or several. He is impossibly good looking. Perhaps it's my hormones or something, it's been a while since my last proper relationship. I can't possibly like him, not when he's such an arrogant chauvinist git. 'I really don't want to disturb a business meeting,' I protest to Nick.

'Nonsense,' he replies. 'Darcy, you remember Miss Johnson?'

I look Darcy full in the face, challenging him not to remember me or be disgusted, but he leaps to his feet and shakes my hand. 'Miss Johnson, always a pleasure. Let me introduce Ollie Wickson, Gregory Mountjoy and Christopher Montague.'

I shake hands with the men in suits, who are polite but seem keen to get on with their discussion. I edge backwards, claiming I need to return to my table, when Darcy suddenly asks, 'And what brings you here, Miss Johnson?'

'I'm on a working lunch with some colleagues from Editorial,' I reply airily, unable to stop myself from taking pleasure in the kudos of being in such exalted company. Hah, you can't still think I sit at home all day in my own Jane Austen dream world now, Darcy (though obviously I do spend quite a bit of the weekend doing just that). I can't resist adding, 'I don't spend my whole life with my head in a book, you know.'

'I would be sorry if you did. It would be a waste of your talent and deprive the world of your witty conversation,' Darcy replies.

I'm not sure how to respond, I can't believe Darcy has a sense of humour after all, so reply rather lamely, 'I haven't been here before but I often dine out with colleagues, you know.'

Darcy looks at me seriously with the hint of a smile playing about his lips. 'I'm sure you do. You look very at home in such luxurious surroundings.'

I'm even less sure how to take this comment, it sounds as though he's being sarcastic, but I don't know him well enough to be certain.

'So, this is a business lunch, huh?' I ask, eying up the glasses of champagne.

'Yes, we do have some work to look through,' Darcy replies.

'It's a tough job but someone's got to do it.' I smile sweetly.

'Actually, it's a major international deal,' Darcy retorts.

'I'm sure. Making money always is.' There's an awkward pause. 'Well, I must get back to my trivial girly chat about fashion and let you boys get on with running the world.'

'Not all businessmen are chauvinists,' Darcy remarks.

'I'm pleased to hear it. So you have no problem with women in the workplace?'

'Not if they do a good job, no. A businesswoman should dress smartly and act in a professional manner, have a good head for figures, and live in the real world.' Darcy reels off this list as though he has given the matter a lot of consideration.

*Not like me then*, I think. 'A woman like that sounds pretty scary.'

'Women are all very well in the workplace until they decide to get themselves pregnant, pop off on maternity leave for a year or two, leaving everyone else to pick up the pieces,' remarks Gregory Mountjoy, sitting on Darcy's left. Mountjoy is a rather portly old chap who looks as though he would be more at home in a gentleman's club in the 1920s, along with his views.

'That's a bit of a sweeping generalisation, don't you think?' I retort. 'Women can actually bring a whole new dimension to business and anyway, both men and women have maternity leave these days.'

'I quite agree,' Darcy replies unexpectedly, 'as long as they are prepared to put in the hours and work hard, constantly trying to improve themselves. Women have a lot to prove in the workplace.'

I peer at him, wondering what point he's trying to make. Surely anyone should work hard regardless of gender.

'Anyway,' he continues, his eyes still on my face, which is making me blush like a teenager and feel totally self-conscious, 'you didn't answer my question as to who you are here with.'

'Oh, I expect you know Bunty, Miffy, Natasha and Nina, editorial team at Modiste.'

'In some respects, to a certain extent, yes, but I'm surprised you are acquainted with them,' he returns so softly I'm not sure I've heard him correctly.

'Sorry?'

'I meant, I didn't know you're part of their crowd,' Darcy says diffidently, sounding quite unlike his usual self. He looks as though he would like to add something but doesn't.

'I am,' I state proudly and, making my excuses, return to the girls who are all speculating and bickering about the size of Darcy's fortune, exactly how many shares his mother has in the business, and whose mother knows her best.

They all stop abruptly to quiz me about where I know him from and every detail of our conversation. I've suddenly transformed from the least popular kid in school to the top of the cool crew. Unfortunately, I'm not very good at answering their questions as I hardly know what to say.

'My mother's been asking that man to her soirees for the past two years and he always says he's too busy,' Nina moans, shooting pouty looks in the direction of Darcy's table.

'Oh leave him alone, he's okay.' Miffy smiles. 'I've known him longer than any of you. He might seem a bit aloof but it's just his way and probably not surprising considering how many dazzling debutantes throw themselves at him.'

'I'm not throwing myself at him,' Nina humphs. 'I've never had to throw myself at any man.' Her haughty tone makes me want to laugh out loud.

'He probably just doesn't need your fortune, sweetie,' Miffy states. 'That might have something to do with it.'

Nina looks unconvinced and returns to her restaurant notes.

All I know is that for some reason, Darcy always seems to make me feel totally unsettled; I can't make him out. I know he dislikes me, so why can't he leave me alone and stay out of my life?

ALL TOO SOON, Bunty looks at her Cartier watch, gasps that it's time for her afternoon Shiatsu massage and we're swooshed back in the luxurious limo to return, in my case, to the daily drudge of sales forecasts, being told to get stuffed, and my old flat with the washing-up left piled in the sink from the morning.

# CHAPTER 10

I t isn't so bad though. Mel and I have a good laugh the next day about my taste of life in the glamorous world of fashion editing. In spite of Mel's disregard for the comforts of life, her love of all things to do with clothes means she enjoys a gossip about Modiste and now I have news from the inside. 'I would do anything for that kind of money,' she says dreamily. 'Think of all the amazing causes I could help.'

'True.' I ponder. 'But I would rather be poor if I had to have friends like that. I don't think they even like each other that much. They are total frenemies.'

'There's a saying about that. I think it goes something like, "better a dinner of herbs where love is, than a stalled ox and hatred therewith".'

'Yes, I remember hearing that somewhere, I think it's Shakespeare or something. Anyway, it's very true.'

Mel laughs. 'It's from the Bible, you saddo.'

'Oh okay, smartass.' I'm quite taken aback. I didn't realise Mel was so clever at this kind of thing.

'By the way,' she continues, 'did you see there was some post for you today?'

'No.' I'm surprised, I don't get much and it's usually bills.

'Yes, I was most intrigued, very smart paper.' She hands me a beautiful thick-quality envelope.

I open it, hoping it's something exciting. 'Oh God! It's an invitation.'

'An invitation for what? Let me see. Who's it from?' Mel tries to snatch the card from my hand.

'You're not going to believe it!'

'Darcy Drummond!'

'Definitely not, he'd never ever be seen out with me, let alone ask me out.'

'Nick Palmer-Wright?'

'No, but it *is* someone who we met the other night. You'll never guess so I'll tell you. It's Rob Bright, chess champion and the world's biggest *Star Trek* fan.' I continue in spite of Mel's snort of laughter. 'Listen to this... Master Robert Aldous (Aldous?! – good grief, what sort of name is that?) Bright, requests the pleasure of the company of Miss Sophie Johnson on a visit to No.1 Royal Crescent, Bath. Please RSVP to R. Bright etc...'

'Welcome to the Sophie Johnson school of crap dates once again.' Mel laughs.

'Ha, ha, you're so funny,' I retort while inwardly cringing. She's so right, why do I always pull the losers?

'You're not going to go. Surely no-one's that desperate.' Mel looks at me anxiously.

'Erm, no, I mean yes... well that is, I don't really know,' I prevaricate. 'To be fair, I haven't exactly been inundated with requests for dates through the agency, or at all actually.'

'Yes, but it doesn't mean you accept a total loser, does it?' Mel sounds really worried, as though she's seeking acknowledgement I haven't completely lost my mind.

'I might go. I've never been to the Royal Crescent and would love to visit. And I've paid my membership. Might as well get my money's worth.'

I FIND myself repeating the same thing rather lamely to Mark at work the next day.

'If you go on accepting mediocre instead of downright amazing, that's all you're going to be left with, darling!' he declares, probably with more accuracy than I would have liked.

'I know, Mark, but when no-one else is offering, beggars can't be choosers,' I grumble. 'It's not like Darcy Drummond or any other fit guy is breaking my door down, ready to carry me off on a white charger.'

'No, but that's because you don't give yourself a chance,' Mark points out reasonably. 'You keep selling yourself short and accepting the Rob Brights of this world when you could have a Nick Palmer-Wright, or even land yourself a Darcy Drummond, but because you keep messing around with the likes of Rob, you'll never know.'

'Do you really think so?' I ask disbelievingly. 'I don't agree, someone like Darcy will go out with a total babe, like Christie or Jessica Palmer-Wright, someone with beauty and breeding. Men are so predictable. You know the type they go for: five feet ten, slim and beautiful, elegant and refined. Not clumsy, romantic-fiction-obsessed feminists like me. Of course, I'd like to go out with those kind of guys, but they never ask me. Not Darcy Drummond though because he has the personality of a slug.'

'That's because you aren't aiming high enough, due to that ridiculous inferiority complex of yours. You're beautiful, you just don't realise it, and that's much more attractive than those ridiculous try-hard clotheshorses and excuses for women Darcy's bored to tears with meeting in his every day social circle. You're funny too and make people laugh. In fact, you are one of the most amazingly talented people I know, yet you're messing around in a dead-end job, which is pretending to be something it's not. If only you could stop acting like Charlotte Lucas when you're meant to be playing the part of Elizabeth Bennet! Stop under-selling yourself, get out there and see what happens, sweetie!'

'You sound worryingly like Amanda, but seriously, that's the nicest thing anyone's ever said to me,' I cry, flinging my arms around Mark. I mean, I'm genuinely touched. 'If you weren't gay, I would ditch Mr Darcy himself right now and marry you.'

Mark is such a good friend and maybe he's right, if only I could stop thinking of myself as Charlotte Lucas – I want to be Elizabeth Bennet. I feel like her, for goodness sake. I can relate to her but somehow, it seems I only attract the Mr Collins of this world.

I'M STILL BROODING on the issue when I get home from work that evening. Perhaps I should try a bit harder.

'Do you think I'm Elizabeth Bennet or Charlotte Lucas?' I ask my sister when she rings up later that evening.

'What do you mean? Oh, you're on about *Pride and Prejudice* again. How do I know which you are? I haven't read it for ages. Okay, I'll relook at it and let you know, but does it really matter? Have you ever thought you should get out a bit more? If you were a bit busier, maybe you wouldn't worry about these things?'

I love Chloe, she's always so matter of fact. But I accept Rob Bright's invitation in any case – after all, I do need to get out more and, quite honestly, no-one else is asking at the moment.

THE DAY of my hot date with Rob dawns sunny and bright, perfect for something exciting to happen to an aspiring heroine. In the words of Jane Austen, 'If adventures will not befall a young lady in her own village, she must seek them abroad.' It sounds great but I'm not at all sure that seeking them out with someone like Rob Bright was quite what she had in mind. Bath is a good start though, I'm so looking forward to being there again as I haven't visited for years. It is a beautiful city and the perfect place for getting into the Regency mood.

Rob turns up punctually in a silver Vauxhall Corsa, just the car I would have picked for him.

'Morning, morning,' he pronounces. 'Perfect day for it. Hope you're ready for the adventure of a lifetime.'

This makes me rather comically think of Coldplay's video with all the dancing chimps, which I think is rather appropriate for Rob. I have a job not to smirk. He's dressed in jeans with turn-ups, scruffy trainers (yuk), a smart jacket and a white shirt with a neck scarf. I really hate this look.

Fortunately Mel is out so I don't have to put up with any of her loaded comments or comic expressions behind Rob's back.

'Your chariot awaits, madam.' Rob points to his car. I try to look suitably excited and get in, hoping I've remembered to pack headache tablets. He hasn't opened the door for me but it's no surprise as I hadn't got him down as the chivalrous type.

Driving with Rob is not what I would call a pleasant experience. He seems to be under the misapprehension he's a rally driver and though not a nervous passenger, I don't really like unnecessarily fast driving, especially when it's also careless. He corners far too fast, drives with his foot to the floor right up to lights which are obviously about to turn red, then brakes abruptly, narrowly missing a pedestrian more than once. All the time he's oblivious to anything, chatting away about this and that but actually nothing at all.

'So, do you play chess?' he asks, clipping the kerb on a sharp bend.

'Er... no.' I reposition myself in the seat and grip the handle on the car door for extra support. 'No, I don't really know how to play.'

'That's okay. I'd probably beat you anyway!' And he haw haws at his own comic ability. 'Of course, I can teach you myself. Think how many cosy evenings we can have pitting our skills against each other. I wouldn't expect you to try to win because that would be an impossibility for anyone, especially a girl. Attractive as you are, girls simply don't have the brain power for a strategic game like chess.'

I am so incensed by Rob's arrogant misogyny that I nearly ask him to pull over by a bus stop so I can go home immediately. But I think better of it, we're some way into the journey and I'm looking forward to seeing the Royal Crescent. But he's a complete and utter idiot.

'I could try my best,' I assure him sarcastically.

'Oh, I'm sure you would.' He smiles in an oily and patronising manner, placing his sweaty hand on my leg. Eww, I'm not sure if he's actually referring to the chess or something else.

*For goodness sake, this is going to feel like the longest drive ever*, I think, shifting in the seat so he's forced to put his hand back on the wheel.

There's an awkward silence. I'm not good at those, they make me want to chunter aimlessly because I have to fill it, even if it's with gibberish.

'Do you have any other hobbies?' I ask, knowing this conversation will keep him busy for some time. Fortunately, I'm right, Rob fills the rest of the journey with chatting about the latest rare edition of *Star Trek: The Next Generation* in his world-record-holding collection. I don't think there is anything I couldn't tell you about the entire plot and series in all its twelve-part glory.

When not talking about his Trekkie addiction, Rob mostly waxes lyrical about Richard Simms. Richard this and Richard that. They have regular evenings together playing chess. If I'm lucky, I too will be able to join them sometimes for dinner. And if I'm *really* lucky... even watch them play chess. Personally, I think this is a pleasure I might easily be able to do without.

I'm beginning to think that even if Rob were the last guy on earth, I'd never go out with him again, when finally, to my great relief, we drive through the beautiful countryside that surrounds Bath.

The roads are busy but we manage to drive up the hill above the city and park in a back street. It isn't a very salubrious area, but according to the map, there isn't far to walk to the crescent. Rob seems completely incapable of any kind of map-reading skills, so it's over to me.

We walk along the road and round by a sort of car lot crammed with mostly smart black cars. Further on around the corner, the scene is transformed as a wonderful vista opens out onto a beautiful green surrounded by railings, in front of which stands the iconic arch of Regency housing – the Royal Crescent itself. It's happily situated high up on a hill overlooking the whole of Bath and I stand drinking it all in. I say 'I' because while having my Lizzie Bennet moment gazing awestruck in front of Pemberley, I suddenly become acutely aware that I'm standing alone and, looking about me, Rob is nowhere to be seen. Though a blessing in some respects, I had sort of thought he was with me.

I look around but decide to wait where I am, thinking he's bound to catch up soon.

AFTER SEVERAL MINUTES of immersing myself in the view, I become impatient. I want to go and explore the tantalising scene in front of me. Where on earth is Rob?

I turn and retrace my steps along the road, back around the corner and upon passing the car lot, I become aware that some dodgy-looking figure is skulking round in between the cars, peering in the windows. It's Rob.

'What are you doing?' I call, looking about me in case someone comes along.

'Have you ever seen so many incredible machines?' Rob rhapsodises. 'They're all pretty new, Range Rover SV Autobiography, Jag XKSS, look at them all.'

'Yes, I'm sure they're all jolly nice, but don't you think maybe we should move along – people will think you're trying to steal them.'

'I'm only looking,' he says petulantly, like a little boy who's been told he can't have a sweetie before tea. 'Anyway, I think they might all belong to someone famous, just imagine!'

'Actually, I think they're owned by the people who are staying at The Royal Crescent Hotel. It's an amazing place in the middle of the Royal Crescent which is around the corner incidentally, if you were thinking we might visit it today?'

Any sarcasm is lost on Rob, he's still lovingly stroking a sporty-looking car. I have no idea what it is, except it's black.

'I'm going to walk round the crescent,' I say. 'I'll meet you there.'

'Wait! This one has a personalised number plate PEZ 1, I might be able to work out who owns it and I can add it to my book of car number plates.'

I turn and stalk back round to the Royal Crescent, figuring that I'll go and explore on my own if necessary. This guy's a complete freak; he really is the limit. Perhaps being single isn't so bad after all.

EVENTUALLY, Rob miraculously appears and practically prances along the pavement next to me, he is so enthused about the number plates. He continues to chunter aimlessly all round the crescent, seeming not to notice the amazing architecture or the view of the city.

At the door to No.1, we are greeted by a lady dressed in Regency servant's uniform.

'Good morning, madam, sir.' She bobs a curtsey. 'Welcome to number one, Royal Crescent, the home of Henry Sandford. You must be Mr Bright and Miss Johnson. Welcome, welcome! I am Mrs Rowley, here to look after your every need during your visit. Would you care for a glass of Ratafia or some sweetmeats?'

She proffers a glass of rose-coloured liquid and some yummy-looking mouthfuls, and I gladly accept as I'm always hungry, and also it has been some time since breakfast. I have often wondered what Ratafia tastes like, having heard about it in many of Georgette Heyer's Regency romances, read in my misspent youth. It is delicious, perhaps a bit too sweet for my taste, but reminds me of mulled wine at Christmas. The sweetmeats are like little bits of candy peel and quite nice actually.

Rob takes an enormous gulp of Ratafia, pulls a face, and plonks it back down on the surprised Mrs Rowley's tray. 'Yuk! Haven't you got a beer and a packet of crisps?' He smirks, looking round at me as though he were Michael McIntyre himself.

'Er no, sir, I'm sorry, sir, but we don't actually know what crisps are, and beer is not generally taken by gentlefolk at this time of day.' Mrs Rowley clings gamely to her little piece of role play.

'I think they're lovely,' I say reassuringly to Mrs Rowley, who's looking a little crestfallen. She smiles pleasantly at me and leads the way to the parlour.

'Your visit starts here.' She bobs a curtsey and disappears off down the corridor, her long skirts rustling behind her.

The parlour is like something in *Pride and Prejudice*, with a small table laid ready for breakfast, with dear little china cups and a teapot. Over the other side of the room is a beautiful wooden dresser and a chess game placed on the edge.

'This is quite a nice little set,' Rob gurgles, blundering across the room to investigate it.

'Er, could sir please not touch that.' A smartly dressed older man, who is obviously the room steward, rushes across to prevent Rob's slimy fingers from messing about with the chess pieces.

I stand for a moment, imagining the women of the house dressed in Regency clothes, sitting at the breakfast table, watching out the window as perhaps a visitor might come to the door to leave a calling card or an invitation to a ball. The view stretches out over the green where I guess children would have been playing, their nursemaids watching over them as they bowled hoops or played ball.

My happy imaginings are rudely interrupted by Rob's too-loud voice. 'I'll have you know, I'm extremely good friends with the Chess Champion for the borough of Bromsgrove and he would indeed agree with me that this set is late nineteenth century not eighteenth century.'

'Sir, I do assure you, we have had an expert from The Bath Trust examine this chess set thoroughly and it is in fact from the eighteenth century. The charity was lucky enough to be given the set from descendants of Henry Sandford himself. If you look carefully at the portrait above the fireplace there, you will see Henry with this exact chess set. Furthermore, in his surviving papers, it is mentioned that he played with this very set with the niched horse heads.'

'I think you will find I know more about chess than any antiques expert,' Rob blusters. 'To settle it, I'll take a photo on my phone and text it to my good friend, Sir Richard Simms, and he will confirm that I am correct.'

I mentally add 'completely arrogant know-it-all' to the ever-growing list of unpleasant qualities I'm compiling for Rob. He's just too much and always manages to rub people up the wrong way with his supercilious tone and ridiculous pomposity.

Having ascended the grand staircase, we're shown into a lovely drawing room with a piano and beautifully ornate furniture. Tea things are laid out and I can picture fine ladies or perhaps an admiring gentleman or two seated on the elegant sofa while enjoying a fine performance on the piano by a truly accomplished woman.

The room guide is a very enthusiastic and inspirational young American woman who has an impressive knowledge of the room and its contents. She's lovely and I'm really enjoying chatting with her but this visit with Rob is a bit like taking an untrained toddler out to a historical house which is not very child friendly. He can't seem to understand the concept of not touching things, even though there are signs everywhere. He's also not in the least interested in any of the amazing paintings or incredible pieces of furniture which adorn each room. To keep him quiet and from annoying any more room stewards, I find myself rushing round the house tour faster than I would have liked, due to sheer embarrassment.

Though quite a large residence, it was only Henry Sandford's town house, not his country estate, so it doesn't take us that long to complete our tour. I would have liked to view the kitchens but Rob seems in a hurry to go and have lunch. I don't bother reminding him that the whole point of our date was to visit the house, not lunch, but I don't bother as I hope I will never have to go out with him again, like ever.

Before we visit the shop, which I'm excited about, I have to say, because I love Jane Austen paraphernalia, we spot a little museum room. The information on gout is interesting as I've read about so many characters who suffered from it. I stand there pondering how awful that something so simple could have caused so much suffering, but I guess that's the case with many illnesses in the past. I'm lost in thought when I suddenly realise Rob has disappeared again. Honestly, this guy is a nightmare. Looking around, I discover him transfixed by the section on gambling.

'This is amazing!' he exclaims. 'I'm definitely joining the agency's Gaming Nights.'

'Great idea,' I reply. 'Look, I'm going to the souvenir shop, okay?'

Rob doesn't reply or seem to notice me go, he's so involved in the rules of play. I know you don't want your date hanging on your every word, but ideally some notice would be good. Although in Rob's case, I conclude no attention is definitely preferable.

The gift shop is great and I have to make a real effort not to buy loads of souvenirs emblazoned with 'Keep Calm and Read Jane Austen'.

It is still a gorgeous day when I thank Mrs Rowley and leave No.1 Royal Crescent.

'Have you lost Mr Bright?' she asks in a concerned manner.

'Yes, thank goodness!' I reply with feeling, and escape into the beautiful sunshine.

# CHAPTER 11

'Please get on and eat. The food's getting cold!' my mum exclaims, exasperated. She always says that at family meals and everyone always ignores her, continuing to chat and faff about.

'At least there's plenty to eat if Chloe and Kian aren't coming,' Ben mumbles, chomping his way through a crispy roast potato he's managed to swipe off the edge of the roasting dish without Mum noticing.

'Ben, that's not very nice, is it? I'm sure we all wish Chloe were here with us, and Kian too really.' Mum deftly dollops out huge portions of succulent roast beef and crunchy Yorkshire puddings.

Ben snorts but is temporarily distracted, making sure Becky, his latest conquest, has enough food on her plate. 'No, honestly, Ben,' she protests, holding her hand over the dish to stop him piling it any higher. 'We don't really eat roast at home.'

'Not eat roast?' chips in my dad, who's already started and managed to drip gravy down his smartest shirt. 'That can't be right, best part of the week, Sunday roast!'

For once, I've come home for Sunday lunch as a treat. I try

not to most of the time as the train fare is expensive but it's just so tempting, my mum cooks the most amazing roasts ever and makes all the trimmings herself rather than buying them ready done. It's also lovely to catch up with everyone, though I must admit, there's pretty much always a drama of some kind or other and I end up trying to smooth things over because I'm the youngest.

This time it had erupted just before lunch as Chloe has been on the phone explaining rather awkwardly to Mum that she can't come because Kian thinks she spends too much time with her family. Apparently we all make him feel uncomfortable. I can't imagine we make anyone feel awkward, my mum and dad are really warm and welcoming, Mum even does a favourite birthday meal for both Kian and whoever is Ben's current girlfriend, so they don't feel left out. But like I said, Kian is a complete b.

My mum had come off the phone upset and flustered, especially as Chloe's call had been right at the point when the potatoes were at a critical moment of roasting. Mum always says timing is everything with a roast and she has certainly got it off to a fine art.

As we sit and enjoy the delicious food, I feel fed up with Kian yet again. For years it has been our family tradition to meet up every Sunday or at least when we can. Obviously, while I was at uni I couldn't very easily, and having moved to London makes it less often than we'd like but this makes our get-togethers even more precious. We've always been a close family until my two siblings married people who didn't want to fit in. Why can't they just get along with everyone?

In fact, it almost puts me off finding my own Mr Right, perhaps I'm best off staying single. I imagine Rob Bright meeting my family for the first time and I nearly choke on a parsnip.

I miss Chloe's cheerful banter throughout lunch, especially as Ben and Becky spend most of their time whispering sweet nothings in each other's ears, which makes me feel sick.

. . .

As soon as they've finished eating, they retreat to Ben's room, much to Mum's discomfort. If Chloe were here, we would have had a laugh about it.

As I'm upstairs grabbing another wiping up cloth, the sound of Mum and Dad's raised voices floats up to me.

'You need to talk to him about it, Phillip. It's terribly bad manners,' my mum says stridently.

'I don't see what I can say at his age. He's a grown man. It's not up to me to tell him what he can and can't do.'

'You have to tell him it's our house and he can't just do that in his room. Besides, isn't she someone else's girlfriend?'

'Probably, but it's not really any of our business.'

'It jolly well is when it's our house, and it's immoral anyway. You always side with him, male chauvinists, the pair of you.'

I hear my dad's murmured reply and return down the stairs.

As I walk into the kitchen, their conversation ends abruptly, always a tell-tale sign they've been rowing.

'Did you look into that course I mentioned, Sophie?' Mum asks casually, passing me a pan to dry.

'Erm, yes,' I stutter. Mum looks at me with her usual X-ray vision and I quail under her all-too-knowing gaze. 'That is, I mean, I've googled it.'

'Sophie! You need to get on with it now, the PGSE is less than a year's course. If you started this coming September you'd be a full-time teacher this time next year on a starting salary of £24,000.'

'Yes I know,' I mumble into my tea towel, trying to avoid this well-worn and oft-repeated argument. 'But I won't get paid while I train and I have to find the money for the course.'

'You get funding if you apply at the moment, they're desperate for teachers,' – my mum's standard reply.

'Yes, I know but I still have to find enough money to live on during that time, and I'm not even sure I want to teach.' I look round for my dad, hoping he'll take up my defence or change the subject, which would work just as well.

He's still clearing the table, but manages to chip in with, 'But Sophie already has a job, darling. Even if it is rubbish, phoning random people and being told to get lost twenty times a day!' He smiles and pats my shoulder affectionately to soften the criticism.

'It's still a job,' I say defensively, 'and most people would do anything to say they work for Modiste. And look at my new jacket – a total bargain from Miu Miu, thanks to a tip-off from Miffy.'

'It is nice,' my mum relents, glancing at my beautiful coat hanging elegantly in the hall. 'But how much money have you had to borrow to pay for it? You could buy more clothes like that on a teacher's wage and you wouldn't have the commute. Who's this Miffy? I haven't heard you mention her before.'

'Just a friend of a friend,' I say vaguely as I haven't told my parents about The Jane Austen Dating Agency. My mum would have fifty fits as she has a pathological dislike of online dating and thinks I should meet someone nice and normal round the corner. Speaking of which...

'Alan still asks after you,' Mum says casually. 'I saw him the other day, he hasn't got a girlfriend yet. I think he still carries a torch for you.'

'I'm not surprised, he's such a square, with greasy hair and spots.'

'Not that many anymore, and his parents are always so lovely.'

'But he still lives with them and he's a total Mummy's boy.' I tut in exasperation.

'Plenty of boys still live at home with their parents and there's nothing wrong with them. Look at Ben!'

'Exactly, I rest my case.' I laugh, but stop abruptly, as looking at Mum's face, I see she doesn't really find it funny. 'Seriously, Mum, there's no spark with Alan, he's really not my type.'

'You mean he isn't tall, dark and handsome, brooding and slightly distant but oh so gorgeous? Be careful, Sophie. If you spend your whole life waiting for Mr Darcy, you might miss someone equally as nice when they come along, simply because you're so busy looking for something that doesn't exist.'

Her speech makes me think, it's the second time lately someone has given me this advice. Perhaps ironically, Darcy Drummond is right after all; maybe I do live in an unrealistic dream world. But the sad reality is that after today, perhaps that is where I would rather be.

BY THE TIME I get home from my parents early that evening, I'm really tired and stressed and not in the mood for anything much.

'What's up with you?' Mel asks.

'Nothing really, I'm just nonplussed about things, especially relationships. They never seem to work out. Does anyone ever live happily ever after?'

'Depends what you mean by happy ever after.'

'I mean happily married, at least.'

'Yes, lots of people.'

'Just not in my family.'

'Your mum and dad seem pretty happy whenever I meet them.'

'Nah, they argue all the time.'

'Yes, but that's normal. We don't live in the world of story-books, you know. Perhaps you shouldn't read so many romantic novels.'

'You're not the first person to say that.' I smile wryly. 'I just despair of ever finding Mr Right.'

'You're not exactly old, Soph. There's plenty of time.'

'Mmmm, I'm old enough to be in a steady relationship instead of a disaster area,' I grumble. 'Marianne Dashwood said "a woman of seven and twenty can never hope to feel or inspire affection again!"'

'That was a long time ago. How about some yoga? It will help you chill out and relax a bit.' Mel pulls on her trainers.

'Nope, not really my thing.'

'I'm off in ten minutes if you want to give it a try?'

Fortunately I'm saved from an embarrassing yoga session by my mum phoning to check I got home safely. Also to tell me about a programme on Channel 4 about student teachers. It will probably be enough to put me off and why oh why does she never give up? I also have two texts, one from Chloe to ask if I can ring her asap. That will be another de-stress session about Kian and his annoying antics, with me struggling to refrain from shouting at her what a pain he is and that she should just ditch him. These calls tend to end with me hoping Chloe might finally see sense about him, but she usually concludes with, 'But he can be so sweet sometimes and he can't help that he was brought up with attachment issues.'

I mean, attachment issues, please!? Maybe I should have gone to yoga; I really do need to learn to relax.

The other call is from Emma at The Jane Austen Dating Agency. She's left a cheery message referring to a possible match and a date involving a picnic at Box Hill. That sounds a lot more like it, things are beginning to look up.

I phone Emma straight back. It's great to hear her friendly voice once more.

'Hi, Sophie. How are you? I hope you got my message.'

'Yes, thanks so much. I certainly can't resist a champagne picnic at Box Hill, I shall be imagining myself as Miss Emma Woodhouse.'

'No, that's my role.' Emma laughs. 'I've always fancied being Emma Woodhouse, I not only have the name but am legitimately supposed to matchmake people. It's my job!'

I laugh, especially as, secretly, Emma has reminded me of her namesake in Austen's novel since I first met her; she has just the same mix of self-confidence which comes from always being indulged by those around her and having plenty of money. She is quite bossy, yet intelligent and likeable, and means really well. In fact, I always liked Emma Woodhouse in the novel. I know Austen thought no-one but herself would be a fan, but ironically there's a great deal to admire, in spite of Emma's snobbishness.

'So, spill the beans,' I beg, 'who's this mysterious guy?'

'He's very eligible, extremely handsome of course and his name's Daniel Becks. He's new on the books.'

'Do you think we'll get on well?'

'Definitely, you'll be perfect together, I think. He's really nice, good fun and easy to get on with but if you're worried, you can meet up at one of our First Dates nights initially.'

'They sound intriguing, what are they?'

'You know the *First Dates* restaurant on TV? It's a bit like that; we have an exclusive premises in Westminster where you come and meet your date for the first time, a nice casual drink at the bar, followed by a romantic dinner. It gives you a chance to chat and chill out in a less-pressured environment – I promise no filming other than a couple of promotional photos for our publicity.'

'Sounds fab and I must admit I think I'd feel better meeting Daniel in a group situation first, rather than on our own. I'm not sure about blind dates.'

'I can understand that, but I'm telling you now, he's going to be the one, you're simply made for each other!' And with that, Emma rings off, leaving me to plan my outfit for First Dates night the following week.

Perhaps it's time for me to move on from Mr Darcy, maybe, just maybe, a Willoughby or Wickham or two might do very well instead.

# CHAPTER 12

I finally decide on a cheeky little black dress because apparently you can't really go wrong with one of these for an evening out. This is the advice I read while idly googling 'what to wear on first dates'. The useful article suggests the LBD will take you anywhere, you can dress it up or down, and you won't clash with anyone. It makes a change from reading 'Left out in the cold... ten ways to survive a career in cold-calling'.

I always find this dating business a bit nerve-wracking, but from my understanding of the evening's arrangements, the room swaps round after each course, so even if Daniel doesn't turn out to be the hunk Emma has suggested, who knows, I might even meet someone else over dessert. But I still feel nervous, what if I can't think of anything to say?

'That'll be a first!' Mel had laughed like a loon when I mentioned this concern. Rude! Just because I'm chatty and outgoing doesn't mean I'm that confident and even Mel doesn't know it's all a bit of a façade. Underneath, I'm nowhere near as self-assured as I come across.

· · ·

I NEED every bit of this cheery mask as I enter the Park Plaza on Westminster Bridge. To my great surprise, like the hotel, the room is minimalist and chic, nothing Regency about it. There are huge mirrors from floor to ceiling which have the effect of making the place look busier than it actually is, as the couples and tables are only on one side and reflected in the other.

An immaculately dressed man shimmies up from nowhere and takes my coat, inviting me to sit at the bar. It's so like *First Dates* – I feel very nervous and am glad no-one is filming my anxious wait on the bar stool for my date to arrive. I glance around the room at the other couples seated at the tables, some chatting animatedly, one or two have already started eating. I'm wondering what to order from the bar when I spot a familiar attractive blonde girl in a lovely blue and white maxi dress enter the restaurant. She catches sight of me and rushes across.

'Sophie!' It's Izzy Fenchurch, who I met at the Regency Dance night. I'm so pleased to see a familiar face, and after an enthusiastic hug, she plumps down on the bar stool next to me.

'A white wine spritzer please, lemonade not soda,' she asks the barman.

'Oh, can you make that two please?' I chip in.

'So, how are things going on the dating front?' Izzy asks with her usual directness. 'It seems ages since we were at the Regency Dance evening, have you fallen madly in love yet?'

'Erm, not exactly.' I briefly recount my disastrous date with Rob Bright.

'Oh no! That's so bad! He's such a loser. I hope he's not going to be here tonight as last time I heard, he threatened to dine with us all. How come you went for a date with him?'

I try not to look shamefaced. 'Desperation, I guess, and I wanted to visit Bath.'

'But you can do so much better; you're attractive, clever and funny. Why on earth would you go out with a loser like that? In any case, he would have only been allowed to approach you with a hint from one of the chaperones.'

'Chaperones? Oh, you mean Emma or Jessica Palmer-Wright?'

'Yes, the idea is you only get an invitation for a date if one of the chaperones hints that there's a possible connection there, that's the whole point of the matchmaking idea. You must have given the impression you like him!'

'Well,' I reply with a smirk, 'I don't think it was Emma, she knows I'm not very keen on him – I suspect my friend Miss Palmer-Wright may have been at work here.'

'Is she your friend?' asks Izzy naively. 'She always seems a bit of a stuck-up cow to me.'

'Er yes, she is a bit hard work. How are things going with Josh?' I figure it's best to change the subject as you never know where Jessica PW is going to pop up next.

Izzy's face lights up with happiness. 'He's just the nicest guy ever. He writes me poetry and quotes Shakespeare's sonnets while we walk in the park. We love the same music, the same films, the same food – we're totally soulmates.'

I must admit I feel quite envious, especially when a good-looking, tanned blond curly-haired man enters the restaurant, his eyes clearly searching for Izzy the moment he walks in.

Izzy jumps impetuously off her stool and runs to hug him. He returns her embrace and swings her feet off the ground. She drags him to where I'm sitting at the bar, feeling like an awkward spectator. 'This is my Josh.' Izzy smiles.

He shakes hands with me politely but his attention is soon straight back to Izzy. 'Shall we find our table? I have something for you.'

She squeals with excitement but then turns to me. 'Will you be okay on your own?'

'Of course.' I smile with a confidence I don't feel. There's still no sign of Emma, who I had thought would already be here, or anyone who could be Daniel.

The bar is quite a good vantage point to check out the other diners in the restaurant. Most of the couples are around my age, but my attention is suddenly drawn to a slightly familiar older gentleman wearing a smart suit and tie, with a signet ring on his little finger. I wrack my brains, where have I seen him before?

The woman opposite him is also more mature, with grey hair piled high, an aquiline nose and far too much make-up. She's wearing an extremely fussy beaded 1920s-style dress, with a shawl around her shoulders. It's rather comic actually as I can tell from their body language they aren't getting along too well. Perhaps I'm becoming as good as Mel at this reading body language thing. I strain my ears to try to pick up a bit of their conversation.

'At Richmond, you will find the pheasant is never served with a jus d'orange or anything else of that sort. A plain gravy works just as well.' She has a cantankerous and piercing yet aristocratic voice which carries across the restaurant.

The man murmurs something in reply but I can tell by his face he doesn't agree with her at all.

'Garçon! Waiter!' The lady snaps her fingers above her head condescendingly. 'Please remove this excuse of a dish from my sight! I have never been so insulted. No-one serves pheasant with an orange jus. It is simply disgusting.'

'I'm terribly sorry, ma'am.' The young waiter's apologies tumble out to her, his face aflame with embarrassment. 'May I serve madam something else from the menu?'

'No you cannot. It would no doubt be the wrong one. This is what happens when one eats with riff-raff in common restaurants,' she adds in what I assume she thinks is an undertone to her companion. 'Bring me a tisane – plain, mind you, and some fresh, that is *fresh*, artisan bread with a little butter. And hurry it up or my companion will have finished his entire dinner by the time I have been served properly.'

The hapless waiter scurries away, bearing the offending

pheasant dish before him. It looks really nice actually, I would love to eat it, but I'm so hungry I'd probably eat pretty much anything.

At a table nearer to me is the elegant lady with her hair swept up into a bun. I think she is the one Izzy said had been jilted at the altar, Maria or something like that. She is seated opposite a smart-looking man in naval uniform but this date night is not looking very successful for these two either. The silence between them is audible. She's picking delicately at her food, as though she wants to be anywhere but here, and he's moodily staring out of the window. Not exactly a match made in heaven.

Across the room, I notice Rob Bright, unmissable in smart jacket, bow tie and jeans, waxing lyrical about something boring, no doubt. His date seems to be as usual a total mismatch; she is very slight and dainty with dark curls, beautiful make-up and a tiny little dress which looks like Gucci. The dress makes me wild with envy but she is obviously not happy with her date either, and is giving Rob short monosyllabic replies, which he doesn't appear to take any notice of anyway.

'Sophie!' Thank goodness, Emma has arrived. I'm so glad to see her as I've been feeling a bit abandoned. 'Is Daniel not here yet?' she asks, surprised. 'He was meant to be here over half an hour ago. Still, I suppose the man is allowed to have some faults and I haven't noticed any others yet. I'll give him a buzz on my mobile.'

The door of the restaurant opens and in strolls a tall, good-looking man with light brown wavy hair and a tanned freckled face with an attractive grazing of stubble. Oh my gosh, can this be Daniel? I can't believe my luck; he's gorgeous.

Emma goes to meet him and brings him over. He responds well to her gentle teasing for his poor timekeeping, his cheeky grin revealing impossibly white teeth. I feel suddenly shy but he comes up and kisses me on the cheek in a heady and expensive whiff of Davidoff.

'Hi, Sophie. Lovely to meet you at last.' His voice is warm and friendly, not too deep with a slightly ironic tone to it as though he has a sense of humour lurking underneath waiting to bubble to the surface.

'Hi, at last?' I can't resist asking.

'Yes, I've heard so much about you from the lovely Emma here.' He smiles and touches Emma's arm with a friendly pat.

'How nice.' I'm so bad at taking a compliment. I think it's an English thing. Even when someone admires my outfit, I find myself responding with, 'Oh, it's only New Look,' or something disingenuous like that.

I notice every female eye in the room has turned on Daniel and I feel a twinge of pride that he's standing and talking to me.

'I'll leave you two to find your table.' Like her namesake, Emma is adept at this matchmaking business and trips away to talk to the maître d'.

'Shall we then?' Daniel gently places his arm round my shoulders to guide me towards our table. He pulls my chair out for me in true gentlemanly fashion and I mentally give him a huge tick. From a nearby seat, Rob Bright gives me a cheery wave and I mechanically smile back, hoping he will carry on talking to his partner. You would have thought my walking off without him on our date the other day might have given him the hint I'm not in the least interested, but it's obviously going to take something far more major than this to get Rob to understand anything.

'Sophie? Hello?' Oh no, Daniel's been talking to me and I've totally missed what he's trying to say and if I admit that I haven't been listening, that's really rude and not exactly a good start to our date.

'Sorry, I erm…' I blush rather awkwardly.

'It's okay.' Daniel smiles. 'I often daydream too, though not generally at the beginning of a date, I tend to leave that till later, unless I'm really bored!'

'Oh, no,' I stutter, 'I wasn't daydreaming, it's just I…'

117

Then I realise he's pulling my leg. Second big tick, this guy has a sense of humour. We laugh and I relax a little. For the first time in, like forever, it looks like this date might be fun. I certainly feel lucky with Daniel. Pretty much every other woman in the room is still sending him admiring glances and I already begin to wish we didn't have to swap round for the next course. This date is worth getting to know a whole lot better.

# CHAPTER 13

The problem is, when I really like someone, I either get tongue-tied and can't think of anything vaguely coherent to say, or I come out with utter gibberish as though I've been drinking, even when I haven't. It's so annoying. When I'm with someone like Rob, it isn't a problem as I don't like him in that way, in fact, strike that, I don't like him in any way, but you know what I mean. Yet, as soon as someone attractive comes along, I become totally useless.

Still, Daniel is such a nice guy; he puts me at ease, keeping up a constant stream of chatter, so I soon feel more able to communicate normally, instead of making a complete idiot of myself.

'So, what do you do?' I ask in between mouthfuls of delicious chicken liver pate. Incidentally the food is incredibly yummy. I didn't like to mention it too much in case it detracts from the whole point, which is Daniel, not the food.

'I work in the city. It's basically freelance consulting in investment banking.'

'Oh.' This is an absolute disaster. Daniel seems too fun-loving to be a boring old investment banker. That's it, I suddenly remember, speaking of bankers, Sir Henry Greaves – he's the old guy sitting over in the corner opposite Miss Snooty who was complaining about her pheasant. I knew I remembered him from somewhere. How hideous. I hope I don't end up with him for the next course; that would be terrible. It was bad enough last time.

Daniel smiles at me, showing his perfect teeth. 'I know what you're thinking,' he says (*probably not*, I think, I hate it when people say they know what I'm thinking), 'that bankers are normally old and boring (yes, actually maybe that is what I was thinking) but we're not all like that as I shall have to prove to you.'

'No, I'm sure you're not, you don't seem boring at all, I mean…' Back to embarrassing, I can tell I'm turning horribly red.

But Daniel just laughs; he is really nice. I like him a lot.

By the time he's recounted amusing anecdotes about his job and I've regaled him with tales from Modiste, the time flies by.

WE'VE ALREADY FINISHED our first course and I'm hoping somehow we can stay at our table and not move, when I notice two men walk in. I can't see who they are, but assume they are here on a date and a bit late. They're both wearing long coats and look very smart.

They seem to know Emma, who greets them with kisses and a warm welcome. They walk to the bar and as I look across, I realise with misgiving it is Nick Palmer-Wright and Darcy Drummond. Nick smiles at me and I wave cheerily, when I suddenly notice the expression on Darcy's face. He looks furious. For goodness sake, what have I done this time? Actually though, his gaze isn't focused on me, he's glaring at Daniel. I turn to check out Daniel's reaction in time to glimpse him giving a slight smile in greeting. How strange. The two men obviously know each other, but as I glance again to see if I imagined Darcy's expression, I merely catch sight of the back of his coat as he swings round abruptly and leaves the restaurant. Emma looks surprised, but Nick says something briefly to her and follows Darcy out the door. How odd.

I'm about to ask Daniel what's going on, but he's already started talking of something else. Before I can change the subject, Emma rings a little bell. 'Sorry to intrude into your lovely evening. Please can I have your attention? If you look under your plate, you will find the name of the next person you will be dating for the following course. Please can I ask you to change now as the chef is ready to serve the mains?'

It's typical, I'm having such a lovely evening and would much rather stay where I am with Daniel. The idea in itself is a good one, swapping round if you have a hideous partner but there should be a get-out clause if you really like the one you're with. I hope I'll be able to meet him again soon for a proper date. That is, if he likes me. I look up at him shyly as we rise from our chairs.

'What a shame, but I'm sure we'll catch up again very soon. I feel I still have a long way to go to prove to you that bankers aren't all boring bastards,' he quips with that gorgeous smile. My heart does a big flip-flop all by itself. I know they say bizarre things about their feelings like this in romantic novels, but it really did.

I pick up my plate, feeling for the piece of flowery paper underneath and this time my heart sinks. You will never guess whose name is written on it. Actually, you probably will. It's none other than Sir Henry Greaves. This man seems to be my fate as the worst dinner partner ever… perhaps in close competition with Rob Bright. More diverting still is the fact that Daniel has approached Sir Henry's table and is introducing himself to the cantankerous battleaxe seated opposite him. I have a real job not to laugh, the thought of Daniel matched with Miss High and Mighty is hilarious.

There is no time to sit and snigger, however, as Sir Henry Greaves trundles up to my table. 'Are you Miss Sophie Johnston?'

'Erm, yes I am.' I don't bother correcting the Johnston to Johnson.

'Speak up, girl, can't stand muttering!'

Yep, this was going about as well as I expected, except looking on the bright side, he doesn't seem to have recognised me from the awards evening, which is a great relief. Then again, I guess I haven't had my make-up or hair done professionally, so I probably look a little more like my usual self.

Sir Henry is everything and more as a dinner partner than I had already imagined. He's one of those people who is all about who you know, not what you know. He's the worst name-dropper I've ever met. It is, 'Of course, I was having drinks with Angela Rippon,' and, 'John Major was at the club that day, we were at Harrow together, you know.'

Sir Henry enjoys reading *Burke's Peerage* for pleasure and is astonished to discover that I don't have a copy. He is totally incredulous, 'Doesn't every young lady have a copy of *Burke's Peerage*? I thought you said you had a degree.'

'Well, yes,' I reply awkwardly, pretending to be very interested in my risotto.

'Wasn't one of these bloody new-fangled polytechnics, was it?' he blusters.

'No, it was Oxford actually.' I can't resist.

'Oh, they take women now, do they? Can't say I agree with it myself. What on earth a girl wants with an education, I don't know. A pretty face and a pleasant biddable disposition, that's all you need, m'dear.' He pauses a second to continue noisily chomping on his steak. 'Make a good wife and preferably come from a decent family. Are you related to the Stevenson Johnstons?'

'Erm, I've no idea.' I am so incensed by the last tirade, I'm having a job not to drink the whole bottle of wine in the nearby cooler, just to get me through the next half hour. Ironically, so far The Jane Austen Dating Agency seems to be full of misogynist men with opinions stuck in the Regency era, apart from Daniel of course. I wonder how he's getting on with the old battleaxe.

'Who's the lady you were dining with for the first course?' I ask, hoping to at least introduce a new topic of conversation.

'Eh? Oh that was Lady Constance Parker. Related to the Parker Sainsburys she would have me believe, but I will need to check my *Burke's* when I get home. Can't be too careful, you know, people will tell you anything. I have a feeling she is one of the more recent Parkers, though still a good family and well known. Lost her husband many years ago and lives on her own with her daughter at Radnall Park. Used to the best of everything, definitely one to watch, I think.'

He seems to suddenly recollect himself as he utters these last words, 'Yes well, that is... ahem... probably difficult to live with, but I spend most of my time at the club in any case and circumstances have forced me lately to consider my situation. It's a disgrace! Three daughters, only one married. In fact, one of 'ems over there, Maria. It was her idea I should come to this agency, had some damn silly romantic notion I should marry again and find love. Not that she's one to speak, thirty-five and still not hitched, I ask you!'

I follow Sir Henry's gaze until it falls on the rather graceful girl, Maria, who I noticed looking so unhappy earlier. Surprisingly she appears rather more cheerful than before, in spite of the fact she is seated with Rob Bright. The woman needs a medal; no-one is happy sitting with Rob, and I thought the Navy guy wasn't bad looking for an older man. I wonder where he is, then I spot him with Louisa, her vibrant auburn hair glinting under the lights. He is a very different man, talking and laughing with ease. Upon glancing back at Maria, I notice her gazing rather sadly at him, then she returns to listening to Rob's all-too-ready flow of conversation.

Thank goodness we all seem to have finished our main course and I look forward to escaping the dubious pleasure of Sir Henry

Greaves's company. I guess at least we've made some progress, he has actually spoken to me this time. He seems quite interested in Lady Constance, by the sound of it to solve his financial issues, but from my reckoning they are a good match.

Sir Henry must be in his sixties, he is quite a good-looking man, rather vain I should think. I noticed throughout dinner he glanced across at the mirrors on a regular basis to check or it seemed rather to admire his cravat and to ensure his hair is neat. Lady Constance, from all appearances, is just as difficult and snobbish about her choices. Yes, I think they would suit very well.

I am startled out of my imaginary matchmaking by Emma ringing the bell once more. 'All change round please. If everyone would like to look under their place card, they will discover their next exciting partner for the dessert course.'

I hardly dare look. No, it can't be. Someone's having a laugh at my expense. I begin to wonder if maybe Emma had chosen my first date and then left the rest rather unadvisedly to Miss PW or perhaps Rob has bribed her, judging from the triumphant expression on his face. I just can't seem to get rid of the man.

HE APPEARS AT MY TABLE, full of himself as usual. 'What a super do!' he exclaims. 'I simply can't believe my luck, so many beautiful ladies in one evening, I'm quite overcome.'

*But not any quieter or less annoying,* I think, but settle with resignation that I am going to have to put up with Rob for the next half hour or so. At least my dessert involves chocolate, which always makes me feel better.

'You'll never believe who's here?' Rob leans in towards me, far too close for comfort. He'd already kissed me wetly on the cheek upon first arriving at my table, causing me to recoil in distaste.

'Er who?' I ask, not very interested. Rob's prolific conversation on the number of attractive women in the room, who are supposedly extremely keen on him, has already bored me to tears.

'Lady Constance Parker!' he announces, after a dramatic pause. 'She's one of the Parker Sainsburys, you know.'

'Oh yes, I already know as Sir Henry–'

Rob, as always, has absolutely no interest in anything anyone else might be saying, so he continues to talk over me. 'Yes, but the point is she is the aunt of Richard Simms, my wonderful employer. She is the patroness of Dafco and owner of Radnall Park. I have never met her but I am sure she would be interested in knowing how her nephew did at the Country Chess Championships earlier this week.'

'I'm sure she would,' I reply, realising this could help me escape from Rob sooner rather than later. 'But not right now, not when you don't know her, especially while she's eating her dinner.'

I try hard to dissuade him from the idea but Rob dismisses any concerns with his usual arrogance.

'I'm sure you mean well, Sophie, and I expect you know best in many things but you will have to allow me to be a better judge in social matters. You must understand that the world of business follows different social rules and therefore it is perfectly acceptable for me to talk to Lady Constance, provided I am humble enough in my approach. Much as I'm sure I can be guided by your excellent judgement in future, on this occasion you will find that my education and contacts within business circles make me much better equipped than you to know what I am talking about.'

With this crushing speech, he scrapes back his chair and manages to squash the lady at the table behind him, causing him to spend far too long apologising and twittering at her. This disturbs all the other diners who are looking round in annoyance. I catch Daniel's eye and he gives me a conspiratorial grin.

Rob, undeterred, makes a beeline for Lady Constance's table, where she is instructing Daniel on the best way of managing staff. It's completely incongruous as I shouldn't think Daniel has any more idea or intention of hiring servants than I have. He's making a good effort to appear to listen in a polite manner, however, when the couple are rudely interrupted by the appearance of an overkeen Rob Bright at their table.

He gives a ridiculous little mock bow to Lady Constance and proceeds to introduce himself. I'm unable to hear exactly what he's saying but can tell by the incredulous expression on her face that she's not at all amused by his interruption. It's possible to just about make out the words: 'apology', 'Richard Simms' and 'Dafco'. Lady Constance inclines her head slightly at these words, but during another of Rob's prolonged speeches, she firmly turns away and continues her discussion with, or rather lecture to, Daniel.

Rob returns to me and ladles dessert in his mouth with a spoon, slurping noisily. 'I was so pleased to meet Lady Constance,' he says, unabashed. 'She was very civil and even remarked that Richard Simms might have mentioned me not just once but a couple of times.'

I realise the only way to cope with Rob for the rest of dinner is to ignore him as pointedly as possible, but unfortunately it doesn't have much effect; he's so full of Richard and Lady Constance and his very likely prospects of promotion.


FINALLY, I've had enough, so it seems a good idea to disappear to the ladies, where I phone Mark for a chat. I've already texted Chloe, but she's out with Kian for once. Mark answers straight away. I had promised I would let him know how things are going...

'Sophie – OMG, what's happening? What's your date like?' he shrieks.

I soon fill him in with details of Daniel, but have to put my hand over the receiver, Mark's so overexcited I'm worried the whole restaurant will hear his screeching. I'm just in the middle of my recital of the downturn of events, i.e. Sir Henry Greaves – which makes Mark laugh uproariously as he remembers my ineptitude at the GQ Awards evening with Sir Henry – when I am disturbed by the sound of sobbing coming from the nearest cubicle.

'Erm, Mark, can I call you back?'

'Of course, you go, girl. Sir Henry awaits!'

'No, I mean… Oh, I'll explain later.' I click off my phone and listen. Yes, there's the sound again; I hadn't imagined it.

'Hello?' I call. There's no answer, no sound either. 'Hello? Are you okay?' I ask again, this time knocking gently on the toilet door.

'Just a minute,' comes the reply, and after more sniffing and a flush, the door opens slowly and out walks Maria, the lady who had been with Rob Bright during the previous course. Her eyes are suspiciously swollen and red-rimmed. I'm not surprised – Rob's just the worst date ever and has nearly reduced me to tears a couple of times.

'Don't worry,' she says. 'I'm fine, I'll be okay in a minute.' In spite of her best efforts, however, the tears roll down her face again. I pass her some tissues from my bag. 'I'm so sorry,' she says between sniffs, 'I don't usually cry.'

'Best to let it out then,' I say sagely. 'After all, coming to a Regency Evening and being stuck with Rob Bright is enough to upset anyone quite honestly.'

This makes Maria smile slightly in spite of herself. 'It's not him, it's me.'

'That's what they all say,' I add darkly.

'No, it's not Rob, honestly.'

I look at her quizzically and she gives another tiny smile.

'Though his conversation is enough to drive you quite crazy, but at least it saved me from giving much reply… It's not that, it's

Charles, you see. I just hadn't expected to see him again, not like this, or have to sit with him all that time. It was just so horribly awkward.' She starts to sob again and I give her a hug as she really looks like she needs one.

'Thanks.' She sniffs once she's recovered her composure. 'I don't even know your name.'

'Sophie.'

'Maria,' she introduces herself diffidently, apologetically almost, 'Maria Greaves…'

'Yes. I had the pleasure of your father's company for the main course.'

'Poor you.' She looks at me speculatively. 'You're not only far too young for him, you're far too nice!'

'He was very pleasant, I'm sure,' I answer politely, not liking to be rude about someone's father whatever I personally think about him.

'Really? He's usually pompous, tactless, and judges everyone on either their ancestry or their bank balance.'

'Yes, that did rather disqualify me as I have no lineage worth speaking of or much money either.'

'You're lucky he spoke to you at all then. If you're not listed in *Burke's Peerage*, you don't exist in my father's world. That's what happened with Charles, you see.'

'So, where did you know Charles from? Was he the guy you were sitting with for the first course?'

Maria nods. 'I haven't seen him for fifteen years. He was my first boyfriend. We met when I was seventeen.'

'Gosh, how romantic!' I'm struck by this as I don't think I'd even had a boyfriend at seventeen.

'Oh yes, it was,' she replies dreamily. 'He was so chivalrous, mature, kind, understanding. I'll never forget the day he proposed.'

'He proposed? What happened?'

'I refused him.'

'You did what?' I'm flabbergasted. (I've always wanted to write that word.)

'I know… it was ridiculous… I loved him, have never loved anyone but him in fact, but he can't forgive me.' Tears fall down Maria's face once more.

'Why on earth did you say no if you really loved him?' I don't want to hurt Maria's feelings as she's so upset, but the truth is, I'm incredulous. This woman had met her ideal man, unlike me, and goodness only knows I know how long it takes to find a man you can put up with for a couple of dates even, let alone marriage.

'My father was totally against it.'

Ah, this makes more sense. 'Did you have to listen to him? You must have been over eighteen by then, surely you could have married anyway.'

'Yes, I could have done, but he persuaded me it would ruin Charles's life marrying a young girl, that he would resent me. I believed him and I loved Charles so much, I felt I should let him go, have a chance of a career and live his life without being held back.'

I'm silent for a moment as I can't imagine being so selfless about someone. 'But what could your father have had against him?' I ask, realising as the words come out of my mouth that it would be quite a lot, knowing Sir Henry.

'For a start, Charles is not from a well-known family and at that time he was studying. He had no money, just student debts. My father felt I could do better and has a bad habit of over-spending so looks to us children to marry well. Look how wrong he was. Charles now has a great career, he is a captain, soon to be promoted to commander. Ironically, he's good enough for my father now but he wouldn't even look at me, not after what I have done to him. Now I'm totally past it, and no man has ever caught my eye since.'

'Nonsense. You're only a bit older than me, which is not old at all. We're not living in the Regency period. And you're so pretty.'

Maria blushes and looks embarrassed; she obviously doesn't have a very high opinion of herself.

'It's an awkward situation,' I continue, 'but surely Charles didn't have to take your first answer. He could have tried again?'

'I expect his pride was hurt. He never did get along with my father and Charles felt as though my family criticised him for not being good enough for me. You can't blame him. Charles carried on at uni, got his degree and was away at sea for many years. Can you imagine the shock meeting him again here as my first date?'

'How did he react? Was he pleased to see you?'

'He was cold, very cold and formal,' Maria answers sadly. 'I could have put up with anything but that. He was always so much fun and we would laugh together, discuss the same interests. He obviously hates me now.'

'I'm sure he doesn't. I expect he doesn't know how to react and, don't forget, it would have been as great a shock for him as for you.'

'I know, I've tried to tell myself that but he's so different with me from everyone else. With Louisa, he's laughing and joking; he hasn't given me another thought. I'll have to move on and try to forget. I'll leave the agency, then I can avoid him.'

'No, you can't do that. It would be such a shame. This is your chance to meet someone new and I'd like you to stay. Goodness only knows I need all the help I can get with all the dodgy dates I've had.'

'I must say, I don't seem to be having much luck at the moment either. Not that I have a great deal of experience with men. I could never find anyone to compare with Charles, and my father puts most of them off.'

'I haven't even found a Charles, although I do like Daniel, the new recruit.'

'Oh, the good-looking chap you were with for the first course? Yes, I think you and everyone else likes him.'

I laugh wryly. 'I know, I guess I'll have to join the queue. Anyway, we must have a girly get together. You'd like my friend Mel, and Izzy is nice too.'

Maria seems to cheer up a little. 'Yes, I've met Izzy, she's really sweet. That would be so lovely as most of my friends are married so I always feel like a spare part and the others my father doesn't approve of.'

'I can't promise he accepts me!' I joke. 'But he has begun to speak to me, which is an improvement. Who knows, by our next meeting we may even be acquaintances. Come on, I have some emergency cover-up in my bag and we'll go back out together. Your next date might be someone nice.'

BY THE TIME I've returned to my table, Rob has obviously become bored and to while away the time, is chipping into the conversation of the couple at the table behind. They look quite fed up with him but I must admit I've enjoyed the break.

Fortunately the evening is drawing to a close. Maria goes home early with her father but at least she looks a little more cheerful and we've swapped numbers. As I go to grab my coat, I bump into Izzy, standing by the door. She doesn't look at all her usual bubbly self.

'Are you waiting for Josh?' I ask, assuming this is the case.

'No, I'm not,' she says with feeling. 'He's still chatting to his last date even though they finished their desserts ages ago.'

'He's probably just being polite. It's difficult to rush off after dinner without appearing rude.' Although of course in my case with Rob, I didn't care what he thought. The weird thing with him is that the more I snub him, the keener he seems to get. He'd given me another kiss as he left, much to my disgust, and has even threatened to invite me to one of his chess evenings.

Izzy looks a little tearful. 'No, you obviously haven't seen who he's sitting with.' She points to where Josh is seated in the far corner of the restaurant.

I must admit he doesn't look too worried about finishing his conversation. His partner is simply stunning, super elegant, probably in her late twenties. She has long straight hair, beautifully cut, and a flowing dress which clings in all the right places, if you know what I mean. Everything about her screams wealth, confidence and luxurious elegance.

'Anyone can see he's crazy about you when he looks at you,' I say firmly. 'I expect he's just being polite.'

'I'm not so sure, and I'm certainly not going to hang around here waiting for him to finish his conversation.' She continues with spirit, 'I'm going home.'

'Izzy! Are you okay?' a familiar-looking guy calls as he appears in the doorway. It's Matthew, I remember him from the Regency Dance evening. 'Do you want a lift home?'

'I'm fine,' Izzy snaps, grabs my arm, and propels me towards the door.

'I wish he'd mind his own business,' she whispers to me.

'Who? Matthew? He seems very nice.'

'That's the trouble,' Izzy grumbles. 'He's too nice.'

I'm not sure how to answer that one. 'Do you want to share a cab?'

'Yes please,' she replies gratefully and we step out onto the street together.

I don't know about First Date, this has been more like first heartbreak evening and has given me quite a lot to think about.

# CHAPTER 14

I'm still mulling over the events of the First Dates evening when back at work the next morning. It was all a bit surreal. And the more I think about it, the more familiar the characters and their stories from last night seemed. It's as though I have entered a parallel Jane Austen universe. I did wonder if it was some kind of set-up but I hadn't spotted any television cameras anywhere and the people appeared to be genuine.

These musings are certainly more interesting than my current sales total. I'm never going to win a place to go to Victoria Beckham's Spring Summer show at this rate. Maybe Mum's right, I should start looking up PGCE courses.

The phone rings, making me jump, and I answer it quickly, hoping it might be a returning customer from my bridal list. It isn't; it's Emma from the dating agency. It hadn't occurred to me she'd have my work number – courtesy of Miffy, probably.

'Hi, Sophie, I have some exciting news!'

'Oh, that sounds good.' I'm speaking quietly as I don't want the rest of the office earwigging again.

'That was a successful evening last night, wasn't it?'

'Erm, yes.' I try to sound enthusiastic.

'And you'll never guess who's been straight on the phone this morning, asking for a second date?' she asks brightly.

'Not Rob Bright.' I'm really hoping against hope it isn't as I can't stand one more date with this guy.

'No. I didn't think you liked him,' Emma replies innocently, and I can imagine her smiling to herself on the other end of the line. 'No, it's Daniel – he loved meeting you last night and has requested to see you again.'

'Oh my God.' I'm amazed and my heart beats rather fast. The thought of meeting up with Daniel again is pretty exciting *and* he likes me. Someone cute, funny and normal actually likes me at last.

'Would you like to go out with him?' Emma persists, obviously not quite sure how to take my response.

'Yes, that would be lovely,' I reply, trying not to appear too keen but simultaneously grinning and punching the air with my fist, to the consternation of the rest of the sales team. Kelli gives me a scornful look from the other side of the partition and I swing my chair round so that I have my back to her.

'I mean, that's great. What happens next? I'm kind of new to all this.' Some complete hunk asking me out is most definitely an unfamiliar experience for me.

'Daniel has suggested a champagne picnic at Box Hill. I told you this man has sensitivity and class.'

'Yes, he has,' I reply. 'It sounds amazing.' (I've given up playing cool, calm and collected by now – I'm at the 'thank you very muchly, thank you' Miranda Hart school of dating stage.)

Emma rings off once we have made arrangements for Daniel to pick me up on Sunday afternoon for a strawberry and champagne picnic. It sounds heavenly and I am totally overexcited.

'YOU'RE IN A GOOD MOOD,' Mark says when he finds me rather

bizarrely humming while photocopying the month's sales forecast.

'Oh yes,' I reply happily, 'I have a date!'

'Oh no. Who is it this time? Sir Henry?' Mark teases.

'Er no, not quite that good. I'm just going to have to make do with Daniel instead. Strawberry and champagne picnic – it's a hard life but someone's got to do it!'

'Oohh, well done you! That's so exciting!' Mark gives me a bear hug. 'I wish I was going to be a fly on the wall on this date, darling. When are you going? Sunday? Make sure you give me a blow-by-blow account afterwards or I'll never speak to you again.'


TYPICALLY, the week drags by really slowly as it always does when you're looking forward to something. Strangely, my sales figures go up drastically as I've bagged a couple of new bridal salons wanting to advertise, who are part of a larger chain. All things considered, I feel a bit more positive about work – perhaps I'm meant to be part of the fashion world after all.

Maybe I can do this. I can really belong.

I'm also overexcited for my forthcoming date with Daniel.


SUNDAY DAWNS FINE and perfect much to my relief. I have been stressing all week about the weather until Mel's got fed up with me.

The short drive to Box Hill with Daniel, in contrast to the start of my date with Rob Bright, whizzes by as we fly down the country lanes in his convertible. Our chat is easy and relaxed, and I feel quite comfortable in Daniel's company in spite of my underlying nervousness. My only concern is that convertibles are a lovely idea in theory, and I have always wanted one, but the reality is they wreak havoc with your hair. I've a horrible feeling

I'm going to arrive at the picnic site looking as though I've been crawling through thick undergrowth.

UPON OUR ARRIVAL at Box Hill, we wander in companionable silence up to a quiet spot where the whole view spreads out uninterrupted before us, with quaint little patchwork fields and tiny trees. Daniel's been very gentlemanly and not only opened the door for me, but also carried the lovely hamper, supplied with compliments of Emma and the dating agency.

I sit on an old-fashioned rug, wrapping my cardigan round me more snugly. I've worn a long flowery maxi dress as I felt it was necessary to act the part but although spring has sprung and the sun is out, the air is still quite chilly.

Daniel notices me shiver and passes across his jacket, which fits very comfortably round my shoulders and smells deliciously of his aftershave. I feel a warm glow fill my whole body, which I suspect has very little to do with the thickness of his jacket.

Daniel expertly opens the bottle of champagne and hands me an elegant flute. The bubbly is beautifully refreshing. He's even sliced a strawberry and placed it on the edge of the glass. We've talked of this and that but so far nothing in particular. I'm itching to ask Daniel how he knows Darcy Drummond. There must be some story behind this acquaintance, but I don't like to broach the subject. Daniel starts the topic himself, however. 'How long have you been at the dating agency?'

'Not long,' I reply, sipping champagne, 'just a few weeks.'

'And who've you met? Emma and Jessica obviously.'

'Yes. I especially like Emma, she's really nice.'

'Definitely, Jessica is a little more scary.' He pulls a face. We both laugh. 'And have you ever met the CEO, Darcy Drummond?'

'Kind of, but I don't really know him,' I reply. 'I believe he's the MD of Drummond Associates?'

'Yes, he's a very wealthy man. Worth ten million or maybe

even more, I should think. I've lost count over the years – I've known him a long time, since we were kids.'

I must look shocked as Daniel continues. 'I can understand you're surprised by this, after seeing his reaction to my presence in the restaurant the other evening. Do you know much about him?'

'As much as I ever wish to!' I cry with feeling. 'From the time I've spent with him, I think he's one of the most arrogant, unpleasant men I've ever met.'

'I can't say I disagree with you because he's not exactly my favourite person. I've known him such a long time that you won't find I'm able to give you an unbiased view, but he's generally well thought of in business circles.'

'I don't know about other people,' I reply hotly, 'but that's what I think of him and I'm sure others would agree, if they knew how rude he is. Everyone I know thinks he's full of himself.' (By everyone, I mean Chloe, Mel and Mark, who I guess haven't really met him, but that's irrelevant.)

'I don't feel he deserves people to admire him,' Daniel continues. 'Everyone's blinded by his money and position, or intimidated by his influence.'

'Personally I take him as I've known him; a bad-tempered arrogant piece of work, used to getting his own way. I hope his being involved in the agency won't scare you away.'

'No, definitely not. If he wants to avoid me, he has to stay out of the way. We're not on good terms.'

'Why's that? What did he do?' I ask, prepared to believe the worst. I mean, this is so the Wickham/Darcy feud.

'We met through a philanthropic cause his father's company supported. I come from a poor background, with parents who had nothing. My dad left when I was young and my mum struggled to cope with my sister and me on her own. The late Mr Drummond was good to me and I always respected him. Sadly, his son had other ideas.'

I'm gripped by Daniel's story but as he stops at this point, I don't like to ask any more questions, he seems genuinely upset about what happened. He begins to talk about work and the dating agency. He's so positive in what he says, without being boastful like Rob, who constantly talks about himself. Daniel is able to discuss most subjects, making everything interesting with his own touch of charm.

'I joined the dating agency because I want to get out more,' he says. 'I can't bear sitting around doing nothing. The way Darcy treated me has made me lose faith in human nature. My life could have been so different. I never expected to end up working freelance.'

'So, what happened?'

'The late Mr Drummond planned for me to join his business at management level. He bequeathed it in his will. He'd been so kind as to give me this incredible opportunity. I thought it was definite. It was what kept me strong, working hard when every-thing else went wrong. But when it came to it, the position wasn't given to me.'

Surely this couldn't be possible. 'How could that happen? If you were legally entitled to the position, a lawyer would have made Darcy honour Mr Drummond's request?'

'Not really.' Daniel smiles wryly. 'You've no idea how powerful these people are. I could have tried legal representation, I suppose, but to Darcy, hiring the top lawyers in the land would be a matter of course. I would have struggled to find the funds to even secure an appointment with a regular legal professional. When the position became available two years ago, just as I was at the age to take it on, it was given to another guy. The only thing I can think of to explain Darcy's behaviour is that I've told him what I think of him a couple of times. I do have occasional anger management issues.'

'Really?' I ask with a smile. 'I can't believe that.' And I can't,

Daniel seems so easy-going. I can far more easily believe it of Darcy Drummond.

'Maybe sometimes I can get a bit grumpy to be fair! I can't think of any other explanation. We're so different, I think he must see me as a rival rather than a friend.'

'That's terrible.' I'm incredulous that anyone can get away with such scandalous unfairness in this day and age. In fact, I'm not sure altogether. I mean, I really like Daniel, but can this be true? It's so like Wickham in *P and P*, all so plausible. I remember when I first read the book, I thought everyone was a bit gullible, believing him so readily when they didn't really know him. I don't blame Lizzie for wanting to be on his side though, especially when Mr Darcy had been so vile. I would much rather believe Daniel than Darcy Drummond. But this is different in any case. Emma really likes him and can vouch for his personality. I must stop living in books; I'm literally losing the plot, this is real life.

Anyway, Daniel is such a nice friendly guy, nothing shady about him at all. 'You should go to the papers,' I suggest.

'I suppose one day the world will find out about it, but not from me. I can't bring myself to do it, I'd feel like I was destroying old Mr Drummond's legacy. He was so kind to me, I owe him everything.'

That's so typical of Daniel, he's such a kind person. I begin to wonder if I've found the perfect guy at last. There's a tiny question that bothers me, however. 'But I still can't understand what makes Darcy so determined to be unpleasant to you?'

'I s'pose he hates me. I put it down to jealousy – because his father was so fond of me, he was prepared to give me a top position in his own company. Obviously Darcy resented this, he must have seen me as competition and couldn't cope with it.'

'I just hadn't realised Darcy is that nasty. I obviously took a dislike to him as he's so arrogant and looks down on everyone, but I never believed he would behave like this. You'd think his sense of honesty and pride would have made him keep the promise.'

'His sense of pride is one of his core values – and I guess this has led him to do a lot of good things. He's very involved in charity work and, rather ironically, apprenticeship schemes for those who need a leg-up.'

I ponder for a moment, trying to work it all out. Certainly Darcy had shown a great deal of arrogance in how he spoke about the dating agency and the sort of people it attracts. At the GQ Awards he'd appeared bored and full of himself. No, this account from Daniel doesn't surprise me at all.

'But what about Nick Palmer-Wright?' I chip in. 'Surely he wouldn't want to associate himself with such a lying arrogant piece of work. He seems a genuinely nice guy, I can't imagine he would support this kind of unfairness.'

'I don't expect he knows about it,' Daniel replies sombrely. 'Darcy can be very charming and even good fun when he wants to be.'

I feel disbelieving at this, but remembering his boyish smile with Christie at the awards, I guess perhaps he could be.

Daniel and I talk of other topics including Rob Bright, when Daniel suddenly asks, 'Do you know Lady Constance Parker?'

'No. The rather snobby lady complaining about the quality of her pheasant at the First Dates evening?'

'Yes, that's the one.' Daniel smiles. 'I had the pleasure of her company for the main course. She's related to Darcy, you know.'

'Is she?' I reply, momentarily surprised, but then not really as her arrogance and oblivious disregard for the feelings of anyone around her makes this seem probable.

'Yes, she's his great aunt.'

'Of course she would be.'

'Sorry?'

'Oh, nothing. Just something from a book.' For God's sake, I've got to stop this whole novel comparing thing going on,

Daniel will think I'm really strange. Unless of course this really is a set-up for a TV programme and Daniel is an actor. I peer at him surreptitiously but he seems sincere.

He continues, oblivious. 'She has a large estate and a very high opinion of herself. It was rumoured Darcy might marry her daughter. Keep the money in the family sort of thing.'

'What's her daughter like?'

'Don't know. I've never met her. I don't mix in those sort of circles anymore.' Daniel looks so sad and I long to give him a hug to comfort him, but am too embarrassed. He's got such puppy dog eyes, sort of mournful and cute at the same time.

'Isn't Lady Constance something to do with Rob Bright?' I ask to divert him from his story.

'Yes, I believe she might be.'

'Rob's been telling all and sundry that he knows her. I think she's something to do with his munificent benefactor, Richard Simms.'

'He certainly seemed keen to introduce himself to her the other evening! But I don't think she was the only one he's interested in.'

I'm embarrassed at this, blushing bright red, and Daniel's teasing blue eyes crinkle at the corners as he meets my glance with a smile.

'Shall we walk?' he asks, as if sensing my discomfort, and gallantly reaches out his hand to help me up.

We wander along the pathway, drinking in the view. Upon finding a sunny spot by a bench, we pause a moment and, noticing Daniel still looking serious, I feel as though I should say something to cheer him up.

'I'm sure things will get better, you know.'

'Of course. They are already.'

It seems natural to reach out and hug him, and we stand like statues clinging to each other at the top of the hill. He smells so nice and brushes his stubbly cheek against mine as he finds my mouth and we share a gentle kiss.

I'd like to say that birds sang, stars shone from the sky and choirs of angels appeared from nowhere, but that wouldn't be strictly true. I had a bit of a stomach ache actually – I'm not sure strawberries and fizzy champagne are a great mixture in reality.

'Are you okay?' Daniel asks.

'Just a bit cold,' I fib, and we walk back to our picnic spot, gather the things, and return to the car.

It's been a day of surprises but the beautiful Box Hill has more than lived up to my expectations. All in all, I feel pretty darn happy, if a little confused.

# CHAPTER 15

Of course I discuss the whole Darcy/Daniel feud with Mel the next day. She's surprised but, in her usual style, tries to defend both Daniel and Darcy without really succeeding in managing either. Mel never likes to say or believe a bad word about anyone. Sometimes it makes it really hard when I want a good gossip as she always has to give a reason why someone's behaving badly, which I don't really want to hear.

In this case, she thinks there must be some mistake somewhere along the line. Having met both men only briefly, she says it's impossible someone as friendly and nice as Daniel can be lying, but she can't believe anyone as respected and well known as Darcy Drummond could have behaved in such a way over his father's will.

'Think about it, Sophie. No-one in Darcy's position could get away with ignoring his father's final wishes, even if he wanted to,' Mel insists. 'And I can't believe his close friend, Nick, would want to go along with this sort of deception either. It's against the law, apart from anything else.'

'I know, you're right. It's just I'd rather believe Daniel. I don't want to even try to imagine he might be lying.'

'I think you like Daniel a lot.' Mel smiles.

'Well, yes.' I laugh. 'He's a big improvement on all the other guys I've ever dated!'

'That's not exactly saying much!'

'Thanks. Either way, I'm a bit freaked out. My life seems to be turning into a Jane Austen novel. It's quite uncanny.'

'I think you've simply been reading too many romantic novels, full stop.'

Suddenly the phone goes. It's Emma. 'Hi, Sophie. How did your date go yesterday?'

'It was lovely. Beautiful weather, good company and a yummy picnic, thank you.'

'And how did you get along with Daniel? He's a bit of a dish, isn't he?'

I blush. 'Oh yes, really nice, good company.'

'I think he likes you a lot too. I can tell these things.'

'Erm, have you known him long?'

'Not really, no. Why? Nothing wrong is there?'

'Oh no, not at all, I was just interested,' I reply awkwardly.

'Anyway, I've had a bit of a brainwave, sweetie. Did you know it's our Regency Ball in a couple of weeks?'

'No. I didn't know it's so soon.'

'It is, and I'm sure Daniel's going to be there. He's a Gold member.'

'Oh,' I reply wistfully.

There's an awkward pause before Emma continues.

'I do have a suggestion to make. I'm allowed to invite a couple of close friends or family members along as a bit of a perk and I'd like to invite you and you could bring your lovely sister and friend along too if you like?'

'Really? You mean we could all come to the ball? But surely you have other friends and family you would like to invite?'

Emma laughs at my amazement. 'Of course I mean it. It would be my pleasure. Quite honestly, I don't see much of my family, they all live miles away, and as for friends, I can't think of any of those I would like to invite as much as you. Please say you'll come.'

'Oh my gosh, I'd love to, but surely I have to be a Gold member?'

'Not if you're invited by one of the organisers.' Emma takes my stunned silence for acceptance. 'So that's settled then. I'll post out your invitations, which should arrive in the next couple of days. Dress code is Regency attire, empire line dresses for the girls, and good old breeches and top boots for the boys.'

After a little more chitchat and repetition of my stammered thanks, Emma rings off. This phone call's put me into a complete dither of excitement. I've always wanted to go to a real Regency Ball and this one is going to include Daniel, which is almost too much excitement to bear.

It's surprisingly easy to persuade Chloe to come, apparently Kian is going to be working that night thank goodness, though I have a horrible suspicion there's going to be trouble when he finds out where she's going.

Mel's oddly keen for someone who isn't into Jane Austen in any way, shape or form, and typically decides to make her own dress. This is going to involve a host of late nights with her sewing away at all hours, but nothing really new there.

Work seems to fly by and bizarrely my sales figures have gone up again, perhaps I could be quite good at this thing after all. Amanda has even smiled at me on a couple of occasions; it was quite unnerving. Mark's thrilled about Daniel, though he keeps asking me how I'm going to move things forward, probably because he knows I'm a complete non-starter when it comes to dating. Having told him about Daniel's harsh treatment at the hands of Darcy Drummond, however, Mark's incredulous.

'How kind of him to give you his whole life story during your first proper date together. God, he's worse than me!' Mark says calmly, sipping his mid-morning latte.

'You think he's making it up? I believe Darcy's been a complete b towards him.'

'I think he's been reading *Pride and Prejudice*. It's scarily similar.' Mark sees my face. 'Okay, joking apart, I'm not saying Daniel's lying exactly, but firstly you don't know him that well and he could be – how do we know? Secondly, if not, to be fair he won't be the first person who's been badly treated by the rich and powerful in this country. He's almost a bit too plausible.'

'That doesn't make it right, and if he's lying, that'll be just typical. He's the first normal guy I've met. It's not fair.'

'Life isn't fair though, is it, darling?' Mark states sagely.

However I feel about Daniel, I'm so excited about the Regency Ball – after much searching, I've managed to hire a beautiful long cream empire line dress with a tiny V-shaped neck finished with a very fine gold thread. I don't even want to think about how much it cost but, put it this way, I had, originally upon hearing the amount, presumed it must be the purchase price. In for a penny, in for a pound, I figure anyway, and as this is my dream to attend a Regency Ball, I have to look the part.

We've decided to stay at a small country hotel in Bakewell, the beautiful little village near Chatsworth. That way we can also get a taxi back and make a real night of it. I still don't know what Chloe has told Kian, but when I asked her about it, she said he'd been fine, which is suspicious in itself considering his usual overprotective behaviour. Mind you, she probably told him it was just a tour of a stately home or something.

THE EVENING of the ball arrives at last, but as I'm trying to get ready, the wearing of Regency dress presents more issues than I had thought possible. Not least the fact that empire line dresses are cut a bit like maternity wear. It may have been all very well in Austen's day, as women were so tiny and dainty. At least I think they were, if the size of clothes on display at the costume museum and at Jane Austen's house are to be believed. The gloves and slippers they wore were miniscule. In any case, the reality is that, from the side, I look at least six months pregnant.

Of course I suppose women still wore corsets under their loose dresses. Hmmm, no corsets in my wardrobe, funnily enough. In desperation, I borrow a pair of Spanx from Chloe, which is ironic as she is much more petite than me, but I figure they might pull me in and the dress will then hang elegantly round my sylph-like silhouette. Squeezing them on, however, is more of an operation than I had thought; they're so impossibly tight.

Finally, I manage, after feeling as though I have been wrestling with a bear and it's won. I look at myself in the mirror. Yes, if I had been going for the red-flushed beetroot sweaty face look, I've succeeded. Worse still, upon examining my outline critically, I now appear to have an extra two pairs of boobs. All my fat has been suctioned up below my chest with the result I look like a freak. Not quite the look I was aiming for.

Angrily, I peel off the offending Spanx, which is easier said than done. It's a bit like escaping from a giant squid. Dress back on – I decide to concentrate on some subtle make-up and tonging my hair into ringlets before securing it high on my head. Okay, it's not a bad effort actually.

As I'm admiring my reflection, I'm disturbed by Mel who's sheathed from head-to-toe in a beautiful soft green dress, delicately decorated by tiny painstakingly hand-stitched embroidered flowers. She really is very talented. Her long curly hair is braided and has tiny ringlets framing her face.

'Wow – you look amazing,' I say, genuinely impressed. Apart from anything else, I have never seen Mel in a dress before; she usually lives in trousers and dungarees. In fact, she's so annoying, she cares so little about her appearance but always manages to look great.

'So do you,' Mel retorts. 'You're lucky being so pretty. Look out, Daniel!'

The problem remains that my dress still makes me look pregnant whatever Mel says. Then I have a brainwave – of course, Regency women damped their dresses down with water so they clung to their figures.

'What are you doing?' Mel asks, probably thinking I'm completely mad.

'Damping my gown!' I reply, liberally sloshing water over my dress. 'Ooh, it's cold and yuk – it feels horrible.'

I come out of the bathroom to examine myself in the long bedroom mirror. I have to say, the water thing has worked; my dress clings in an intriguing manner and I no longer look so pregnant, or maybe just at the starting-to-show stage, which is an improvement anyway. As long as I don't freeze – I'm feeling pretty cold wearing a damp dress. The quote 'il faut souffrir pour être belle' springs to mind. I can't remember who said it, but they're obviously right.

Ideally, we should be travelling by horse and carriage to fit the occasion, but as that isn't available, a taxi will have to do. Chloe knocks on the door, looking dainty in a pretty long dress she managed to find in a local charity shop. It was so clever of her as it's all lace and I think it would be worth a lot of money in a vintage store.

I can't contain my excitement at the idea of going to Chatsworth House, aka Pemberley in *Pride and Prejudice*; imagine, I am going to be dancing in the same room as Keira Knightley and Matthew Macfadyen. More to the point, I'll dance with Daniel. Whether he's spinning yarns or not, I just want to be with him again. Maybe we could even have some pics taken together so I can prove to Mark and my parents that I actually have a real-life decent boyfriend rather than fictional ones.

IT'S STILL light as we ascend to the crest of the hill above Chatsworth, where the view down to the valley below and the imposing stately building takes my breath away. A stream runs in front of the main house, with contentedly grazing sheep dotted about the green landscape.

'This is paradise,' I breathe. 'If I were Lizzie, I'd have put up with a lot of arrogance just to live in this place.'

'Darcy wasn't arrogant, if I remember correctly,' Chloe retorts. 'We had to write an essay on this in school – he was simply misunderstood.'

'Like Kian?' I ask, then regret my usual habit of speaking without thinking. 'Sorry, I didn't mean it.'

'That's okay,' Chloe says, surprisingly. 'Actually, I agree with you – he's a complete and utter loser. All men are. It's just a matter of whether you marry a greater or lesser one.'

I smile. Chloe has always told me this, even when I was little. You would have thought it would teach me to lower my expectations somewhat, but instead I still live in hope of finding better.

The long driveway to Chatsworth House is aglow with bright lights and smart cars queuing to set down their elegant occupants.

I feel unusually nervous as we alight from the taxi, relieved to have Mel and Chloe with me. Arriving alone would have been terrifying in this crowd.

IN THE GREAT ENTRANCE HALL, we give our invitations to a smart young doorman who has opened the doors especially for us. I could get used to this treatment.

As I walk into the hall, I am blown away by the grandeur and beauty of the huge staircase, framed either side with twin balconies fashioned in gold. I would have loved to stand and stare, losing myself in the amazing painting on the ceiling which looks as fresh and immediate as though it had been painted yesterday. I'm forced to keep walking forward, however, propelled by crowds of people funnelling in behind us.

There's a formal welcoming party comprising Miss Palmer-Wright, Emma Woodtree, Nick Palmer-Wright, Darcy Drummond, and the diamond-laden lady from the awards evening, who I assume is his mother. This is confirmed by Nick Palmer-Wright's introduction – Mrs Veronica Drummond. They're lined along the side of the room to meet and greet, before each guest mounts the staircase up to the ballroom. This crowd has obviously not patronised the local costume hire or charity shop – their outfits positively scream wealth.

I try not to look at Darcy as I can't trust myself not to hit him with a barrage of accusations, but hold my head up, greeting Miss Palmer-Wright with a confident smile which doesn't quite reach my annoyingly shaky legs.

She simpers in her usual fake manner, just uttering, 'Miss Johnson. Oh, and you've brought all your friends with you,' sarcastically.

Nick, however, is warm and genuine in his greeting, and I don't know whether it's my imagination, but he speaks to Chloe with an added friendliness. As I reach Darcy Drummond, I have a job to control my nerves. He bows his head but as he raises it again, I feel a jolt as his eyes meet mine. They are such a deep brown, strong and warm, yet challenging. Why does he have to be so good looking?

I dismiss a distracting image of touching his handsomely chiselled face as he shakes my hand politely but moves swiftly on to greet a horsey-looking girl dressed from head-to-toe in shimmering diamanté. Not very Regency, but I have to admit she looks amazing. Darcy's mother vaguely acknowledges us, but is already focused on the horsey lady. She is obviously wealthy, I think cynically.

I don't really care though, I'm too busy scanning the room for Daniel.

'Lovely to see you, Sophie.' Emma comes forward and gives us all a hug and a kiss. 'So glad you could come.'

'This is beautiful, Emma, every bit as gorgeous as I imagined,' I say breathlessly.

Emma looks pleased. 'It takes months of planning, but is always spectacular.'

We move on as more guests are arriving. I link arms with Chloe and Mel and we ascend the dauntingly huge staircase together. It's amazing, I feel as though we have been transported back in time as I sashay up the great wide steps.

At the top, we enter the ballroom through a huge archway. It's simply crammed with people, but the scene in front of us is breathtaking – candles burning, an orchestra in the corner playing Regency music with couples already moving elegantly on the floor. It's as though someone has waved a magic wand and we've slipped back a couple of centuries. I stand in the doorway for a moment, transfixed, drinking it all in.

'Sophie!' a familiar soft voice calls to me.

'Maria, so good to see you.' I give her a hug. She looks really beautiful in her long gown, her hair swept up into an elegant chignon. 'Isn't this gorgeous? So, what have I missed so far?' I ask eagerly.

'Nothing really. I've already danced once, though it was a bit more vigorous than I expected.' She smiles in the direction of an enthusiastic Rob Bright, who's cavorting with some poor suffering young girl in the line-up.

'Lucky you!' I laugh. 'And is Charles here?' I immediately wish I hadn't spoken as Maria's lovely face falls.

'Yes, he's here,' she replies, and then in barely a whisper, 'he's dancing over there.'

I follow her gaze and notice Charles looking pretty happy arm in arm with Louisa Mills, the lively young redhead from the restaurant. He obviously hasn't suddenly realised the error of his ways yet then. We desperately need Jane Austen to help sort this situation. Regency romance, it seems, is still way out of reach for us all, especially when I discover that Daniel is nowhere to be found. Every time someone arrives, I find myself watching the doorway, my heart in my mouth, only to be disappointed once more.

'Miss Johnson!' It's Rob Bright. *Oh no, that's all I need.* 'Would you do me the honour of dancing the next with me?'

'Erm, well... I don't...' Darn it, I meant to have an excuse ready but with one thing and another, it had slipped my mind. I find myself being led to the dance floor by an exuberant Rob, and I can tell Chloe and Mel are both struggling not to laugh, the rotten things.

The dance, not unlike our last one, is torture. Rob's ability doesn't seem to have improved at all, in spite of his boasting that he'd taken a couple of private lessons. Whether he has a terrible teacher or two left feet, I don't know. I'm inclined to think the latter most likely.

AFTER WHAT SEEMS LIKE AN ETERNITY, the dance ends and I am swept off by my rescue team, i.e. Maria and Chloe, who probably figure I need a break. Mel earns my gratitude by kindly disappearing to the dance floor with Rob to get him off my back for a while as he seems intent on shadowing me all evening for some reason. Goodness only knows I've given him little enough encouragement, but he doesn't seem to care, he has such a high opinion of himself.

Looking at the dance floor, I notice with misgiving that Josh is dancing with the beautiful and expensive-looking creature he was dining with at the First Dates evening. Izzy is nowhere to be seen.

Suddenly my phone bings from within my bag. 'Why on earth have you got your phone with you?' Chloe asks sarcastically. 'Not exactly Regency, is it? Soph?'

I've gone quiet as I am reading a text from Daniel. *Hi Sophie, I'm really sorry but I'm not going to make it tonight – have had to work late. Hope you have a good time anyway, will be sorry not to be there with you. Was hoping to have the first dance but maybe next time...*

'You okay, Soph?' Chloe asks.

'Yes fine. It's Daniel, he can't come tonight. Had to work late,' I reply shortly, trying not to look as disappointed and crushed as I'm feeling.

'I've heard that one before. I'm sorry.' Chloe can obviously see how upset I am. Another text bings its arrival.

*It's no good, I can't lie to you, Sophie. It's not that I have to work, I just can't face meeting Darcy Drummond tonight, it would bring back too many memories and I don't want to spoil your evening. Hope you understand. Daniel x*

'Ooh he's put a kiss.' Chloe's peering over my shoulder. 'He certainly can't stand Darcy.'

'I'm not surprised. How would you feel if someone had promised you a chance out of nowhere, offered you a lifeline, having come from a difficult background with no money, and you were relying on that opportunity, maybe your only hope. Then this insufferably arrogant rich bastard comes along–'

'Soph...' Chloe tries to stop my tirade as we are approached by none other than Darcy Drummond. I don't know what's wrong with this guy, he always pops up without warning at the worst bloody moments.

'Miss Johnson? Would you do me the honour of accepting the next dance?' he asks diffidently.

'I... erm... well... I don't... erm... okay.' I'm floored by his request. I can't think how to refuse him at all.

A million thoughts flood my mind as Darcy takes my hand and leads me to the dance floor. Why has he asked me? Maybe he makes it a point to dance with everyone so there is no favouritism. This seems unlikely though as, glancing round the room, there are so many women at the ball. If that were the case he'd be dancing all night. I have a comic mental image of Darcy needing a lie down at the end of the evening, after being whirled round by hordes of women. I can't imagine him dancing at all; he's so serious and uptight.

We take our places opposite each other in the line and for the first part of the dance, my mind is focused on the steps as it involves weaving in and out of the other dancers and I don't want a collision. Fortunately, it's one we had practised at the Regency Dance evening, formal and slow, and I miraculously find I can remember the steps, which is an added bonus.

Annoyingly my body is letting me down again. Every time Darcy approaches, I feel shaky and my legs are unsteady. I put it down to my simmering anger over his treatment of Daniel. He returns to my side for the next bit of the dance – I have to concentrate on not meeting his glance, his eyes are so intense and I'm struggling to battle against some strange instinct which wants to rejoice in his touch and attention. No, I must remember I hate him, especially after his rudeness about me.

'Er, are you enjoying the dating agency so far?' he asks as we descend through the line together hand in hand.

'Yes, really good,' I reply carefully, not wanting to give him any ammunition. 'I've met lots of lovely people anyway, some true friends.'

'Oh,' Darcy replies noncommittally. 'What did you think of the First Dates evening? It seems to be quite popular.'

'It was lovely, though I probably wouldn't have chosen all the partners I was placed with. Some bits of it were better than others.'

Darcy looks dangerously close to a smile at this point. It makes him even more attractive. 'Oh?'

'When you came into the restaurant, I had just met a mutual acquaintance,' I can't resist mentioning. Darcy goes quiet and as we are naturally parted by the movement of the dance, I assume he'll ignore the topic and move on.

As we meet again, however, he continues with, 'Daniel Becks is the sort of guy who finds it easy to make friends. Whether or not he manages to keep them is another thing.' Darcy states this as a fact, his tone low and aggressive.

'He's been unlucky enough to lose your friendship in a way that will affect his whole life.' I stop in the middle of my steps and glare at Darcy momentarily. His impassive face makes me feel furious.

'Oh yes, he's been so unlucky,' Darcy retorts sarcastically.

He makes me so mad, I don't know how to carry on the dance. 'Guys like you just don't realise the effect you can have on another person's life.'

'Really?' Darcy's curling his lip. God, I've really rattled him. 'What do you mean guys like me?'

I feel uncomfortable at this. 'I mean your wealth and influence place you in a position of power, with the ability to change the lives of others. It's a really big responsibility that I hope you take seriously.'

'Extremely seriously. Can I ask why the inquisition?'

'I'm just trying to understand you.'

'I wouldn't bother at the moment.'

The dance ends, which is probably a good thing, but I want it to continue. Just as your tongue won't leave a sore spot in your mouth alone, I want to carry on probing Darcy Drummond. I want to shout at his self-satisfied drop-dead gorgeous face. Anything to get a reaction.

Instead I meander casually across the room to where Mel, Chloe and Maria have been apparently trying to attract my attention, leaving Darcy to his own devices. He's better off staying with his business associates and friends anyway – why can't he just leave me alone?

'Sophie – we need you,' Chloe hisses.

'What? What's going on?'

'You're good friends with Izzy, aren't you?' Maria asks. 'You need to stop her.'

'Stop her what?'

Mel, succinct as ever, quickly fills me in. 'She's fallen out with Josh who's been dancing all night with Lady Cara Lyttleton, and Izzy's distraught – she's just stormed off to confront him.'

'Oh my god, I must go and find her.' I dash off towards the smaller refreshment room to the side of the ballroom, but I'm too late. I walk in on an extremely embarrassing scene.

Josh is standing amongst a crowd of people near the drinks, his handsome face shaken and guilty. He is rather like a cornered rat. With her arm linked in his is Lady Cara, resplendent and sparkling in a vivid scarlet dress. She has a self-satisfied smirk all over her face. Poor little Izzy is in the middle of a full tirade at Josh... she has obviously lost it completely.

'You wrote me poetry,' she sobs. 'You said we were soulmates and I believed you. What a load of total and utter crap!'

I galvanise myself into action as the scene is drawing many spectators, not least Mrs Drummond who's been making small talk with the horsey girl in the corner and is now glaring in our direction. Someone mutters something about calling security. I mean, security at a ball at Pemberley. Jane Austen would be horrified. Something has to be done and quickly. Out of desperation, I breeze towards the assembly in a casual manner I certainly don't feel.

'Izzy, how nice to see you here. You must come and tell me what you've been up to.'

Grabbing her arm, I propel her gently across the floor, surrounded by the protective circle of Mel, Chloe and Maria, leaving Josh in the company of Lady Cara and her posse of snobbish and glowering acquaintances.

# CHAPTER 16

'What are you doing?' Izzy demands breathlessly as we plonk her down in an elegant chaise longue out on the veranda.

'Trying to get you out of the room with some shred of dignity still intact,' Chloe says.

'Look, hun,' I say gently, 'I know Josh has won first prize for jerk of the night...'

'With some pretty close runner ups.' Chloe smirks, peering through the window at Rob Bright who's cavorting with another victim.

I glare at Chloe. 'Admittedly, Josh has acted badly, but Izzy you can't confront him in there, it's not the time nor the place.'

Izzy's crying, great shuddering heartfelt sobs. 'I can't understand what has come over him. He was so loving and kind, such a romantic – the perfect man...'

'Hmmm, no such thing,' Chloe remarks.

'I thought he was the one, for God's sakes, and now he's cold, distant, like it never happened. It's like I imagined it all.'

'Maybe there's a reasonable explanation,' Mel persists, ever the optimist.

'Huh, they always say that.' Chloe, bizarrely, is quick to notice the faults of total losers, unless she is going out with them herself. This must come under the 'love is blind' category.

'Is everything all right?' Nick Palmer-Wright appears at the doorway looking genuinely concerned, earning himself huge brownie points from me.

'Yes, just a misunderstanding,' I reply, smiling gratefully at him.

'Oh good. We don't want anyone to be unhappy.' He glances rather doubtfully at Izzy's tear-stained face. 'I was going to ask Chloe to dance if she's free.'

Chloe blushes and having glanced at me shyly, accepts, and they disappear back into the ballroom. I notice what a handsome couple they make, mentally dismissing my misgivings that this can only end in tears.

'Getting on very well together, those two,' Mel says drily.

'Yes, it's nice for Chloe. She's lived in Kian's shadow for so long, it'll do her good to have someone make her feel better about herself. If you guys will stay with Izzy, I'll go and get her some water.'

I brave the crazy melee of the ballroom once more. It is a gorgeous splash of whirling colour, filled with smiling happy people. Before I manage to make my way very far across the ballroom, I feel Rob's sweaty hand on my arm.

'Miss Johnson, I've been looking for you all evening,' he recriminates, his beery breath betraying the fact he's slightly the worse for wear. 'You'll never guess who's here.'

'I'm sure I can,' I mutter.

Rob carries on oblivious. 'Hattie Parker – Lady Constance's daughter. She isn't very often out in society as she spends a lot of time abroad.'

'Don't blame her. Which one is she?'

'Over there.'

I wince as Rob points across the room in an embarrassingly

obvious manner to where the horsey-looking girl is standing talking to Mrs Drummond.

'She would be.'

Eventually I manage to detach myself from Rob, making the excuse that I'm expected elsewhere. He wanders off, muttering about introducing himself to Darcy Drummond. Good luck to him if he does, he won't receive much of a reception there. Speaking of Darcy, I spot him standing in the corner talking to his mother, with Hattie Parker. To be fair, he looks bored as usual. He catches my glance and looks away again immediately as his mother's trying to capture his attention.

As I approach the drinks, I bump straight into Jessica Palmer-Wright, who's holding a couple of glasses of champagne – I bet one's for Darcy. I almost feel sorry for her, she is wasting her time with Lady Hattie around.

'Ah, Sophie,' remarks Jessica PW, 'I hear you're a real fan of Daniel Becks. I assume you're unaware that he comes from a broken home and was brought up on an estate in Brixham. Also, he has behaved so badly to poor Darcy,' she sneers bitchily, making me want to slap her. 'I'm sorry to be the bearer of bad news about your hot new man, but quite honestly, considering his background, you can't expect much better.'

'Really? Thank you for your information, Miss Bingley,' I remark incredulously. 'What did he do to Darcy that was so bad?'

'Miss Who?' Jessica snaps. 'I can't remember the exact details but I know it was really awful,' she simpers insincerely.

'You haven't told me anything I didn't know already. Daniel told me about his background himself and why should I care where he lived when he was growing up?'

'No, I don't suppose you would,' Jessica sneers and stalks off.

It is all I can do to grab a bottle of mineral water for Izzy and start to make my way back through the throng to the gardens.

Emma's dancing with a tall chap with dark hair and sideburns, but is looking happy and carefree.

Mel whirls past. I notice she's been captured by Rob again but she seems to be enjoying herself in spite of this handicap. She's more than capable of getting herself out of anything if she needs to. Also the good thing about Regency dancing is at least you can move around the room away from your partner for some of the time.

Chloe returns with Nick. She looks flushed and pretty, she hasn't been like this for years, not since she met Kian anyway.

I repeat to her what Jessica Palmer-Wright said about Daniel.

'She's such a bitch,' I add grumpily. 'Then again, she's bound to be on Darcy's side, she's so desperate to marry the guy. Good luck to her with Lady Hattie around.'

'I hate to be the bearer of bad news,' says Chloe, 'but I talked to Nick about it and he says that it was Daniel actually who screwed Darcy over some business deal.'

'Does he know Daniel then?' I ask.

'No.'

'Then how's he supposed to know what happened?'

Chloe looks upset.

'I don't mean to blame Nick, he's a really nice guy,' I continue, 'and it's nice he's just trying to stick up for his mate but he will of course have heard the story from Darcy. It doesn't mean it's true.'

Chloe's unconvinced. 'I know what you mean but I still can't believe Darcy's quite as bad as Daniel's making out. It doesn't make sense.'

'I can. He's such an arrogant everything-is-okay-in-the-name-of-business guy. I can tell his type a mile off, as long as he's making a profit he doesn't care what happens to anyone else's. Look at Bill Bellingham – bought up all the local parks and built on them, raking in a fortune, even paying off the jury when the protestors appealed.'

'I don't think you can accuse Darcy of acting like Bill Bellingham – he's a real lowlife.' Chloe laughs.

'If the cap fits,' I retort.

'Are you sure it isn't because he upset your pride that you hate him so much?'

I'm about to reply when I notice Mel coming back with Rob. 'Look out, maybe we should act as though we're going somewhere. I can't bear any more of Rob's conversational wit.'

'I think we should try to get Izzy home,' Maria interrupts, appearing suddenly. 'She isn't feeling too well. It's such a shame Matthew isn't here.'

'Matthew – from the dance evening?' I ask.

'Yes, he's totally crazy about Izzy and is such a nice guy, but all she cares about is Josh,' Maria says sadly.

Izzy certainly looks rather worse for wear. I think she had probably taken to drinking more than she should have earlier in the evening, for a bit of Dutch courage. We feel responsible for her; she seems so young and vulnerable and evidently has precious little support from home. Her stepmother obviously wants her out the way and her dad's pretty oblivious, so it isn't surprising she is a bit of a mess.

'I'm not leaving.' Izzy starts crying again. 'You have to make him come and talk to me. I can show you the texts he sent. He told me it was forever. I want to know what can have happened to make him turn against me like this.'

'We can't, love,' Maria explains gently. She really is a sweet person. 'Why don't you come back to the hotel and tomorrow you can come and stay with me for a couple of days.'

'But he told me he loved me…'

'I know,' Maria soothes, 'but nothing more can be done tonight. The others are right, this isn't the place.'


AFTER SOME EFFORT, we finally manage to persuade Izzy to come back with us all to the hotel. Our abrupt departure upsets Rob but he soon rallies, announcing he has an important chess tournament in a few days, so he ought to have an early night.

And that's the end of my first Regency Ball – I'm not sure I could exactly call it a success, more like a rollercoaster ride. After all my hopes and imaginings, romance is as far out of my reach as ever and it's increasingly looking as though nothing less than the matchmaking genius of Jane Austen can sort out this muddle. I wonder if The Jane Austen Dating Agency has any relationship counsellors.

# CHAPTER 17

Not surprisingly, the next day is a bit of an anti-climax, to put it mildly. It's inevitable that after really looking forward to a wedding or party, it's all a bit of a damp squib when everything is over, as reality strikes again. Although to be fair, we had a pretty healthy dose of real life the night before.

Once back in London, we go our different ways. Chloe has been very quiet and reserved on the return journey. I tell her to phone me whenever she needs to. I have five missed calls and two texts from Mark who's obviously itching to find out how I got on with Daniel. I don't feel like talking about it.

Maria texts me to say that Izzy is reasonably okay considering, but is still heartbroken. She is apparently barraging Josh with endless texts and calls, all of which he is totally ignoring. I feel utterly despondent; perhaps romance only belongs in Regency fiction after all. This feeling isn't helped by returning to our flat which is long overdue a clean, and we'd left all the washing-up from Friday to come back to, always a bad idea.

I often think there must have been some dreadful mistake somewhere along the line with regard to my background. I feel that some freaky twist of fate propelled me into the wrong family. In my opinion, I should have been born into a wealthy household as I have a definite taste for the finer things in life.

I love to daydream about being rich enough to have a butler, housekeeper, cook and perhaps even a PA, which would all contribute to a really luxurious and comfortable existence. Something like the team of servants who looked after Lady Mary on *Downton Abbey* would be amazing. I could just waltz down to dinner in my latest couture gown and after I have eaten a healthy and ethically sourced dinner, prepared by the chef, I could leave the washing-up and curl up with my favourite romance. (Though thinking about it, I already postpone the clearing up, but then I still have to do it the next morning.)

Or better still, I could snuggle up to my handsome hero and watch a movie. Oh no, back to escapist daydreaming again, I must stop this. But I do truly believe I could do really good things if I had lots of money, and having met rich people, they often have no taste at all. If it belonged to me, I could buy such gorgeous clothes, have designer furniture, and of course give loads to charity. I read about some guy a few years ago who won twenty-one million on the lottery and then said he didn't know what to spend it on. 'Give it to me… GIVE IT TO ME!!! I know what to spend it on, it's really not a problem…'

It's one of life's ironies that people who have lots of money don't spend it or maybe don't want to. Or perhaps that's why they have money and I don't.

My philosophical contemplation on the unfairness of life is broken by a ring at the doorbell, probably someone trying to sell me something. Although, actually, that ring sounds like Mark's. Fab, I fancy a good gossip about the events of the ball over a cup of tea.

I trot to the door, swinging it open with gusto, but then want to run back inside slamming it behind me again, as it's none other than Rob Bright. He still looks a bit bleary-eyed and rather more ponderous than usual after the revelry of the night before.

In spite of our early departure, it had been late for him; he probably goes to bed at nine every night with a large volume entitled *50 Shades of Chess*. He must have driven all the way home this morning and come straight round.

'Miss Johnson.' He smiles crookedly. 'Can I come in and talk to you for a moment?' I don't know how he's got hold of my address, surely Emma wouldn't have given it – she knows how I feel about him.

'Erm, I'm just on my way out actually,' I reply. Hah, I'm getting better at this being assertive thing.

'It'll only take a minute.' Rob pushes heavily past me into the lounge and plumps himself down onto a comfy chair.

Oh dear, epic fail, maybe not that much better then.

'You can't be in any doubt as to why I'm visiting you at your home.' Rob launches into conversation without preamble as I perch gingerly on the edge of a chair on the other side of the room, as far away as possible. He continues unperturbed. 'You must've noticed I prefer your company over that of anyone else.'

'Erm, not really,' I mutter. Here we go again. I seem to be irresistible to weirdos.

'Nearly as soon as I met you at the Regency Dance evening, I chose you to be my long-term companion, the one with whom I can share the triumphs and tribulations of being a chess champion. But before I'm run away with by my passionate feelings, it's probably best I tell you my reasons for wanting a partner and why I joined The Jane Austen Dating Agency.'

At this point, I'm so busy trying not to laugh, I'm unable to prevent Rob continuing his obviously much-rehearsed speech.

'Ahem,' he noisily clears his throat. 'I joined The Jane Austen Dating Agency, not because I've ever read any of her books...' (what a surprise) 'but because I hoped I would meet the right sort of serious, educated young lady such as yourself. My reasons for wanting a partner are...' He pauses ceremoniously, he's totally loving this...

'Firstly, I think everyone should have a partner, and besides, it sets a better example at work events if I have a beautiful lady on my arm. Two, I'm sure it will make me happy. Three, actually I probably should have made this number one – my mentor Richard Simms has advised it... He suggested it a few weeks ago, over a chess match.

'"Rob," he says in his deep authoritative voice, "you need to get yourself a partner, young man. Choose carefully, not someone too intelligent, nor someone stupid, as that would be very irritating as a housemate. She must be able to cook, clean up and be an excellent hostess so she can make herself useful on our chess evenings. Find this woman as soon as you can and I will come and visit her."

'So as you can see, I have connections in high places, which makes my offer extremely tempting for you. Now I'm aware you don't have the best job in the world – cold-calling isn't exactly a high-earning position, but I promise there will be no recriminations about this after we are living together.'

I have to interrupt. 'Living together?' I splutter. 'Aren't you offering marriage?' Oh God, that came out wrong. I don't want to marry Rob, but that's not the point, how insulting is this? However gross Mr Collins was, at least he was suggesting making Charlotte Lucas a respectable woman. I'm not even worthy of playing the part of Charlotte Lucas, that's so rubbish.

'I am suggesting you move in with me,' Rob replies in a tone that makes this sound as though it's the biggest prize in the world. He hoists himself to his feet and clumsily comes to sit next to me, grabbing my hand in his. 'Of course, if you play your cards right and things work out, perhaps we could consider marriage at a later date, if that's what you want. You're only human.' Oh yuech, his oily smile makes me feel sick.

This guy is the limit. It's totally necessary to stop him right now. 'Wait a minute,' I cry, leaping to my feet in order to create some distance between us. 'I haven't said anything yet. It's kind of you to think of me, I'm sure...' (see, finally no more thank you very much, please, thank you, sir) 'but I wish you wouldn't. It's a very nice offer but one I really can't accept.'

'Come, come, Miss Johnson, Sophie!' Rob smiles ingratiatingly. 'I know most of you girls think it's fun to play hard to get. So I shan't be downcast by your refusal. Come out for dinner with me tomorrow and you can give me your real answer then. I know all you women like to be wined and dined a little, before anything else.'

'Rob, you're making a big mistake. I'm not the sort of girl who plays hard to get, it's not even in my vocabulary, for goodness sake. With me, what you see is what you get.'

'You *are* pretty charming!' agrees Rob, advancing ominously towards me.

'No!' I exclaim hastily, dodging his now sweaty advances. 'You wouldn't make me happy at all and I know I would make you extremely miserable.' (Given half a chance!) 'No!' I put my hand up in front of Rob's face as he's looking amorous again. I wonder if I am going to need to rugby tackle him to the ground, but I'm worried he might like the attention; he's such a creep. Quite honestly this guy is beginning to make Mr Collins look a bit of a catch.

'Really, it's a definite, absolute no, like not ever.'

'You can't be serious,' Rob replies heavily, 'and I believe once you've had a chance to think about it and talk to your lovely girl-friends, you will reconsider.'

'I can assure you, I won't ever change my mind, I never change it, well only with clothes sometimes when I get home and find they make my bottom look huge, but certainly never with important things like relationships.'

'You're so amusing.' Rob advances towards me again. 'I hope after a girly chat with your friends, you will be ready to agree.'

Oh my God, what do you do with a guy like this? He's a bit like Dean with his sheer persistence and obstinate refusal to accept a simple no. I consider storming out of the room but decide against it, that would leave Rob loose in my flat; he'd probably make himself at home and start watching TV.

'Helloo!' It's Mel. Thank goodness, what perfect timing. She wanders in with her bags of shopping, takes one look at my demeanour and Rob's florid face and reads the situation pretty quickly.

'Rob!' she says brightly. 'How are you today? I think Sophie's a little tired as it was rather a late evening for her.'

'Yes, yes, I must go, need to brush up on tactics for this week's tournament.' And to my great relief, Rob makes as though to go out the door, then startles me by briefly reaching over and placing a horribly wet kiss on my cheek. 'Till we meet again.' He gazes at me in what I think he believes is a meaningful manner, and finally leaves.

'Oh my God,' Mel splutters and I join her in fits of giggles, total relief at his departure making me giddy with mirth.

'So, when can I wish you joy?'

'Never ever in his case, or at all.' I feel thoroughly deflated. It's beginning to look as though losers are definitely my lot in life.

## CHAPTER 18

Just when you think things can't get any worse, they invariably do. Work drags unbearably and even a supposedly glamorous evening with Miffy and Co. at Natasha's house is unable to take my mind off things. I then stupidly make the mistake of telling my mum about the price of the chandelier in Natasha's entrance hall during a particularly long and trying phone conversation.

'Did you just say £5,000? Ridiculous amount of money.'

'No. *Eighty*-five thousand,' I repeat patiently.

'That's totally sick,' she snaps. 'There are people in the third world dying of thirst and old people dying from lack of health care in this country and yet these ridiculous young bimbos are spending obscene amounts on a lamp. The world's gone mad.'

'I agree with you, it is pretty ridiculous, but that's the way these people live, Mum.'

'I don't care if it is, it doesn't mean you need to mix with them. And how have they got their money, that's what I want to know?'

'Modelling, I think, in Natasha's case.'

'Huh, she wouldn't make enough doing that, more like drugs

or something dodgy. I've read all about it in the paper. I'll show you the article when I see you.'

Oh dear. I knew I shouldn't have told Mum about my evening with the editorial team, but the fact is she's so busy suggesting I should change my job, I thought she'd be pleased I'm doing something proactive. Maybe not.

I hadn't wanted to go in the first place but the draw of seeing Natasha's expensive London town house had been too great for me to turn down. The evening had been pretty tedious actually and I made an excuse to come home early but not before I had been amazed by the appearance of Jessica Palmer-Wright while we were eating dinner. She had pretended not to know me, which was odd in itself, but I have to say I was happy with the arrangement as I hardly wanted the editorial team to discover I'm a member of The Jane Austen Dating Agency. The result would be social annihilation.

Odder still, while I was waiting for the butler to bring my coat, inanely examining a huge piece of art on the wall – I think it was art but I'm not really sure – Jessica Palmer-Wright had suddenly appeared beside me, grabbing my arm.

She had spoken in an alcohol-fuelled whisper, her face horribly close. 'Sophie darling, just wanted to have a teensy word before you go.'

I was too stunned to speak, so she continued, 'I don't really feel I know you yet, Sophie, you're a jolly mysterious girl. (Am I? That's the first time I've been told that.) We really are going to have to see more of each other.'

'Erm, I'm quite busy at the moment actually,' I muttered, stepping back to put some distance between us. Jessica PW is easier to cope with when she's being bitchy and aggressive, this sudden effort to be friendly quite frankly scared me.

'Yes, yes of course, but while we're talking, you won't mention to anyone from the agency that I was here tonight?' I looked at her, puzzled for a moment. 'It's no biggie, but best to keep these things separate, don't you think?'

I shrank back from her murky grey eyes. Boy, this girl is used to getting her own way.

'I'm sure you wouldn't want your new fashionable friends to find out you belong to a literary dating agency, would you?' she added bluntly. Ah yes, this is the Jessica Palmer-Wright I am used to – back to her bitchy self. I don't know what her game is, but I'm certainly not interested in having anything to do with it.

'No, it's just – look, I don't care what you're doing here, or who you are friends with, I'm not going to mention it, okay?' I said.

'Fine,' Jessica relinquished her grip on my arm, which was too firm for comfort. She turned and called loudly, 'Bye then' from the doorway with an insincere smile, before returning to the others in the drawing room.

So, the whole thing was very strange but I'm certainly not going to tell my mother – she would demand I leave my job immediately.

I get off the phone from Mum as quickly as I can but the call has still lasted over half an hour, and in that time, Mel has disappeared out before I have a chance to catch up with her. I don't know where she was going, in fact she has been acting a bit bizarrely the last week or so. I have hardly seen her to speak to properly since the ball.

At least I have a date with Daniel to look forward to – his text asking me out for the day in the country was very welcome if not as romantic as a written invitation. After, we're having dinner with Mum and Dad as I'd like them to meet him.

DANIEL TURNS up on time and kisses my cheek. Just the warmth of his hug and infectious smile makes me happier. The uncertainty of the evening at Natasha's and all the rubbish with Rob has simply melted away.

'So, did you miss me?' Daniel asks, grinning.

'Maybe a bit.'

We drive to Box Hill again as it's a sunny day and we enjoyed it there so much last time.

UPON OUR ARRIVAL, we walk hand in hand, enjoying the beautiful scenery. Who needs an expensive chandelier – with Daniel I feel maybe money isn't so important after all.

'Was the ball eventful in spite of my absence?' he asks.

'Yes, it was pretty full-on, perhaps a bit too much drama for my liking.'

'Surely not at a Regency Ball?' Daniel mocks.

'There were nearly a couple of punch-ups, but it was fine really.'

We reach the top of a field of freshly mown grass, sloping away gently down the hill.

'It's a shame we can't stay carefree like when we were children. I used to love rolling down hills like this when I was little,' I say wistfully.

'What's stopping you then?' Daniel smiles cheekily.

He helps me over the stile and sits himself down at the top of the hill. 'Come on!' he calls, patting the ground next to him. I lie on the prickly grass a short distance from him. He pushes off and rolls away down the hill, picking up both tufts of grass and a fair bit of speed as he goes.

I roll more slowly, over and over, it's amazing actually. I feel like a little girl again, no preconceptions, no prejudices, just amazing freedom. I get faster and faster, rolling down the hill, catching Daniel up, bumping along until we both end up in a tumbled heap at the bottom.

I must look a complete sight, covered in grass from head to foot, but most of it's in my hair. 'Come here,' says Daniel, picking pieces of grass from my jumper. He looks at me intensely, then raising his hand to my chin, draws me to him and we kiss. He pulls me down onto the tumbled grass beneath him. His lips feel warm and firm. Mmmm, this guy knows what he's doing.

It's heavenly, the sun beating down on us, the grass deliciously cool, tickling my back, and the feel of Daniel's arms around me. We kiss for what seems like an age but I don't want to move. Then his hand travels down to find the hem of my skirt, which he expertly starts to lift, stroking my thigh with his other hand. Distracted, I push his hand away gently, not wanting him to stop kissing me, but not wishing him to go any further. Undeterred, he insistently places his hand down again, deftly pulling up my skirt. He obviously intends more than kissing.

'Daniel.' I manage to break away and with effort push him off as he doesn't seem to be getting the hint. I feel distracted and awkward, picking grass off my top.

'Mmmm?' He follows me with his mouth. 'Come on, Soph.' He pushes me down again.

'Look, Daniel.' I pull myself free and wait a few seconds. 'Can we take things a bit slower?'

'Oh?' He looks momentarily grumpy.

'It's just I'm a slow-burn kind of girl,' I explain gently.

'That's okay, I can wait,' he remarks jauntily, recovering his equilibrium and giving me his hand, pulls me to my feet.

We walk in silence to the end of the track, the magic somehow broken.

❧

WHEN BACK IN the car on the way to Mum and Dad's, however, Daniel is chatty again and things feel more comfortable – he's so easy to get along with and I wonder if I imagined his momentary grouchiness earlier.

MY PARENTS LOVE DANIEL – not surprisingly; he is charming, polite, easy-going, happy to eat everything and join in with everyone's plans without a murmur. Even Ben likes him.

'Where did you find this one, sis?' he jests. 'He's not from your usual pile of social rejects.'

'Yes, not bad, is he?' I reply, pausing momentarily to admire Daniel's toned upper body, nicely fitted into his polo shirt. He's talking to my mum in an animated way about his work and she's looking impressed for once.

'How's Becky?' I ask.

Ben goes a bit quiet. 'We kind of...'

'Split up?' I add helpfully.

'If you put it like that.'

'Not again, Ben.'

'It's fine, I don't really want to talk about it. Anyway, I'm going out with Tiffany now, you know, from the squash club. She's really nice and bubbly.'

'Not the Tiffany who's been going out with Johnny for the past two years – aren't they together anymore?'

'Maybe, I don't really know.' Ben's looking sheepish.

'Ben?'

'No, I don't think so.'

'So, you're seeing her behind his back?'

'Yes.'

'That's going to end in tears,' I reply matter of factly.

'Yeah, like you're a dating expert. Like you know anything with your track record.'

At that moment, Daniel appears at my side. 'What's that?'

'I was just saying Sophie's a triumph in the dating department,' Ben sneers.

'I'm not surprised.' Daniel smiles, placing his hand on my behind in a meaningful manner. I move away from him under the pretence of getting another drink, but he's really annoying me with his persistence. This is definitely not the behaviour of a potential Austen hero.

'Sophie, can I have a word?' Dad asks.

'Yes, sure. Daniel can have a chat with Mum for a minute.' I follow Dad into the lounge and he firmly shuts the door.

'Everything okay, Dad?' I ask anxiously, as he looks serious.

'Just wondered if you've seen Chloe lately.'

'No, not really, not since the ball, but I spoke to her on the phone a couple of days ago. Why?'

'She came round here last week with a black eye – a great big bruise, it was.'

'What? How did she get that?'

'That's what's worrying your mother and me. Chloe says she fell and banged herself as she was leaving for work the other morning, but it didn't look like she could have done it like that to me.'

'You think Kian did it?' I whisper.

'Your mother and I are worried he might have.' Dad looks so upset. 'We all know what an unpleasant person Kian is, but I don't like to suggest it to Chloe as you know how defensive she is. Besides, she's adamant it was an accident and keeps changing the subject when I bring it up.'

'This is terrible,' I cry, sinking down onto the chair. 'What are we going to do? I have had my suspicions he might be violent, but would he hurt Chloe?'

There's an uncomfortable silence as Dad and I consider this unthinkable question.

'The thing is, I happened to speak to Chloe's neighbour, Lionel, the other day. I popped round to see her – she was out, but he happened to be out emptying his bin when he asked me if everything's okay with Chloe. Obviously I was a bit surprised as I only see him occasionally to say hello and goodbye to. He said he didn't like to be rude, but he was worried about the shouting and crashing he'd been hearing next door.'

'Oh my God. Does he think they're fighting?'

'I guess so. I was so taken aback, I didn't really know what to say to him except thanks. It's so difficult, he seemed reluctant to say any more.'

'Probably embarrassed,' I suggest.

'From what I've seen of Kian, I'm worried he could be capable of some pretty nasty behaviour,' Dad says quietly.

'I wonder if he found out about the ball and was angry.'

'How would he have known about it? None of us mentioned it and he wouldn't know anyone who was going, would he?'

'No, I guess not. I'm going to have to talk to Chloe, not that I can ask her outright, she'd be so offended. She still won't even hear a cross word against Kian.'

'I'm sorry, love. I didn't mean to worry you with it.' Dad puts a comforting arm around me.

'It's okay, Dad. You were right to tell me. We've got to help Chloe somehow. If only she would confide in me.'

'Perhaps this is too bad to tell you, or maybe even admit to herself.'

I love my dad – he's so wise, my mum too. I know she only gets so stressed out because she cares. In fact, I don't know how I'd cope without them. Our family might fight like cats and dogs, live in each other's pockets and drive each other mad generally, but together we're a pretty amazing force. It's just that Kian is proving too strong to deal with even for us.

'Daniel seems nice, by the way,' Dad says casually.

'Yes,' I reply, waiting for the but...

'Yes,' he continues. 'It's only...' (yep here it comes) 'that you haven't known him very long.'

'I know, Dad. He seems nice though.'

'Yes, very charming...' Dad pauses. 'It's just that these investment bankers usually are very plausible.' He hesitates, then continues, 'His story about Digby Drummond or whoever he is…'

I laugh. 'You mean Darcy Drummond.'

'Yes, Darcy, funny sort of name for a fella – I thought Daniel was talking about a woman when he first started telling the story… I just think Daniel's tale of woe is a bit hard to swallow.'

This is serious talk from Dad. He doesn't normally say too much about our choices of partner, figuring we have our own lives to lead.

'I think Daniel was treated unfairly by Darcy,' I protest.

'Huh… do you really think lawyers would allow him to get away with this if it was in his dad's will? I know there are legal loopholes, but it seems a little farfetched to me. Anyway, your mother says it's straight out of the plot of *Pride and Prejudice*. Perhaps this chap reads too many novels.'

'Don't you like Daniel then?' I ask outright.

'It's not that exactly. He's very pleasant, charming even, but he's almost too nice on the surface. I don't feel I can get to grips with him somehow. It's nothing tangible really, I might be wrong. Just watch your step around him. You're a sensible girl, Sophie, take it steady.'

'Of course I will, Dad.' I give him a hug just as Mum comes in.

'Did you ask her about Chloe?' She sits down in a chair with a heavy sigh. 'We're worried sick about her and this wretched business with Kian.'

'I know, Mum. It's really upsetting.'

'He's so controlling; she isn't allowed out anywhere without him. He accused her of being unfaithful the other day just because she wore her hair up for a change. We hardly ever see her at the moment.'

I give my mum a hug too. 'I'll talk to her, there must be some way round this. Don't worry, we'll work something out.'

. . .

AFTER DELICIOUS CAKE AND COFFEE – my mum is the most amazing cook – we all leave feeling totally stuffed.

'Your parents are great,' Daniel says enthusiastically as we begin the drive back to London.

'Yes, I'm lucky,' I return, and yes, I would agree with him, they are pretty amazing. It doesn't make dealing with other relationships any easier; unfortunately, to me, they're as much of a mystery as they ever were.

# CHAPTER 19

I'm pretty busy at work for the next few days as it's reaching the month's end and Amanda is cracking the whip over our sales targets. I've just about managed to scrape through, thank goodness, but am not in any position to be winning tickets to The Victoria Beckham Spring Summer show. Oh well, I guess I wouldn't have fitted in any of the clothes anyway, although I'm fairly tall and slim, I'm nowhere near the waif-like gazelles who wear designer clothes.

I still haven't seen much of Mel lately, so am pleased when I get home that evening to find her cooking yummy vegetable tagine for us.

'I owe you a thank you, by the way,' I say, testing a mouthful.

'What for?'

'For getting Rob Bright off my back the other day – you were heaven sent.'

Mel laughs. 'Yes, I could see you were in hot water. Rob doesn't give up easily, does he?'

'No, he doesn't,' I reply with feeling. 'Hopefully now he's gone forever with any luck.'

'Er, no, I don't think he has actually.' Mel becomes suddenly strangely awkward. 'I think we may be seeing quite a lot more of him.'

'What do you mean? You don't think he'll be back to ask me again?'

'No. I've managed to distract him a little more permanently.'

'Mel, you're the best friend ever! How have you managed to do that? Did you tell him I have a personality disorder, or that I'm gay?' I'm in fits of giggles at my own ready-made excuses.

'Soph, can you be serious for a minute?'

I stop laughing abruptly; this is most unlike Mel.

'The thing is… I don't know how to tell you this, but I've agreed to move in with him.'

There's a prolonged silence where, if we had one, you would have only been able to hear a clock ticking or if, for some bizarre reason, we were living in a desert, just the tumbleweeds blowing across empty sand.

'You what?' No-one in their right mind would want to move in with Rob, he's hard enough to put up with for half an hour, let alone a day or more. 'Why would you do that? I mean, I didn't know you like him.' I try to be tactful, but it's proving difficult.

'I don't,' Mel replies shortly. 'Though why do you think just because a guy isn't successful with you, he won't get lucky with the next girl?'

'Yes, but oh my God, Mel. This reminds me of the guy at uni who used to go round asking randomly "Do you want a f***" and in the end got lucky. You're that poor misguided individual who said yes.'

'Thanks a lot,' says Mel, angrily dolloping large spoonfuls of tagine onto a plate. 'Some friend you are.'

I'm stung by this; Mel and I are really close. I take a deep breath. 'Mel, you know I will always be your friend, we've been through too much together to fall out. Remember the time we turned up at the wrong wedding?'

'Oh yes, we hid behind the door and snuck out, giggling like loons as the bride made her grand entrance.' Mel smiles at the memory.

'Nothing's ever going to change that… and if you think Rob Bright's the guy to make you happy, then I am willing to try, *try* mind you, to tolerate him.' I gulp at this horrendous thought.

Mel gives a wry smile. 'Sophie, you know me better than that. Do you really think Rob's the guy for me?'

'No, so why are you moving in with him?'

'I'm trying to get a foot on the ladder with my design business.'

'You're using him? But what does Rob have to do with the fashion world except that he's a danger to it?'

'It's not him.' Mel laughs. 'His patron Richard Simms has links with Lady Constance Parker.'

'Yes, Rob's been telling me till he's blue in the face, but she's not got anything to do with fashion. Lady Constance? No, that's laughable.'

'She's the sister of Vivienne d'Artois,' Mel announces dramatically.

'Not the Vivienne d'Artois of Beaux Arts?'

'The very same.' Mel's triumphant.

I'm still lost. 'But how is being with Rob going to help you with that? Couldn't you just date him and get him to introduce you to Lady Constance?'

'Not really,' Mel replies sheepishly. 'I need to be with her a great deal to make any impact. You've already told me how difficult she is. I'll need to spend a lot of time inveigling my way into her snobbish little circle.'

'But how can you put up with someone like him?' I still can't believe it.

'I don't actually find him that bad,' she says stubbornly. 'He's annoying, for sure, but he'll be at work most of the time and perhaps he has hidden assets.'

She raises her eyebrows ironically at this, causing a release in the tension that has arisen between us and we both dissolve into giggles. 'Oh, Soph,' she says when we've recomposed ourselves, 'I don't know if I'm doing the right thing, but I'm sick of struggling at the bottom to get my label even vaguely noticed.'

'I thought you were doing better lately.'

'Not really.' Mel sighs. 'We both know it isn't an easy industry to get into. You need a leg-up and this is mine.'

I guess there's no arguing with that. Mel has made up her mind, and when she does that there's no moving her, whether it's about animal rights or eating meat. She digs in her heels and refuses to budge.

But I can't get over the shock of the news – Mel and Rob. It's a horrible thought, so degrading for her to have to be with him. I can't help feeling bad too, as maybe if I had a more influential position at Modiste, I might have been able to help without her having to sacrifice herself on Rob.

As is typical some weeks, things go from bad to worse. My conversation with Chloe doesn't go well at all. She refuses to talk about Kian, brushing away my concern about her eye, making me feel as though I'm fussing. She banged it herself and that's the story she's sticking to. I noticed she won't come out for a girly night with Mel, Maria and Izzy, however. Chloe says she has too much on at work, but I figure it's more likely that Kian has once again put a stop to any freedom.

My other issue is that of Mel going to live with Rob, I'm short of a flatmate.

'Isn't there anyone from work you could share with?' my mum asks helpfully when she phones later that day. 'What about a nice student from the uni, a trainee teacher would be good company?'

The trouble is, it's such short notice. Mel's decided to move out next month due to an exhibition coming up in the autumn. It's a huge event and she needs to get all the work prepped in time. Rob's already promised her the use of her own room to use as a design area. You have to hand it to her, she's ever practical. I'll miss her so much though. I know she's only moving an hour or so from London, but it seems the other end of the world.

Our girly evening is a really fun diversion, however. We go to see the new film version of *Emma* at the cinema – the cast is fabulous, with dinner afterwards. Izzy is still pretty down though, in spite of Maria's best efforts to keep her cheerful.

We're part way through our pizza when she jumps up dramatically from the table.

'Everything okay?' I ask, concerned, as she's nearly knocked everything over in her excitement.

'No,' she says, sinking back down in her chair crestfallen. 'I just thought I had a message from Josh but it isn't.'

'I bet he'll contact you when he's ready,' Mel says kindly.

I am not so sure. I have heard from Maria that he's continued to ignore Izzy pretty consistently in spite of her never-ending stream of texts. I have also been told he's been spotted in a couple of happening bars with Lady Cara draped all over him.

'So, when do you move in with Rob?' Maria asks Mel.

I have to try to hide an involuntary shudder. Even the words give me the creeps.

'This week,' Mel replies cheerfully. 'Though I hope we'll all meet up quite often.'

'I think you'll need to,' Izzy retorts surprisingly. She seems to have been in her own little dream world most of the evening.

'Yes, it'll make a change from all the chess evenings!' I joke. 'Anyway, what are you going to do about the catering? Does Rob know you're a veggie?'

'Of course. I told him I'll serve ready-bought hors d'oeuvres at his chess evenings but I'm not cooking meat.'

'So, who's going to take over from Mel as your flatmate?' Maria asks.

'I don't know, I'm still looking for someone.'

'What about Izzy? She's looking for a place to stay till she finds somewhere more permanent,' Maria suggests.

'That would be great,' I enthuse, feeling more cheerful. 'How about it, Izzy?'

'That would be fab, if you don't mind having me?' she says, brightening instantly. 'It would be really nice and I'd rather be in London.'

'I'd keep Izzy with me,' Maria says, hugging her fondly, 'but she's getting pretty fed up with the sofa and I don't have any other room.'

'We'll have a great time together.' I'm thrilled; things are looking up after all. Izzy's good fun, or she was before the problem with Josh, but the company will be nice and much better than living with someone I don't know.

'THAT'S ALL SORTED THEN,' Mel says later as we arrive back at the flat. 'You won't miss me at all, but I do have a small favour to ask.'

'Yes?'

'You will come and visit me at Rob's, won't you?' she asks, unusually shy.

'I suppose so. As long as you promise me a visit to Lady Constance.'

'I think that probably goes with the territory, don't you?' Mel smiles and I grimace, knowing she's probably pretty darn right, there's going to be no avoiding it at all.

# CHAPTER 20

*You are cordially invited to our Regency Gaming Night – a unique opportunity to join in genuine Regency gambling at Le Salon des Barcarolles, Mayfair. Entertainment, champagne and canapés included. Saturday 14th June 8pm*

'So, are you and Rob going to this Regency Gaming Night?' I ask Mel, waving the invitation under her nose. It had plopped through the letter box earlier that morning.

'Yes, there's going to be no choice,' she says glumly, 'no choice on this at all.'

Mel's moving out in the afternoon and has packed all her stuff into boxes which are spilling much of their contents all over the floor. Rob's apparently coming along with his car to pick her up as she usually either bikes or tubes it.

I haven't bothered trying to talk to Mel any further on the subject of Rob as I know her well enough to realise that I'm not going to change her mind. But the idea of Mel at a Regency Gaming Night is laughable; it's entirely against all her principles.

'You will come along, won't you?' Mel twirls a strand of wavy hair between her fingers. 'I'd appreciate you being there for support.'

'I s'pose I can, but Regency Gaming Nights don't really sound my thing.'

'I bet Daniel will be there and a whole load of other fit and wealthy city guys.' Mel's tone betrays a hint of desperation.

'I haven't heard much from Daniel lately,' I say rather lamely. Just a couple of brief texts about being busy at work. I haven't really missed him though; maybe he's not the one for me. I feel numb about it all.

'Oh okay,' I relent. I do feel sorry for Mel, in spite of the fact I still don't really understand her motives. 'Come on, let me give you a hand with those bags.'

Mel duly leaves with Rob, cases stuffed in his car and just a few things remaining for her to pick up another time as they won't fit. Mel next to Rob is a humiliating sight, so bad I find myself hurrying them off to avoid prolonging the distressing spectacle.

I don't have long to feel lonely; Izzy moves in the next day and although she isn't as great a friend as Mel yet, I have high hopes we'll get on well together. She's still extremely depressed as she's obsessed with Josh.

WE'RE EATING TOGETHER that evening when Izzy's phone goes off. She grabs it suddenly, making me spill my wine, only to return looking crestfallen. 'Just my dad,' she says flatly.

'Aren't you going to speak to him?'

'No, I'll phone him back later.' She seems really quiet and withdrawn, nothing like the lively happy-go-lucky girl who was so full of fun when I first met her.

'Have some more carbonara. I know it's your favourite,' I ask, holding the dish in front of her.

'No, I'm fine thanks, not really hungry at the moment. Thanks all the same,' she says politely.

She's picked at her plate but hasn't eaten properly and has

obviously lost weight. It doesn't really suit her; she's beginning to look thin and gawky.

'DO YOU WANT TO WATCH A MOVIE?' I ask after dinner.

'In a minute, I just need to send a couple of texts.' She disappears into her room and shuts the door. I know she'll be in there typing away, waiting for a reply that'll never come. Maria's already warned me of her depressed moods. I do feel sorry for Izzy, but am unsure how to help. Josh seemed such a nice guy, so loyal, and I think she had truly believed he was the one. He was always incredibly romantic – I mean, how many guys spout poetry, real romantic verse like Shakespeare? Mind you, I don't think I've ever gone off my food for anyone, so maybe I've never really been in love. Of course I'm upset, put out even, that I haven't heard from Daniel, but my appetite is its usual healthy self, so maybe I don't like him that much after all.

A COUPLE of weeks pass in a pattern of boring work and a pretty non-communicative Izzy in the evening. I really miss Mel and her easy chat, and am holding out for next weekend when I've been invited to dinner with her and Rob. Obviously I'm not looking forward to seeing Rob again, but I guess missing Mel so much has made my disgust for Rob lessen a little. I'm going to stay the night at their house in Marlow and then go to Lady Constance's the next day as she's holding a garden party of some kind.

Izzy's going home to her dad and stepmum for a couple of nights, so I don't need to worry about her. In fact, I'm pleased as I hope somehow her family might help her get over Josh, where her friends are failing to succeed.

. . .

I'M QUITE excited when I arrive at the station at Marlow. It's actually very pretty, with a quaint village centre and a surprising number of funky bars and fashionable little bistros. Rob and Mel's place is a typical, small semi-detached box with character-less walls and blandly decorated rooms, without much personality. It's the total opposite of what I would expect for Mel, but suits Rob perfectly.

It's so good to see Mel again. She looks her usual happy self and excitedly leads me to a room upstairs at the back of the house. It's overlooking the tiny square courtyard garden and is a reasonable size. I peek in the door and notice Mel's sewing machine, all set up on a large worktable, her fabrics in a cabinet, neatly stored in rolls, boxes of tiny buttons and pins all beautifully organised in wall units.

'Wow, this is great,' I enthuse. 'And you're usually such a messy person!'

Mel laughs. 'This is my domain,' she announces proudly, 'and I love it.'

'In spite of Rob.'

'In spite of Rob. Actually, he isn't here that much. He's at work today and although the office is only up the road, he has to travel often and spends all his free time playing chess with Richard Simms or the rest of the chess team. When he is here, he likes to watch episodes of *Star Trek* on the widescreen in the lounge.'

It strikes me as a little lonely, but Mel seems so caught up in her next project, I don't think it bothers her that much.

'So, what's Richard Simms like?'

'Boring as hell. Makes Sir Henry Greaves look like personality of the year.'

This makes us laugh raucously. I've so missed our gossipy chats.

'Normally we would be going to dinner with him tomorrow, but can't obviously because we're going to Lady Constance's instead,' Mel explains.

'I can't wait!'

THE EVENING soon passes with Rob insisting on showing me his entire geeky collection of *Star Trek* memorabilia, which I try to look interested in for Mel's sake, but it's a struggle.

I finally manage to escape under the pretence of needing an early night to be ready for Lady Constance the next day.

THE MORNING IS INTERRUPTED at regular intervals by phone calls from Richard Simms to finalise arrangements for the next month's worth of chess tournaments. At least, as Mel had pointed out, Richard keeps Rob busy and from annoying the rest of us.

AS WE DRIVE to Waddesdon that afternoon, Rob regales us with detailed instructions on how to behave and not be overwhelmed, interspersed with rapturous statements about how lucky we are to be invited to Lady Constance's house.

'Don't be overawed by Lady Constance and her daughter, Sophie.' He smiles superciliously. 'Of course they're very superior people, but won't judge you for wearing your everyday casual attire.'

Mel and I exchange amused glances.

'In fact, I think Lady Constance prefers it because she says it helps sort the wheat from the chaff,' Rob continues, managing to stall the car and making me want to giggle.

WE ARRIVE in due course at Radnall Park, Lady Constance's residence. Large gates open automatically, allowing us a glimpse of an impressive Elizabethan property standing at the top of a beautiful long drive. It is astonishingly grand, a proper stately home, and to be fair, I guess this explains a lot as to why Lady Constance is so full of herself. These charitably empathetic feelings soon vanish, however, within a couple of minutes of meeting her again.

We're ushered into a vast room where Lady Constance is seated in a seemingly most uncomfortable attitude on an ornate Queen Anne decorative sofa, from which she presides over the room in true queenly fashion. Through the large windows which overlook the gardens behind her, staff are bustling to and fro through the entrance to a large white marquee.

'You must see the view from the window!' she commands us imperiously.

We obediently go and admire the vista before us.

'You will notice the extensive work Lady Constance has had carried out,' Rob chunters enthusiastically, sweeping his arms in large exuberant gestures in the direction of the garden.

'Yes, lovely,' I respond politely.

'The work on the bridge cost thousands alone,' he continues.

'Over a hundred thousand to be exact.' We are interrupted by a middle-aged, slightly balding man with a small black shiny moustache and an incredibly sharp suit. I'm fascinated by his shoes, they are so highly polished they hurt my eyes. He reminds me of an exceptionally smart used car salesman.

'Hello, Richard. Here's Richard everyone!' enthuses Rob, practically knocking me over and strongly reminding me of a clumsy overenthusiastic Labrador in his hurry to get to Richard's side.

'Delighted to meet you, charming.' Richard shakes my hand, proving to be yet another worthy candidate for limp handshake of the year award. He then brushes me aside with uncivilised haste to get to Lady Constance. He bows low over her hand and kisses it ingratiatingly.

She swats him away as though he were an irritating fly. 'At last! I thought I told you to be here early, Richard. You know how incompetent that lot are without someone to tell them what to do.'

'I'm sure Forster is managing it all beautifully, Lady Constance,' Richard says, smiling in an oily manner. Lady Constance's face darkens in a way that would make the strongest man flinch and run crying for his mother. 'Of course, I'll go and check the arrangements are being correctly managed,' Richard mutters, obediently backing his way out of the room.

'Robert, you go with him!' Lady Constance instructs. 'These two ladies will entertain me while you are gone.'

My heart sinks as the men leave the room. I have no ideas for suitable topics of conversation to interest Lady Constance. Fortunately, she appears to be happy to hold the floor herself and seems pleased with our subdued compliments on the elegant arrangements she has made. Lady Constance has an opinion on every subject, and the manner in which she discusses issues convinces me she is totally unused to ever being contradicted. She asks Mel in minute detail about every part of her and Rob's life, interfering in the most trivial of matters. There's nothing too small for her notice, if it allows her to dictate to everyone around her. I begin to wonder if maybe one of her intimidating ancestors, pictured on the wall around us, could have given Jane Austen the inspiration for Lady Catherine de Bourgh.

When Constance starts on Mel's creations, I don't know how to hold my tongue. 'Of course I am aware Mel likes to do a little needlework,' Constance says to me casually, emphasising the 'little' as though it is some random hobby.

'Yes, Mel has created some beautiful designs,' I reply politely.

'What? Yes, I have seen a few bits and pieces she has sewn. She might become quite talented if she works hard at it. Creativity for some does not come naturally.'

'Have you ever designed clothes?' I interrupt impatiently, finally unable to bear any more.

'Who me? No, of course not, I have people to do that for me!'

Lady Constance snaps. 'But there is no other woman in this country with such excellent taste in design and needlecraft, except for my sister of course. If I had learned, I would have been outstanding, but there is a limit to how much time I can give to these things. There are always so many demands on my time.' At this, she glowers at us both, as though it's our fault that she doesn't have the opportunity to do the things she wants to.

'Quite so,' agrees Rob, who unbeknown to me has crept back into the room. 'Pardon me for interrupting, Lady Constance, but I believe the marquee is complete and looking quite splendid. Forster says they will be ready for you to commence the grand opening ceremony at 2pm.'

'Two o'clock?' snaps Lady Constance, her venomous tone causing Rob to back away slightly, 'No, no that won't do, won't do at all, three o'clock is what I said. I must have time for my luncheon.'

'Certainly. I will tell Forster to sort it, madam,' Rob replies and trots out of the room like an obedient dog. I watch, fascinated at the speed with which everyone does exactly what this woman wants. She doesn't even need to order her servants about, she has Richard and Rob to do that for her, the two Rs, I think, smiling to myself.

DINNER IS an awkward but lavish affair. We are joined by Lady Constance's daughter, Hattie; the horsey-looking girl from the Regency Ball. There is another gentleman, probably in his late thirties, who's introduced to us as Colonel Anthony Meyrick, who owns the neighbouring estate. He seems a very laid-back sort of man who obviously lives the country life to the full, looking at his long boots and tight gaiters. He is a pleasant enough chap, but I don't feel I have a lot to say to him as I don't know much about pigeon shooting or hunting.

I hoped our new companions would add to the conversation, taking the onus off us, but I needn't have worried, Lady Constance continues to hold forth about everything as usual. Lady Hattie seems content to be quiet and eat, and at least she has a hearty appetite unlike most of the editorial team. I try to engage her in conversation as she is placed near to me, while Lady Constance chunters on at the head of the table.

'Do you ride?' I ask, thinking this is probably a bit of a random question, but it seems to suffice.

'Oh yes,' replies Lady Hattie. She has quite a deep and hearty voice. 'There's nothing better, I'd spend my whole life in the saddle if I could, wouldn't you?'

'Erm, absolutely, although I haven't ridden properly for years and I don't have my own horse, so no.' Oh dear, back to talking gibberish again.

Lady Hattie doesn't seem to notice. 'Well, you must borrow one of ours, we have hundreds in the stables and Mummy simply isn't bothered anymore.'

'Bothered about what?' Lady Constance interrupts. 'I simply refuse to be left out of the conversation – what are you talking about?'

'Horses,' I interject helpfully, as Hattie seems to have retreated back into her food.

'Oh horses, yes well, of course Hattie will be riding at Badminton in a couple of months. Have you seen her medals in the trophy room at the back of the house – perhaps there may be time to show you after the garden party.'

I look suitably impressed; she must be good then. Hattie, who is obviously like everyone else; crushed by her mother, doesn't say a word in between times. She probably prefers talking to the horses rather than her family, and I must say I don't blame her at all.

'No disappearing off to your apartments after luncheon. Hattie, you know Darcy is going to be here, and his mother has suggested you show him round the party.' The mention of Darcy's imminent appearance makes me start wildly and drop my fork. Why does that man always have to be everywhere?

Mel looks at me expressively across the table.

I laboriously fold my napkin to give me time to try to recompose myself. I don't want to see Darcy. Neither does Lady Hattie by the look of it. 'I'm not sticking around to see him,' she mutters. It doesn't seem as though she's enamoured with the idea of looking after Darcy either. For goodness sake, putting up with Rob Bright and Lady Constance is bad enough – who next? Probably Jessica Palmer-Wright.

I'm becoming used to the amount of cutlery at these dos, but am nevertheless daunted by the number of courses that seem to come and go. Lady Constance at the head of the table raps out orders at the rate of knots. She is, of course, surrounded by the two Rs, seated like bookends either side of her, ready to respond to her every comment and whim.

Mel and I are sitting opposite each other, but she is unusually quiet, leaving the others to monopolise the conversation. I'm rather hoping she's plotting her way out of this situation and into the successful design career she deserves.

HAVING WAITED some time for an opportune lull, or at least for Lady Constance to stop talking for a minute, I ask hesitantly about her sister.

'You must have heard of her, working for Modiste,' Lady Constance states tersely.

'Yes, I know she is a fashion icon,' I reply meekly, 'but I would love to hear more about her.'

Lady Constance leans towards me for emphasis. 'I can tell you this, young lady, what my sister does not know about fashion is not worth knowing. I have many of her creations in my wardrobe upstairs. She has a royal warrant, you know.'

I'm not at all surprised, this is impressive stuff – I notice Mel's eyes widen.

Before I can make any reply, Lady Constance continues. 'Of course, I do not buy anything available to other people. One likes to stand out from the rabble. My shoes are handmade by John Lobb, shoemaker to the royal family, there is no way I would ever wear anything mass produced.' She glares at me through narrowed eyes as she speaks, as though daring me to defend anyone crass enough to wear any items from the high street.

It takes some time for Lady Constance to exhaust her list of prized possessions, provided by those lucky few who are skilled enough to have a royal warrant. Having tired of this topic of conversation some time before, I think it will be fun to liven things up a bit. We've heard more than enough of her authoritarian droning on and on.

'Erm, did you enjoy the First Dates evening the other day?' I ask boldly.

'Oh!' she exclaims, 'don't remind me of that dreadful evening, having to sit and eat with such terribly common people. It was my personal maid, Anna's, idea to attend a Jane Austen evening. Never heard such nonsense – Anna is a very good sort of woman and she does know how to arrange my hair, but spends all of her spare time with her head in a book. Constantly spouting about lovey-dovey claptrap. Total balderdash I call it. Rather have my Labrador, Bessie, she gives me more loyalty than any man. Even Lord Parker, God rest him, could never remember to fold his pyjamas or take off his waders in the house. Used to track mud everywhere... No, it was a dreadful evening, couldn't serve pheasant properly. The young man I sat with in the second course was tolerable, I suppose, but probably born the wrong side of town, judging by his accent.'

I'm shocked at this comment. I presume she's talking about

Daniel, who's ironically lost the chance he might have had of bettering himself as a result of the machinations of Darcy Drummond.

Rob, ever helpful, chips in, 'I thought you were getting on pretty well with Sir Henry Greaves, he seemed a nice chap.'

'Oh him! He was reasonable company, I suppose, but a bit of a crusty old bore. The man went on and on, made it difficult to get a word in edgeways and I have never met someone so terribly opinionated.'

I have a job not to choke on my dessert. This is such a brilliant example of the pot calling the kettle black. It's one of life's greatest ironies – how people never seem to be aware of their own faults when they're presented in front of them. Yet they're always so quick to spot them in others. Totally bizarre.

Lady Constance continues without pausing for breath. 'Sir Henry Greaves is one of those people who have a rather exalted opinion of themselves, always primping and preening and expecting others to do the same. Continually on about who he is connected with and how important they are, waffling about lineage... Do you know,' she spits out, pointing a bony finger angrily at me, 'he even asked me if the Parkers are listed in *Burke's Peerage*! I have never been so outraged!'

She draws herself up to her full height in her seat, her back straight. 'I said to him, I'll have you know, my man, that my great grandfather, Lord William Parker, wrote *Burke's Peerage*!' She sits back in her chair, glowering at us all, waiting for the gasps of 'oh really' and 'amazing' which she inevitably receives in plenty from the two Rs.

I'm still trying to work out how *Burke's Peerage* could be written by someone other than Burke, satisfying myself with making a mental note to Google it when I manage to escape later – it will certainly be more interesting than listening to Rob's review of *Star Trek* – episode 523.

. . .

THANK GOODNESS, at last lunch is finally over and our ordeal finished. Lady Constance stalks ahead, leading our little procession out to the garden party. She is flanked either side by the two Rs.

Mel and I follow at a distance, with me trying not to sink into the lawn in my heels. Perhaps if I had been born into a wealthy country family like this, I would know how to walk in high heels on grass. There's definitely an art form to it – if you put your weight down as usual on the back of your foot, the heel sinks straight into the turf and you end up looking drunken, lurching from side to side in a most unflattering fashion. This then makes me try to walk without putting my weight down properly, with the result that it hurts all up the back of the calf, and you look as though you are a part of the Ministry of Silly Walks.

Lady Hattie, I notice, has, against her mother's wishes, quietly sneaked off to her room under the pretext of getting changed, and not returned. I guess with a mother like Lady Constance, Hattie has to use any kind of defence mechanism she can.

# CHAPTER 21

L ady Constance's opening speech is everything I expected; pompous and full of the amazing feats she and her family have achieved for the past few centuries on their estate. Most of the nearby village seems to have turned up and there are lovely stalls run by the quaint little school and local church. It appears that in this picturesque place, the ancient feudal system is still alive and well. Lady Constance is certainly the first port of call in both managing charitable events and keeping everyone in order. I was told by Colonel Meyrick, when we spoke earlier, that Lady Constance is also a Justice of the Peace, so she obviously enjoys dictating local law and order in her spare time. I can imagine she fits the role admirably.

Colonel Meyrick is friendly and chatty, with nothing dictatorial or proud about him. He obviously is happiest in the countryside and strides out alongside us talking about the best picnic spots in the area. He also seems to have taken on the position of escorting us round the garden party, for which I am extremely grateful. The two Rs are pandering to every whim of Lady Constance as always, leaving Mel and me to shift for ourselves. The colonel is at least pleasant to talk to.

'Do you know Darcy Drummond well?' I ask as we meander between the stalls, Mel munching on some flapjacks she's bought from the Scouts' cake sale.

'Yes, I've known him all my life – and Nick Palmer-Wright. Our families are related several generations back,' Colonel Meyrick replies. 'They're like brothers, both decent guys who work hard and are well respected.'

'Yes, I got the impression they go around together. Nick Palmer-Wright is a lovely guy, so kind and non-judgemental.' I put particular emphasis on this last part of the sentence, as though to infer that Darcy is totally the opposite, but the colonel continues without seeming to notice.

'I understand Darcy looks out for Nick – since he lost his father especially, he is rather easily put upon by those less deserving of attention.'

'Oh?'

'Yes, I believe that happened quite recently, as Nick became entangled with a married woman, so Darcy sent him to head up their office in New York till it all blows over.'

'Really?' I ask, horrified. 'I must admit I haven't seen him for a while but I didn't know he has gone abroad.'

'Yes, he's been out there a few weeks now. Apparently, Darcy suggested it as soon as he knew the affair was getting serious.'

I wondered why Chloe had been so quiet about Nick, but had assumed it was because Kian was being difficult. I had no idea he'd been sent out of the way deliberately. Typical of Darcy. There was nothing in it anyway, just a harmless friendship, but right now Chloe needs all the friends she can get. Honestly, Darcy has no idea about life's every day issues – he says I live in the land of storybooks, but he lords it at the top of his controlling business empire, changing people's lives, it's all a game to him.

'I don't see what business it is of Darcy's who his friend's dating,' I retort.

'Oh, do you think it was out of order?'

'Actually, yes I do. What if they really cared about each other?'

'Perhaps they didn't and he's better off away from her... Are you okay, Miss Johnson? Would you like me to fetch you a glass of Pimms?'

Oh dear, he must have noticed my horrified expression.

'Yes, that would be very kind,' I reply gratefully.

As the colonel disappears to join the queue for the Pimms, Mel takes me to one side to whisper in my ear.

'Can you cover for me for a bit?' she asks, looking about her furtively, acting as subtly as a comedy spy.

'What are you talking about?' I ask. 'No-one's exactly taking any notice of us. Where are you going?'

'I need to do some research. Just tell Rob I've needed the loo or something, if he even notices I've gone.' Without waiting for a response, she disappears off in the general direction of the house. I have no idea what she's doing, but there is no time to question as Colonel Meyrick is already returning and... oh great, he's accompanied by Darcy. This day's getting better and better and I begin to feel slightly miffed with Mel as it's her fault I'm here and now she's disappeared.

The colonel passes me a sparkling glass of Pimms, from which I take a fortifying sip. 'Miss Johnson, you know Darcy Drummond, I believe.'

'I sure do, as much as I ever want to,' I mutter, but feel a little childish so end up saying, 'Yes, hello,' bizarrely, slightly too loud and over-polite.

'Where do you know each other from?' the colonel asks pleasantly.

'Work,' I say a little too quickly, causing Darcy to look startled, but there's no way I'm bandying about the fact I've joined a dating agency here.

'Of course, you work for the very glamorous Modiste. Trust you, Darcy, always keeping the most beautiful girls to yourself.'

The colonel gives Darcy a hearty slap on the back, which he does not appear to appreciate at all.

'Not exactly, Anthony. Miss Johnson works in Classified Sales,' Darcy replies.

Oh that was a burn, awkward. How to well and truly put me back in my place then. This guy is such a b.

'Yes I do, actually.' I hold my head up high. 'We can't all be supermodels and world-class business leaders.'

'Oh here we go, someone has issues,' Darcy snaps.

'No, not really. You need to stop judging others simply because of what they do. I have a very good degree, actually, and I do have a brain, believe it or not, some of us women do.'

'I'm sure you're a highly intelligent woman, and maybe if you used your brain, instead of wasting your time in a dead-end job like cold-calling, you might be a lot happier and less desperate to hide yourself away in a book the whole time.'

I feel as though he's hit me, his words sting my very being, as intense as a real physical pain.

'You're totally wrong,' I say defiantly. 'I'm just biding my time in Sales until a better position arises in Editorial.' (Oops, I didn't want to tell him that, it was supposed to be my secret until I'm a bit more integrated.)

'If you think those bitchy girls in Editorial are going to let you in, you are very much mistaken,' Darcy states firmly. 'You know better than anyone else how it works in Modiste. More to the point, you're getting yourself into very hot water being involved with that group of social climbers. Sophie, you're so naïve.'

'What's it to do with you anyway?' I demand. 'Why do you care? Or am I too much of an embarrassment to you and your agency?'

Darcy pauses, seemingly about to say something, then stops himself.

'Not at all. I leave membership issues to Jessica and Emma. It's nothing to do with that – why would we be embarrassed of someone like you? Your problem is you lack confidence and keep pitching yourself too low.'

'And your problem is your propensity to think you're above everyone and everything. And you're not, not at all. One day it'll all catch up with you and you'll see how hard it can be to try to fit into a world different from your own.'

'Er, would anyone like another glass of Pimms?' the colonel asks politely, shifting about awkwardly from one foot to the other.

'No thank you, Colonel, I'm not feeling very well. I'm going to return to the house,' I reply.

'Are you all right, Miss Johnson? Would you like me to walk with you?' The Colonel looks concerned.

'No, it's okay, I'll be fine – it's just a headache – I'll be better for a bit of quiet, thank you all the same.'

I stumble off towards the house, not caring if my heels sink into the grass or not. I need to get away to think.

# CHAPTER 22

'Can I help you, madam?' A sombre-looking butler steps into the path of my rapid stomping into the house.

'I need the ladies if you could please tell me where it is?' I ask, hastily dabbing at my tear-blotched eyes. I hope my mascara hasn't run. Bloody Darcy Drummond, he knows just how to get under my skin. I hate him.

'Straight on and round to the left, madam.' The butler ignores my tear stains and scruffy appearance in a truly professional manner and waddles off on his way. From the back, he looks rather like a penguin.

ONCE IN THE elegantly tiled and over-the-top bathroom, I clean my face and take some deep breaths. I mustn't let Darcy get to me, he's not worth it. Next thing is to get hold of Mel, wherever she is, and get out of here. I don't want to stay one more minute. Perhaps she can drive Rob's car home and we might be able to pick him up later, or never, with any luck.

Feeling extremely furtive, I begin the task of searching for Mel. I've already tried her phone several times but it's going straight to answerphone. She'd said she was returning to the house so she can't be outside – I would have passed her anyway as I came back in. So that narrows it down to about a hundred rooms or so – I should be done before… well, either way, I figure I had better get on with it.

HALF AN HOUR later I'm fed up and tired, my feet hurt from my heels digging in, so I decide to take them off and tiptoe in my bare feet. I hope to goodness I won't bump into anyone as I probably look like a complete and utter weirdo. Fortunately, however, the place seems to be deserted as most of the staff are out helping with the garden party.

The house itself is simply vast; I trail past room after room, not liking to call for Mel as I have a feeling she's up to something she shouldn't be.

Suddenly, as I'm passing yet another large oak door on the third floor, I hear a noise from within. I haven't liked to wander in and out of the rooms in someone else's house when the door is shut, so have tried to listen out for any sounds instead. There's definitely a rustling inside this one. I creep to the door and gently push it with a couple of fingers, just a little, and poke my head round.

It's a large boudoir with a great curtained bed in the centre, with thick velvet drapes. I could swear as I came in there was a tiny movement from behind the bed.

Taking all my courage, and hoping against hope there are no ghosts or vermin in the house, I tiptoe towards the end of the bed and peer round the other side. There, crouched on the floor, with her head partly hidden under the bed sheet, is Mel.

'What are you doing?' I ask incredulously.

'Shhhh! What are you doing, more like? You frightened the life out of me. I thought you were Lady Constance!' Mel scrambles to her feet, brushing bits of fluff off her clothes.

'For goodness sake, of all the bizarre things to do. This looks like Lady Constance's room. What the heck are you doing in it? She'll go mad if she catches you.'

'I was checking to see if she has any vintage outfits designed by Vivienne d'Artois of course.'

'Oh, of course, silly me. I should have guessed! And what are you going to do with them if you find any, nick them?'

'Of course not. What sort of person do you think I am?'

'I don't know what sort of person you are when I come across you stealing about in other people's bedrooms without permission, especially when that person is one iota as scary as Lady Constance. You must be crazy!'

'No, just desperate. I don't seem to be getting anywhere talking to the woman, so I'm going to have to check out her gear, and research the competition when no-one's around.'

'Good grief, Mel. Can't you just ask her to look at them?' I ask naively. I take one look at the expression on her face. 'Okay, maybe not. But this is going to end in tears, I can tell you.'

'Pssst, Mel... Pssst!' I look to see where the noise is coming from, then catch sight of Mel's face – she looks definitely sheepish.

'Come on out – it's only Sophie!' she whispers loudly.

'Sophie, darling, what are you doing here?' It's Mark, draped in a 1920s feather boa with a fascinator in his hair.

'God, I wish you people would stop asking me that when I'm only here because of you lot,' I snap. 'Why on earth are you involved in this, Mark? Don't tell me you know Lady Constance as well.'

'No, darling, never met her before, but your friend Mel here got in touch to ask me to help her out with a little fashion detective work, and who am I to refuse an adventure?' Mark looks so hilarious, I smile in spite of the stressful situation.

'I needed Mark to help me identify the really popular stuff. I found his details on your phone,' Mel whispers defiantly. 'I'm not copying the designs, but I must check out the opposition first hand if I'm going to be really successful in this industry.'

'I think you're both mad,' I grumble. 'And I for one am getting out of here before we are discovered and Lady Constance calls the police.'

Unbelievably, as I'm speaking, I hear the shrill and authoritative tones of Lady Constance coming down the corridor.

'Under the bed!' Mel shrieks as she returns to her previous hiding place. I look wildly about me and climb quickly into an old antique wardrobe, wedging myself tightly between an old coat, which I think rather horribly is made of real fur, and a mothbally old dress. It makes me feel dangerously as though I'm going to have to sneeze. I don't know where Mark's gone but I keep jolly quiet as I for one don't want to get caught by an irate Lady Constance.

I need not have worried, the ever-faithful Mark has taken one for the team. Instead of hiding he brazenly wafts out of the bedroom into the path of Lady Constance, stopping her abruptly.

'Who are you?' she booms in a voice of total outrage. 'Why are you wandering around my house without a by your leave?'

'My dear Lady C, I may call you Lady C, may I not? I am Mark du Croix – from Carter Whitrow Publications, I am one of your greatest fans – I have just heard how you were the sole inspiration for Vivienne d'Artois's latest collection. You little minx – you simply must tell me how you have achieved it.'

I wait in vain for the roar of annoyance one would expect to hear erupt from Lady Constance at this brazen introduction. Yet I can distinctly hear her simper, ask for Mark's name again, and trot off along the corridor chatting away animatedly. Mark's a genius.

Despite my uncomfortable surroundings, I wait a little longer before gingerly opening the door to my awkward hiding place, in case Lady C makes a comeback.

Eventually, however, my foot has finally gone to sleep, so I ease myself out of the cupboard and tiptoe quietly across the carpet. Suddenly to my horror, the door opens abruptly and in walks Darcy Drummond.

'Oh my gosh, you made me jump!' I exclaim, my heart hammering, not helped by the look of outrage on Darcy's face.

'Made you jump? What the hell are you doing in Lady Constance's bedroom?'

'Erm, well, I was checking where Mel had gone as we were separated, and I came in here because I heard a noise.'

'And was she in here?' asks Darcy, a curious expression on his face.

'No, there was no-one. It must have been my imagination. Silly me.'

I start to walk towards the door, trying not to look at the other side of the bed where Mel had been hiding, though fortunately the space is now empty and she appears to have escaped.

'Wait a minute!' Darcy firmly places his arm across the door, blocking my exit. God, he's so handsome close up, it makes me feel a bit dizzy.

'What?' I ask, hating the slight tremor in my voice.

'I need to talk to you,' he says urgently. 'Sophie, I...'

'Look, I don't think this is the time or the place for a talk. I'm sorry I was in Lady Constance's room but I expect Mel–'

I'm interrupted by Darcy saying a little too loudly, 'No! This isn't right!'

'I said I'm sorry, okay? I didn't mean to be in here.'

'It's not that, I need to explain something,' Darcy repeats. 'It can't wait. I've tried to work it out but I can't. You need to understand, realise...' He pauses, seeming to be struggling for the right words... 'I really admire you. In spite of your ridiculous gaucheness, your bizarre friends and ability to burst out laughing at random moments, I think maybe... well, I really like you. You're not like anyone else I've ever met.'

It's one of those moments where time seems to stand still and

I must have stood there looking completely stupid as I can't take in what he's said.

'I'm aware that in saying this, my mother and friends will be furious and I'm probably ruining my chances of any sensible relationships, but it can't be helped. I want to get to know you better. Will you come out with me on a proper date, just the two of us?' Darcy raises his eyes to my face, waiting for my response.

My goodness I'm ready to give it to him too. 'You really think I would consider going out with someone like you? Someone who's been rude about me and my personality right from the very first time you met me. You're against everything I stand for, my background, my choice of reading matter and friends and family. We live in different worlds, you and I, yours is one of profits and shares and mine is the land of romantic storybooks. We're not exactly compatible.'

'We *are* different,' Darcy states slowly, 'but surely that's okay, it can work. Even if you do spend your whole time living in a literary dream world. As to your background and friends, what do you expect? I've been brought up in the fast-paced high-pressure world of commerce and am proud of that. Do you expect me to like the fact you hate businessmen and that you belong to some gimmicky dating agency named after a spinster who's been dead for two hundred years?'

'That's rich,' I exclaim, 'coming from you when it's your company. How can you be the CEO of The Jane Austen Dating Agency when you don't even agree with it?'

'It's business,' Darcy snaps. 'Haven't you heard of investments? Anyway, it was the pet project of my grandmother's – she was a huge Jane Austen fan. She came up with the idea shortly before her death and we founded it for her sake. I've never read an Austen novel and after the amount of stress the agency causes me, I never want to.'

'I can believe that,' I reply angrily. 'Though I'm sorry about your grandma, but look at how you've treated Daniel Becks.'

'What are you talking about?'

'You've cheated Daniel, totally disregarding your father's will! You've taken away any chance he had of improving himself.'

'Is that what he told you? I don't know how he's managed to survive such terrible misfortune!'

'And you've sent Nick abroad, away from my sister, Chloe. Is that true?'

'Yes it is. She's married, for God's sake, and you know full well it can come to nothing. Nick's young and single, he has every rich woman in the town at his feet. He doesn't need to be mixed up in your sister's tawdry problems. And maybe you might have forgiven me if I hadn't been truthful. If I had flattered you, whispering sweet nothings and romantic crap to you. But that isn't my way, I say what I mean because I'm honest in business and every other part of my life.'

'You are mistaken, Darcy,' I snap. (OMG I have always wanted to say this line.) 'You couldn't have asked me out in any way that would have tempted me to accept. For a long time now I've considered you to be one of the last people I'd ever go out with.'

Darcy steps backwards as though I have slapped him. 'Okay fine,' he says, removing his hand from the doorway. 'I won't keep you any longer. I'm sorry to have upset you and hope things work out as you have it all mapped out so perfectly.'

With that, he leaves abruptly and I'm left to sink onto Lady Constance's bed, exhausted and shaky.

# CHAPTER 23

The return journey with Mel and Rob is a silent affair, both Mel and I are lost in our own thoughts. I'm trying to work out what's just happened. Darcy Drummond likes me? He wants to go out with me? It's all so bizarre. I know I've always wanted to be Elizabeth Bennet, but can my life really resemble hers? Perhaps without the Regency dress or much of the romance either, for that matter. I mean, what happened to 'You must allow me to tell you how ardently I admire and love you.' At least Mr Darcy only criticised Lizzie for being tolerable, he did not annihilate her entire personality and offer advice in the style of her mother.

But Darcy Drummond does seem to like me. I can't believe he really means it, perhaps he's joking. Yet his expression and body language were clear enough. I can't stand him though, he's insufferably arrogant; the way he spoke. He feels no remorse for his treatment of Daniel, or for breaking up Nick and Chloe's friendship. Worst of all, the man is a complete chauvinist with opinions from the dark ages.

Rob doesn't seem to notice our silence, chuntering away as usual about the incredible success of Lady Constance's garden party and how lucky we were to be able to attend. Unfortunately, I'm staying the night with Rob and Mel, returning home the next day.

'How did you manage to get out of Lady Constance's room?' I ask Mel curiously, when we'd managed to lose Rob for a short while. As soon as we'd got back to their house, he'd disappeared to study his week's chess timetable.

'I snuck out while Mark was distracting Lady C,' Mel replies, smiling. 'He's amazing, isn't he? Now they're best buddies. Mark is sure she'll allow him to borrow some of her prime collection Vivienne d'Artois, as he has told her it will be on show at the V&A Museum.'

'Is it really going on show at the V&A?'

'Of course not, silly! But Lady C won't find out as she's hardly likely to travel to London to check out her own clothes, is she?'

'You never know,' I reply seriously. 'With her, nothing would surprise me.'

'Well, I'm thrilled. Mark's solved all my problems. I just need to borrow the stuff, get some ideas from the style and quality of the fabric, then start thinking of my own collection.'

'That's great,' I try to sound enthusiastic. 'Then you can leave Rob and get back to some kind of normality.'

'Shhh!' Mel whispers. 'We'll have to wait a bit for that, I don't want to be too obvious and he's not that bad, I suppose.'

'Really? Hmmm… seems it to me.'

'Anyway,' Mel continues, 'what happened between you and Darcy Drummond? The atmosphere was practically crackling when you came downstairs. And how come you were up there together?'

'Just coincidence. I can quite honestly assure you there is nothing going on between us.'

'Huh.' Mel smiles cynically. 'I think he likes you.'

'Me? I hardly think so. You've been reading too many romance novels!'

I RETURN HOME the next evening, throwing my bags on the comfortable old bed with relief. Izzy's not due to return until the following day, so I'm hopefully going to chill out, have a nice cosy chat with Chloe on the phone later and get an early night. I didn't sleep well at all at Mel and Rob's, so will be glad to catch up on some much needed shut-eye.

AFTER A PLATE of my favourite pasta, accompanied by a thera-peutic dose of Northanger Abbey, I'm lying on the sofa feeling completely chilled. I've even nearly forgotten about the fact that Darcy thinks he's in love with me. This seems to be beyond comprehension – he could have anyone at all, any number of glamorous women. Not good old Sophie who doesn't fit in anywhere.

I think maybe he only imagines he likes me, perhaps he just has a taste for something a bit different, more challenging than his usual female companions. Whether my life is morphing into some ridiculous Jane Austen spin-off or not, I'm definitely not ever going out on a date with him anyway, he's far too like Darcy in *P and P*. Rude and arrogant and used to having his own way. Nope, it's not happening.

Just as I'm beginning to figure it's time to get to bed, my phone rings. I answer it blearily. I hate it when I'm nearly asleep and that happens.

'Sophie, thank God.' I think it's Daniel but it's hard to make out his voice, there's so much noise in the background.

'Daniel, is that you?' I ask, instantly awake. *What's going on, and why haven't you called me for like forever?* I add silently.

'It's Izzy. She's not well.'

'What? What's wrong with her? Is she with you?' My words tumble over each other. It takes me a moment to register who he's talking about. I didn't know Daniel knows Izzy that well, and more to the point, she's meant to be at her dad and stepmum's house.

'She was with me, but I've had to go.' Daniel sounds odd, distant. 'I got called away but I didn't really want to leave her in the state she's in. I think her friend Tamara was there, but I'm not sure.'

I swear I can hear a woman's voice in the background talking to him.

'Is that Izzy?' I ask. 'What's wrong with her, is she okay?'

'Yes, I mean no, I don't know, look I've got to go.'

'Daniel... Where is she?'

'Outside Blush,' he mutters. 'King's Road.'

'But, Daniel...' The line goes dead.

I stand there for a moment, goggling at the phone in my hand.

I'm totally confused over what's happening but galvanise into action, knowing that somehow I must get to Izzy as soon as possible. I run to the door, grabbing my keys while simultaneously dialling a cab to get to King's Road.

'It'll be at least ten minutes, it's a busy time of night,' the man at the other end of the line growls.

'Please be as quick as possible,' I squeak impotently.

I spend the time waiting for the taxi to arrive, repeatedly pressing speed dial, desperately trying to get hold of Izzy. Unsurprisingly she isn't picking up. I leave a couple of messages and send her a text. In between, I phone Maria who isn't answering either.

FINALLY, the taxi arrives and I dash out into the street like a mad woman. The journey seems to take ages, but in reality is only about twenty minutes. At Blush, I jump out onto the street. It isn't somewhere I've been much except one time with the girls from uni and even then I'd gone home early, and I've no idea where Izzy might be.

❧

THERE'S a large bouncer on the door who has obviously no intention of letting me past without paying. Fortunately for once I have some cash left in my purse, which I thrust at him and dash on in. I look out of place in a denim skirt and white shirt, but thankfully inside it's really dark apart from the flashing lights. There are people everywhere, all crammed in a small space, my idea of the worst nightmare. I take a breath like a deep sea diver about to enter a marine world and plunge into the surging mob. For a while I'm carried along by the tide until I finally manage to find a small inlet, a tiny gap where I can stop being moved and look about me.

I see someone who looks like they might work there. 'Have you seen a blonde girl, pretty, bubbly?'

The bloke looks at me incredulously and disappears off into the crowd. He's quickly swallowed up into the melee and I can no longer see him. Perhaps he wasn't the right person to ask. After a sudden brainwave, I pull out my phone, find a pic of Izzy with Chloe and Mel and show it to people. I blunder along, tapping random people on the shoulder, asking them if they've seen Izzy.

'Wish I had seen her, pretty hot, huh?' one guy lurches. His mates around him laugh raucously.

'Wanna join our crowd, love?' another bloke mutters, draping his arm round my shoulders.

'Erm, maybe another time, thanks.' I politely remove his arm and push though the throng to another part of the room, the noise is getting louder as I seem to be nearer the DJ.

I look about for some sign of Izzy, or even a group around someone who might be feeling unwell, but am getting to the point where I want to give up when an attractive girl with tawny dreadlocks shouts in my ear, 'Dunno who you're looking for but there's someone huddled on the floor in the loos.'

I thank her gratefully and push my way through the crowd, following the signed directions to the ladies.

They are dark, almost black, row after row of cubicles, loo roll all over the floor and a horrible smell. I cautiously advance round the corner, when I come across a figure slumped on the tiles. I run up and touch her gently. 'Izzy?' She seems to be unconscious. Beside her, it looks suspiciously as though she's been sick.

'Izzy? Are you okay? Can you hear me?'

She groans, mutters something incoherent and promptly passes out again. She reeks of alcohol, I'm not sure what, but it's pretty pungent. I half drag, half pull her onto one side into the recovery position. No-one ever warns you how heavy someone is when they are totally out of it. Next, I quickly dial the ambulance and give our location. This whole situation feels surreal, me squatting on the floor of a disgusting public toilet, my arm round Izzy who's still unconscious. I sit there for ages, wondering how on earth she got into this mess and why she was with Daniel.

It seems to have been forever and my legs have gone to sleep when a familiar head peers round the door.

'Maria? What are you doing here?'

'Oh my God, is that Izzy? What's happened?' Maria rushes over and squats down at Izzy's side.

'I think she's passed out, I presume that's all it is?'

'Oh God, I knew she was in a bad way, but I've been dealing with Louisa,' says Maria distractedly, checking Izzy's pulse.

'Louisa?'

'We were all here having a few drinks, you know a group of us: Charles, Izzy, Tamara and everyone, and Louisa fell down the stairs,' Maria explains, looking distressed. 'I left Charles with her for a minute while I came to the loo. We're going to get her to A&E in a mo.'

'So, how come you were all here together? How did Izzy end up on her own?' I'm still puzzled as to what's going on.

At that moment, a friendly voice calls round the door. 'Can I come in?' It's a couple of paramedics, calm and capable. To my exhausted mind, they seem like angels. They gently ask us a couple of questions while examining Izzy, one of them jotting down their obs.

I hear an altercation outside the door. It's a man's voice shouting, 'I don't bloody care if it's the women's loos! I know the girl who's sick in there and I'm going in.'

The door bursts open and in storms Matthew, dishevelled but determined; a young woman with nose piercings and an interesting feather tattoo behind her ear, at his heels. 'Matthew, what are you doing here?' I stutter.

The feisty young woman retreats back out of the door, having evidently seen that I know this man.

'I came as soon as I could, I got a text from Daniel,' Matthew pants as he wedges himself inside the door. 'Is she okay?'

I glance haplessly at the female paramedic who turns out to be called Rita.

'We don't know yet, she's in a pretty bad way. Do you know if she ever takes anything recreationally?'

'Drugs?' Matthew exclaims. 'She'd never do that, she wouldn't be that stupid.'

'You'd be surprised,' Rita replies ominously. 'Sometimes it's just the once for fun, and in minutes it can all go horribly wrong.'

Matthew's face contorts with worry, and Maria looks shocked.

'I don't think Izzy would take them even once,' I say firmly. 'Anyway, she reeks of alcohol.'

'Yes, she must have had a fair amount to be in this state,' Rita replies. 'Though sometimes they mix the two, or she could have had her drink spiked,' she adds cheerfully as an afterthought.

Matthew and I exchange glances.

'Surely that's not likely,' Maria says weakly. 'We were with her all the time until the last half hour or so.'

'Don't worry, we'll get her to hospital, then we can find out what's going on,' says the other paramedic. I think his name's Gary. I like him, he's steady, calm, somehow reassuring. 'Rita, give me a hand, we're going to get her on the trolley.'

'Can I go with her in the ambulance?' I ask.

'You can, but it might be better if your friend here, Matthew isn't it, takes you in his car. She's certainly going to be staying in overnight.'

Matthew readily agrees to give me a lift. We watch numbly as Izzy's taken off on a trolley to the ambulance. She looks frighteningly young and vulnerable, her blonde head poking out the top of the hospital blanket, her face pallid. I'm frightened by the fact she's still unconscious.

We're joined at the doorway by Charles and another guy propping up a wilting Louisa, who's left ankle is horribly swollen. She also has an ugly-looking gash on her head.

Matthew hurls questions at Charles. 'What the hell's going on? How on earth did this happen? How did Izzy end up here?'

'I don't know,' Charles replies uncomfortably. 'We all stopped off here for a few drinks. It isn't my style at all, but everyone seemed to want to come, apart from Maria of course.' He glances at her briefly, then looks away. 'We had a couple of drinks but next thing, Tamara started doing this drinking game with shots, you know, Jägerbombs, then Louisa and Izzy followed suit, which I must admit I was a bit worried about, but I thought they must do this all the time. I didn't want to seem like a spoilsport.'

'Surely you must have noticed things were getting out of hand?' Matthew glares right into Charles's face. 'Izzy's very vulnerable, she needs looking after, not bloody encouraging into a worse situation.'

'Please, guys, this isn't going to sort things out,' Maria pleads. 'Charles, I really think we should be getting Louisa checked out at the hospital.'

'Yes, you're right.' Charles seems to recollect himself.

'Can they come with us?' I ask Matthew diffidently. 'It would make more sense, surely.'

'Yes fine, as long as they're quick – I must get there as soon as possible to make sure Izzy's okay.' Matthew's face is ashen. He's obviously smitten with her and is worth twenty of Josh, whether he gushes poetry or not.

Louisa's unable to move very fast, but the two men half carry, half support her to the car. She still seems pretty immobile and the wound on her head has become sticky and slow moving.

ONCE AT THE HOSPITAL, we stop at the twenty-minute parking slot and pile out. We are a sorry sight. Matthew strides ahead, his usually immaculate hair dishevelled, he has sick on his shirt, and Charles and Maria half carry Louisa towards the doors of the hospital. I hurry on behind, holding everyone's belongings, still desperately hoping Izzy's okay. I feel responsible, she's only young and I should have been looking after her but then I'd been sure she was with her dad.

AS WE REACH THE ENTRANCE, I notice a smartly dressed guy in a long coat who looks completely out of place, standing at the reception desk with his back to us. As we enter, he turns and I gasp as I realise it's Darcy. He does a double take as he notices me.

'Sophie, Miss Johnson? What are *you* doing here?'

I have a horrible feeling I'm wearing my old scruffy denim

skirt, I think my mascara has smudged and I'm worried I may smell slightly of sick. It seems to me it's always some kind of sod's law that if you rush out of the house without make-up, or changing first, it's pretty much guaranteed you're going to run into someone you really don't want to meet. Like an extremely hot and arrogant guy who's recently asked you out, or your future mother-in-law or something. It's just the way it is.

'Darcy,' I mutter, wishing the ground could swallow me up. 'I'm just helping my friends into the hospital.'

'So I see.' He looks edgy and awkward, almost as though he wants to get away. Not that I can blame him.

'So, are you visiting someone?' I ask politely, keeping my eye on the proceedings at the desk. Matthew's already dashed off down the corridor, presumably to discover what's happened to Izzy. Maria and Charles have found a nearby wheelchair for Louisa and are checking her in at reception.

'Yes, well no, yes sort of,' Darcy stutters, eyeing the wound on Louisa's head uneasily. 'I'm visiting my cousin in the maternity unit, but I'm in the wrong place, it's the Lindo wing.'

'Oh, isn't that where Princess Kate had her babies?' I twitter stupidly.

'That's what everyone asks!' Darcy smiles wryly, and for a second the tension between us breaks.

'We're off to A&E,' Maria calls softly. Charles is already in a rush to push the wheelchair round the corridor, following the red footprints marked on the floor.

'I'd better go.' I smile awkwardly at Darcy. 'Enjoy the Lindo wing.'

I don't look back to register his reaction, just follow the others down the soullessly blank corridor. What with hospitals, drunk heroines and head wounds, the cosy world of Elizabeth and Darcy seems to be getting further away than ever.

# CHAPTER 24

Three hours later, Louisa's been seen by the triage nurse and the gash on her head neatly dressed. Her X-ray shows the ankle is sound, probably just a sprain. She's waiting with Charles and Maria, who are then going to take her home to her parents. Thank goodness Maria's with them. Charles seems to have gone into some kind of stupor. I guess he's shocked, but I can't help thinking, as he is a little more mature, he should have taken better care of Louisa.

It's a weird fact that when in hospital, time seems to stand still. I feel like we've been here forever. Izzy is still unconscious, the hospital staff have attached her to a drip and some kind of machine which is connected to a mask over her mouth, but other than the occasional moan, she's shown no signs of waking. A bustling nurse moves the oxygen to one side, checks her obs and replaces it again.

After what seems a lifetime, a doctor appears. 'Do you have any idea how much she drank?' he asks us after carrying out a brief examination.

'No, neither of us were with her, or we'd have done something about it,' I reply. 'I understand she was drinking shots, but don't think she had any drugs with it.'

'Right. She's had a fair skinful by the look of it but I've seen worse. We'll keep her on the monitor for now to keep an eye on her oxygen levels. Any next of kin present?'

'No, her relationship with her parents is strained, to put it mildly,' I reply sadly.

'They should be informed,' says the doctor firmly.

'I'll contact her father,' Matthew replies, jumping to his feet. I think he's glad to actually do something at last. Until now, he's been either pacing the floor or sitting staring into his hands. He disappears out into the corridor.

'I'm afraid you can't stay, love.' The nurse touches my shoulder gently. 'Best go home and get some rest. We'll let you know how she is in the morning.'

I nod dumbly, give Izzy's hand a gentle squeeze in case she can sense I'm there, and leave.

BACK OUT IN the car park, Darcy comes jogging up behind me out of nowhere. 'Sophie, can I drop you home?'

'That's kind, thanks, but I'm waiting for Matthew – he's going to give me a lift.'

Darcy's face drops slightly. 'Oh okay, as long as you're not planning on going home alone on the tube at this time of night.'

'No, definitely not.' I smile to myself. No need to tell him I'd been too scared to go on the tube in the daylight until recently. 'How was your cousin and her new baby?'

'What? Oh, lovely,' he answers absently. 'Yes, very cute. Hard to tell if it's a boy or a girl though, I always think when they're that small.'

'Yes, I s'pose so. I guess it helps if they're dressed either in blue or pink,' I suggest inanely. This is just so awkward. Darcy's brown eyes meet mine. Oh God, he's so impossibly good looking and slightly glowering. I don't care what anyone says, the brooding dark look definitely does it for me. Next thing he'll take me into his arms, kissing me passionately and...

'Yes quite, that always helps.' His matter-of-fact words jolt me out of my slightly bizarre musing. The shock and tiredness must be having a strange effect on me.

Matthew reappears. 'Hi, Sophie. Good, you're ready to go. I need to call in on Izzy's dad, explain to him properly. The line kept breaking up. He was obviously pretty shocked and... Oh, hello.' He stops abruptly as he notices Darcy.

'Matthew – this is Darcy, Darcy this is Matthew.' I make polite introductions, thinking how bizarre and awkward this whole situation is. Darcy eyes Matthew in a slightly hostile manner.

'Right, I think we should go. I'll drop you home on the way,' Matthew says, typing something frantically into his phone.

We walk away briskly, leaving Darcy staring after us. Goodness only knows what he thinks of me now, not that I care. It's just that my head and my heart seem to have totally different responses to the man.


THE NEXT MORNING I wake up with that horrible slightly sick feeling you get when you know something bad has happened, but you can't quite remember what. Then within seconds, it all comes flooding back to me. It was surreal really; Louisa and Izzy, both ill – what had they been doing? Mind you, Izzy has been a total mess since breaking with Josh – that boy has a lot to answer for. Also, my confused mind mulls over the events again, like they're in slow motion, what was Daniel doing there with the others and why did he dash off and leave them?

I check my mobile in case he messaged me but there's nothing. It's really bizarre the way he phoned and then disappeared like that. It doesn't add up at all.

I phone the hospital early and can't get much sense as I'm not next of kin. Fortunately, after a few tries, I reach Matthew on his mobile.

'Matthew – how's Izzy, have you any news?'

'Yes, I'm here now with her dad. She's going to be okay,' Matthew adds quickly, probably sensing my fear.

I breathe a huge sigh of relief and sit down shakily on the sofa. 'Has she got to stay in long?'

'A couple of days probably. She's had pretty severe alcohol poisoning so they will need to keep an eye on her. At least she's conscious and able to talk a little.'

'Has she explained what happened? Where she's been? I thought she was meant to be staying with her dad and stepmum?'

'No, apparently she was at Tamara's flat. Izzy didn't want to go home because things are difficult there. Also, I think she hoped if she stayed in London, she could somehow meet up with Josh.'

'God, don't mention that loser,' I mutter. 'If I ever meet him again, I'll be tempted to tell him what I think of him.'

'You and me both, though from what I hear, he needs to find himself someone wealthy; there's been rumours of gambling debts.'

'Doesn't make it right,' I snap. 'Izzy's still young and vulnerable, with no proper family, and he let her down badly.'

'I'm not going to disagree with you there,' Matthew replies with feeling. 'But I've been talking to her dad who's actually a really nice guy, by the way, just doesn't know how to cope with her or his new wife. The hospital has suggested some family counselling sessions which might help. Are you coming in to visit today?'

'Yes of course, I need to get to work but I'll call in after. Send Izzy my love and let me know if there is anything she needs.'

· · ·

I STRUGGLE through the morning on autopilot, going through the motions but feeling nothing. Probably partly because I had a really disturbed night with restless anxious dreams about Izzy being on a boat in the middle of a rough sea and I couldn't get to her. Doesn't take a psychologist to work out the meaning of that one.

AT LUNCHTIME I dash out into Oxford Street to grab a get well card and a huge fluffy teddy for Izzy. As I'm legging it down the street, clutching my purchases, my phone rings. It's Mel.

'Hi, Soph, just wanted to check you haven't forgotten the Regency Gaming Night?'

'Oh no! I had. When is it?'

'Tomorrow evening. Please say you'll still come.'

'I guess, it's just Izzy's in hospital and it's all been a bit of a nightmare.'

Mel's suitably shocked and I briefly outline the events of last evening. 'At least she's going to get help now. And what about Matthew? He sounds like he's genuinely really keen on her.'

'Yes, he was amazing last night, so calm. Hopefully Izzy might begin to see what a nice guy he is. Have you heard from Maria?'

'Yes, she left a garbled message about Louisa having an accident last night, but no details.'

'I know – I was there, she was with Izzy and Tamara. Apparently they'd been doing Jägerbombs and Louisa fell and gashed her head. Izzy was in a terrible state – it was a complete nightmare.' I recount the sorry tale as briefly as possible.

'Poor you. For once I'm almost glad I've just been here enjoying the pleasure of Rob's company.'

'How's that going?'

'Hmmm, I'll fill you in with the details when I see you tomorrow night. You *are* coming, aren't you?'

Mel rings off, having expertly extracted a promise from me to go to the Regency Gaming Night. I can't believe I'm such a soft touch; I really don't want to go, but can't let Mel down.

AFTER A STRUGGLE back into the office and an afternoon that seems to go on forever, I race for the tube at Oxford Circus as usual but get off at Paddington, wishing all the way up the usual rush-hour escalator scrum that I hadn't bought quite such a huge teddy. A couple of times I think I might fall back down as those impatient individuals who have to run past, because it's not going fast enough, nearly shove teddy and me back down again.

Just as I manage to reach the entrance at Paddington, my phone rings. It's Mum.

'Hello, Sophie, darling. Is that you?'

'Yes, Mum. Of course it's me.' *Who else would answer my phone?*

'I can't hear you very well, there's so much background noise. Are you at a party?'

'No. Paddington Tube Station.'

'Where?' She shouts even though she's the one struggling to hear. I can hear her perfectly.

'At the tube station, they're always noisy.'

'Can't you go somewhere quieter?' she snaps.

'Not really. I can phone you back later if you like, though it won't be for a while as I'm calling in at the hospital.'

'Why, you're not ill are you?' Mum always thinks the worst scenario.

'No, I'm visiting a friend who's ill. She became unwell on a night out yesterday evening and had to go to hospital.'

'Oh dear, she hasn't been doing drugs, has she?' My mum's been reading the paper again; *The Daily Mail* has a lot to answer for.

'No, she hasn't.'

'You can't be too careful.' Mum sniffs. 'You will watch yourself, won't you? And you know they can spike your drinks – I'll give you an article about it when you're next round. I really don't like you going out in London in the evening.'

*Or anywhere else for that matter*, I find myself silently adding.

'Anyway,' she continues glibly, 'I was wondering if you can come down soon? We're trying to plan a little family get together.'

'I'll see what I can do. Of course I'll come if I can.'

I manage to get off the phone before I drop either my bag, the teddy or my mobile.

THERE'S a foolish part of me that makes me look wistfully towards the signs to the Lindo Wing at St Mary's. I don't understand it, it's not like I want to see Darcy or anything. My life just doesn't go down that kind of path. Instead I follow the little red steps to Izzy's ward.

🐌

I'M RELIEVED to find she's propped up in bed, pale and wan, the drip still in her arm, but the fact she's conscious is a great relief, she had looked so deathly still last night. Matthew's standing by the bed, holding open an old book. He appears to be reading poetry.

'I must go down to the seas again, to the lonely sea and the sky,

'And all I ask is a tall ship and a star to steer her by.'

I stand listening, mesmerised, but Matthew notices my presence and stops, looking embarrassed. I could kick myself; I feel as though I have interrupted a special moment.

'Erm, hi – I just popped by to see how you're doing, Izzy, but I can come back in a while.' I turn awkwardly as though to go out the door again.

'No!' Izzy exclaims weakly. 'No, Sophie, please stay. I want to thank you for helping me last night.' She holds out her arms, I drop my stuff, bending to hug her awkwardly, and she starts crying.

'Hey, come on, you're okay now,' I murmur.

'I know,' she says half smiling, half crying. 'I'm such a mess. I didn't mean to put you all through this and I'm sorry I lied to you.'

'It's okay, Izzy, I understand.'

'No, you don't, I need to explain – it was because I wanted to go and confront Josh, so I bunked over with Tamara, but it all went wrong and...' Izzy starts crying again.

'Look, Izzy, it doesn't matter. The main thing is you're going to be okay, you've got all of us. You don't need Josh.'

She smiles weakly. 'I know I've been really stupid. And... anyway...' She catches Matthew's eye and stops. 'Matthew says he's going to stay with me till the end of the evening. I hate being in here but he's going to read to me. He's a big fan of John Masefield. I'd never heard of him but his poetry's dreamy. So full of passion.'

I glance at Matthew, who still looks embarrassed.

'The nurse has said I can stay late,' he smiles shyly, 'and if I'm very lucky I might get to share your hospital food! Mash potato and sausages, yum.'


AN HOUR OR SO LATER, I make my excuses to leave. Izzy's propped up, still looking fragile but a little more cheerful. My teddy is tucked in bed next to her and Matthew sitting on the other side, with his ready smile and comforting calmness and dependability. I think those two make a much better couple than Josh and Izzy ever did. He might be older, probably nearly forty, but I think maybe Izzy needs this steadiness. In any case, Josh doesn't deserve her after his behaviour.

·  ·  ·

IT'S REALLY late by the time I get home and I can't even be bothered to scratch around for dinner. The fridge looks horribly bare and the flat feels so empty. At times like this I still miss Mel. Then again, Izzy's coming home in a day or so and she's going to need plenty of looking after, so I won't have much time to miss anyone.

I slump down on the sofa, wondering if I should phone Chloe about the weekend. I haven't heard from her for ages. Since her black eye, we've barely spoken. It's as though there's this invisible barrier between us. I feel bad as I should probably call her, but I can't face speaking to Kian right now.

The front door bell goes. Great, who's that so late? I hope it's not my neighbour upstairs, who has a habit of going out and returning at stupid times, ringing the wrong doorbell. I peer cautiously through the spyhole. It's Maria.

I open the door in a hurry. 'What a lovely surprise. Come on in.'

'Are you sure you don't mind?' she asks, fiddling with her scarf.

'No, of course, come in and have a drink. I was feeling at a bit of a loose end actually, after all the drama.'

She takes off her jacket and we wander into the lounge.

'Yes, it's been a bit of a shock, hasn't it?' She sits gingerly on the edge of the sofa and I pass her a glass of wine and help myself to one. It's funny but it's always so much more sociable to eat and drink when there are two of you.

'How's Louisa?' I ask.

'She's going to be okay. Her head's pretty sore but it will heal and she may need crutches for a while till her ankle is stronger.'

Something about Maria's tone makes me feel she's ill at ease.

'Did Charles take her to her parents' place last night?' I ask tentatively.

'Yes, he said he did. He dropped me home on the way.'

There's a silence. I feel like there's something awkward going on here. It's not like Maria, she's normally shy but not with me.

'Is everything okay? You seem a little on edge. I know last night was pretty stressful but hopefully everyone's going to be okay.'

'I know, I mean it was very upsetting but yes, it's just...'

'Just what?'

'I need to talk to you, Soph.'

'Yes?' I reply, thinking we are talking. Or have I just gone into a parallel universe?

'About Daniel,' she blurts.

'Daniel?' I repeat stupidly.

'Yes, Daniel.' She speaks more firmly. 'He was there.'

'Last night.'

'Yes.' She pauses, seeming to struggle for the right words.

'I thought he was,' I say. 'In fact, I knew he was because he phoned me and told me about Izzy.'

'Oh,' Maria exhales, apparently relieved. 'You know then.'

'Know what?'

'That Daniel was at the club with Izzy and Louisa.'

'Yes, I know that,' I repeat, 'because he phoned me.'

'Oh,' Maria pauses for a moment, 'but did you know he was there on a date with another woman?'

# CHAPTER 25

There's a heavy silence as I digest the full meaning of Maria's words.

'Daniel's seeing someone else?' I repeat dumbly.

'It seems so. I'm really sorry, Sophie, but I felt I should tell you.' Maria's staring at me anxiously, as though I might burst into floods of tears any moment.

'I guess I'm a bit surprised, but actually it's okay.' And it is. I'm feeling a bit put out and shocked, but surprisingly not a lot else.

'What?'

I try inadequately to attempt to articulate what I'm feeling but it's proving difficult as I'm not sure exactly. I like Daniel but…

'I feel a bit cheated and maybe a little indignant about it, but I don't think I was in love with him. Who was he out with? Another woman from the agency?'

'I don't think she is. I haven't seen her before.'

'What's she like?' I ask.

'I'd like to say she's really ugly with no personality, but that would be lying.' I can see Maria's trying to choose her words carefully.

'You can tell me the worst,' I say with a bravado I don't feel.

'She's attractive in an obvious way, pretty but not naturally so. Fake eyelashes, fake hair extensions, fake boobs, you know the kind of thing.'

'Yes, I guess so,' I say sadly. Everything I'm not – perhaps I should have worked harder at it. Daniel's the only boyfriend I've had who was anything like normal.

'She was hard though, no nonsense, with thin lips. And she has money, you could tell by her clothes and high-maintenance appearance.'

'The opposite of me then.' I try to smile and fail.

'She wasn't half as lovely or nice as you. He obviously doesn't know what he's missing.'

I gulp and try to pull myself together. 'So, what was he doing with Izzy?'

'He wasn't with Izzy at all. Charles, Louisa, Tamara, Izzy and I all went out for a pizza. But you know what Tamara's like; she wanted to go on to a club and Louisa was all over it, living for the moment.'

'I know, she's always a bit full-on.'

'I did say I was worried and tired and that I would rather go home. Charles was very civil and offered to order me a cab but...'

'But?'

'I didn't want to leave Izzy on her own with Tamara as we all know how she is when she's had a few, and I was worried Izzy's been on the edge lately. She'd hardly eaten any dinner and had been drinking steadily on an empty stomach.' She takes a gulp of wine herself. 'And I feel like Charles is always judging me for being totally boring. He admires Louisa for her youthful exuberance, the fact she's never tired, never listens to anyone...' Maria breaks off, looking as though she might cry.

'Anyway, while we were in the club, the girls kept drinking, Charles too, and they all started having Jägerbombs. I refused, even though Louisa tried to persuade me.'

'Sounds like you were the only one with any sense,' I remark.

'They taste disgusting, like Calpol, not that I've ever tasted Calpol, but it smells like it.'

Maria cracks a small smile before continuing her story. 'While we were sitting there, Daniel and this girl came in, they went to the other end of the bar and he bought her a drink. He didn't recognise me... or if he did, he didn't say anything.'

She takes another sip of wine.

'Next thing, Louisa decided to go out the front for some air with Charles. Apparently she fell on the stairs while messing around, seeing how many steps she could jump down or something. You'd have thought he would have stopped her. I rushed to help as she'd gashed her head on the handrail and landed awkwardly on her ankle. While I was distracted with all this, Izzy must have passed out in the loos. Tamara had already disappeared off out the back a while before with some guy she'd just met, and didn't reappear.'

'That Tamara seems a total nightmare.'

'She's a bit of a one,' Maria agrees. 'Anyway, I guess Daniel must have seen Izzy was in a state and phoned you. Why he didn't come and find us, or look for her, I don't know.'

I can't stop myself from replying. 'Because he's a selfish moron. Quite honestly it all makes sense now, his rushing off and a woman's voice in the background.'

'I'm really sorry.' Maria puts her arm round me.

'It's okay, I feel pathetic somehow. I'm so rubbish with men. Why would someone like Daniel want to be with me?'

'Don't say that. You're too good for Daniel. He's a player, anyone can see that, he's obviously with this girl for the money.'

'I guess in the words of Elizabeth Bennet, handsome men must have something to live off as well as the plain ones.' I laugh cynically.

'But this isn't the eighteenth century, so he has no excuse except that he's a two-timing little shit.'

'Maria!' I've never heard her swear before. 'I suspected something was wrong as he hasn't exactly been contacting me much lately. I didn't really buy the busy-all-the-time line. Oh my gosh, I just thought of something!' I laugh.

'What?' Maria appears relieved to see me seeing the funny side of anything.

'Daniel's obviously a Wickham. I said I wanted one but maybe now I've found one, I've changed my mind.'

'Yes, I think he's about as useless as George Wickham in the novel.' Maria smiles. 'Hey, do you think he's making all that up about Darcy too, just like Wickham?'

'I don't know.' I stop and think about it for a moment. 'He's certainly good at lying. Whether that makes Darcy a nice person suddenly though, I'm not sure. He's still an arrogant stuck-up moron.' Then I remember he was quite kind the other evening offering me a lift home. 'Most of the time anyway,' I falter.

'You don't sound too sure. Sophie... I think maybe you rather like him, love and hate can be very similar emotions,' Maria suggests.

'Anyway,' I continue, hastily changing the subject, 'here I am moaning about my problems and ignoring yours. I guess Charles stayed at Louisa's house.'

'No, actually. It was very odd. Apparently he dropped Louisa home and then instead of going to check how she is, he's gone away for a couple of weeks. Matthew told me.'

'How bizarre. I thought he'd be round with bunches of flowers and apologies to her parents for not taking better care of her.'

'Apparently not, but he obviously likes her; they've been a couple at every agency event.'

'Maybe he's embarrassed and, being a typical man, is sticking his head in the sand.'

We sit and contemplate life for a moment.

'We are a sad pair, aren't we?' I smile wryly. My stomach

rumbles loudly and we laugh. I'm never very good without food. 'If you haven't had any dinner, would you like a takeaway?'

'I would, actually. I didn't really eat much today, all too stressful.' Maria smiles, looking more cheerful for the first time that evening.

AS IT HAPPENS, we have a nice relaxed girly night watching *Mamma Mia* for the hundredth time and stuffing ourselves with chicken chow mein. We both agree that if you can't go to Greece, it's the next best thing.

AFTERWARDS WE SIT AND CHAT, Maria telling me about her romance with Charles. By the end of the evening, I've concluded that her relationship with him had been the real thing, making Izzy's brief infatuation with Josh seem like a feather in the wind in comparison. I don't tell Maria this, for the simple reason that she already knows it and is bitterly regretful.

CHAPTER 26

'Good evening and welcome to our Regency Gaming Night,' announces Miss Palmer-Wright. 'Now, for those of you who are new to our exclusive little gatherings, tonight we will be playing Hazard, a well-known Regency game utilising two dice. Interestingly, the expression "to be at sixes and sevens", meaning to be in a state of chaos or agitation, derives from this game.'

'Sounds like me,' I remark to Mel who's standing nearby. 'I'm frequently in a state of chaos.'

We've made it to the dreaded Regency Gaming Night, although I had tried to pull out with the excuse that Izzy's only just been discharged from hospital and needs looking after. Unfortunately for the purposes of this excuse, Maria not only stayed over last night, but also kindly offered to sit with Izzy for me while I came to this lovely event. Actually, it was my suggestion that Maria stays round for a few days as I have to work and Izzy shouldn't be on her own. I think it's going to be really fun, like having a girly pyjama party. Or it would be if I didn't have to come to this tedious evening.

Tedious is the word that immediately springs to mind while listening to Jessica Palmer-Wright drone on and on about the

235

rules of the game. Games aren't really my thing and gambling is a definite no. In fact, one of my disastrous ex-boyfriends took me out for a twenty-four-hour booze cruise with his sister and her partner, which involved whiling away the long trip to France playing poker for pennies. I hated parting with every single penny I lost. (I obviously wasn't very good at it.) Sad, I know, as I think it was only a few pence at a time but I just can't cope with the fact you lose money you've earned – to be fair I was a student, so had very little at all – simply because you haven't got the right combination of cards or the required number on the dice. So, as you can tell, I am not exactly the right material for a gambler.

'If you would like to find your tables, all that remains is for me to wish you an enjoyable and lucrative evening.' Jessica Palmer-Wright concludes her little speech with a fake smile, which by its very nature defies anyone to enjoy themselves or to win.

Mel and I stand watching the scrum as people push their way towards the tables, shoving and jostling as if their lives depended on it. I stare incredulously, I had no idea this would be so serious; it's just a game.

The room itself is impressive, the exterior being a typical town house, the windows therefore are huge with thick velvet drapes. The tables are heavily decorated with wine-coloured cloths, the ceiling dripping with diamanté chandeliers. The ambience is opulent yet somehow dingy, the lights are dim and the place seems to me sort of gloomy and seedy.

I notice Rob is at a nearby table with Sir Richard Simms and a couple of old gentlemen I don't recognise.

'Talk about incestuous. I've heard about keeping it in the family but this agency seems a little too small and cosy for my liking,' I grumble.

'We've met some lovely people through it, look at Izzy and Maria,' Mel says.

'That's true, I wouldn't be without either of them, they're fab.'

'And where would I be without Rob?'

'Not at a bloody Regency gambling evening,' I mutter. 'How's it going with the business anyway?'

'Pretty darn good. I've finished borrowing the dresses and Mark's going to safely return them to Lady Constance. I'll have to burn some midnight oil dreaming up impressive new designs. Now I know what's already been done, I can get creating some groundbreaking stuff.'

'Sounds fab.' I'm really pleased for Mel, she deserves this. I know how hard she works and how talented she is. She's every bit as good as the designers at work, yet it's all about getting that lucky break. 'How are you coping with Rob,' I lower my voice, 'you know, on a personal level?'

Mel looks a bit embarrassed. 'His demands aren't that many – he spends a lot of time at chess tournaments and when he's not doing that, he's at work or running after Sir Richard or Lady Constance. I think I'm more like a trophy wife or something – in fact, I sometimes wonder if he's gay. He certainly doesn't show much interest anymore, but that suits me.'

I'm almost speechless. 'But, Mel, you can't be satisfied with that kind of relationship, surely?'

'I am, actually. Anyway, it suits me for now while I sort myself out. You've no idea how hard it is to have a dream and not be able to fulfil it.'

'That's what you think,' I mutter. My dreams are so unrealistic I think I've stopped dreaming about them.

We're interrupted by the appearance of Jessica Palmer-Wright. 'Would you like to find a table, ladies?' she asks patronisingly.

'Erm, we're happy watching for a moment,' I say politely with a smile.

'Nonsense, you must join in, that is the best way to learn.

And…' she leans in conspiratorially, 'it's one of the rules of the evening that all attendees must play.'

'Of course.' I surreptitiously glare at Mel.

'We were just choosing a table,' Mel says, grabbing my arm and propelling me towards the one nearest.

'What are you doing?' I hiss.

'Getting you out of trouble. Let's join this group.'

We push our way into the circle of players around the game.

To my alarm, I'm standing opposite, in fact have come face to face with Daniel. I automatically look away, hoping he hasn't spotted me, then glance up again to meet his piercing blue eyes. He has the grace to go a little red. I smile at him out of habit and he grins back.

'Sophie, how are you doing?' he asks, sounding the same as he always has, no real embarrassment evident in his tone. 'Come and join me.'

'Fine, thank you. Been busy, you know.' I don't know what I'm trying to do; prove that I've been too engrossed in my work to notice that he's been off with another woman? I push through the throng to stand next to him and he reaches over and kisses me on the cheek. He's as cute as ever, but I don't feel anything being so close. He reminds me of a spoilt and good-looking young lad who has no real substance, he simply hasn't grown up yet.

'I hear you're going out with the very glamorous Wynter Trent?' I ask diffidently.

'You must hate me.' He has the grace to look embarrassed.

'Not really,' I reply, and actually mean it.

'Mr Becks?' The caller points out that it's Daniel's turn to throw the dice. He throws them in a much-practiced manner.

'Chance,' the caller says. 'You can throw again.'

Daniel throws the dice once more, getting a seven and a three. The caller tells him he can re-throw. I don't understand this game at all. At the next throw, Daniel is out. I can tell he's annoyed but he tries to cover it.

'Did you lose much?' I ask casually.

'Not really, and I won over a grand last time anyway.'

I've just taken a large sip of my wine and nearly choke. 'A grand?' I had no idea anyone bet anything like that kind of money at these dos. Then again, maybe I am being a bit naïve, looking around the room at the hugely expensive Rolex and Tag Heuer watches on display. I should have realised this was a big pull. That's what Izzy had said; a lot of rich guys enjoy gambling – of course they're not here for Regency romance, are they?

At that moment, none other than Josh wanders up with a couple of glasses of fizz, one of which he passes to Daniel before he sees me. He casts a stricken look at Daniel, then back at me.

'Hello er, Sophie,' he bleats.

'Josh.' I barely acknowledge him, wondering if he realises what he's done to Izzy.

'How's everything?' he asks politely.

'Been a bit stressful actually,' I snap.

'Work troubles?' Daniel suggests casually.

'No, I've been in hospital the last couple of days visiting Izzy.'

'What?' Josh spills his drink all over the table and a couple of bystanders.

'Watch out, mate,' a well-dressed man to his right scowls.

'Sorry, look, Daniel, mate, hold my place, I need to talk to Sophie.'

I'm not sure I want to listen to him, but it looks as though I have no choice. We walk out into the foyer, which seems to be pretty deserted.

'I feel I owe you an explanation, but how's Izzy? What happened? You said she's in hospital... Is she going to be okay?' Josh is genuinely distressed. Maybe he does care for her after all.

'She's out of hospital now and going to be okay.'

Josh audibly breathes a sigh of relief.

'But no bloody thanks to you.' I feel so angry, I don't want to give him a break. 'She's young and trusting, no proper family to help her through this and you picked her up for a bit of fun, and then cast her aside when you found something different.'

'Is that what you think happened? That's not it at all. I did genuinely love her, I do love her. It's just…'

'Just what? You can't keep your pants on? Someone else came along and forced you to go out with them?' I'm on a roll now.

'No, if you'd listen, I can explain.' Okay, so maybe I am getting a bit carried away. I let the man speak.

'When I first met Izzy, I really liked her and thought it was fun hanging out with her.' I snort disbelievingly. 'Can I finish?' I let him carry on. 'I could see she was fragile and lovely and over time I fell in love with her, I figured this was the woman I wanted to spend the rest of my life with.'

'So, what went wrong?'

'My debts.'

There's a silence.

'They can't be that bad,' I say briskly. 'What's that got to do with Izzy?'

'The thing is, they are that bad, like tens of thousands of pounds, so I needed to get money fast. My boss's daughter, Cara, is wealthy and has had a thing for me for a long time. So, I agreed to go out with her. She lent me money; I told myself it was just temporary. I hoped to go back to Izzy and explain but as time went on, things got more and more complicated.'

'So you left her heartbroken, ignored her texts, let her screw herself into the ground over you?'

'No… that is yes. I did reply to a couple of her texts but Cara found them on my phone. She went nuts, wrote a really bitchy message to Izzy saying it was all over and then made me promise never to contact her again. I was devastated but there was nothing I could do; I owe so much money.'

Phew, this is all a bit heavy but I must admit, in spite of myself I almost feel sorry for Josh.

'So, what are you going to do now?'

'I'm going to win it back.'

'You're what? You must be nuts. Hazard, even though I don't know much about it, is a game of chance. There's a bit of tactic in choosing which number to start the bet on, but other than that people have lost whole fortunes on the throw of a dice.' Josh stares at me dumbly. I continue, 'I don't mean now, I mean historically, in Jane Austen's time anyway.'

'But I've already won a couple of grand.'

'Yes, but how much have you lost?' I'm so exasperated with him.

'A few hundred, but I'll win it back.' I stare at him impatiently. 'And I'll win Izzy back too, I just need time.'

'No you bloody don't. You're to leave the poor girl alone. If you'd been honest with her about the money from the start, you might have had a chance. She loved you and maybe you could have worked something out, but the underhand way you've gone about borrowing more money from Cara, going out with her for financial reasons and now gambling, getting into more and more debt. Quite honestly, you, Josh, are the last thing Izzy needs.'

We stare at each other angrily.

'I know what's going on,' he says suddenly. 'It's that Matthew chap who was sniffing around before.' Josh gives a bitter laugh. 'Poor bloke, he's wasting his time there; she'll be back to me as soon as I click my fingers.'

'Matthew's a nice guy, and more to the point, he's been there for Izzy, instead of messing her about,' I say firmly.

'If she's happy with old and boring that's fine by me,' he snaps, reminding me of a particularly unpleasant spoilt little boy. 'Daniel's looking for me. I expect it's my turn, you'll have to excuse me.'

Josh stalks off towards the gaming room. Then he turns back to me. 'But you'll tell her, won't you? I'd like you to explain if she'll listen.' His eyes are like a spaniel's; sad and pleading.

'I'll do my best,' I say and he walks away.

# CHAPTER 27

I spend the rest of the evening in a daze, watching the proceedings of the gambling night as though I'm trapped in a bubble, far removed from what's going on. For a start, I really don't understand the rules of Hazard. The only thing I can see about it is that it is a hazard playing it, due to the serious amounts of money won and lost. No wonder people in the old days squandered whole estates by gambling. Before this evening I used to be confused as to how something so outlandish might have happened, but having been at the Regency Gaming Night, I finally understand. It's like a drug to these people, there's an air of expectancy, excitement, it's electric, almost palpable, people laughing and joking, drinking steadily, the excited rattle of the dice and the 'oh's and 'ah's when someone dares higher and higher stakes.

'Oh for goodness sake, not again!' a loud voice grumbles. It's Rob who's obviously been losing steadily all evening. Mel whispers something in his ear, but he just bets a higher stake and goes again. He's going to be sulking the whole way home.

'Not playing, I see.' Jessica Palmer-Wright notices my inertia and accosts me in the doorway.

'Not at the moment. Is Emma not here?'

'No, she never comes to the gaming nights, not really her thing. Can't think why, I simply love them.'

I can see that. Jessica Palmer-Wright is in her element, flitting from one table to the next, leaning provocatively over the tables, flirting with this man and that, all expensive-looking city types. Certain individuals seem to get royal treatment, striding in as though they own the place, with personal bodyguards and Jessica Palmer-Wright signalling to a private butler to serve them with plenty of drinks and hors d'oeuvres. I have to say she is damn good at this job, acting like a 1940s society hostess.

'Madam!' a smart-looking butler attracts her attention with a low bow. 'You are required in the salon.'

'Oh yes, of course.' Jessica expertly excuses herself and sashays out of the room.

I watch her go, fascinated. I have to give this woman points for flair, even if I hate her whole attitude. While I'm observing, my attention's caught by the back view of a familiar tall, dark-haired lady who sweeps past the foyer and is ushered through a doorway. Miss Palmer-Wright glances behind her surreptitiously, following her into the room, and firmly closes the door.

I'm confused at who I thought I saw because I'm sure I recognised her. No, it's impossible... but it looked like Natasha from Editorial at Modiste. It can't have been.

'You all right?' Mel's managed to escape the grumblings of Rob for a moment.

'Yes, no, I mean – I could have sworn I just saw Natasha from work with Jessica Palmer-Wright.'

'Perhaps you did. It wouldn't be that weird, would it?'

'It is a bit because she isn't a member of The Jane Austen Dating Agency and I'm sure you have to be to attend events. Also, she doesn't really know Jessica Palmer-Wright that well.'

'I thought you said she was at that dinner you went to at Natasha's house.'

'She was, but I thought Miffy had invited her. They were getting on pretty well though.'

'For f***'s sake, this thing is bloody rigged!'

We look as Rob angrily pushes his chair back from the table so hard it falls on the floor. He takes the caller by the scruff of the neck and shoves him against the wall.

'For God's sake, Rob, leave him alone, it's just a game.' Mel dashes across the room and pulls on Rob's arm. He's such a weakling he's soon overpowered long before the security guards grab him.

'THAT WAS EMBARRASSING,' I say in the taxi on the way home, wondering for the millionth time how Mel puts up with this nerd.

'I tell you it was rigged; they'd done something with the dice,' Rob blurts, then promptly passes out.

'He never was good with his drink,' Mel says drily. 'He'll probably wake up with one hell of a hangover and then act as though nothing happened.'

'Is he often like this?' I ask. 'I don't know how you put up with him.'

'Fingers crossed it's not for much longer.' She smiles and I hope she's right. Personally, for me, a little of Rob goes an awfully long way.

IZZY'S ASLEEP when I get back but Maria has waited up.

'I hope you don't mind but Matthew dropped in tonight,' she says diffidently.

'Of course not, he's always welcome and he's very attentive.' I smile.

'Yes, Izzy seemed a whole lot more cheerful this evening and he's left her a book of John Masefield's poetry to read. Apparently they're going to discuss it tomorrow.'

'How romantic.' I pause for a second to sigh. I don't know how Izzy does it; attracting two handsome poetry-reading guys in a few weeks, when I can't even find one.

'How did your evening go? Was it as bad as you expected?' Maria asks.

Briefly I recount the happenings of the soiree, keeping the bit with Daniel especially short as I really don't want to talk about him, he's such a waste of space. We discuss the situation with Josh at length, however. Maria's still angry about his behaviour but sorry for him at the same time.

'It sounds like he loves her really.'

'Do you think we should tell her? I don't want to upset her again,' I ponder aloud.

Izzy wanders in, rubbing her eyes blearily. She looks touchingly young in her fluffy rabbit onesie. 'Tell me what?'

Maria and I exchange glances.

'I saw Josh this evening,' I say carefully. Of course I tell her the details of our conversation as gently as I can. Maria and I are both almost holding our breath, hoping this isn't going to set her back.

'I guess at least I can take comfort from the fact he does love me,' she says weakly after an uncomfortably long silence.

'Of course, that's true,' says Maria.

'But not enough,' Izzy continues.

'He's just a very mixed up young man who's in rather a lot of trouble,' Maria says sensibly.

'I guess, and who's to say he would have been happy with me? I reckon he's the kind of guy who's always going to struggle with money, gambling and stuff.'

'I think you're right.' I smile encouragingly at her. 'And anyway, more excitingly, I hear the gorgeous Matthew was here all evening reading to you.'

'Yes.' Izzy gives a watery smile. 'In fact, I promised him I would check out the poems he brought for me. I'd better get reading the rest; I want to ask him about something in one of them.'

'I'll bring you a hot chocolate,' I call as she disappears back to her room.

'She took that well.' Maria heaves a sigh of relief. 'By the way, Emma phoned while you were out.'

'Oh?' I pour milk into three mugs.

'She wanted to tell you about a seminar or something. She certainly seemed surprised you were at the Regency Gambling Night, didn't think it was your thing.'

'It certainly isn't,' I remark with feeling.

# CHAPTER 28

The next day I'm back at work and it's a bit of a relief. In spite of my tiredness – I think I was on autopilot on the tube this morning and was almost surprised when I got to work so quickly – I'm ready to kick butt. As soon as I arrive at Modiste House, I mount the stairs with purpose and stride onto the sales floor as though I'm someone, instead of my usual apologetic bumbling entrance.

'Morning, Sheena, Gina, Kelli, Caitlin – good weekend?' I breeze past casually.

Once at my desk, I rearrange my sales folder. Today I'm going to sell a lot of advertising space, I can do this. I flick past my embarrassing trickle of sales from the previous week and pick a fresh page with columns neatly laid out.

Suddenly I notice Heidi's desk is empty. 'Heidi not here yet?' I ask, surprised; she's always incredibly punctual.

The girls exchange conspiratorial looks, then Caitlin nods to Gina. She sneaks up to my desk, having taken a quick peek to see if Amanda is around. 'Heidi's quit,' Gina says in an excited whisper.

'What, just like that?'

'Yes, you missed all the drama – as you're always late.' Gina rolls her eyes at the listening sales team.

'Actually, I was on time this morning.'

'Yes, but, darling, the rest of us always get here at eight,' Caitlin bitches, self-satisfied as ever. The girls titter. As far as I'm concerned I've always been told the day starts at nine and that's the way it is. Besides, my train doesn't get in till 8.50am.

'So, what happened?' I ask.

'She rang up this morning and spoke to Amanda. I thought Heidi must have phoned to say she's sick, but Amanda spent some time talking to her on the phone. Amanda sounded quite upset. Anyway, Sheena happened to be walking past to get to the stationery cupboard and overheard that Heidi's left.' Gina has the satisfied smirk of a newspaper reporter with an exclusive.

Amanda sails in… 'Girls!' she exclaims loudly, 'I thought you would all be on the phones by now. The weekend is over, you know.'

Gina scuttles away to her desk like a startled rabbit and the others immediately pretend to be busy and in the middle of something.

'While I have your attention, darlings, I'm sorry to announce that Heidi has left us.' Amanda's tone makes it sound as though Heidi is a soldier who has defected to the enemy camp. The fake sad expressions of the rest of the sales team are so insincere I have to bite my lip to prevent myself from laughing. It's a good job Mark isn't in the room, because I would lose it completely.

'This of course is a great pity, but Heidi was obviously not aware of the incredible opportunity Modiste represents, so it is her loss.'

I gasp audibly and have to turn it into a pretend cough. Heidi's quite a nice girl, certainly a darn sight better than the rest of the team and a hard worker; she was at Modiste when we joined. In fact, she's the only one who's ever been vaguely kind to me. I'm sorry she's left. She never seemed fed up or unhappy but then you never know, she must have hidden it well.

I crack on with the sales calls, zinging through the list in a businesslike manner, even taking it cheerfully on the chin when Tina from Brides at Home tells me in no uncertain terms that she doesn't need to advertise, but phrasing it in a very uncouth way as to where I should stick the magazine and slams down the phone.

I don't know why I'm so much more positive this morning, I guess it's because after the recent events I realise that none of it really matters, not in the same way as being in hospital or really ill. I mean, it's just a job. Suddenly I feel sorry for the rest of the team, constantly striving for supposed physical and fashionable perfection. For some reason today, it seems petty and somehow irrelevant.

MID MORNING, I wander off to grab my coffee, carefully managing to avoid the rest of the team who are bound to be having a bitch somewhere, holding a post-mortem on why Heidi left and whether she was told to go. Mark is out on a course so I'm missing our usual gossip. If he weren't at Modiste, I don't think I'd have made it this long.

I'm idly sitting flicking through my e-mails on my iPhone when a message pops up from Darcy Drummond. It's entitled *Just wanted to say...* How bizarre, I didn't even know he has my e-mail address.

For no apparent reason, I surreptitiously check no-one is watching as I quickly click on the message. Oh my gosh, it's really long. For a moment I panic, thinking he's asking me to leave the agency, so hurriedly scan the screen.

*Dear Sophie,*

*Please don't think I'm stalking you or asking you to go out with me again, or anything like that. It's just that when we spoke the other day, I didn't get a chance to explain some of the things you're so angry about.*

*Firstly with regard to your sister, Chloe, I could tell right from the start Nick really liked her. While I could see that she obviously enjoyed being with him, I assumed she wasn't really interested as she's married. In fact, it is against regulations for anyone to attend agency events if they are married, or in a long-term relationship, for obvious reasons. I notice she hasn't been at any others since the ball, so will let this pass without repercussion, but you can understand that for a professional agency such as ours, we can't be mixed up in divorce cases and being sued for being an accessory to the fact.*

(Oh, typical pompous Darcy. Who the hell does he think he is, a divorce lawyer?)

*Nick on the other hand, I could tell was pretty smitten and therefore thought it best to remove him from the situation. I haven't got any other apology to make about this – it was the right thing to do, that's all there is to it.*

(I scowl at the screen, this guy is so full of himself it's not true.)

*As for Daniel, I've known him since I was a kid, we used to hang out together as teenagers but knowing him as well as I do, I can honestly tell you he's a born liar. I don't know what crap fabricated story he has given you, but I suspect he's been making me out to be the bad guy.*

*When my father was alive, he was very fond of Daniel and took pleasure in overseeing his upbringing as he came from a very deprived home. As part of the charitable causes supported by Drummond Associates, my father arranged for Daniel to be included in the apprenticeship scheme. I know his background was maybe against him, but he had every opportunity to improve his chances in life. It soon became apparent to me, however, that he was prone to late-night drinking binges, getting himself involved in fights and general bad behaviour. This side of his life he managed to keep away from my father and I felt it was not my place to disillusion him. In any case, it would have just looked like jealousy.*

Dad was impressed with Daniel's "transformation" and pleased with his metamorphosis into polite society. He maintained this belief right to the end of his life, therefore leaving in his will instruction for Daniel to join our business at management level. I had my doubts about this as Daniel's background was so different, his mentality so unsuited to corporate city life, but I honoured my father's wishes and tried to welcome him to the company. At first, Daniel appeared to attempt to fit in, attending meetings and turning up punctually, but as time went on, huge cracks began to show. Daniel took issues into his own hands, he got on the wrong side of the board members who have been here for years and know the system inside and out.

I won't go into details but worse still, Daniel acted in a completely unethical way on a large deal with Branscombe Holdings, going behind the board's back and causing us not only to lose face publicly, but the eventual loss of the deal. It was the cause of a major PR disaster and required a lot of covering up. This of course had no other possible conclusion other than his appearance before a tribunal and his immediate dismissal. I admit in this maybe I could have tried to intervene, perhaps even plead his case and inexperience, but I could not bring myself to do so. I must admit this gives me an occasional twinge of conscience, but it is too late to do anything about it so I have no more to say on the matter.

I believe Daniel went off to work for various shoddy companies of a dubious nature, at the same time as getting himself a really bad reputation with women, drink and drugs. He also racked up numerous gambling debts in his spare time. He has stayed out of my way until now. When I discovered he had joined the dating agency, it was a horrible shock. He can only be attempting some kind of revenge against me. I have consulted with Jessica Palmer-Wright on the matter, but unfortunately he was allowed to join by Emma Woodtree who obviously was not aware of his history. As you know, Daniel can be very charming and persuasive when he wishes.

I realise this e-mail is more like one of your novels (Don't I know it, I think), but I wanted you to understand where I am coming from *and to realise that just as Daniel is not totally blameless, neither am I as black and heartless as you seem to think.*

*As far as our relationship goes, we're polar opposites and you can't expect me to have chosen to be with someone who is so naively prejudiced against the world of business. Your background is very different from mine so it's not something you can understand. If it weren't for companies like ours, the city would not exist. Business, not love, really does make the world go round.*

*I hope your friends have recovered and everything is going well for you. And just for the record, your mum and Mel are right; I believe you can do so much better for yourself than Modiste.*

*With very best wishes,*

*Darcy Drummond*

❧

I SIT and stare blankly at my phone; my head is whirling. Darcy really is a totally arrogant piece of work. How dare he decide whether Chloe should be in the agency or not? Though to be fair, the sensible part of me does see some kind of sense in this. I really hate being able to see other people's point of view, it makes life so complicated.

As for Daniel, hmmm, seems like he is George Wickham to the very core. Why on earth couldn't I have seen through his lies earlier? I'm no smarter than Lydia Bennet. I know I thought it would be better than nothing to go out with a Wickham, but quite honestly, he is no different from the other sad losers in my dating history.

I guess it was kind of Darcy to try to explain about Daniel, but his arrogance shines through every word. To be fair he has a privileged background and no idea what it would be like if his and Daniel's situations were reversed, perhaps he too would be out drinking and gambling. I try to imagine Darcy in low-cost housing and fail.

What does he mean by saying I can do better for myself than Modiste? I guess that is a compliment of sorts, but the patronising way he says I don't understand business. Hah, he's right, I don't understand it and I don't bloody want to either.

I suddenly realise I've been some time sitting staring at my phone and that I'd better get back to work.

THE REST of the morning goes in a blur, and in spite of an unexpected sale to a small bridal shop in Cork, my misguided joie de vivre from earlier has disappeared.

I wander out to lunch, avoiding the sales team, and traipse aimlessly round the shops in Oxford Street. It's depressing, I can't afford any of the designer clothes so I don't know why I'm looking. I still don't fit into this glitzy world of glamorous purposeful-looking people, all walking as though they know where they are going. Instead I just feel like I'm drifting, struggling and bobbing about, like a rowing boat in a sea of sun-seekers and million-dollar yachts.

Suddenly my phone rings, making me rummage about in my bag. A shop assistant glares at me suspiciously. I grab the phone and leave the store, their clothes were pretty weird anyway.

'Hi, Sophie, it's Emma. How's it going?' Her bright cheery tone contrasts starkly with my gloomy mood.

'Fine thanks,' I reply automatically, trying to put some zing into my voice. I look about the crowded street for somewhere quiet to talk. I end up cutting down Holles Street and into Cavendish Square Gardens where I gratefully sink onto a bench.

'I'm sorry to hear about Daniel,' Emma says sympathetically. 'I really owe you an apology.'

'Why would you apologise to me?'

'I kind of feel as though it was my fault as I matched you with him. All I can say is, I didn't know what he's like, otherwise I wouldn't have let him into the agency, let alone suggest him as your partner.'

'You know me, if I can attract a weirdo or loser, I will,' I joke sadly.

'I just hope it hasn't upset you too much.'

'No, actually, at one time I really liked him but there was no real spark, so I'm okay.'

'Are you sure? I feel so terrible about it,' she whispers conspiratorially. 'Jessica was furious about me letting him into the agency. Apparently he used to know Darcy – they have some long-standing feud. I don't know how I was supposed to know, he obviously didn't put that on his application form!'

'I wouldn't worry about it.' I laugh lightly. 'It seems to be it's pretty much impossible not to fall foul of Jessica Palmer-Wright and Darcy Drummond. In fact, wouldn't they make a perfect couple!'

'Oh, didn't you know? Darcy's engaged to be married to Hattie, Lady Constance's daughter.'

There's a silence and somewhere deep inside, within some traitorous part of me, I feel a sense of hollow emptiness.

'Darcy's engaged?' I repeat stupidly, recalling Lady Constance's keenness for them to get together at the garden party. 'But I thought... well, it doesn't matter.'

'Yes, they're old family friends, so it's a fait accompli. Mind you, he's generally surrounded by a string of heiresses and she is usually at horsey events with a roguish Rupert Campbell Black-type character in tow, but hey ho, people are all different.'

'Yes, that's true.' I recover my equilibrium. This is silly, I don't like Darcy anyway, he's an arrogant bastard. I'm probably just hoping that little message at the end of his e-mail means he still sort of admires me, because it makes a change from the ego-bashing crowd I usually end up pulling. People like him live by a different social code. Who am I to understand the lives of rich businessmen, or country estate heiresses for that matter?

This is not *Pride and Prejudice* and I'm not Elizabeth Bennet. I'm only Sophie Johnson, from a sleepy seaside town on the south coast. Where do I fit in? I don't belong here. These questions keep coming to me and shrieking louder and louder until I want to run and hide like a child, safely back in the world of storybooks.

'Anyway,' Emma continues, 'other than apologising to you for my mess up with Daniel, I wanted to mention something which might make up for it.'

'Sounds intriguing.'

'Yes, we're holding our annual conference on "Love and Romance in Austen" at Chatsworth House in a couple of weeks and wondered if you would like to be included.'

'Oh gosh, yes – it sounds amazing. Is it over a weekend? Do you have a programme of events and stuff?'

'Of course, you should have had an e-mail about it but our system's been playing up. I'll flick you across another copy. It is over a weekend but obviously you need to allow time to travel up. I don't know if Maria and Izzy are coming – I've sent them an e-mail but have had no reply yet. Mel can't come as she's working towards her first exhibition or something.'

'I know, I'm so pleased for her – this is her chance to really show off her creations. You won't have heard from Izzy and Maria because there was a bit of an incident last week.' I don't like to go into too much detail with Emma as she might be worried hearing that Izzy got into such a state, so I briefly recount her hospital visit, saying she had become unwell. Emma is concerned to hear the story but is not one for sad tales so we soon return to more cheerful topics.

As Emma continues chatting about The Jane Austen Dating Agency conference, I idly watch a pair of pigeons near my feet, bowing and cooing at each other in their comical courtship dance. The sun breaks through the cloud and I'm bathed in a shaft of light, the shadows dappling through the branches of the trees.

A short stay at Chatsworth House and a nice escapist conference on love and romance Austen style? Perhaps things aren't so bad after all. Darcy can keep his reality and world of business acquisitions and mergers. I'm ready to escape back into the reassuring world of Jane Austen.

# CHAPTER 29

A couple of weeks later, I'm happily sitting on a very elegant sofa within a beautiful room, sipping some really delicious coffee. This is the life.

'So, this would have been the morning itinerary for the mistress of a great house such as Chatsworth, or indeed the mistress of Pemberley.' A bespectacled lady, Professor someone or other, enthusiastically explains to us. 'Of course, women wore morning dress and, having either dined in their room or at a breakfast table with a variety of dishes including kippers and smoked salmon, would adjust their toilette, ready to come into this room to receive visitors as we are doing now.'

I smile across at Maria, who's also enjoying the surroundings. Izzy, I'm pleased to see, is helping herself to a tiny pain au chocolat and munching away happily. She looks fragile still but has more glow in her cheek than previously. All thanks to a certain person, I think satisfactorily. Matthew has proved to be a total rock these past couple of weeks, constantly round with little thoughtful gifts, everything designed to take Izzy's mind off things. He has been unable to get here this morning but is coming along later for the evening dinner.

.   .   .

THE DAY so far has been bliss. We arrived at the station of Matlock quite late last night, the journey from London having been hard work as the train was packed out of Waterloo. The twenty-minute bus journey with all our luggage and the baleful stares of the local farming community was also somewhat of an endurance test. But the cottage on the Chatsworth Estate more than made up for it. Some thoughtful person had put out a welcome pack with Bakewell tart, hot chocolate and a nice cold bottle of white in the fridge. My idea of a perfect combination. There had even been a roaring real fire in the grate, so all that had been left for us to do was to unpack, eat and chat, or read our latest fave books.

This morning had been a leisurely start, with Emma greeting us warmly over breakfast like old friends. We were then ushered through to the red drawing room for a seminar with Professor Stafford about Austen and life in a great house.

The talk is an hour or so and very interesting. It feels so much more real somehow being in an actual stately home where, if not Jane Austen, certainly other Regency women would have lived out this lifestyle. In fact, I get a kind of buzz thinking that Jane Austen, like me, would have visited this house as an outsider, an interloper, but she could at least dip in and sample its delights, even if she had to return to the real world, in her case, of genteel poverty and spinsterhood, and reliance on her male relations, and in my case, a rubbish job in sales, an overbearing mother, and a string of hopelessly failed romances, if you could even call them that.

WE ALL HAVE lunch in the great dining hall; haricot mutton, which was apparently one of the dishes served at the dinner table in Regency days. It's actually very pleasant. Emma eats with us and we fill her in on recent events.

'It sounds as though The Jane Austen Dating Agency is providing some mixed results,' she says pensively.

'I'm very happy with it.' Izzy smiles shyly. 'I wouldn't have met Matthew if it hadn't been for the agency and he's so kind to me. I can't imagine life without him now.'

'That's true,' Emma says, smiling at Izzy's naïve happiness, 'and there's Mel and Rob.' She's met with an awkward silence at this.

'This seminar is lovely, we're all really enjoying it,' Maria says reassuringly.

'Definitely,' I add, 'and I can't wait to wander around this afternoon.'

The door to the dining room opens and a windswept Charles blunders in. 'Sorry I'm late,' he says breathlessly.

Maria looks up, sees him and quickly looks down again, blushing.

Emma, noticing their awkwardness, jumps to her feet and pulls up a chair for Charles opposite Maria with the grace of a true hostess. 'That's okay, Charles. You're very welcome, you did say you might be late.' Emma passes him a plate.

'Journey up was terrible,' he grumbles, helping himself liberally to new potatoes, mutton and haricot beans.

'Oh, did you drive then?' I ask, to cover the awkward silences.

Maria seems to have buried her head in her dinner and is not looking up.

'Yes, I did.' He glances at Maria. 'It was kind of a last-minute decision. Matthew's with me too, he's stopped off at our B & B to sort out arrangements.'

Izzy looks up with delight. 'Oh, he's here already?' she squeaks. 'He said he wouldn't get here till this evening.'

'I expect he wanted to surprise you,' I say, smiling.

·  ·  ·

AFTER LUNCH, we all decide to wander through the house, Izzy and Matthew going on ahead, arm in arm so they are very much on their own. Maria and I follow at a discreet distance, and I can't help but think about the Regency Ball. Although there are about thirty people on the course, they've all dispersed, and Chatsworth is so vast, it feels as though we have it all to ourselves. This huge silent staring house is a stark contrast to the floodlit shimmering splendour of the ball at Pemberley, crammed with people in elegant dresses and hustle and bustle.

'I think you could rattle about living somewhere like this,' I whisper. 'It's almost unnatural how quiet and echoey it is.'

'I suppose you get used to it, and of course they would have had lots of servants,' Maria says.

'Maria, Sophie, wait up!' We turn to see Charles jogging after us and stop for him to approach. Maria looks instantly uncertain.

'Maria, I wanted to talk to you,' he says shyly. 'If that's okay with you, Sophie?'

'Of course. I want to go and check out the Sculpture Room anyway,' I say hurriedly. I definitely don't want to get in the way of this. I wonder what Charles has to say. Maria is such a lovely person and they were obviously destined to be together, until Sir Henry got involved.

'Sophie.' Maria grabs my arm.' You don't have to go, we'll walk with you.'

'No,' I say firmly, 'I'd like some chill-out time on my own if you don't mind.' I walk determinedly away. I'm telling the truth; I actually feel like I do need some time on my own. All these couples and the talk of romance and relationships this morning, it's made me realise and maybe see things a little more in perspective.

At least it's not like in Jane Austen's day, I don't need to find a husband or partner as my only choice of a career. I can do anything, anything I choose. And suddenly the day becomes brighter, and I enter the Sculpture Room happier and ready to be impressed in a sort of calm soulful way.

Nothing could have prepared me for the wonder of this place, it's simply beautiful. The sun shines down through the glass roof and onto the dazzling white marble. The enormous white statues are life-size, almost like a scene from Narnia but not creepy or deteriorated, just beautiful, smooth Italianate. I move soundlessly from one to the next, gazing at their simple beauty. These sculptures have captured expression and mood so beautifully and I'm transfixed. In my head, I wonder about the story behind each figure, who made them, what they were feeling.

I gaze, lost in thought, when suddenly I hear a noise and before I can quite register who or what it might be, Darcy comes into view and walks towards me.

'Darcy!' I mutter, feeling foolish, not knowing how long he's been here. I hope he didn't think I was weird standing there gawping at statues. Not that I care, because I don't like him anyway.

'Sophie,' he says. 'All alone?'

'Yes, I thought I'd take a stroll for a moment to get some headspace. You know, it's all been a bit hectic.' I stop, realising I'm burbling.

'Oh right,' he says, and there's silence again. He's looking at me with those deep brown eyes and I can't cope with it, he's too intense, it's making my heart race and my legs feel like someone else's. Not a good sign. *Sophie, get a grip, girl.*

'These are very… impressive.' I sweep an arm vaguely in the direction of the nearby sculptures.

Darcy follows my arm with his eyes. Unfortunately I'm gesturing at a prostrate figure of a naked man, who is quite frankly extremely well endowed.

'Very…' Darcy says seriously, his eyes meeting mine once more and I could swear his mouth curves up slightly at one corner. The tension, the atmosphere between us, is electric, it practically crackles. It's as though everything else has disappeared and there's no-one in existence but us. I'm mesmerised by him but…

'I… I think I should continue my walk, otherwise I'll be late for this afternoon's seminars.' I awkwardly break the silence and move away slightly.

'Good idea. Why don't I walk with you?' he suggests and we wander together past more statues.

'I didn't think this would be your kind of thing,' I say blithely.

'What, Chatsworth, or the seminar?' he asks with a smile.

'Both, I guess. I didn't think you would be interested in either Regency romance or old stately homes.'

'You're probably right as always on both counts. I came to do some quality control checks in my very senior capacity as CEO of the agency, but actually while I'm here, even I can't fail to be impressed by these surroundings.'

I stare at him, disconcerted, this is no time for him to turn into a normal person.

'Of course, I'm only thinking about it in terms of business, it would make a fantastic hotel for example, or a casino.'

I'm about to give him a blast of my opinion when I catch sight of his expression. 'Oh, you're joking – good job or I would have had to slap you.' Oops, I didn't mean to come out with that.

But he smiles wickedly. 'What a shame, I might have enjoyed that, perhaps I should annoy you more often.'

'I don't think that's humanly possible,' I quip and we laugh and walk onwards, the ice broken.

᠅

WE'VE REACHED the huge doors out to the park and stroll into the beautiful sunlight. I peek at him, this Darcy is totally new and unexpected.

'So, did your grandmother like Chatsworth?' I ask shyly.

'Yes, she adored the place, she loved a good romance.'

'At least someone in your family had some sense then.' I laugh.

'I suppose so.' Darcy smiles. 'She was an amazing person but I didn't see enough of her, I was always too busy with work and she and my mother didn't really get along, then Gran became ill.' He broke off... 'The Jane Austen Dating Agency was an idea she came up with and I promised her I would make it a reality. Sadly she didn't live to see it.'

'She must have been a pretty inspirational person – it's such a great idea.'

'Yes, she was. Actually, you remind me a little of her; you have the same passion for life, exuberance, sheer optimism, and she had a great sense of humour.' He stops, flushing awkwardly. 'So, what do you think about Chatsworth, Miss Sophie Johnson, lover of all things romantic?'

'I think it's perfect,' I say dreamily. 'Right now I can feel like I'm Elizabeth Bennet and...'

'I could be Mr Darcy?' he asks quizzically. 'And yes before you ask, I do get those sort of jokes all the time. Perhaps that's why I've doggedly refused to ever read the book.'

'Why are you called Darcy? Was your mother a fan of Jane Austen too?'

He laughs. 'Not likely, I don't think she's ever read it. Not really her thing. No, I think I was called after General Darcy or someone like that, or maybe my grandmother persuaded her.'

I laugh because that doesn't surprise me.

'What about your family?' Darcy asks. 'Are they all as romantic and bookish as you?'

'Not really. My parents love books, of course, and have been married for years, but still argue about the same old things. My sister, Chloe, doesn't get much time to read; she's always working and trying to cope with her husband who's an abusive philanderer. My brother, Ben, is too busy going out with the next woman he meets, whether they're in a relationship or not.'

'Oh, that explains it then.'

'Explains what?'

'Your unmitigated desire to run away from reality.'

'Maybe.' I colour slightly. 'But what about you? You must have things you wish to escape from.'

'All the time,' he says slowly. 'We all have our issues, Sophie. Sometimes it would be nice to switch it off and do nothing.'

'Why don't you then? It's not like you need the money.'

Oops, that was a bit blunt but Darcy seems to take it on the chin. 'Because it's not that simple. I have to work, the business needs running. It's just the trips involve the same people from a narrow social circle, always talking about stuff that really doesn't matter, always networking. It's all such a bore and there's never a break.'

I look at him sympathetically, I've never seen Darcy like this before and everything suddenly becomes clear. He's just a poor rich boy, with little or no attention from his mother, spoilt at times, ignored at others. Not enough expected from him and then too much responsibility too young.

He looks so vulnerable, I put my hand out involuntarily to touch him, but my mobile rings. 'Sorry, I'd better check it, might be important.' I grab the phone out of my bag. I can never answer it quickly enough, it's one of those really annoying things that by the time I get it out, the person on the other end has gone.

'Everything okay?' Darcy asks politely.

'It was my sister, Chloe,' I reply, checking the screen, 'but I don't think it's anything urgent or she'd have left a message.'

My phone bings again. It's a voicemail from Chloe. She's crying so it's difficult to make out what she's saying.

'Soph... you there? ...Need to speak to you. It's Kian. He's gone... don't know where. Not like for a while... been gone... couple of days... no-one knows where.' She stops and all I can hear is muffled sobbing. 'Soph, can you phone me back... soon as you get this. I... don't know what to do.'

I immediately press redial on Chloe's number but it's engaged. 'Excuse me a mo. I need to make an urgent call,' I tell Darcy.

I get Chloe on the next try. 'Chloe, are you okay?'

'Not really.' She sounds terrible. 'Kian's gone. Left me.'

'Okay,' I say carefully. 'Has he given a reason?'

'No, that's the thing, he's disappeared, but hasn't taken his stuff, no message, nothing.'

I hesitate before asking the next question, but steel myself anyway. 'Have you tried Rosaline?' She's his supposedly ex-girl-friend, the one he was having an affair with.

'Yes, I have.' Chloe starts to cry again. 'She saw him last week.'

Oh dear, Kian's obviously back to his old ways. 'Chloe, I'm so sorry.'

'It's my own fault,' she sobs, 'I shouldn't have trusted him again, you all warned me. I'm so stupid.'

'No, you're just too nice,' I say gently. 'So, has he gone back to Rosaline then?'

'No, that's the thing, she said he was due to see her the night before last but didn't turn up. She's worried as he's been hanging out with a dodgy crowd he met through some online gambling thing. He'd been acting very strangely with me but I ignored it, hoping it was work pressures.'

'But, Chloe, he puts stuff in packages, it's not exactly high up on the league table of stressful jobs, is it?'

'No, but I was giving him the benefit of the doubt. Anyway, I was getting phone calls with no-one at the other end, the line kept going dead.'

'Creepy. Why didn't you go to the police?'

'I sort of assumed it was one of his exes and stuck my head in the sand.'

'Oh, Chloe, you're going to have to report it now he's gone missing, aren't you?'

'I know, but I don't feel I can cope with this right now, Soph. Do you mind coming over, I know you're probably busy but...'

'Of course I'll come. You know that, but you'll have to give me a few hours, I'm in Derbyshire.'

'Thanks, Soph, I don't know what I would do without you.'

I click the phone off and absentmindedly put it back in my bag and sink onto a nearby bench. Without noticing it, we seem to have arrived at a beautiful vista overlooking trees and sweeping lawns, grazed by picturesque cattle. Must have been designed by Capability Brown, I think absently. Poor Chloe, what's Kian up to now? It's all too much. I sink my head in my hands.

Darcy sits next to me. 'Sophie, are you okay? What's wrong?'

I'm too upset to really take in the fact he has his arm around me. It feels right, warm, safe.

'It's my sister, Chloe...' I feel unable to say more.

'It's okay. Take a minute and breathe,' Darcy says, surprisingly comforting.

I pull myself together and briefly explain the situation.

Darcy removes his arm and stands up. 'I guess you'll be leaving straight away then.' His expression is unreadable. I can see him withdrawing emotionally just when I thought... I don't know what I thought.

'Yes, I must get back and pack.' I leap to my feet and pace towards the house.


As we get to the main hall, we're accosted by Emma who seems distracted and in a hurry. 'Darcy, I need to speak to you urgently.'

'Oh okay.' He gestures as though he was going to help me to the door but stops when Emma continues.

'It's extremely important,' she says. I've never seen her like this; really stressed.

'It's okay, I've got to go and tell the others I'm leaving anyway,' I say quickly.

Emma's so distracted she hardly seems able to take this in. 'What?'

'Family trouble,' Darcy snaps.

And that just about sums up our parting, at the end of a day which had seemed so much more promising.

# CHAPTER 30

The next day I heave a sigh of relief as I open the door to our flat. Inside there are fresh flowers on the table and everything looks clean and tidy.

'Hello?' I call, hoping either Maria or Izzy might be in.

'Welcome back,' Maria calls. She's been baking cakes and generally clearing up, by the look of it.

'Thanks so much, Maria,' I say gratefully, giving her a hug. The flat has never looked this good.

'That's okay. Come and have a cup of tea and one of my carrot cake muffins,' she says, proudly getting them out of the oven. They look yummy. 'I bet you're exhausted. How's Chloe?'

'Not brilliant, I'm afraid. She's gone home to spend a few days with Mum and Dad.'

Maria passes me a muffin and bites into one herself. 'Any news of Kian?'

'No, none at all. It's like he's totally vanished. These cakes are delicious, I think you're going to have to stay here permanently.'

She smiles. 'What did the police say?'

'They think it's probably just another domestic, especially given his history, though they say they'll investigate further.'

'I don't like to say it but it looks as though he's off messing around with another woman. It's nothing new for him, is it?'

'I think you may be right, but the odd thing is, there's no activity in his bank account and historically (because, as we all know, he totally makes a habit of this) he's taken his stuff and Chloe's money. In fact, last time he signed several IOUs with both his and Chloe's name, so she's been repaying the debt.'

'God, he's a nightmare, isn't he?' Maria says with characteristic understatement.

'Anyway,' I take another muffin – they really are delicious – 'what did I miss? How was the rest of the weekend?'

'Oh, pretty good.' Maria smiles mistily. 'Izzy enjoyed it too, she's out with Matthew for dinner.'

'I can't believe I missed it,' I moan. 'I was so enjoying myself, especially the talks and the surroundings – it was amazing.'

'Yes, they were good, especially the one on Jane Austen and dancing.'

'More to the point, what happened with Charles – how come he turned up without Louisa or is she still ill?'

'It's funny you should say that, she's better but has left the agency.'

'Oh? She seemed such a fixture.'

'I know, but apparently after the accident, Charles made sure she was safely back with her parents and then he went to stay with his brother for a while in Weymouth.'

'I remember you saying that but I thought he really liked her. Didn't he go to visit her again?'

'That's the funny bit,' says Maria ecstatically. 'She has this almighty crush on her physiotherapist and is going out with him. Apparently he's pretty good looking.'

'Oh, so Charles came rushing back on the rebound…?' I can't help asking.

'No, he wasn't upset at all. He said he realised when Louisa fell down those stairs, because she was messing around and I stayed calm and helped, he found he didn't really like her that much as she's rather young and...'

'Silly and spoilt?' I add helpfully.

'I'm sure she's quite nice really, but I do think Charles is maybe a little more serious and mature than her.'

'So, what happened at Chatsworth? Come on, Maria, this is no time to hold back.'

'Charles explained all this to me when we left you and went to walk in the grounds. It was just so beautiful – he explained that he loves me more than ever, he bitterly regrets those years we've been apart. He has always loved me, he was just resentful that I turned him down and let my father tell me what to do.'

I'm silent for a moment, touched by these beautiful words, perhaps Regency romance is alive and well after all.

'I'm so happy for you, Maria.' I give her a big hug. 'Does that mean you're an item?'

'Very much so. In fact, he's taking me out to dinner later, so you'll be able to meet him properly.'

Maria looks so happy and radiant. I'm really pleased for her, she totally deserves this.

There's a loud banging on the door so I go and open it. It's Mel, but she's practically unrecognisable, her hair is windblown and she looks a mess. The steps outside our flat are piled with a million bags.

'I've got more bits to grab from the taxi,' she says, disappearing off and returning with another handful of stuff, fabrics and patterns flying everywhere, cascading from various baskets and pots.

I rush to help, wordlessly carrying it all in as she returns several times to the taxi. It is rather like Mary Poppins's bag; bottomless, more and more stuff comes out, a mannequin in various different pieces, row after row of outfits all covered in plastic.

'I should bloody well have charged double for all this stuff,' the driver mutters.

'You haven't exactly helped!' Mel shouts from under a pile of fabric.

After raiding our secret emergency stash we keep for last-minute girly nights and chocolate, I pass the driver several notes and he wheelspins off, still mouthing something rude.

I shut the door and walk into the lounge. Mel's standing forlornly in the middle, surrounded by a sea of stuff.

'What's happened?' I ask.

'I'll get a cup of tea,' Maria says and pops the kettle on.

'I've left Rob,' Mel announces dramatically.

'About bloody time too,' I say, 'but where are we going to put all this stuff?'

'It's all right, we'll find somewhere,' says Maria. 'Anyway, Mel was here first, I'll move out.'

'No you won't,' Mel and I say at the same time.

'It'll be like one big sleepover, a real laugh,' I say cheerfully.

'Yeah something like that,' Mel grouches.

'So, what happened?' Maria asks.

'Lady Constance is what happened.'

'Oh no.'

'Uh-huh. She found out there was never an exhibition of Vivienne d'Artois clothing at the V&A, under her patronage or anyone else's.'

I grimace. 'Oh dear. I bet that wasn't pretty.'

'Not at all – and she was *pretty* darn angry.'

I try not to laugh. 'Glad I wasn't there to see it.'

'Of course, Rob went mad, saying all sorts of ridiculous stuff about how I had stolen from Lady Constance and acted inappropriately. That then set me off, telling him some home truths, like I really hate *Star Trek* and it was me who gave the entire second series to the charity shop in the village.'

'So I left.' Mel sits down and deflates like a withering balloon.

'It's probably for the best,' Maria says cheerfully.

'Not when I've got my first exhibition in under two weeks and no backer and nowhere to prep the stuff.' For once Mel is stumped and my joy at having her back, and the fact she has seen sense about Rob, is blown away by the huge disappointment she must be feeling about her show. This is her one big chance and because of blimming Rob and Lady C, it's gone.

We sit and look at each other in silence. No-one quite knows what to suggest.

We're shaken out of our stupor by a sudden loud and insistent ring on the doorbell. Before I can get to the door, it's blasted again several times. Someone is obviously very keen to see us.

I open the door and am unceremoniously brushed to one side by Lady Constance, who comes sweeping into the room and stands there goggling at Mel.

'You!' Lady Constance seethes, pointing her finger at poor Mel, who's looking shell-shocked. I have a job not to laugh, this is a true comedy moment. Lady C just needs a fur coat and black and white hair to be the perfect Cruella de Vil.

'Would you like to sit down?' I ask, polite as always, though not gushing. Perhaps I'm beginning to learn to control myself.

'No, I would not like to sit down in an establishment like this. My God, it's like student accommodation,' she snaps. 'Who on earth would live in a place like this, it's so tiny.'

'Er, we do,' I say incredulously. This woman is the limit, who the hell does she think she is? 'And to what pleasure do we owe this visit?' I ask. I'm proud of this, no stuttering, just extremely calm and polite.

'To find out what else this thieving little hussy has taken from me!' Lady Constance snaps.

'I haven't taken anything from you,' Mel says calmly.

'Yes, yes you have, you lying little baggage, you!' Lady Constance's tremulous voice is getting higher and higher.

'I borrowed some clothes and I know it was wrong, but I

wanted to know the sort of quality needed to achieve the high standards of your sister. I knew you would never lend them to someone like me, so I borrowed them under false pretences and for that I'm truly sorry.'

'Some admission indeed,' snarls Lady Constance. 'I would expect nothing more from someone of your ilk. You intend to steal my sister's ideas and that's a fact.'

'That's not true,' Mel says. 'I can show you my stuff. It's nothing like Vivienne d'Artois.'

'I'm sure it isn't, there's no way someone like you can have the skill of my sister, she is a true artisan.'

'You're probably right,' Mel says humbly, 'and I don't pretend to be.'

'I know your sort – totally designing and calculating. You took poor Rob in, using him heartlessly. You waited your time and then you pounced.' Lady Constance paces the room, prowling like an angry panther.

'As you can hear, Mel is very sorry and there's no real harm done,' I say. 'I'm sure you have plenty to do, Lady Constance, and would rather be on your way to do it.'

'That's enough from you, madam. I've heard all about you, dangling yourself under Darcy's nose, trying to get yourself a rich man.'

'I can assure you I'm not.'

'That's not what I heard from a very reliable source. I was told that you've been deliberately hanging round him. And you're wasting your time.'

'Why's that?'

'Because he is engaged to my daughter, Hattie. What do you say to that?'

'Nothing really, because if that's the case, you can't be worried he might be interested in me.'

'How dare you!' Lady Constance shouts. 'Their engagement has been known by our social circle since they were very young.

And to think you, a trashy little sales girl pretending to work for Modiste, is scheming to stop this, I don't think so.'

'Would you like a cup of tea?' Maria breaks in, trying to soften the mood. Everyone ignores her.

'I think it's high time you left,' I say firmly to Lady Constance, opening the front door. 'I don't expect you to walk into our house uninvited, accusing my good friend of things she has not done, and insulting me to my face over your potential future son-in-law. Who, I might add, is one of the most stuck-up pompous arrogant men I have ever had the misfortune to meet, so you and your daughter are bloody well welcome to him!'

'Well! I have never been so insulted. If you ask my opinion, this Jane Austen Dating Agency has an awful lot to answer for!' Lady Constance sweeps out of the flat, banging the door behind her.

I must admit, with one thing and another, for once, I can't help agreeing with her.

# CHAPTER 31

Mel and Maria burst into a spontaneous round of applause as I watch Lady Constance stalk angrily down the steps, get into her limo, and before even closing the door, order the driver to leave immediately.

'My God.' Mel half laughs, half cries. 'Sophie, I've never seen you like that before. You certainly told her!'

Maria smiles. 'Shall we all have that cup of tea now, or something stronger?'

'Something stronger, I reckon.' I sink down weakly onto the sofa. 'I think that's the first time I've ever got tough with someone older than me, or with anyone ever actually. To their face anyway.'

'Maybe you're finally growing up a little?' Mel suggests. 'No more nice, kind Sophie who's looking for a man to complete her life. Instead move over everyone for the new sassy independent Sophie, ready to take over the world.'

I laugh. 'I'm not sure I'd go quite that far, but it's a start.'

'Even a worm will turn.' Maria smiles.

'Are you calling me a worm?' I joke.

'No, of course not, but I could do with taking a leaf out of your book, especially when it comes to telling my father that Charles and I are engaged.'

'Engaged?' I exclaim. 'Really? You didn't say.'

'I hadn't quite got that far,' says Maria shyly, 'but engaged we are, whether my father likes it or not.'

'That's the spirit. You tell him.' Mel has a large sip of wine. 'Or take Sophie and get her to talk to him, she's scary!'

'Yeah right, anyway I propose a toast – to Maria and Charles, congratulations!' I say. We all clink glasses noisily. 'Now, what are we going to do about Mel's show?'

Mel groans. 'I'm going to have to give up and try again next year, if I can get another sponsor that is.'

'No, I don't think so,' I say firmly.

'What do you mean? There's no choice.'

'That's what you think. I, on the other hand, have a cunning plan. Just give me some time.'

I leave the others to watch *Poldark*, although they're on strict orders to call me if I miss any scenes with Aidan in a wet white shirt. At the moment, however, I have more important matters to deal with. I retreat to my room with the phone.

'Mark?'

'Hello, darling. It seems like ages. How are you?'

'Good thanks. How was Marbella?'

'Simply gorgeous, of course,' he says glibly. He chatters on for a while about the fashion shows, the parties, in fact mostly the parties, and makes me laugh with a couple of risqué stories which may or may not be true.

'Look, Mark, can we catch up tomorrow morning? I need to ask a really big favour.'

'Of course, darling, anything for you.'

'It's not for me actually, it's for Mel. She's got a problem with her fashion show.' I briefly recount the saga with Lady Constance.

'Oh no, complete disaster. Anything I can do to help. You

know your wish is my command and I am a huge fan of Mel's work.'

'What I need, if you can manage it, is a meeting one day this week at lunchtime with anyone you can get who's big in the fashion world. You, obviously, and Tim if he's free. I'll ask Miffy what she can do too, oh and anyone else in Editorial.'

'You betcha, you can count Tim in, and I'll see who else I can get to help. Tell Mel to bring samples of her work with her and layouts for the show – she'll only have a few minutes, if that, to impress these people. You know how it is.'

'Thanks, Mark. You're simply the best, you know that.' I ring off and get up to go and tell the others.

Before I make it out of my room to spread the news that I have things in hand, the phone goes again.

'Hi, Sophie, it's Emma.'

'Hi, Emma, lovely to hear from you.' It suddenly comes back to me there had been some kind of crisis when I left Chatsworth on Saturday and I had forgotten all about it. 'Is everything okay?'

'No, not really. It's all gone horribly wrong,' she blurts, totally unlike her usual well-measured self.

'What's the matter? You're not ill, are you?'

'No, I'm fine, though stressed as hell. But I received some upsetting news on Saturday while at Chatsworth.'

'I'm so sorry. What is it?'

'I don't know how to put it, but you need to know and it will soon be common knowledge...' There's a pause as she takes a deep breath. 'Jessica Palmer-Wright and Daniel Becks have run off together.'

'Really? I didn't think they knew each other that well.'

'Neither did we.'

'Oh my God. Darcy Drummond must have been upset to hear this news.'

'Not half as upset as he was when he heard the rest of it,'

remarks Emma. 'They've disappeared with the profits of The Jane Austen Dating Agency – cleared us out.'

'Oh… my… God…'

Emma continues, her voice wobbling, 'And more serious still, they've been running an illegal gambling ring under the cover of the Regency Gaming Nights. So not only are we done financially, the agency is in trouble with the police. I'm sorry, Sophie, but The Jane Austen Dating Agency is finished.'

## CHAPTER 32

It takes a few moments for me to register the full meaning of Emma's revelation. For once, I'm lost for words. I hadn't seen this coming at all. My mind's full of a million questions; none of it makes sense. I'm so shocked, I don't really know what to say to Emma. We agree to speak again soon but when she rings off, I'm left with a feeling of total emptiness.

Why on earth would Jessica Palmer-Wright get involved with Daniel? I know he's persuasive, but she must see he's nothing but trouble. Not that I believed for a minute that Jessica Palmer-Wright was a true supporter of the agency, or that Daniel wasn't capable of anything after the lies he spun.

'It's over,' I announce dramatically, upon returning to the lounge.

'What's over?' Mel asks, stuffing popcorn and distracted by *Poldark*'s Demelza and Hugh.

'The Jane Austen Dating Agency, it's no more.'

'Why? How come?' I have the others' full attention and *Poldark* is summarily dismissed.

'Our dear friend Miss Palmer-Wright has run off with Daniel Becks, taking all the profits with them.'

'No!' Maria says. 'That's terrible.'

'I know, and worse still, the two of them were involved in some illegal gambling deal and have got the whole agency pulled into major trouble.'

'Rob was right,' says Mel, spraying popcorn everywhere in her excitement. 'For once he was right about the game being rigged.'

We all pause for a second, momentarily diverted by the thought that Rob could be right about anything.

'I expect it was a one-off,' I suggest.

'Yes, you're probably right, he doesn't usually make a habit of it,' Mel agrees with a smile.

'Poor Emma. What's going to happen about her job?' Maria asks quietly.

'That's a point,' I reply.

We sit, considering a moment.

'She has contacts,' Mel says, ever practical. 'I reckon Miffy at your work will get her in somewhere.'

'That's true, though I don't know what Emma's qualifications are,' but I cheer up momentarily, 'and she doesn't strike me as badly off, she can always ask her family for help. I think they're quite wealthy.'

'It's such a shame though,' Maria murmurs, close to tears.

And it is. I feel lost. I had such high hopes of The Jane Austen Dating Agency; it was going to solve all my problems. I was lined up to meet the man of my dreams, have some fun, marry him (he'd be wealthy, of course) and we'd live happily ever after...

But would we though? How likely is that to have happened?

About as likely as Jane Austen herself was ever likely to find a Mr Darcy of her own and marry him. Her reality was the charming Tom Lefroy, but it came to nothing when his family intervened and that was the end of that. Romantically, he still remembered her years later, after he married a wealthy woman, but that didn't help, the end result was the same.

The nearest Jane ever came to marriage was Harris Big-

Wither. I mean, come on, the name says it all. No wonder she had second thoughts, having initially accepted him and then run away home. I can imagine that was a sleepless night, checking out the size of his library, his estates, the enticing inducements of a comfortable financially worry-free future and weighing it against the fact she would have to accept, perhaps forever, the death of romantic dreams, imaginings and hope.

This would all be exchanged for the nitty-gritty reality of a bore of a husband, probably a Rob Bright-alike, droning on and on, and the endless drudge of repeated pregnancies and child-birth. Poor Jane, no wonder she ran away. Thank goodness for all our sakes she did; we would probably never have her wonderful books today if she had shackled herself to such a man.

LATER THAT EVENING, I scroll through The Jane Austen Dating Agency website, then sadly close the page with an air of finality. I sit aimlessly staring at the screen and idly flick on to my Twitter account. I'm browsing through the usual mixture of this and that, when a random tweet catches my eye. It's a quote saying, 'She needed a hero so that's what she became.'

And then, just like that, it suddenly becomes clear to me. I don't need The Jane Austen Dating Agency. I can do it by myself. Darcy's right, not that I will ever tell him that, but I've been living in a dream world. That's okay because we all need to sometimes. I'm not promising never to dabble in those happy imaginings again, but it's not right to live in it. The time has come for me, Sophie Johnson, to kick ass and sort out my own happy ever after.

I START the very next day at my meeting with Mark over the obligatory smoked salmon blinis.

'Sophie, darling, you look… different,' he says, eyeing my outfit in an impressed manner. 'New suit?'

'Yes it is, cost a small fortune but I thought it's about time everyone began to take me a bit more seriously.'

'Ooh hark at you… but you look good. It suits you, this new businesslike image.'

'Thanks.' I try to bask in the compliment for once, instead of brushing it aside as usual. 'I have an idea and I need you to tell me how I can manage it,' I say to him conspiratorially, simultaneously checking the rest of the sales team aren't around to overhear.

'How exciting, you know how I love ideas, darling! Fire away!'

'Have you heard of Scoop?'

'Scoop? No, what's that?'

'It's a trade show of womenswear held at the Saatchi Gallery. I understand it's an opportunity for niche designers to exhibit to an international audience, and I think it would be perfect for Mel.'

'Look at you, knowing all the goss. How did you hear about that?'

'I didn't!' I confess. 'I've been spending a lot of time doing research and I don't even know how to get Mel in, but it sounds the right sort of place for her to have a chance. I need your help with this though, Mark. Do you think Tim would know anything about it?'

'He's bound to; there isn't a model with a broken nail that Tim hasn't heard about practically before it even happens. I'll phone him at lunch and we'll get a plan together. Mel has talent and I love that. She also beats me every time at arm wrestling, an attribute I find simply irresistible.'


HAVING COMPLETED phase one of the new Sophie, after lunch I begin phase two. This is partly the reason for my sharp new suit, which I took the rest of my savings out to buy. It's more than I have ever even considered paying for an outfit, but I figure this is a business investment. I take a brief moment to go in the ladies, reapply lipstick, brush through my hair, which for once is doing what it's told, and straighten my shirt. Yep, I look like I mean business. You can do this, Sophie.

Because today, I'm going up those stairs to Editorial.

I check my surroundings briefly on leaving the loos, to make sure none of the sales team or Amanda are about. The coast is clear, I sneak along the corridor and on to the staircase. The next flight looks imposing and scarily empty. Then I give myself a little shake, these are just stairs and the people at the top of them are ordinary people, they eat, drink and use the toilet like the rest of us, so I have nothing to be scared of.

It's surprisingly easy actually. I climb the steps and reach the top. It looks very much like the sales floor but a little more homely, with books and papers, all more eclectic in style. I look about to see which way I should go.

'Can I help you?' a willowy girl with a perfect complexion asks.

'I'm looking for Miffy Pemberton-Smythe,' I announce as firmly as I can.

'Just through there.' The girl gestures vaguely towards a blue door and disappears off down the corridor. I wander into a room with a couple of empty desks, computers and loads of magazines. On the wall is a pinboard with a mock-up of this month's copy of *Modiste*, all pieced together.

'I think we should move this page back in the copy, or the flow is affected by this article here,' says Penny Sanderson, Editorial Director. I've never met her before, but I've seen her picture in the magazine and on our website's staff listing. She looks up quizzically as I blunder in.

'Yes?' she asks, not unkindly.

'I'm sorry,' I stutter, but then I think, *No, I'm not sorry. Why should I be sorry? I have every right to come and knock on this door and speak to these people. I work for this company, for goodness sake. I'm not doing any harm.*

I try again. 'I just wanted a word with Miffy, but I can come back in a while if you prefer.'

'No, that's fine. I need to go and speak to Jocasta about the Jennifer Lawrence cover.' Before I can reply, Penny bustles out of the room and I'm left alone with Miffy.

'Sophie, darling.' She gives me a couple of perfunctory air kisses in greeting. 'You'll have to forgive me this morning, we're on a copy deadline and a couple of people down. Nats and Bunty have gone awol and I was out at a shoot till 1am.'

'Oh.' It doesn't sound quite as glamorous up here as I thought. In fact, looking around me, it all looks pretty ordinary, although to construct the next magazine would be really something. I'm still clutching my folder of written work. 'Miffy, I won't stop you long, it's just that as you know, I work downstairs in sales.'

'Yes,' Miffy mutters, scanning through a couple of pages of typewritten copy. She looks up briefly. 'Did Amanda send you up with some papers for me?' She holds out her hand to take my file.

'No, it's my work,' I say boldly. Miffy looks surprised. 'I'd like to write, you see. I've always wanted to work in Editorial but I started in Sales, hoping I could move across, but now I'm not sure that happens and I've got kind of stuck.'

Miffy is still staring at me, her mouth slightly open.

This wasn't quite how I planned this. 'I understand if it isn't your kind of thing, but I've got loads of ideas and wondered if you might have a quick look at them when you have time?'

'Oh right,' Miffy says tightly. 'I'll see what I can do, but it's a tough gig to get into, you know. Is your CV included?' I nod. She sees my crestfallen expression. 'I'll have a look at them, okay?' She takes my folder and shoves it on top of the pile of magazines on the corner of her desk, where no doubt they will stay for some time untouched, I think cynically.

Just then the phone on her desk rings. 'Excuse me a mo. Miffy Pemberton-Smythe,' she answers in a very posh voice. 'Hi, how are you? Yes, yes. You can't be serious!'

I back away towards the door as I feel I'm encroaching on a very private conversation but Miffy motions for me to stay.

Finally she gets off the phone and distractedly pushes her hands through her hair. I look at her uncertainly; she looks pretty sick.

'Are you okay, Miffy? Can I get you a sweet cup of tea or something?' I wait for her to answer, she doesn't seem to be with it at all. 'If not, something stronger?'

I dash off down to the café, grab an Earl Grey, add loads of sugar and a sweet biscuit for good measure and bring it back up.

Miffy is still sitting staring into space. 'For God's sake, I don't know what to do,' she says slowly.

I wait, patiently, to see if she wants to talk about it.

'It's Nats and Bunty. They've been arrested.'

# CHAPTER 33

I feel like everything's falling apart all around me. It turns out that Natasha and, to a lesser extent, Bunty, were involved in the scam Regency Gaming Nights. Natasha was obviously the money behind the set-up. It all begins to slot into place, that's why Jessica Palmer-Wright was at Natasha's house. No wonder she wanted to keep her presence there quiet. What I couldn't understand is how it was worth the risk, but apparently there's huge money to be made by the house if the dice are weighted.

'So, Natasha and Bunty are detained at her Majesty's pleasure?' Mark asks when we meet for lunch the next day.

'Miffy says they've been released temporarily on bail, but the trial is at the end of the month. I just don't understand why Natasha needed to be involved in this sort of stuff when she's already stinking rich?'

'The wealthiest people always need more money, darling. You should know that after a trip or two to Harrods.'

I remember the size of Natasha's huge diamond ring. I guess you do need a lot of money to fund a habit like that.

'What happened to your best friend, Jessica Palmer-Wright,

and your sexy ex-lover Daniel?' presses Mark, his mouth full of noodles.

'Oh please! Still nowhere to be found. No-one has any idea where they've got to. And that's the end of that.'

'Good riddance, I say,' Mark says blandly, 'and quite honestly the dating agency wasn't getting you very far, was it?'

'No.' I smile ruefully. 'It was a pleasant little daydream, the reality was something very different, as it usually is.'

THE NEXT FEW days pass by in a blur of work and not much play. It's nearing the month's end once again, so the sales team is under a lot of pressure. Bizarrely though I'm not too worried as I've finally realised that maybe this isn't going to go anywhere. But I'm not giving up hope, if writing is what I want to do.

I'm going to keep trying until someone sees that I might have some talent. I become a hive of industry, writing in every spare minute as I used to do when I was younger and perusing the job ads on the net, eagerly sending off my CV, but as usual the silence is deafening.

'Why don't you come home?' Mum asks on the phone late one evening. 'Dad and I would love to have you back and you can study for a PGCE in less than a year.'

I come up with my age-old arguments. 'That's still a long time. Besides, I don't want to teach. I think it's a vocation like nursing, you should really want to do it, for the children's sake, not because you can't think of anything else to do.'

'I couldn't agree more, but the point is, once you start you'll probably find you enjoy it. The kids loved you when you helped at my school and you were really quite good, you know.'

'I'll think about it, Mum. How's Chloe?'

'She's okay, considering, but still no sign of Kian, he seems to have vanished. Though your dad and I are relieved. Awful man.

We're glad to see the back of him, but he's left Chloe in a total mess again.'

I HAVEN'T HEARD any more about the dating agency, everything's gone quiet. Though I try to put a brave face on it, I feel as though something's missing. I was so looking forward to more picnics, Regency Balls and seminars – it was a wonderful escape from reality.

The good things to have come out of the agency are still apparent, however. Maria and Charles are engaged, though I'm still not sure anyone has actually mentioned it to Sir Henry. Izzy and Matthew also seem to be a lovely couple and there's no recognising Izzy these days, although a little quieter than she was, she's more mature somehow and contented. Matthew's even persuaded her to go for dinner at her dad and stepmum's this weekend with him for support. So maybe some happy endings are possible after all, just not my own.

I'm pretty busy this week in any case. I'm helping Mel prepare for her fashion show. Tim's been a complete star and got her a slot as part of the Scoop exhibition and it's going to be totally amazing. Next Sunday is the night at the incredible Saatchi Gallery. I just hope we're going to get the publicity right, but with Tim around it should be pretty impressive.

TODAY'S BEEN EXHAUSTING and I'm pleased to be making my way back down the stairs to escape the endless calls. I'm going through the big revolving doors at the entrance to Modiste when I'm stopped by someone calling my name.

I turn to see Miffy clopping down the stairs after me. 'Sophie, darling, wait up!'

I stop and turn. 'Hi, Miffy, everything okay?'

'Yes, I'm sorry I haven't got back to you about your work but it's been crazy without Nats and Bunty.'

'That's okay. I've been busy too.'

'Anyway, I just wanted to tell you your work's great, I like your style. Some of the ideas we've already done, but it shows promise. You've definitely got something, you should keep going with it.'

'Really? That's so kind of you and it means such a lot.'

I feel like dancing around like crazy. Not how I was after my first sale on *Modiste Brides*. This is different, it's bigger somehow – this is about me, something I've worked hard for and achieved myself, and it feels... amazing, actually. Somewhere inside me, the tiny hope I've been carrying that I can do this grows a little brighter, a little stronger. This is the best feeling ever.

Feeling bold, I ask, 'I don't suppose you need someone to tide things over for Natasha and Bunty, do you?'

'No, darling, 'fraid not. I wish we could but you know what it's like up there, they're advertising already and you really need experience.'

'That's okay, I understand.' I turn and start to walk back out the doors.

'I tell you what though,' Miffy calls after me, 'what about freelance?'

'What do you mean?' I ask, stopping abruptly.

'You have style and a good grasp of what people want to read. I could have a word with Penny about you working for us on a freelance basis, selling us the odd article. That way you can build up your profile working for us and other publications?' I look at Miffy's aristocratic but kind face and to her great surprise, envelop her in a huge hug.

'Careful, darling!' She laughs. 'This is Christian Lacroix, you know!' But I can tell she's secretly pleased. 'I'll take that as a yes then, shall I?'

. . .

THE REST of the week passes by in a blur. All my spare time is spent either helping Mel plan her show or scribbling down my ideas for articles, which are coming thick and fast. Amazingly, Miffy has asked me to write a piece on Mel's show for *Modiste Magazine* and I won't even tell you the amount I'll get for it, because it's not bad, not bad at all. She's also promised to pass the word around Modiste about Mel's label, which is an incredible introduction for her.

Most amusingly, Mel's been offered Natasha's tiny little dogs to be part of the show, which I think will be fabulous, and may even rival the work of the legendary Vivienne d'Artois.

# CHAPTER 34

'Ladies and Gentlemen, if you would like to take your seats, the show is about to start.'

It's the evening of Mel's debut and the air of excitement and anticipation is simply electric. The Saatchi Gallery is the most amazing venue ever, I've never seen anything like it. The set is all tiny trees with dazzling lights and real birds – brightly coloured budgies and lovebirds with vibrant plumage either on the branches or in elegant bird cages suspended from the ceiling. The whole room is cream with scrolls and elegant swirls and crests. Mel's in her element backstage, still stitching alterations at the very last minute with unflappable calm.

'Hold on, everyone, it's okay, we're here,' Mark announces, stalking into the room in a pair of Louis Vuitton heels, surrounded by ten tiny dogs. 'The show can start now.'

I dissolve into laughter as he totters across and gives me far too many air kisses.

'Oh, here he is, the star diva of the show,' Tim comments, blandly looking up from his work, pinning the back of a bodice.

Everywhere is a brilliant colour, like a peacock's display of Regency dresses but with a modern twist. The sheen of the satin and contrasting net cut an inspirational dash and even though I know Mel's talented, I'm still blown away by this show. Everything all blends to one: the music, the models with hair piled high on their heads, decorated with tiny feathers, each one sporting a tiny Chihuahua in a miniature version of the model's Regency dress.

I'm spellbound, right up to the end of the show when the whole room stands to rapturous applause as the models take a final turn.

'Where's Mel?' Tim calls. 'She needs to take the stage.'

Mark and I grab Mel, who's fiddling about under the pretence of folding fabrics and putting things away, which she never does, and propel her towards the runway.

She walks the platform, flanked on either side by a gorgeous model and two delicate Chihuahuas, she's flushed and laughing, drunk on the applause.

I notice there seem to be several smartly dressed women seated in the front rows with notepads, and I have every hope Mel as a designer is going to be the next in *Vogue*. If not she certainly will be when my piece is published in next month's *Modiste*.


THE EVENING CONTINUES with its surreal dreamlike quality and we all drink champagne, toasting Mel and Mark and Tim – who also take a bow at my insistence. It's like a family party with Izzy and Matthew – who look overwhelmed by the dogs, and Maria and Charles, all congratulating Mel at the same time. I manage to get her on her own for a minute.

'Congrats, Mel – I knew you could do it,' I say hugging her, so she spills her champagne.

'I couldn't have done this without your help,' she says seriously.

'Nah.' I smile. 'You always had Rob Bright as a backup!'

Just as we're laughing and wondering which chess tournament he's playing, my phone rings out shrilly.

'You and your bloody phone!' Mel jokes.

'I'll grab it – it's Emma.'

I press 'answer' and try to find somewhere quiet so I can actually hear what Emma has to say, which is pretty near impossible.

'Hi, Emma, how are you?' I ask, probably shouting.

'I'm okay, but I have some news which I think you should know.'

'What? Just a mo, I still can't hear you very well... Okay, that's better.' I sit out in a small lobby, near a coat stand and some beautiful images of Audrey Hepburn.

'Are you sitting down?' Emma asks, which worries me.

'Yes, but please tell me quickly, is it something bad?'

'Yes and no, it's about Kian.'

'Kian?' I repeat stupidly. Isn't it always the case that you associate certain people in your life with certain other people, in their neat little slots, and if they get mentioned out of context for some reason, it confuses us totally.

'Yes, your brother-in-law, Kian,' Emma explains patiently.

'Oh my God, do you know where he is?'

'I do; he's in prison.'

'In prison? What for? What's he done?'

'He was involved in this gambling scam.'

'What? Another gambling scam?' I ask stupidly.

'No, he was one of the fixers involved in Natasha, Bunty and the others' business.'

'But... but that doesn't make sense because he didn't even know them. He can't have known them.'

'He obviously did, somehow, probably through some kind of organisation, hired by Natasha, I should think. You did say he was a dodgy sort of person.'

'Yes, but I didn't realise just how dodgy.' I go silent as I don't know what else to say.

'This has been a mess from beginning to end,' Emma says sadly.

'Does Chloe know?' I ask, suddenly realising it'll be better for her knowing where Kian is, although I think this will be small comfort.

'She will do by now; the police will have phoned her, I should think.'

'Oh my God, I must get hold of her, try to warn her, apart from anything else it'll be a shock, and… my poor parents.'

'Before you go, I must tell you something quickly,' Emma says diffidently. 'It's about Darcy.'

'Darcy?'

'Yes. I don't know how well you know him, but he's been instrumental in this.' I fall silent, trying to digest the meaning of her words. 'He's worked tirelessly to catch up with the gang behind the scam, to regain some of the money from the agency, apart from anything else. He hired a private investigator to track Kian and his comrades, to bring them to justice. It means, when all this is said and done, your sister will get her money returned to her.'

'I can't believe it. But why? Darcy's not really anything to do with me.'

'Are you sure? Because the way he spoke of you, I assumed you both… well, I sort of thought…'

'Thought what?'

'Nothing. My mistake. Anyway. I'll let you get hold of Chloe. Send her my love. I hope you can help her recover from this, although from what I hear of Kian, it's no great loss.'

'You're so right, it's getting Chloe to see that. If only Nick were around to help her take her mind off him. I think she really liked him.'

'Didn't you know? He's back from New York, has been for a while. I could give you his number if you like, it can't be against agency rules as there's no agency anymore.'

'That would be amazing and thank you a million times, Emma. I owe you so much.'

This call has changed my entire evening. I try Chloe on her mobile but there's no reply, and my mum and dad's home phone is engaged. I walk back past the gallery – the antics and celebrations in the other room seem far removed from my reality. I leave a quick message with Maria, who offers to come home with me.

'No, stay. I'll see you later anyway, and you need to help Mel celebrate in style.'

I MAKE my way home in a taxi, ignoring the driver's efforts to be chatty by continually dialling both Chloe and my parents, but don't get very far.

I arrive at my flat tired and dispirited.

As the taxi pulls up, I'm surprised to see a smartly dressed elegant lady waiting by the door. She's vaguely familiar but I can't remember where from. Her hair is dark, cut short and stylish, her eyes carefully highlighted and her make-up flawless. I see she's wearing Jimmy Choos and a classically cut long coat.

'Hello?' I say as politely as I can muster, considering I'm tired and just want to get in my flat, put on my slippers and speak to Chloe.

'I'm looking for Sophie Johnson,' the lady says, forgoing the hello.

'Yes, I'm her, or should that be I'm she?' I blur. I'm too tired to cope with any more conversations.

'I am Mrs Drummond.' The woman extends her hand formally.

'Oh, pleased to meet you.' My voice catches slightly but I shake her hand politely. 'Would you like to come in a moment?'

Mrs Drummond waits in awkward silence as I rummage in my bag for the door key and fumble with the lock. This woman makes me anxious. My mind's gone into overdrive – why would Darcy's mother have come to visit me? It's all very odd.

I walk into my flat, hoping against hope that we left it fairly tidy. Thank goodness it looks reasonable, Maria's beautiful flowers are still blooming on the kitchen table. Unfortunately some of Mel's original patterns and dresses are left strewn across the sofa.

'Please sit down,' I say. 'Sorry for these, I'll move them.' I grab Mel's creations and shove them behind the sofa as the lounge is where she's had to stay for now; the flat being full to capacity. 'My friend, Mel, has just had her debut fashion show at the Saatchi Gallery,' I say to fill the awkward silence.

'Really?' Mrs Drummond says in a disinterested voice.

I finish clearing a space and come to sit opposite her on a comfy chair. 'Would you like a cup of tea or a glass of wine?'

'No, nothing, thank you.' Mrs Drummond continues to stare at her surroundings in total disdain. 'You must be wondering why I'm here.'

'It is a bit of a surprise,' I say. 'We haven't been introduced.'

'No, indeed, and that is my point.'

'I'm afraid I don't understand.'

This woman is talking in riddles.

'The fact is, we do not know you and you do not really know my son,' she states matter of factly.

'No, I don't know him very well. That is to say I've bumped into him a couple of times but...' I drift off, unsure where I'm going with this.

'No,' she says in an I-told-you-so sort of voice. 'The point is, you and he move in very different circles and have nothing in common.'

'Absolutely. I totally agree with you.'

'You do?' she says, her pre-rehearsed speech momentarily halted.

'Yes I do, I've told him so several times,' I say glibly.

Mrs Drummond visibly heaves a sigh of relief. 'Thank goodness. I thought this was going to be like one of those tawdry cases in the paper where a trumped-up call girl ruins the CEO's career.'

'Excuse me?' I am incredulous now. 'I can tell you I am no call girl, I am not used to moving in the same circles as you, that's true, but I'm an intelligent well-educated woman who knows her mind.'

'That's for sure,' Mrs Drummond retorts, 'but who are your parents, you have no title, no fortune, no listing in *Country Life* magazine.'

What is it with these people and their magazines?

'My parents are normal individuals, we are a loving family and no, I don't have a title or lots of money but I have a great deal to offer.'

'But look at your sister, a complete disaster, her husband is in prison, and your friends so drunk they end up in hospital.' Mrs Drummond's on a roll.

'How dare you criticise my family and friends,' I say quietly but firmly. 'You don't know them and quite honestly, it is through your son's agency that both my sister's husband and my friend got caught up in all this trouble.' (Okay, so Kian was a pain before that, but there's no way I'm going to admit this right now.)

'I am aware of all the issues your relations and friends have and they are not at all what we are used to,' her voice rises querulously. 'Your association with my son is a disgrace, you are out of your league and you should know it. Stay in the circles you are used to mixing within.'

I stare at this woman in her fine make-up and clothes, and laugh outright. 'You're suggesting I will pollute the shades of Pemberley?' I say blithely.

'I have no idea what you are talking about.'

'No, I don't suppose you have read any Austen. Darcy said you probably hadn't. If you had, you would understand.'

'What I do understand, Miss Upstart, is that you are wasting your time with Darcy and this family. It will never work. He is destined to marry an heiress and that is what will happen. Have you any idea what it costs to run the empire his father left us?'

'No,' I say simply, 'and I don't care as I'm not interested in money or anything else from Darcy. As he told me himself, I love books, nothing more, and am not interested in you or your family's tawdry dealings in stocks and shares and any other profit-making schemes you have.'

'Don't you play the innocent with me. I have heard how your sister has been throwing herself at Nick Palmer-Wright, and you've been meddling in Lady Constance's affairs too, slyly getting your friend, Mel, to steal her famous sister's ideas. Your sort stop at nothing.'

'I'm sorry but I'm not going to sit here and put up with you insulting me. I think perhaps you should leave.' I jump to my feet and open the door.

'I will go with pleasure, but before I do, you are to promise me you will never see my son again.' Mrs Drummond stands menacingly close to me, like a threatening black cloud in her fur coat.

'I'll do nothing of the sort. In spite of never having read about them, you seem to be under some misunderstanding, Mrs Drummond, that we are still in Regency times, but we are not, you can't threaten me and tell me who I'll speak to and what to do.'

'You are a rude, insolent little social climber,' Mrs Drummond hisses. 'Very well, if that's how you want to play it, you're on.' With that, she sweeps out the door to a waiting Daimler driven by a miserable-looking chauffeur.

I shut the door quickly and sink down on the sofa, totally confused about what just happened.

# CHAPTER 35

'Have you seen, your Jane Austen Dating Agency's in the paper?' Dad remarks, munching away on his morning toast and marmalade.

'No?' I feign ignorance as I peer over his shoulder. (I'd come clean about the agency a few days ago and my parents have been surprisingly upbeat about it.)

'What a mess!' he says, looking at a picture of Natasha in her mink coat and diamond earrings, obviously at a premiere of some kind or other and looks fabulous. 'These rich girls, they have it all, yet it's never enough, they always have to go and screw it up.'

'Money isn't everything,' I say philosophically, helping myself to more bread and jam. I don't know why, but Mum and Dad's homemade bread always tastes so much better than the stuff we have in London, for all the smoked salmon blinis and glamorous dinners.

'There's a picture of Digby Drummond, or whatever his name is. He says he has no comment over the illegal gambling run under cover of the genteel dating agency. I bet he hasn't. These rich guys think they can buy people off and get away with a different set of laws from the rest of us. Wasn't he the one who diddled that Daniel you were going out with out of a job?'

'Actually, that turned out to be lies, Dad, and anyway Daniel was also caught up in the gambling ring; he's run off with the profits of the agency with Jessica Palmer-Wright.'

'Good grief. What a tangled web this lot do weave. I can't help but think you're better off here without them, Soph.'

I keep silent, munching my toast. London, Mel's triumphant show, Darcy, they all seem a million miles away since I've run home to sleepy old Bampton.

'Have you seen this?' Dad says eagerly. 'Look, Chawton House – the original home of Jane Austen's brother, Edward Austen Knight, where she spent many happy hours and is said to have written some of her work – is under threat as the previous backer, businesswoman, Xavera Merinata, has pulled out to invest in other causes.'

'Huh, why doesn't that surprise me?' I say bitterly.

'No, actually,' my mum enters the room and conversation unexpectedly, 'she had invested a great deal of money in the property and it was thanks to her the women's library was set up in the first place.'

'I know that. The collection of women's writing there is amazing.' I've really enjoyed wandering the grounds and visiting the library. 'You remember, Mum, I went to some study courses there. What are they going to do about it? '

'They're doing everything they can to raise funds,' Dad says. 'There's a donate page linked in with Jane Austen's House in Chawton. Why don't you write an article for the local mags to increase awareness, Soph?'

'Good idea,' I say enthusiastically, although I know this will only be a small help. I wish I had loads of money so I could invest in something as amazing as this. A real piece of our heritage which celebrates the work of so many women writers. Mrs Drummond doesn't know the half of it. It's nice my parents seem to have understood that I want to take this writing seriously, on the surface of it anyway, and I've finally made a decision about work once and for all.

Chloe walks in looking tired. 'Chloe!' I jump to my feet. 'Are you okay?'

'I've been better,' she says quietly.

I can see she's looking pretty shattered. 'Any more news on Kian?'

'Not any that I'd like to hear, we're a bit past all that. After how he's behaved, I don't want to ever hear his name again.'

'No, we don't,' Mum agrees. 'He really is the lowest of the low. And he's going to get his comeuppance now.'

'Don't you believe a word of it,' Dad says. 'He'll be off on bail in the next five minutes scot-free and able to annoy the next poor victim.'

'It won't be me,' Chloe says in a firm voice, which thank goodness sounds much more like her old self. 'I'm going out later, Soph. Fancy coming up to help me choose something to wear?'

I follow her into her old room, which she seems to have taken over once more. It's like going back to the old days when we were kids; there are clothes all over the bed and floor, perfume bottles, hairspray, everything strewn everywhere.

'You'd better watch out or Mum will be after you to tidy up this mess,' I joke.

'Yeah, I'll do it later.'

'You always said that and never do.'

'Shut up,' says Chloe good-naturedly. 'Look, I need to talk to you about something exciting.'

'Exciting, that's sounds good after all the crap we've been through lately.'

'Guess who phoned me last night.'

'Please not Kian.'

'Of course not.'

'Your old school friend, Jazz?'

'No, you'll never guess so I'll tell you. It was Nick.'

'Really? Nick?'

'Yes, Nick Palmer-Wright.' Chloe's practically squealing with excitement.

'Oh yes, Emma said he was back from New York. She was getting his number for me.'

'Thanks for telling me. Anyway, he got my mobile number from Mel and has asked me out tonight.'

'That's the best news ever!' I'm so excited I nearly fall off the bed.


CHLOE and I spend the rest of the day shopping and picking out clothes for her to wear for her night out with Nick. 'I don't know where this is going to go,' she confides in me shyly, 'but I'm going to enjoy it while it lasts.'

'You need to learn to accept that you deserve a genuinely nice guy, instead of an idiot. You always pitch yourself too low and get total morons. Now, for a change, you've bagged yourself a hand-some prince, make the most of it!' I say meaningfully.

'What about you though, Soph? It sounds just like you, always settling for second best?'

'Not anymore,' I say firmly, and I mean it.

# CHAPTER 36

On Monday morning there is a grim job to be done. I've finally decided to grow up and follow my dreams instead of waiting for them to magically happen. Bizarrely I put on a decent outfit, a bit of lip gloss, and make sure I look businesslike. I know it's strange to feel the need to look smart when you're going to be on the phone rather than meeting someone face to face, but I need every bit of poise I can get. With steely determination, I pick up the phone.

'Modiste, good morning. Can I help you?' It's Veronique on reception.

'Hi, Veronique, can you put me through to Amanda on the sales team?' I ask politely but firmly.

'Hi, Sophie, are you off sick?'

'Not exactly.'

'Oh okay, I'll put you through,' Veronique says, ever professional.

'Morning, Sophie darling. Are you unwell?' Amanda asks, distracted. Monday mornings are always busy. I can picture her there, lecturing the sales team on this week's targets. I don't miss it one little bit.

'Not exactly. I'm sorry, Amanda, but I've decided to leave Modiste.' There, I've done it, I've said it, it's out there.

'Sorry, Sophie darling, for a moment there I thought you said you're leaving.'

'I did, I am. I mean, that's what I said.' I pause, unsure what to say next.

'But why? You can't be serious? Think of all the training you've done, you're just getting started.'

'No, Amanda, it's too much, it's not what I want to do. I'm sorry.' I suddenly feel bad. After all, Modiste have invested their time into training me and I think Amanda had become quite fond of me in her own little way. There's a silence.

'Sophie, have you really thought about this? You are giving up an incredible opportunity. Hundreds of girls would give anything to work for Modiste, to be in your place.'

'I know,' I squeak, 'but not me.'

'But you've got so much potential and you want to throw it all away?' Amanda is incredulous, disbelieving almost.

'No, I mean, yes. I think your heart's got to be in whatever you do, don't you think?'

'I believe you make the most of whatever opportunities you're lucky enough to be offered,' says Amanda firmly. 'Your resignation is accepted... if you're not going to change your mind.'

'No.'

'Then I wish you all the best.'

'Goodbye and... thanks,' I say sadly, but she's already gone. And just like that, I've done it. I'm free.

I should feel like I've thrown away the best opportunity of my life but I don't. One day in the distant future, maybe I might regret this decision but not right now. For the first time in ages I feel like me, and free, like dancing and skipping with joy with it all.

. . .

OVER THE NEXT few days I make endless lists, write a couple of articles for a local magazine, listen to Chloe rhapsodise over Nick, moan to Mel on the phone, and think about what I'm going to do about the future. Mel is full of the fashion show and I've had one brief e-mail from Miffy to say thanks for my article and that it will be in next month's *Modiste*. And just like that, my glamorous life in London is over.

My endless applications for editorial positions and copy-writing continue to meet with a wall of silence. But I keep trying anyway in the hope that if I persevere, something will come up. It will have to as my share of the rent is due on the flat and I can't expect Mel to keep footing the bill, though Izzy and Maria are still camping out there at the moment, which will help tide things over.

AS THE DAYS GO ON, I begin to feel slightly empty as, although I don't miss the pretentious rubbish of Modiste, life back at home is pretty mundane. It feels like a huge anti-climax. Chloe is at work or mostly with Nick, which is a good thing of course, I'm pleased for her, but somehow I feel a bit as though there's still something missing.

'Come back up here with us for a few days,' Mel suggests when I speak to her on the phone. 'We're all missing you and it sounds like you've had enough of your parents' bickering and Ben's womanising to last a long while.'

'You're right,' I say gratefully. 'Tidy up the flat, I'm on my way.'

LATER THAT DAY, having shoved a few things in my bag and after a two-hour train journey, which involved a bus trip due to works at Basingstoke, I arrive back at the flat, hot and bothered.

I open the door wearily and, 'Surprise!' I jump out of my skin as Mel, Izzy, Maria and, to my delight, Emma, all rush to hug me.

There's a banner across the ceiling saying, 'Welcome home!' and glasses of fizz at the ready. I'm flabbergasted.

'Thanks, guys, but what's going on?' I gasp, dumping my heavy bags on the floor.

'It's a welcome home party for loyal members of The Jane Austen Dating Agency,' Emma says, laughing.

'Look, we've even got *Keep Calm and Read Jane Austen* balloons and everything,' Izzy says proudly.

For a moment I'm speechless, and so pleased to see these girls, they are such good friends.

'Well, here's to The Jane Austen Dating Agency,' I toast. 'Even though it's no more, we're all friends because of it.'

# CHAPTER 37

The next morning I'm wrestling with a long article I've been trying to write with suggestions for next month's *Modiste*, when there's a ring at the doorbell. I'm all alone as Mel has gone to a meeting with a colleague of Tim's who is interested in signing her label, and Izzy and Maria are out. I sidle to the door and peer through the side window, hoping against hope it's not Lady Constance or Mrs Drummond. I really don't feel strong enough today to cope with them or Sir Henry Greaves, who might be coming to complain about my part in encouraging Maria's engagement to Charles.

Thank goodness it's none of the above, but I still stagger back in surprise. It's only Darcy Drummond, on my doorstep. He's looking more rugged and handsome than ever this morning as he hasn't shaved, but his pale blue shirt and dark trousers are smart, as always. It crosses my mind momentarily to hide and not answer the door, but he rings the doorbell again. It's as though he knows I'm here.

I give in and open the door. 'Darcy.' I smile in a friendly manner.

'Hi, Sophie, I was passing and wanted to check you're okay.'

'Yes, yes I'm fine.' Passing? Islington is somewhere he's probably always passing and driving on by.

There's an awkward silence and I'm not sure whether I should invite him in, so instead I dither and hover on the doorstep undecided. 'Erm…' I stumble.

'Er…' he says at exactly the same time, and we both laugh. At least it breaks the ice.

'Are you doing anything today?' he asks.

'Yes, I'm working, writing, you know, another article for *Modiste*.'

'Of course, yes I saw your feature in this month's magazine, it's very good,' he says, sounding surprised that I can actually write something that might be.

'I didn't know you read *Modiste*?' I say, raising my eyebrows.

'I don't usually, but I thought I might make an exception just this once as I may have a vested interest in it.'

'Oh?' I reply, still feeling puzzled.

'If you're busy I can go away again, but I wondered if you might like to come for a drive with me. I have something I would like your opinion on.' Darcy appears unusually diffident and humble. It suits him.

'If you could give me a few minutes then yes, that would be lovely. I can always write later this evening.'

Darcy waits in our lounge, prowling like a caged lion, while I grab a jacket and my bag. I'm so relieved that I actually look okay today. I'm wearing my new pale pink Miu Miu top, smart jeans and my favourite pair of heels, so not bad. It's part of my 'be ready for anything' motto. The old scruffy Sophie, constantly feeling not good enough, she's gone. I add a touch of lippy and trot out the door after Darcy.

'You don't take long to get ready,' he remarks.

'No, I'm used to having to go everywhere in a hurry,' I say glibly, following him along the pavement to a stunning silver Aston Martin. He opens the door for me and I get in as though I have spent my whole life climbing into Aston Martins. Mmm, I could get used to this.

Darcy pulls out smoothly. This car makes me think of a thoroughbred horse; he's having to rein it in amongst traffic, but I reckon out on the road it is super fast. I reflect on Darcy's comment on my make-up, I guess he's used to dating supermodels and waiting ten hours for them to be ready for a date, and having seen his mother, she must spend ages getting that lot on her face. Then again, this isn't a date. In fact, I'm not sure what it is exactly.

We glide through the streets of London then hit the M4, as though we are going south.

'Is this a mystery tour?' I ask.

'You could call it that.' Darcy smiles. 'You'll have to wait and see.'

I feel like a little kid with all my birthdays come at once. I don't like to mention Mrs Drummond's visit, or the news about the agency or anything else, but it hangs in the air unspoken between us. I just want to live in the moment, enjoy this incredible experience, almost as though I'm travelling in a bubble and if I acknowledge it, it will somehow burst and disappear back in to my usual humdrum everyday life. So, we chat companionably about this and that, but nothing at all, and I enjoy watching the beautiful fields pass by, the hedgerows and green plenty of the warm July day.


FINALLY WE TURN off at Alton and I am more confused than ever. This is a long way to go for a pub lunch. We continue on into the beautiful little village of Chawton, to where Jane Austen's house nestles on the corner, and then take a right turn down the picturesque drive to Chawton House.

'Oh, are we going here?' I gasp. 'This is where I used to study, women's literature, you know.'

'Yes, I know,' Darcy says softly.

I look at him uncertainly, but he's concentrating on manoeuvring the car into a space alongside the great house.

Darcy walks round my side of the car and opens the door for me.

'Thank you,' I say, and get out as gracefully as possible.

'Like to go for a walk around the grounds?' Darcy asks, and I nod. This is such a thoughtful place for him to bring me. I can't believe it. It's so unlike him.

We walk side by side, our arms brushing every so often from our proximity to each other and I feel a frisson of electricity dart up my arm and travel down to my knees whenever this happens.

I try to focus and steel myself to say, 'Darcy, I want to thank you for everything you've done to help sort out my sister's situation with Kian. Getting him brought to justice, she's finally realised he's a no-hoper and is moving on.'

Darcy appears embarrassed. We're climbing up the steps by the side of the house and towards the rose garden. He turns to help me up by giving me his hand. I hold it, revelling in its warmth, but he then releases it again. 'You don't need to thank me, I was only seeking justice for the dating agency, I needed to get my money back. You know me, I'm a businessman and I never do anything for personal reasons.'

'Oh,' I ponder this for a moment, 'but…' I look up at his face and realise he's teasing. 'Never?'

'Nearly never. All right, I did it for you as well.' He continues to stride on ahead, obviously uncomfortable with this conversation.

'What happened about Daniel and Jessica?'

'No-one can trace them, but I believe they're hiding out in the US – I have people working on it and have already managed to recoup a lot of the funds.' His face is stern, impenetrable.

'That's something, I guess. At least you'll have some of the money back then,' I say cheerfully.

Darcy stops, turns to face me and takes my hands in his. 'Is that still really what you think about me?' he asks angrily. 'That I'm all about money and trust funds and stocks and shares?'

'Yes, I… suppose I do,' I stammer. His eyes are intense and I feel a little intimidated.

'I guess that's my fault, it's the only side of me I've ever shown you.'

'Maybe, but you can change that.' My voice pitches down to nearly a whisper.

'Yes, I can and I will, look!' Darcy keeps hold of my hand and pulls me past the rose garden and to the vista overlooking Chawton House, the parkland stretching out in front of us, horses happily grazing. 'I have a proposal for you.'

I stumble slightly but he supports me, preventing me from falling.

'Not that kind of proposal, Miss Johnson,' he smiles, 'but I very much hope it is one you will accept.'

I gaze at him, confused. 'And what might that be then?' My throat is so dry it comes out as a croak.

'This…' He sweeps his hand towards Chawton House and the parkland around us. 'I've bought the lease for 125 years, so your collection of women's literature is safe.'

I stand and gawp at him, uncomprehendingly. 'It's not my collection, but are you serious? You've really saved it? That's fantastic.' Without thinking, I throw my arms around him and he holds me surprisingly tightly. My head is just below his chin and I feel his stubble on my forehead. He smells so good, I wonder idly what aftershave he wears. Whatever it is, it's delicious. I'm also confused as to why he hasn't let me go yet, but then he dips his head and his lips meet mine and… Put it this way, neither of us speak for a very long time. In fact, we can't stop kissing, his tongue is insistent, causing little explosions in my tummy, and he has to support me as my knees annoyingly feel like giving way.

Finally we break apart. I'm still too surprised to say anything and he looks a bit shocked.

'Sophie… I'm sorry.'

'For what? That was very nice actually.' I try to recover my usual sangfroid.

'For being a total and utter arse. In fact, I was called Arsey Darcy at public school, you know. Perhaps they were right.'

I have to fight back a smile.

'You're right too. I was brought up in a social sphere where everything was handed to me on a plate. I was raised to be polite but that's it, to think our way was the only way, that we're superior to everyone else. I was bored with it but stuck, if you know what I mean. Until you came along and jolted me firmly out of my comfort zone.'

'Me? But you hated me.'

'Hated you? What makes you think that?'

'Maybe the fact that you said I lived in a fantasy world and wouldn't know reality if it hit me?' I repeat his words, although it feels a long time ago.

'Oh that.' He rubs his face awkwardly. 'I was such an idiot. I'm surprised you didn't punch me there and then, to knock some sense into me.'

'It was tempting.' I smile.

'You came in like a whirlwind and I felt irritated by you, threatened almost. I'd never met a woman like you, but right from the beginning I was transfixed. I still am, you know.' He pulls me to him and kisses me again, long and slow.

With difficulty, I pull myself away. 'But we're so different. I mean, I still find business boring and I'm not sure I can promise to totally give up reading romantic novels. And speaking of which, aren't you engaged to Hattie?'

'No. I never was. We don't even like each other. It's just what my mother wants.'

'Oh God, and what about your mother?'

'I'm so sorry. I couldn't believe it when she told me what she had said to you, but I knew then I must see you again, try to explain. I'm not like her. She has always wanted me to be a certain person and I can't live my life being something I'm not. I need you, Sophie.'

'Lots of people do,' I joke modestly.

'No, I mean it. I really need you to remind me how to be a decent person. I might slip back into my old hard-hearted, scheming "profit is everything" businessman ways.' He smiles, an irresistible boyish smile. 'I also require your help for the agency.'

'What agency?'

'The Jane Austen Dating Agency,' he says simply.

'But I thought it was over, finished.'

'That was the old, fake, Jane Austen Dating Agency. I'm talking about a new one, headed up by an amazing new Managing Director – Miss Sophie Johnson, and Head of Membership, Miss Emma Woodtree.'

I stand and stare at Darcy in amazement. 'You mean me? To run the agency?'

'Don't you want to do it?' Darcy asks, his eyes on mine, hopeful, pleading, expectant.

'Of course I'd love to.' I fling my arms round him again, then I recollect. 'But what about my writing? I need to carry on, I can't stop now I've really started to get somewhere.'

'There's no reason why you can't do your freelance writing as well. Emma will help you and you'll have plenty of space here to write.'

'Here?'

'Yes, here at Chawton House. Didn't I tell you? This is where you'll be running The Jane Austen Dating Agency. You approve, don't you? Surely there could be nowhere more appropriate other than Jane Austen's house, but I think that's a little small and it's only just down the road from here anyway.'

He smiles at my face, which must be a picture. Because I can't believe how happy I am, I think this must be how Lizzie Bennet feels at the end of *Pride and Prejudice*, but I don't really have time to consider this, or anything else for that matter, because Darcy's kissing me again and I feel that we might just live happily ever after.


The End

# ACKNOWLEDGEMENTS

It has been a lifelong dream to become a published author and now it has finally come true, there are several people I would like to thank for their help along the way.

Firstly thanks go to my agent Kate Nash, for believing in me in the first place, also my lovely editor, Morgen Bailey, for her tireless work on the manuscript, Tara Lyons for her help, Heather Fitt for publicity and to Betsy Reavley my publisher.

I must mention the incredible support I have received from the Romantic Novelists' Associations New Writers' Scheme. This is a fantastic idea and the critique was of great help.

Thanks so much to Rachael Featherstone and Samantha Tongue, both wonderful writers, who have been so patient and kind in encouraging me along the way.

I must also thank my writing friends, Debs and Viv, who I met at the inspirational Winchester Writer's Festival, for the wonderful chats, yummy food, and for generally understanding the constant dilemmas of writing.

I couldn't have written this book without the amazing influence of Jane Austen's books. *Pride and Prejudice* in particular has helped me through some very difficult times and Jane Austen remains a huge inspiration.

Thanks to my late Auntie Ba, who when I was a teenager, introduced me to Jane Austen's books – I remember those cosy afternoons watching various dramatised versions and we spent many happy hours discussing which were our favourites.

Then there are my incredible inspirational parents, Margaret and Brian to whom I owe so much in many ways. They have been my friends and companions as well as parents and it was thanks to them I have such a love of books and writing. They gave me my first notebooks, encouraged me to put down those first thoughts or holiday memories. It was they who took me to Jane Austen's House, to Chatsworth, to many other magical places as a child and who gave me such a deep love of books and history. We have had some amazing times and I am truly grateful for this and for their ongoing support and encouragement. Mum also kindly frequently looked after the girls, with my dad helping out, whilst I wrote the first draft of this novel.

To my sister Lorna, to whom I've been rambling on about this book for ages and whose incredible support I really appreciate.

I must thank my talented daughter Grace for her excellent editorial skills – in fact she was the first person to read this book and says she enjoyed it in spite of generally preferring psychological thrillers!

Thanks especially to my wonderful, long-suffering husband Keith for his support, kindness and patience, especially when visiting stately homes and for being the chauffeur on research trips. Also for putting up with all those times I jumped out of bed at stupid o'clock to scribble down an idea. I told you it would make a book though and it has!

Finally I would like to thank my lovely, brave and inspirational girls, Marianne, Grace, Madeleine and Francesca for all their love, support, encouragement and for putting up with the ups and downs of having a writer as a mum!

Made in the USA
Columbia, SC
24 May 2020